Bob's Book
Exchange
22.6.10
72

THE WINNERS

It began at a dinner party: Laidlaw, the host, galloping towards his first million; Moulton, the physicist, already plagued by dreams that only a cyclotron could interpret; Arnott, the doctor, successful, married to a beauty; Fitzgerald, the painter, wary still of a success that might become monotonous. . . . Four men who had been to the same provincial grammar school. The four men who had made it. Big. And Madge Innes, the woman who had watched them do it.

A reunion for the successful ones. . . . And yet the only thing Laidlaw seemed to be celebrating was hate. One of his guests was about to be demolished, and Laidlaw was enjoying the demolition.

This is a novel about power: its demands and sacrifices – and rewards. The money, women, prestige that power gives – and takes away. The ambition, the urge to power, first experienced in a childhood of bitter poverty; power bought and paid for – with hate, with lost values, even with love.

Throughout this superbly entertaining novel a brilliant series of lightning flashes illuminates the life – and the Achilles heel – of each of Laidlaw's guests. First one and then another is struck with a fork of light that has its origin in the far-off years of childhood, when all of them, though drawn from very different backgrounds, studied and played and fought together.

Also by James Mitchell:

ILION LIKE A MIST

THE WINNERS

James Mitchell

CASSELL · LONDON

For Delia

CASSELL & COMPANY LTD
35 Red Lion Square, London, WC1
Melbourne, Sydney, Toronto
Johannesburg, Auckland

© James Mitchell 1970

First published 1970

ISBN 0 304 93645 6

Set in 10-on-11 point Intertype Baskerville and
printed in Great Britain by
Cox & Wyman Ltd, London,
Reading and Fakenham
F.670

NOT GOOFY ANY MORE

'I'll see,' said the girl, 'but Mr Laidlaw's very busy.'

She pressed a switch and murmured into a white telephone, the Geordie vowels well under control, the prettily clothed body relaxed and competent. I sat on a bench that sloped at far too acute an angle from the wall, an elegant, viciously uncomfortable slab, covered in Thai silk, and looked at the picture on the opposite wall. It showed the heads of three miners, face-men, two young, one fighting middle-age, just coming off shift. It was an honest and very moving picture. All three faces showed exhaustion, but the two young men were grinning. The older one, jaws clenched, eyes staring straight ahead, looked angry at first, but it wasn't anger. He was just tired. Worn out. The picture was signed in tiny, neat italics: *J. Fitzgerald*. I looked at the older miner again. It was Moulton's father.

The girl said, 'Mr Laidlaw will see you now, Dr Arnott.' She sounded surprised. 'Straight through that door and second right.'

I stood up. From the window I could see the shaft and wheels of the Coronation Pit where Moulton's father had worked all his life.

'Do you like the picture?' I asked.

'It's interesting,' she said. 'Interesting' was a safe word.

'I know the old man. I know the chap who painted it too,' I said. She looked at me again.

'It's about the only thing a painter round here could tackle,' she said. 'That and the shipyards.' And she went back to her filing-system, but as I went through the door she was looking at the picture.

The second door on the right had no name on it. I knocked and went in. Laidlaw was sitting at a desk, a great slab of mahogany, his chair tilted back, his feet up.

'Come in, Bob,' he said. 'Sit down. Make yourself at home. Have a drink?'

'Please,' I said. It wasn't going to be easy. A drink might help.

He got up and went to a wall cupboard, unlocking it with a key he kept on a chain.

'We like to trust the workers,' he said, 'but not with Dimple Haig. What'll it be? Scotch? Gin? Sherry?'

'Scotch,' I said. 'Ginger ale if you've got it, Tommy.'

'Of course,' he said, and smiled the smile of a man amused by the suggestion that he hadn't got ginger ale. That wall cupboard had everything.

He gave me my drink and a cigarette, then settled back in his chair, tilting it carefully, his drink on the floor beside him.

'What can I do for you, Bob?' he asked.

I looked at him. Stomach flat as a board, Riviera suntan; the calm sanity of a man with a first-rate digestive system.

'I've come about Jim Moulton,' I said.

'Jim? Is he back up here? That's wonderful,' he said, and I swear to God he meant it.

'He's looking for a job,' I said.

'Same old trouble?' I nodded. 'Pity. . . . He's absolutely brilliant. You remember him at school?'

'Yes,' I said.

It was all going far too easily.

'Open Scholarship to Cambridge, State Scholar, Captain of the Fifteen, Captain of the School. Remember how he used to tease me about the way I played rugby?'

I remembered very well, though 'tease' was not the word I would have chosen. Until he was sixteen at least, Jim Moulton had found it impossible to criticize without using his fists. In the street he lived in, every male criticized that way. It was part of being a male. Once, when Laidlaw had spoiled a fine run by the form's three-quarter line (he dropped a pass that was almost put into his hands), Moulton had twisted his arm till he screamed. I can still remember the scream, and the way Laidlaw stood after he had dropped the pass, his lower lip trembling, his short-sighted eyes already peering round for Moulton. He was in a hopeless position. Without his glasses he couldn't see to catch a ball; with them he wasn't allowed to play rugby, and everybody had to play. Week after week, from autumn to spring, from his first year to his fourth, Laidlaw had been beaten by Moulton. Success had mellowed him right enough. Now he called it teasing.

'You must bring him up to the house some time,' he said. 'I've lost touch with too many people.'

'Moulton might feel a little embarrassed,' I said.

'Why on earth should he? We were all good friends at school.' If Laidlaw chose to remember his time with Moulton as friendship, that was fine with me. My business was to help Moulton find a job, and Laidlaw was far and away the best contact we could get.

'All right,' I said. 'When shall I bring him?' And I awaited the usual tycoon-play with desk diary and secretary.

'Friday night,' he said at once. 'Bring your wife. Is Moulton married?'

'Separated,' I said. 'He's up here on his own.'

'I'll find a spare woman,' he said. 'Dark suit. Six thirty. O.K.?'

'Fine,' I said.

2

'Just one thing,' he said. 'You called me Tommy just now. Well, I know you all used to call me that at school, but my wife doesn't like it. Nowadays I'm called Tom. You might tell Moulton that too if you see him. O.K.?'

'Of course,' I said.

He was wrong about that. It was his parents who called him Tommy. At school he was known as Goofy, a popular cartoon character of the thirties: amiable, well-meaning, and totally inept in physical action. Moulton had decreed it, and the rest of us obeyed with pleasure. As nicknames go, it was accurate enough. I don't suppose we ever thought that it was cruel, too.

ARTHUR SAYS WE CAN GO

My wife spent almost all of the next two days making up her mind what to wear. This is a recurrent problem for Sue, who is both tall and sensitive to the fact that many of my friends earned far less than I did, so that her best clothes, the ones made to use her height rather than submit to it, were not worn as often as they should be. This time the problem was a different one: aesthetic rather than moral. What could she wear that wouldn't disgrace me in the eyes of Tom and Sybil Laidlaw? She chose something rustling and elegant in green silk, I remember, and the Chinese ear-rings I'd bought in Malaya, and as she dressed questioned me endlessly about Moulton, whom she'd never met. How brilliant was he, and was his temper still as bad, and did I think Laidlaw would really help to find him a job?

'You know, I'm looking forward to this,' she said. 'It'll be like hiding under the table at an Old Boys' reunion.'

'I only ever went to one—and that was a mistake,' I said. 'I should have thought myself lucky just to get away.'

'You make it sound like Dotheboys' Hall,' she said.

'That's about right, I suppose,' I said. 'Except it wasn't residential.'

'I expect you quite liked it really,' said Sue. 'Everybody pretends their school was awful.'

Nowadays there's a brand new glass and concrete palace on the hill, with machine-shops and swimming-pool and a pottery kiln, staffed with cheerful-looking M.A.s all somehow earning two hundred above basic Burnham. In my day the school looked and felt like a condemned prison, a gaunt, brick box hedged in with barbed railings like the spears of charging Goths. Inside, it smelt, summer and winter, of boy and cast-iron pipes and paper kept too long. Mr Futters's blackboard squeaked, I remembered. Mr Futters once hit me on the head with a blackboard rubber, because I had failed to use π to three decimal places. I told my father about it, thinking it would amuse him, and he lost half a shift in the shipyard, came up to the school and hit Mr Futters on the head with his fist. Afterwards, Jameson, Sybil Laidlaw's father, and a J.P., sent my father to prison for a month and the headmaster, old Bickersley, caned me in front of the school. During that month, and for the first and last time, my mother had to ask for money from the guardians.

'It really wasn't a place to get nostalgic about,' I said.

4

'But look at the people who went there—even in your time,' said Sue. 'Laidlaw's the richest man for miles, then there's Fitzgerald—his paintings are doing terribly well—and your chum Moulton . . . well, I mean, he may be on a bad patch at the moment but he's a big shot in the C.N.D. and all that. And you, Bob. You've got the biggest practice in the county, I should think. And you all started from nothing, so the school must have helped.'

Then the phone rang, and it was Arthur Harkness, my assistant, being unsure about whether he knew enough about Mr Dumble's case to treat him on his own. Sue saw the way things were going, and sulked in a bitter little silence.

'Look, Arthur,' I said. 'All he's got is haemorrhoids, for God's sake.'

'Oh no, there's far more to it than that,' said Arthur, and he told me about Mr Dumble's neuroses, which were many and strange, and of which the haemorrhoids might or might not have been a physical manifestation.

'You can treat him,' I said.

'Of course I can, but can I cure him?' Arthur asked.

'Psychoanalyse him,' I said. 'Let him lie on his stomach and he'll tell you anything.'

'Just as you say,' said Arthur, and he rang off, having defeated me, as he always did. I would spend the next four hours wondering if he really had made Dumble lie on his stomach and tell all. He was perfectly capable of it, and of telling Dumble that I'd suggested it. He'd told Miss Danks, who weighed fourteen stone, that I'd suggested she take up ballroom dancing. She did, too, and won a prize at Butlin's. None of this hurt my practice—in fact it gave me some good word-of-mouth advertising as an eccentric, always the most popular kind of G.P.—but it left me puzzled and wary, as Arthur intended. He was a sound, if reluctant, physician, who extracted endless amusement from leaving people bewildered. Sue loathed him.

'Is he going to let us go?' she asked, and, when I said yes, 'Then for heaven's sake let's do it before he rings up again.'

I went to show the baby-sitter how to work the telly, then sat in the car for ten minutes while Sue found a coat. She came down at last in the musquash—her best—and we went to collect Jim Moulton.

He was staying at his father's house in the old South Park housing estate, a bewildering warren of Groves and Avenues and Crescents. I hadn't been there for twenty years, yet I drove there automatically, without thinking, surprised only that we arrived so quickly. In the past we had got there by tram, or on a bike. Often enough we walked. There had always been so much time for walking then.

5

The house was of yellow brick, with tiny bow windows on the ground floor. The front garden had been completely crazy-paved with broken flagstones, except for a little circle in the middle, where a monkey-puzzle tree grew. Some wilted ivy clung despairingly to the wall.

'Good gracious,' said my wife.

Yet the back garden, I knew, would be crammed with giant cauliflowers, leeks you could have used as clubs, chrysanthemums like the heads of Old English sheepdogs. And in the greenhouse great red balloons of tomatoes, inflating slowly, vine upon vine of them, like a well-kept jungle. Old Moulton had no use for garden produce that you couldn't sell, or win cups with, and the front garden was too handy. People could just help themselves. Paving-stones cost nowt, and they didn't nourish weeds. His sister Sarah, who had kept house for him since his wife died, scrubbed them with a yard-broom once a week, while old Moulton measured his leeks.

'It's ghastly,' said my wife.

'So are all the others,' I said. 'They're all the same.'

This was Jasmine Crescent. Before was Jonquil Avenue, behind Juniper Grove, and the houses were identical, all five hundred of them. Three up, two down, bathroom and toilet combined, kitchenette and coal stove. And telly aerials now on every chimney, cars and motor-bikes and sidecars on both sides of the road. Democracy not so much on the march as providing its own transport.

'What's ghastly about this one?' I asked.

'It's . . . like a defeat,' said Sue. 'Whoever lives there has just given in. They're beaten.'

JIM

MOULTON's family had moved there in the spring of 1935. Before that they had lived in Eda Place, which had been condemned in 1927, in a second floor two-roomed flat that shared a yard and earth-closet with three other families. Water came from a standpipe in the yard, and was carried, bucketful by bucketful, up the back stairs. Old Moulton was hewing in the Coronation Pit, and when he worked he needed six buckets a day for his bath. Mrs Moulton had to carry it, and she had pulmonary tuberculosis. That spring the mines were on strike, and her health improved a little—he didn't fetch the water, of course, but he didn't take so many baths. He had an allot-ment, and there was somehow enough to eat. Then she had a piece of luck: her roof fell in. Nobody was hurt, and her doctor, old Sil-verstein, went at once to the Town Hall and demanded a council house. Jasmine Crescent had just dried out, and they moved next day, cheered on by neighbours now looking at their own roofs with renewed interest. A year later, Eda Place was demolished. Two men with sledgehammers did it with ease. One old woman refused to go, and had to be dragged out to the workhouse by police. The rest of the Place had already gone, and nobody wanted her.

But Jim's family were first to go, and they went in style, in Goofy Laidlaw's granda's cart. Old Mr Laidlaw at that time kept a pub, the Lord Nelson, and Moulton had been a regular customer. Twice old Laidlaw had flung him out, but in a friendly way, and only be-cause he had a licence to lose. When the Moultons had the chance of a house he moved them for old times' sake.

The cart was the then standard coal-cart, high-wheeled, with steel tyres and a hinged back, but this one had been scrubbed and cleaned, and painted a glowing green, picked out with yellow. It was drawn by a vast, handsome black horse called Todd. Mr Laidlaw wore a black and white check suit, a red waistcoat and a square bowler hat, the only one I ever saw in my life. Horse, cart and man between them contained more colour than the whole of Eda Place. They were magnificent. Laidlaw had come down from the Border country, where his family were farmers, and still kept animals, simply because he chose to. He was a very powerful and determined man, who ruled his family, his barmaids, his horse, dogs, rabbits, ducks and even goldfish with a calm and frightening geniality. Nobody answered

7

back to old Mr Laidlaw. I realized this at once, when I saw him sitting in the cart that very first day.

The rest of Eda Place realized it too, even when he reached inside the cart and hauled out a little boy, handling him easily and deftly, as he would a rabbit. The boy submitted (no use struggling against Mr Laidlaw), and when he banged his knee on the wheel Eda Place and I knew it was his own fault. He was a tall, thin boy, narrow-chested and very pale, who wore spectacles with round fake-tortoiseshell eye-pieces and wire shanks that pulled his ears forward. They were large ears, red and unattractive. His clothes were neat, and better than mine, or Jim's. He wore shoes, not boots, and they were the kind you bought in a shop, not the kind you got from the Shoeless Children's Fund when your teacher wrote a letter, and your mother took you in mortal terror to the police-station. He was a boy to be despised.

I looked round for Jim, the born leader of Jameson Road Junior Mixed, stocky, handsome and deadly, even at nine years old. Without his invitation I wouldn't have dared come to watch him moved, but when he asked me I ached with pride. Nobody else had been asked. I was his lieutenant, his Blondel, and, whenever he chose that we should walk with our arms round each other's necks, his bride. This was a painful business. Being loved by Jim Moulton was always a painful business, yet something always to be desired. There was fire in him, even when he was a child; consuming fire, that was the more attractive because it was so dangerous.

The Moultons didn't have much, and Granda Laidlaw organized them out of their house with ease. Their terrible furniture (not terrible to us, who knew no other kind, but by any objective standard appalling) was humped down the stairs by volunteers, or slung from the window on a rope, then stowed in the cart while the old man fussed about his paintwork. Piles of worn blankets were put on top, then a great wash-basket full of crockery, a poss-tub full of boots and work-clothes and three battered suitcases—their wardrobe. Then Moulton symbolically slammed the door for the last time, and he and his wife went to catch the tram to prepare for our arrival. Jim and I were going to follow the cart. If possible we were going in it. As always he tried the direct method, and walked up to the kid with spectacles.

'I'm sitting in the front,' he said.

The kid looked at him. It was a comprehensive look that recognized the breadth of Jim's shoulders, the power of forearm and fists.

'All right,' the kid said. What else could he say?

Jim went to old Laidlaw then, waiting until the great man had time to spare for a nine-year-old.

8

'Please, mister, can me and me pal ride in your cart?'

Old Laidlaw looked at him.

'It's a good cart is that,' he said. 'Won three prizes in carnivals that cart. And the horse, of course. Bit of a hobby. An interest. Money too. Can you sit still?'

'Yes,' said Jim.

'All right. Get on.'

We climbed up like monkeys, using the wheel's hub as a step. Jim settled down at once on the perch beside the driver and I huddled down behind him, moving gently back and forward on a sewing-machine treadle. Old Laidlaw walked slowly across. It was time to go. His ascent to the driving-seat was slow and majestic. The cart swayed under his weight. He settled himself deliberately, and looked at Jim.

'Gerroff there,' he said.

Jim looked at him, appalled.

'Gerroff there,' said Laidlaw. 'You're in Tommy's seat.'

So Jim sat on the sewing-machine treadle, and I sat on a bag of coal. Laidlaw reached down an enormous arm and hauled up Tommy into his seat, then clucked at the horse and off we went. When we reached the corner, I looked back. Without the gleaming cart the gritty dullness of Eda Place was over-whelming. The Moultons' neighbours watched us go, but nobody cheered, or even waved. The miners hunkered down at the kerb-side, the women and the rest of the men just stood, the way my father used to stand, in an attitude of defeat. There wasn't any work.

When the cart reached Priestgate, old Laidlaw pulled in the horse and looked at his watch. Tommy took the reins, and the horse stood, bracing itself, as the huge old man clambered down.

'Three minutes,' he said. 'Mind you boys stay on the cart.'

The Adam and Eve opened its doors for his coming. You didn't argue with old Laidlaw.

'Is he your da?' asked Jim.

'Me granda,' said Timmy.

'When he comes out of the bar, tell him you want to change places with me.'

'I can't,' said Tommy.

'Look at this,' Jim said.

Tommy turned, and saw Jim's fist, and the expression of menace, foolish to an adult, terrifying to a child, on his face. Tommy's lip trembled.

'Honest, I can't,' he said. 'He won't let me.'

Jim hit him in the back, again and again. Tommy clung to the side

9

of the cart and endured it until his granda came out of the Adam and Eve and went into the shop next door.

'If you tell him, I'll really hit you,' said Jim. 'Won't I, Bob?'

'He will,' I said. 'Best do what he says. He hits hard, Jim does.'

The old man clambered up again, felt in his pocket, and produced three packets of aniseed-balls. We took them and thanked him, then he looked at his grandson, who was weeping very quietly.

'What's up with you then?' he said. Tommy shook his head. 'One of them hit you, didn't he? Which one?'

He looked round at us, and his face was terrible in anger.

'Was it ye?' he asked me, and I answered at once. I had no choice. Nothing has ever frightened me, before or since, as he did then.

'No. Him,' I said, and pointed at Jim. There was nothing else to do.

The old man's hand flashed, and he cracked Jim across the face—one-two-three-four. Jim whimpered once and his face twisted with the effort of not crying. Then old Laidlaw did a very strange thing. He took Jim's packet of aniseed-balls, and confiscated half. Then it was my turn.

'And ye sat there and let him,' he said. His hand swung again, once, and I cried for ten minutes. He took a quarter of my aniseed-balls away and we finished the journey in silence.

Unloading the cart took longer. Moulton had only a couple of friends to help him, and Granda Laidlaw offered nothing but advice. After all, he had supplied the horse and cart. At the end of it, while he was shaking hands with Mrs Moulton, Jim went up to Tommy once again.

'I'll be seeing ye again, son,' he said. Tommy didn't move.

When they drove away, it was my turn. Jim chased me through a maze of new council houses and building-sites, but lost me when we reached the Farthing Meadows, broken countryside with plenty of cover. Then I was free to worry about what would happen next day, for betrayal was the worst of crimes.

'WILL he expect us to go in?' Susan asked. 'Couldn't you just toot the horn or something?'

'I'd better knock,' I said. 'He's a bit touchy.'

I got out of the car, and Sue stayed where she was. She had met Jim only once before and decided that he was 'impossible', a useful, vague word that she kept handy for the unsatisfactory failures of a small town whom it was best, unobtrusively, to drop.

The door opened before I could knock, and Jim came out, bustling me down the path, slamming the door, talking all the time.

'I've been ready ten minutes,' he said. 'I knew you wouldn't want to be bothered with Aunty Sarah.' He looked at the front-room windows, where his aunt lurked behind the curtains, savouring the bouquet of my Rover and Sue's fur coat.

'What about your father?' I asked.

'One of his leeks is ailing,' he said. 'You can't be bothered with a son at a time like that.' And then, very quickly, because he hated to say it, 'D'you think it's a good idea—going to supper with Goofy?'

'Let's get it straight,' I said. 'It isn't supper, it's dinner—and it isn't Goofy either. It's Tom.'

'He'll always be Goofy to me,' said Jim.

This had to be stopped. At once.

'Not to his face,' I said. 'Not if you want a job.'

He turned and looked at me, then back over his shoulder at 52, Jasmine Crescent.

'Goofy's come a long way,' he said. 'So have you.'

'It isn't a crime,' I told him.

'No, 'he said. 'Sometimes I think it ought to be.' Then he bellowed at the trellis-gate.

'Hey, da! Come here a minute.'

An old, wizened face peered, chimpanzee-like, through the trellis bars.

'This is Dr Arnott,' said Jim. 'Why don't you get him to examine that leek? He could call in a specialist if he wasn't sure.' The old man turned away. 'Wait a minute, da. It won't cost you nowt. He's a National Health doctor.'

The old man said, 'Fuck off,' very clearly and distinctly, and Sue wound up her window.

'Obstinate old bugger,' said Jim, and went out in front of me. I opened the rear door of the car for him, and he sat behind Sue, who turned, and was carefully polite, as he was. Introductions from the front to the back of a car are never easy, and Jim was nervous, Sue prejudiced. I drove to Laidlaw's house as fast as I could.

It stood all on its own, in a little fishing-village five miles from the town: big, modern and very well designed, with a lot of mahogany and glass and a beautiful formal garden that must have cost a fortune to keep alive in the North-East of England. I rang the bell, and Laidlaw opened the door at once, as poised and ready as Jim had been, but he was grinning with pleasure.

'You're prompt,' he said. 'That's good. Mrs Arnott, I can't tell you how pleased I am to meet you. And Jim—my God—it's been years and years. Come in, come in.' And he bustled us inside as if we were all out of Dickens, and the snow piling up outside in eight-foot drifts, then turned to Jim again.

'I can't tell you how much I've been looking forward to this,' he said.

The words were gentle, the manner benign, and yet I was afraid of Laidlaw, afraid for Jim, and a little for myself. Suddenly, for reasons I couldn't explain, not then, I was back in Korea, and the end of that sad and clumsy war. I remembered the hills stretched out into the distance. Blue-grey, rough, deserted hills. Below, a road twisted its way, seeking for valleys. The north–south road that linked Pyongyang in the North to Seoul in the South, the only way an armoured column could move; the only way the war could be won. On the American side was wire, twenty yards deep, and before the wire were mines to a depth of fifty yards at least. Behind the wire there were infantry entrenched to enormous depth, bazookas, heavy-calibre machine-guns, napalm traps, all the bestial gadgetry of war, and behind the infantry there were guns, a primeval forest of guns: a hundred-millimetre cannon for every twenty square yards of disputed territory. Then came no-man's land, and then the Chinese positions. They were the same: except for one thing. They had even more guns, more men, more mines than the Allies. Nothing moved, no one spoke. The silence was total—and terrifying. In war, noise means a danger that is familiar only. Silence brings with it the fear of the unknown, the about to be discovered.

Two Negro G.I.s had climbed the hill, looked around like tourists at the vast concentration of power. They moved slowly, on tiptoe, anxious not to disturb the still silence.

At last one of them said, 'What you make of it, Harry?'

His voice was low-pitched, almost reverent, as was Harry's answer.

'Looks to me like it's over,' Harry said.

12

'You really think so?'

'It has to be over man,' Harry said. 'Just look.'

They looked again: self-propelled guns, heavy tanks, backed up for miles.

'Jesus,' Harry's friend said. 'You're right.' He opened his mouth to yell, but no sound came. The whole place was so deathly still. But at least he could grin in silence. Harry did not.

'What you looking so sad about?' his friend said. 'It's over, man.'

'Yeah,' Harry said. 'The war's over. Now we got to fight the fucking peace.'

I could see Harry very clearly, remember well the intensity of disillusionment his last words expressed, but then it was gone, wiped off. Words like Harry's didn't belong at dinner with the Laidlaws, especially as Sue was with me. I watched Sue absorb the worn and well-used elegance of hall and sitting-room as Laidlaw fussed us out of our coats and took us in to meet his wife and the spare woman. Sybil Laidlaw was slender and elegant, and far from plain. If Laidlaw had married her for her money, there was a bonus of sexual attraction that must have made it a pleasant enough decision. She was small and dark, with a quick, low-pitched voice, nervous, and yet at ease with her nervousness. And that too was attractive. The woman beside her was Madge Innes.

'You know Madge, don't you?' Tom asked.

'Oh yes. We've known each other for years,' said Jim.

'We used to be very good friends,' Madge said. 'It's silly—the way one loses touch.'

Jim started, as I did, at the smoothness of Madge's voice. There could be no doubting the threat it concealed.

'I thought you two knew each other,' Tom said. 'I'm glad I was right. Now what about a drink?'

And he did some more Dingley Dell business with glasses and decanters.

'Did he tell you he'd invited Madge?' Jim whispered. I nodded. 'The bastard must have known about us.'

Then he turned to answer a question from Sybil.

'I thought you said he was educated,' said my wife.

'Laidlaw?' I whispered.

'No. He's charming. *Moulton*. He's ghastly. And if he has been after that Innes woman, there's no need to show it so much. It's indecent.'

'How did you know?' I asked.

'I didn't,' said Sue. 'It's just obvious.'

Madge came over then, and Sue prepared to be social. Madge had learned to be good at it too, just as she had learned from somewhere to choose the right clothes, the right make-up. When I had known her, she had never had time to learn. It was at once shocking and delightful to watch Sue and Madge fit phrases together like pieces of a jigsaw puzzle, like two little girls who would infinitely sooner scratch each other and scream, if only the grown-ups weren't watching. Tom put glasses in their hands, then stood beside me and watched.

'We're very lucky men, aren't we, Bob?' he asked. 'We're having dinner with the three best-looking women in a fifty-mile radius.'

He may well have been right. Sue, at twenty-seven, was the youngest, but all three still had good faces and disciplined bodies; they had, besides, a zest for life, a sexual knowingness, that no younger woman could use without offence, yet in them it was charming. Tom stood and watched my wife and Madge Innes deciding not to quarrel, velvet-pawed, and was completely happy. This, said his smile, was what life was for. This, and the dry martini he was drinking, and the *poulet en cocotte* sizzling in the oven. Once, his wife looked at him, and the two of them grinned, they were so happy. And all the time Jim stood, puzzled because he was prepared for the worst and not getting it, baffled as a bull ignored by the entire corrida. He tried of course. I heard him say to Sybil, 'I don't think I've eaten "dinner" since I was at Cambridge. The people I know all have supper.'

'It'll be like old times, then, won't it?' said Sybil, and looked up at him. The backward tilt of that small, beautiful body was delightfully flattering to a male of even average height, like me, and Jim was six feet two. But Jim only looked away, eager now for the fluttering cape, the golden, pigtailed killer, the jeering crowds. This was his moment of truth: if he was going to be butchered, he wanted people to notice him. He'd never doubted that Tom was going to humiliate him from the moment he saw Madge Innes. Madge was there to remind him that everything has to be paid for some time, and he, if not eager to pay, was anxious to be noticed, to be seen in action, preferably fighting for his life. Instead of that, Tom and Sybil were just nice to him and offered him drinks. He couldn't stand it.

They were like that all through dinner, too, a remarkable meal by any standards, and startling by those of our home town. It was prepared by a French Basque cook, and served by her Spanish Basque husband, a squat and likeable man, who talked freely to Tom and Sybil in Spanish throughout the meal. None of the rest of us spoke Spanish, and it seemed that he was commenting on us pretty frankly. At any rate Sybil looked at Jim after one thing he said and laughed, then promptly apologized. Paco, she said, was worried because such a big man had such a small appetite. Nobody believed her.

The conversation was mostly about old times. I mentioned the

14

picture of old Moulton in Tom's office, and he told us how he'd collected Fitzgerald's work from the beginning.

'A very wise investment,' said Jim, and I wished he'd been content to eat his dinner.

Tom said, 'It was. The only way I can remember, *really* remember what it used to be like when we were boys, is by looking at those pictures.' And there was Jim being menaced once again, or thinking he was, and hating the uncertainty far more than the threat.

'Do you really want to remember all that much?' I asked.

'Why, yes,' he said. 'Of course I do. It's very fashionable to have been poor in the thirties.'

'And rich now,' said Jim.

'Oh, it's always fashionable to be rich. That doesn't count,' said Sybil, and Paco cleared away the remaining plates.

'I never got on with Fitzgerald much,' said Jim. 'He was a bloke who cared for nobody but himself.'

'I don't remember him like that,' said Madge.

'I do. He was all grab, even at school.'

'Weren't we all like that then?' I asked.

'Probably,' said Jim. 'That's why it's significant I can remember *him* so well. The rest of us were just selfish when we remembered. He was like that all the time.' He turned to Madge. 'You tell me once, just once, when he did anything for anybody.'

'At least you'll agree he's got talent,' she said.

'Oh he can *paint*,' Jim said. Then he smiled. 'When he did that one of my father, the old man played hell.'

'Because he looked so tired?' asked Sybil.

'Because he looked dirty. He wanted to go home first and have a bath and put his best suit on. Fitz talked him out of it.'

'He's good at that too,' said Madge.

'Irish blarney?' Sue asked.

'No,' said Tom. 'Fitz is a Geordie like the rest of us. I don't think he's been to Ireland in his life.' He looked at his wife.

'Sue, Madge,' she said, and rose. Tom and I stood up too, then Jim followed, awkwardly, as if this kind of standing up were an infrequent exercise.

'Forgive the formality,' Tom said. 'Bob and Jim and I have some business to talk over. We don't want to bore you with it.'

Sybil went at once, and Madge and Sue followed her out. Tom watched them go, and slid down in his chair.

'There's wine and fruit on the table,' he said. 'I thought we might save the coffee and brandy for the drawing-room.' He looked from Jim to me.

15

'Well now,' he said. 'Suppose we get down to the agenda? We don't want to keep the ladies waiting.'

'I'm an agenda?' said Jim.

Tom laughed. 'You must forgive me,' he said. 'It's a way of speaking I've got into ... quite recently. Please try to bear with it.' But there was no plea in his voice. Tom was there to command. The politeness was just so much social grease to ease the grit of an order given to a dependant.

'All right,' said Jim, more relaxed than he'd looked all night. He'd seen the threat too, and welcomed it. 'Where do we start? Minutes of the Last Meeting?'

'We can skip that one,' Tom said. 'We haven't met for years.'

'Nineteen fifty-six,' said Jim. 'The Three Leopards. Old Boys' Reunion Dinner.' He laughed. 'Floreat Etona. Forty Years On,' he said.

'Not Forty Years On,' said Tom. 'That's Harrow.'

That kind of knowledge was an obsession with him still. Jim didn't waste time in argument.

'Swing swing together then,' he said. 'If I had my way they wouldn't do it in boats—there'd be a gallows provided.'

He had made the same poor joke at the reunion. It was the year our headmaster, Old Bickersley, had retired. Bickersley had got his job because he knew classical Greek, and he was the only man in a ten-mile radius, other than a parson, who did know classical Greek. He was talkative, lachrymose, addicted to high-church christianity and snuff, and he could cane harder than any other master in the school, including even Gobby Lipton, who weighed fourteen stone and taught P.T. Sometimes, when he caned you really hard, Old Bickersley wept. He had wept the day he caned me because my father had hit Mr Futters. . . .

OLD BOYS

BICKERSLEY had always been Old Bickersley, for as long as I could remember, though there had always been older men than he on his staff. In 1936, when he'd caned me, he'd been under fifty, and yet to me, to all of us, he'd always seemed unbelievably old, Tithonus old, as if death had overlooked him centuries ago, and couldn't be bothered to come back for him. He was by choice a leftover from an Edwardian era he himself could only just remember. He dressed the part—narrow, peg-top trousers, double-breasted waistcoats—and he played it. Reminiscence of Oxford, the organ in the chapel, mellow old stone and rosy, sun-warmed brick; house-parties and the Irish Question and George V's coronation: he could turn the stuff on as if it were as immediate as this week's newsreel, and up there in the North-East in Depression time it was meaningless. For him it was a warm and weepy nostalgia for the lost promise of his youth; for us it was history, so ancient that Old Bickersley might as well be dead—and he hated us for it, though at the time we never understood why.

It was Jim Moulton who probably analysed it first. I say 'probably', because Laidlaw was on to him early too. But Jim had it all worked out in terms of politics by the time he was fourteen. Bickersley's nostalgia was for wealth. If you wanted to go and live in all that mellow stone and sun-warmed brick you had to *pay*—and the people who had house-parties were bosses, so if you wanted to go to a house-party (God knows what we thought *that* was) you wanted to be a boss too. There could be no compromise with that. And yet Jim got away with it. Bickersley had no choice, because Jim was always top of his year and played for the county boys' fifteen at rugby football. When he had to make Jim Captain of the School he wept freely, not least because Jim was a miner's son, and the mass of his pupils were lower middle class.

With Goofy it was different. Goofy's father had money and his son was dressed accordingly. Very early in life Goofy began to moderate the broadness of his Tyneside accent, and—once he'd seen how things were—to go to the same church as Old Bickersley. (He stopped going, I remember, two days after Bickersley had given him his reference in his final term.) He was interested in money always, and the things that money could buy—and among these were Eton, Winchester, Oxford, Cambridge, weekends at Woburn or Longleat, the

Members' Pavilion at Lords—and the Anglican Church. In that way he was a natural for Old Bickersley, and he exploited it for all he was worth. He'd been aware that Bickersley's nostalgia was firmly embedded in economics, but, unlike Jim, Goofy had seen nothing wrong with it. The haves always had a better time than the have-nots, and if, like Old Bickersley, you were only just a have-not, it was right that you should lament not being a have. Old Bickersley never caned him once. . . .

Jim and I arrived together, I remember, and, the reunion being what it was, we'd had a few drinks first. On the way up the stairs we met Goofy, who treated us as if we'd last met three weeks ago (in fact it had been three years) and began at once to talk about a visit he'd just made to Düsseldorf, and the big deal he'd pulled off there. I could tell Jim hated him for it. Anything involving the Germans brought out that hatred in him, even then. Even now. But he went up the stairs quietly enough, on his best behaviour for once.

Old Bickersley waited for us at the head of the staircase, and with him was Harry Lewis, chairman of the reunion committee, in the shiniest blue serge suit I've ever seen. He was oozing confidence, but Bickersley wouldn't even look at him. I gathered that Harry hadn't done as well as the careers master had predicted. It was our entrance that brought the old bastard back to life. He looked from Goofy to Jim, then back to Goofy, and for once he suffered a dilemma I could appreciate. How can you laugh and cry at the same time? His whole body seemed to reach out to them both, but all he could do was gibber: love and hate so perfectly in balance they rendered him inarticulate. Goofy was looking very smart I remember, and already making money. Jim was Spalding Reader in Theoretical Physics at one of the London colleges, and a sartorial disaster. I was in uniform. I was an acting major and young for the rank, and I was wearing the ribbon of the Military Cross. Old Bickersley didn't even look at me. Love and hate were all he had time for.

'You're looking well, sir,' Goofy said. The words soothed like syrup.

'Thank you,' Old Bickersley said. 'I am in excellent health.'

'And keeping busy?'

'I make it a rule,' said Old Bickersley, 'never to be without occupation. It is essential if the mind is to preserve its tone.'

'Mens sana in corpore sano,' said Goofy.

'Very happily expressed, if I may say so,' said Old Bickersley, and at that point Jim Moulton simply walked away. Old Bickersley brightened enough to spare me a glance.

'Wardropper, my dear boy,' he said, 'how surprising to see you in uniform. And with the insignia—do you so phrase it?—of the

18

R.A.M.C. Are we to assume that your academic studies were successful?'

By the time I'd finished explaining that I wasn't Wardropper—an explanation complicated by my outrage that he should even think I was (when last heard of, Wardropper had been imprisoned for a series of offences involving pigs)—Old Bickersley had lost interest and gone back to Goofy. They appeared to be discussing the Thirty-Nine Articles. I edged round them, apologizing, hating myself for doing so, and went into the reception-room. It was small and nasty, in a Gothic sort of way: stained glass, phony oak beams, too many chairs and tables with carved protuberances that could catch you a vicious clout on the patella if you turned round quickly, but it had a bar, too, and at the bar was Jim, talking to Madge Innes.

Madge had long awoken to the fact of her own beauty. It was a rare and unfashionable beauty, but so overwhelmingly perfect of its kind that I could only, for the moment, gawp at it like a kid at a sweet stall. She was a big girl, five foot seven at least, and with a lot of flesh on her. Ten years before, when I'd been doing my locum at the University Hospital, her mother had brought Madge to see me because Madge was fat. Her mother had no special faith in me as an expert on adipose tissue, but for her I had one special recommendation all the same—she knew my aunty, and she knew that my aunty would give me hell if I ever let on that her daughter was afflicted. Because Mrs Innes believed that her daughter was no ordinary fatty: to Mrs Innes, her daughter's excess pounds were attributable to a fact that terrified her: Madge might be glandular, and glands to Mrs Innes meant sex. Whether Mrs Innes's worry was remorse for the tempestuous passion of her conception or fear that she might turn into a nymphomaniac I was too embarrassed to ask, and anyway the tests I ran on her were all negative. And yet Madge was bloated in an era when sweets were strictly rationed. Her face, even then, would have been beautiful were it not for the spots—pretty nose, grey eyes with a warmth to them you never associate with the colour grey, a perfect mouth, and thick masses of curling brown hair, but her body was at least fifteen pounds overweight. But then Mrs Innes kept a combined cake and sweet shop. I gave her a diet sheet, and advised her to stop helping her mother in the shop. I had seen her once more, not long after, briefly and disastrously, and even then the diet was beginning to work. Now, ten years later, it worked superbly. I felt like Pygmalion. Her body was big, and in another fifteen or twenty years weight might again be a problem if she didn't lay off the starchy foods, but for the moment her very bigness was in exact proportion. Breasts and hips were large but shapely, her waist supple and narrow, her legs long, elegant, and strong. Her whole body exuded a strength and vitality that underlined its rich elegance. Her face was exactly as I remembered it, except that it too was now as alive and eager as the rest of her, and with an informed intelligence that nougat and chocolate creams had hidden from me.

Big, beautiful women are usually referred to as earth-mothers, I know: if a classical goddess is invoked for comparison, it's not Diana or Venus, but Demeter. They belong, we are told, in farm kitchens, their hands white with flour while they cope with half a dozen rosy children. But Madge wasn't like that at all. Her goddess was Venus right enough, though perhaps she owed a sacrifice to Diana too, the hunting Diana whose pride and pleasure is her body's strength. And of course Jim Moulton had got her. There were forty or so men in that room, all healthy, all presentable, the proportion of small-town successes the grammar school threw up year by year: doctors, solicitors, architects, bank managers, local government officers; chaps who, if they hadn't already joined the golf-club, were beginning to think it was about time they did, but Madge Innes was with Jim. They didn't exactly love him for it.

Jim saw me coming and turned back to the bar. It took me some time to reach him—there was a great deal of milling about and back-slapping, my-God-I'd-never-have-recognized-you, Where-on-earth-d'you-hide-yourself, You've-put-a-bit-of-weight-on; the embarrassed exuberance of men who have nothing in common but the remembrance of a lost youth that most of them, in retrospect, despised. When I got to them Jim had bought me a whisky.

'Bloody Romeo and Juliet,' he said.

I was still preoccupied with Madge, and assumed at once that the reference must be to himself and her. I envied him.

'Old Bickersley and Goofy,' he said. 'Playing the bloody balcony scene. What's he after, Bob?'

'Goofy? Why should he be after anything?'

'Who'd be nice to Old Bickersley if they weren't after something? Particularly Goofy?'

'And they say women gossip,' said Madge. 'Hallo, Dr Arnott.'

'Hallo,' I said. 'I'm glad you recognized me. I'd wait for ever for Jim to introduce us.'

Jim showed the faint bewilderment he always showed when social behaviour made its demands on him. Good manners were a language he'd never been taught and he was too bloody busy to teach himself.

'How can you possibly qualify as an Old Boy?' I asked.

She smiled then, and to the warmth there was added an appraising quality. I was in the game too, making a bid, and the idea delighted her.

'I'm covering this thing for the *Courant*,' she said.

The *Courant* was our local newspaper: a venerable sheet that had existed for years on its ability to get the names right.

'You're—what's the expression—a cub reporter?'

She made what I believe is called a moue. Until that moment I had no idea that such facial contortions could be considered sexy.

'Certainly not,' she said. 'The *Courant*'s been taken over. It's got a new image. I'm Hope Still.'

'You're who?'

'Hope Still. The dear little lady columnist taking a look at the world of you great big rough adorable men. Or I will be till the end of the month. I got promoted, thank God.'

Before I could ask her more, Jim butted in to ask if she knew Goofy, and before she could answer Harry Lewis came up and said it was time to go into the dining-room and we'd better leave now because the waitresses were on overtime after ten-thirty. But I turned round at the dining-room door for a last look at Madge. So did Jim. She was talking to Goofy Laidlaw.

'Well I'll be damned,' Jim said.

'You talk like an American,' I said.

'Why shouldn't I?' Jim asked. 'I married one.'

It was the first I'd heard of it.

'I wish to God I knew what Goofy was up to,' said Jim.

A PRESENT FOR OLD BICKERSLEY

THE reunion was the only one I ever attended, so I can't tell you whether its nastiness was in any way remarkable, but nasty it certainly was: in food, in drink, and especially in atmosphere. We had come to take dinner with a headmaster we none of us had liked and most of us had loathed. In all our years of school we had made no more than a handful of friends, and from these we had been separated by Harry Lewis's seating arrangements, which appeared to be not so much haphazard as positively vindictive. I for example found myself sitting between Jeavons, formerly the biggest thief in the school and now the manager of a hire-purchase firm, and Faraday, who even in the second form was renowned for an unctuous hypocrisy as nauseating as that of Old Bickersley himself. I'd last seen him on the day my father and mother were buried. He'd been a fire-watcher, then, as I had. 'Jesus understands,' he'd told me. The fact that I didn't never occurred to him. And now he was a bank manager. We sat exchanging conversation as if it were notes in a devalued currency, mangled tough chicken and sipped Algerian plonk like the connoisseurs we were, and all we had to look forward to was a series of speeches in praise of the sanctimonious old sod at the head of the table and his presentation with a solid silver tea-service to which we'd all contributed. A fine if self-inflicted irony, this last. Harry Lewis had displayed abilities as a tribute-gatherer unheard of since the heyday of the Turkish Empire. When I'd accepted his invitation, largely because he'd told me Jim and John Fitzgerald would be there, he'd nicked me for a fiver by return of post. And John Fitzgerald hadn't even shown up.

Still, if I had my worries, Old Bickersley had his, too. Harry Lewis had put him between himself and Jim Moulton, and Lewis he despised for the state of his suit, Jim he detested for what he had achieved. It was apparent too that Lewis and Jim were arguing, about politics as I afterwards learned. Lewis at that time taught in a secondary modern school and spent his nights doing voluntary work for the Labour Party, his eventual aim a seat in the House of Commons. His views on any kind of deviation from the Labour norm were therefore as sympathetically informed as a lesbian nymphomaniac's views on heterosexual brothels. And between them sat Old Bickersley, puce with rage, his big night in ruins, offering as compromise his own brand of Liberalism, the kind that made Gladstone look like a rabble-rousing Leftist. I couldn't overhear much of it, but I enjoyed it anyway. Anything was better than exchanging tatty symbols of goodwill with Jeavons and Faraday. It even got me through the cheese and biscuits.

Then the waitresses came round whispering, 'Brandy or whisky, sir?' and handing me two cubic centimetres of the one I hadn't ordered, and Harry Lewis bashed the table with the butt-end of his fork so hard he spilled my coffee and his own. And even that was another gain. It won him the first laugh of the evening, and anyway the coffee was undrinkable.

Poor Harry. At school I remembered him as an earnest, bulging sort of boy. Forehead bulging with ideas, stomach bulging with school dinners, eyes bulging with the need to impress people with the fact that he was Harry Lewis and one of these days by God you'd be glad to say you'd met him. And running. Always running. Always frantic to catch up, because wherever he was the knowledge, the excitement, the one elusive, perfect thing that would change his whole life, was somewhere else and if he didn't run he'd never catch it, so he kept on running and the elusive, perfect thing kept on eluding him, as elusive, perfect things so often do.

I looked around for Madge Innes, but she sat at a corner table in shadow, and anyway Harry was making his speech. Golden days. The hopes and aspirations of youth. Wordsworth's immortal lines about shades of the prison house begin to close about the growing boy not true in our case. On the contrary. Mr Bickersley exemplified throughout his life the true meaning of education—a leading-out. Loyal and devoted service to the cause of youth. Scholarship. Christianity. Plain living and high thinking. He could turn it on like a tap, but even so I began to admire him for it. There he stood: eyes glowing, face shining with sincerity, demanding from us—and getting—nostalgia for a dreamworld that existed only in his imagination. In reality he knew as well as I did that Old Bickersley was, by any rational system of evaluation, awful.

Yet he sat down to roars of applause. I'm not sure that here and there some of us didn't dash away a manly tear, though that may have been the Algerian plonk. I think for the moment Old Bickersley even forgave him his suit. Then he was on his feet again almost at once, asking Jim to present this handsome solid silver tea-service. I don't know which of them was the more appalled, Jim or Old Bickersley, but they were both trapped and they knew it. They clambered to their feet like two wrestlers with a grudge, Lewis shoved the tea-service at Jim and Jim shoved it at Old Bickersley, whose snarl of disgust Madge Innes described next night as the expression of a man overwhelmed by emotion, which in a sense it was. Then some idiot shouted, 'Speech!' At least I thought it was an idiot at the time but it wasn't. It was Goofy Laidlaw. When others took it up he shut up at once. Even at the time I was struck by how much he seemed to be enjoying himself.

When the shouting died, Jim said: 'Gentlemen, Harry Lewis said that he wanted me here to undertake a task of considerable importance. I gather that this is it.' The words, as you can see, were fine if only he hadn't got that note of incredulity in his voice. Anyway that was the last relevant sentence he uttered. From there on until he was howled down, he harangued the audience on the necessity for instant unilateral disarmament. Later Madge told me that there should have been a photographer there, but he arrived too late, having been detained at a Masonic. It was a cause of great regret to me. I'd have loved to have that photograph: Jim spouting fall-out statistics and Old Bickersley handling his tea-pot and milk-jug like weapons.

In the end Harry Lewis practically pushed Jim down into his seat, sprayed a little oil about our well-known and distinguished friend's heartfelt if misguided feelings on a controversial topic and called on Old Bickersley to reply. By this time the old pest had turned a colour I'd rarely seen, even in general practice, and I reckoned the evening had knocked a good three years off his life, but he'd prepared a speech, and he made it. At first I was surprised that he didn't take the opportunity to hit back at Jim individually, but then I saw why. Jim was a drop in the bucket, a more concentrated drop than most, but that was all, for Old Bickersley detested the lot of us. Through all the sobs and exhortations and pieties, that message came through loud and clear. Old Bickersley detested us for not being gentlemen or the sons of gentlemen: for being on the contrary Geordie brats with dreadful manners and impossible accents. The one note of hope in his speech was the announcement that he was off south on an early train next day, never, he feared, to return to the scene of his pedagogic labours. We gathered he wouldn't even have waited this long if it hadn't been for the solid silver tea-service. As he talked, I noticed, his colour improved, but I was conscious to the very end of a curious flexing movement he made with his hands—and then I remembered. Usually when Old Bickersley had talked at such length, his hands had been holding a cane.

For a moment, the farce died on me. It's a sad business to hear an elderly man admit in public that his entire working life has been lived in hate; that after thirty years in one town he can take away not even one moment of affection. I remembered the beating he'd given me, my father in gaol and my mother pleading at the Guardians—these are things I shall always remember—but I couldn't hate Old Bickersley any more. The very detestation he showed proved that all his life he'd missed the things every one of his pupils had taken for granted: friendship, co-operation, in the last analysis love.

Then Harry Lewis put on his toastmaster's voice and asked us all to be upstanding while we drank the health of Mr Bickersley, and those of us who'd absent-mindedly consumed our ration covered our glasses with our hands and swallowed anyway. After that we sang 'Auld Lang Syne'. I've never heard it sung with less conviction.

When it was all over, a lot of people wanted to talk to me: to remember; to reminisce. When I looked round for Jim, he was alone. That speech had finished him. On the way out we passed Madge Innes, and Jim invited her for a drink, but she couldn't come: she had to get back to the *Courant*.

'We'll walk you to your bus then,' said Jim, and I remember she smiled then, the zest and strength as beautiful as ever.

'It's sweet of you,' she said, 'but Mr Laidlaw's giving me a lift in his car.'

'Who?' said Jim.

'Mr Laidlaw. He tells me you once called him Goofy.'

'We did,' I said.

'It's strange how even the stupidest children can grow up into quite perceptive adults,' said Madge. 'Good night.'

And then she was at the door, and Goofy was waiting.

Jim said, 'Well, I'll go to hell.'

A GOOD YEAR FOR CHAMBERTIN

'I don't think I'll ever forget that dinner,' said Jim.

'To be honest—I never thought you'd turn up,' Tom Laidlaw said. He noticed the question in Jim's eyes and added, 'I suggested that Harry Lewis invite you.'

'What on earth did you do that for?'

'Why did you come?'

'I was up on a visit anyway. And I wanted to see Bob again. . . . But why ask me at all?'

Laidlaw shrugged. 'It seemed appropriate. You were our most distinguished old boy—academically. Old Bickersley seemed the type who set a lot of store by that sort of thing.' He turned to me then, watched me peeling an apple. It's something I enjoy doing, if the apple and the knife are good—spiralling off the peel, tissue-paper thin, then savouring the taste of the apple with just a whisper of steel in it.

'What a very competent surgeon Bob must be,' he said, and of course I broke the peel. I think he'd intended that I should. 'Try a little of this Wensleydale with it. You'll find it does wonders for the Chambertin.'

We were getting social again, and Jim grew restless.

'I thought Harry Lewis was in charge of the whole business.'

Laidlaw smiled. 'So did Harry,' he said. 'But he needed a helping hand from time to time—like so many of my contemporaries.'

'Old Bickersley didn't even like me. Why pick on me?'

'Old Bickersley didn't like anybody.'

'He liked you,' said Jim.

'That was because he didn't know me properly. I'd just got back from Germany that night. Do you remember?'

'Düsseldorf,' said Jim.

'It seemed to me at the time you rather disapproved of that fact. Am I right?'

Jim was eating a slice of pineapple. He spoke with his mouth full.

'Perfectly,' he said.

'May one ask why?'

'I don't like Germans.'

'Isn't that rather a sweeping statement?'

'Of course it is. It's irrational, subjective and prejudiced too.'

26

'And yet you act on it—and expect other people to act on it.' Jim said nothing. 'I'd gone there on business,' Laidlaw said. 'It was a cheerless place. All schnapps and sausages, and an economic miracle that was just beginning to work. Oh—and call-girls. The place was stiff with them.' He paused and smiled. 'Would that be what some of your crowd would call a Freudian slip?' he asked me.

'It would,' I said.

'But really—it was all very strange. I'd come across the same thing once before, but this was different. They used to hand them round like cigarettes. It was the other way to prove one's manhood, I suppose. The only acceptable alternative to war. And that is very important to them after all. So one worked at one's call-girls as one worked at one's contacts, or one's bargaining. And soon, if one were honest, one found one's call-girls by far the least exciting of the three—not that they couldn't produce some quite remarkable stunts on occasion. What d'you make of it, Bob—the boredom I mean?'

'Perhaps you take your manhood for granted,' I said. 'In which case having to prove it would be boring.'

'But you do think that as an alternative to blitzkrieg it has its points?'

'I always have,' I said.

He went back to Jim. 'They had a new typewriter,' he said. 'I wanted to produce it here—under licence. It's small and compact, good typeface, cheap to make, easy to sell. It's been modified twice since I got the concession. Twice in fourteen years. Even the Japs can't make one as cheap. I sell it big in the States—for dollars. The factory on the trading-estate employs over three hundred people—two-thirds of them adult males. If I closed down they'd be on the dole. And you don't like Germans?'

'That's right,' said Jim.

'I even employed your father for a while—as a storekeeper.'

'I don't like my father either.'

'Now there I'm inclined to agree with you. He drank a great deal. It made him . . . truculent. I think we were obliged to get rid of him.'

'Most people are,' Jim said. 'You, the N.C.B., the Army. I got rid of of him myself as soon as I could. There's only my Aunty Sarah can stand him. He drinks because his head hurts, and his head hurts because it was bashed in when a seam cracked in 1949. Or that's what he says. Trouble is he forgets. I knew him long before 1949, and he was drinking as long as I remember. Maybe it was the Somme—he was there all the time it lasted, and never took a scratch. Trust a pitman to dig a hole—or maybe it was the Black-and-Tans. He was dishonourably discharged from that lot——'

I thought of Fitzgerald. 'I didn't know that was possible,' I said.

'He sold his rifle to the I.R.A.,' said Jim. 'No doubt he needed the money to buy booze. In his sober moments he used to tell me the Germans had a lot of good in them. They had discipline and they put the Jews in their place and they nearly won two world wars. He also admires them because they're hard workers. That's always a virtue in my father's opinion when it applies to other people.'

'Must you always hate what your father likes?' Laidlaw asked. 'Wouldn't you say that's a rather aggravated case of over-compensation, Bob?'

'No,' I said. 'I wouldn't. Not until I had a few more facts.'

'Just as well,' said Jim. 'I didn't come here to be analysed with the fruit and nuts.'

'And the Chambertin,' said Laidlaw. 'Or, more accurately, Gevrey Chambertin, I'm afraid. But the sixty-three. Really a quite excellent year. Or am I boasting?'

'D'you mind if I ask you something?' said Jim, and I froze. The very way he said it warned me that he was going to ask something appalling.

'My dear fellow, of course,' said Laidlaw.

'Why do you talk like this?' Before Laidlaw could answer, he continued, 'I don't mean the content—we can get to that later. I mean the form. "One worked at one's contacts." "Gevrey Chambertin." "A quite excellent year." What d'you do it for?'

'I don't understand you,' said Laidlaw.

'It's like bloody P. G. Wodehouse or Henry James or something. It isn't you, man—how can it be you? You're Tommy Laidlaw from Cobden Street. Your dad kept a corner shop. I used to buy bullseyes there.'

'No,' said Laidlaw. 'You bought aniseed-balls when you bought anything. Mostly I gave them to you.'

I could remember that, all right—the giving, I mean. It was poor Goofy's Danegeld, his tribute, his protection money. If Jim fancied a few sweets, then Goofy was safe for the moment. And when he was safe he could be very entertaining. He was a clown all right, because it was expected of him, and Laidlaw was always far too scared not to provide what was expected, but a witty clown, even a satiric one. From the beginning he'd had an eye for human weakness, and knew how to mimic it. There'd been the matter of Miss Fitton—the headmistress of our junior school. Goofy had gone there when his father took the shop, and paid, over and over again, for the clouting his grandfather had given Jim, paid too for the fact that Miss Fitton liked him because he wore a suit and talked nicely. Miss Fitton was a snob, and a strait-laced virgin approaching the menopause at a gal-

lop, who one day shattered staff and school alike by announcing in
the *Courant* her engagement to the headmaster of the senior school,
an austere and rather grubby widower. Goofy's description of their
nuptials convulsed the playground for days. Where he got the stuff
from I've no idea. A lot of it, I realized later, sounded as if it were
lifted from *The Perfumed Garden*. But the best act was the delivery
of Miss Fitton's first-born—and very educational I found it. Until
Goofy's act I'd only the vaguest idea of how babies got born—but
Goofy cleared that up for me and made me howl with laughter at the
same time. Miss Fitton's baby, you see, would be born wearing his
school-cap and covering his penis modestly with his hands as he
recited the seven times table. . . .

'Aniseed-balls then,' said Jim. 'What's it got to do with Gevrey
Chambertin?'

'But my dear fellow,' Laidlaw said, 'my father was T. T. Laidlaw,
Provisions and Sweets. Not me. I'm Thomas Laidlaw Limited, and
Thomas Laidlaw (Holdings) Limited, and Arnold and Co., and
Easimarts, and ten per cent of this and fifteen per cent of that. My
daughter's at a convent school and my son goes up to Repton next
term. Of course I talk like this. I *am* like this.' He sounded genuinely
aggrieved.

'You really believe that, don't you?' Jim asked.

'Of course I do,' Laidlaw said. 'It's true.'

'Let's get to the content then,' said Jim.

'By all means.'

'We've had reminiscence of the good old days, and why you got on
with Bickersley and I didn't, and what an old bastard my father is.'
Laidlaw tried to interrupt then, but Jim ploughed on. 'I won't quarrel with you over that one, except that I think he's a sad old bastard.
We've had your money and your wine and the way I hate the Germans—all very polished stuff, full of nuances and all that——'

'I'm glad you think so,' said Laidlaw. 'I enjoy nuances.'

'I don't,' said Jim. 'I like things clear. Tell me something—what's
Madge doing here?'

Laidlaw sighed. 'Nuances again. The question's straight
enough—but the answer . . .' He shrugged. 'She's a symbol, I suppose.'

'Of what?'

'Our hopes, our aspirations—yours and mine, that is. Not Bob's. Of
all the things we wanted, and the price we were prepared to pay for
them.'

He paused then, but Jim made no answer. For the first time, his
driving urge to fight had faltered: he seemed almost afraid.

'Then she has a practical purpose as well,' Laidlaw said.

'And what might that be?' asked Jim.

'If you treat her right, she might help you find a job.'

'Madge?' said Jim. 'Help me?' and I groaned inside. This really wasn't the way to set about being a suppliant.

'Why not?' said Laidlaw. 'I've no doubt she'd be able to find something for you herself—if she chose. She's big stuff in local television now. Buys her wines from my fellow. But of course that won't be necessary.'

'I'm glad to hear it,' said Jim.

'Madge and I want to work on this together.' He paused, and the bull-ring image came back to me. Jim was a dazed bull now, the brilliance and glitter had unsettled him, made him unsure, and now he confronted an elegant and very graceful gentleman with two barbed hooks in his hand.

'Tell *me* something,' Laidlaw said. 'Who would you rather be grateful to—Madge or me? Or both of us?'

MADGE

She had really been lucky in her timing. To be a *jeune fille en fleurs* weighing a hundred and twenty-five pounds and five foot seven in her nylons wouldn't have been all that easy in the days of miniskirts, but back in the early fifties it hadn't been all that bad. In those days to a woman bras and girdles had seemed as inevitable a part of life as breasts and hips, and an unavoidable compensation for over-endowment. Not that she had been overendowed, not really, but a figure like hers had had its disadvantages—even running for a bus, for example, could provide enough embarrassment to last for the rest of the day—and the realization of this tended to make her clumsy. The right kind of bra and girdle helped.

Looking back on it, it seemed that she had achieved beauty over-night. One day she was the gross white hope of the school—spotty, overweight, excused hockey to work on old scholarship papers—the next the spots had gone and she'd shed four pounds. Not enough, not nearly enough, but sufficient to make Mr Eades—brought in from outside to coach her in Latin—actually look at her twice one cold March morning, instead of burying his nose in Sallust. As if he'd been Michelangelo looking at a lump of marble and suddenly aware of the statue inside it. As a compliment it wasn't much—Mr Eades, terrified of nubile girls, never exceeded his self-imposed ration of two stares per hour, and anyway he had warts—but it was enough to get her started. From that day on she'd kept to a diet, just as Bob Arnott had suggested she should, and the flesh had fallen from her like snow in spring. It hadn't been easy. Chocolate creams and nougat were im-portant to her, and one day no doubt she would go back to them, when sex demanded too much expenditure of energy for the return involved, but that day, thank God, wasn't yet. Not by a long chalk. Sex so far had meant almost no expenditure of energy except the strictly carnal, and its returns were enormous. Chocolate creams and nougat could wait.

In her way, Madge thought, she'd been an innovator, almost a pioneer. Women like herself were common enough now: women who made money, lived well and indulged in genteel promiscuity. But after all, she'd been at it for fifteen years, and it was still remarkably good fun. Mind you, you had to have a talent for it. She looked at the other two women in the long, over-elegant drawing-room, sipping Chartreuse and babbling about babies. Maybe talent was too weak a word. Take Susan Arnott, for instance. All posh accent and Polly Peck clothes and a fur coat she wore like a Victoria Cross. Where would she be without poor old Bob? Once she'd thought Bob had possibilities: not bad looking, witty when he chose, gratifyingly aware, from the start, of the promise of her body. And with a wildness in him, she was sure. That Military Cross for instance: he'd earned it for a display of violent courage that, battles apart, would have been called insanity, even among men. But he'd settled for Susan with the Roedean vowels and the *Woman's Own* sex-life, and the violent courage was back in the deep freeze. . . .

Sybil Laidlaw moved an ash-tray of Venetian glass fractionally towards Susan Arnott. The movement made her aware of the long, rich curve of Madge Innes's leg. She looked up quickly, to the other woman's hands. They held a glass and it was empty.

'Another drink, Miss Innes?' she asked.

'Please.'

'B and B, isn't it?'

'That's right,' said Madge Innes.

'What's B and B?' Susan Arnott asked, brightly social, invincibly cheerful.

'Brandy and Benedictine,' said Madge Innes. 'Mixed. What the Edwardians would have called a bounder's drink, I imagine.'

'Really?' The brow wrinkled a little, the single word implying that she didn't quite understand, and that therefore what followed might very well be vulgar.

Pity to disappoint you, love, Madge Innes thought, and said aloud: 'You know, flashy and expensive, but none the less exciting—and potent.'

'D'you mean the bounder or the drink?' Susan Arnott asked.

Thick as two planks, but Christ she's a sticker, Madge thought. Sybil Laidlaw put a refilled glass into her hand, and she reminded herself: Careful, baby. Make it last. This is a night you want to remember.

'Miss Innes is very gifted with words,' Sybil said carefully, and the penny dropped with a thud that shook the district.

'Of course,' Susan Arnott said. 'I've seen you. On the television.' (Why was it people like her always called it *the* television?) 'You're awfully clever.' And why should she make that last sentence sound pitying, Madge Innes wondered. 'But really, you should have warned me.' The Arnott was looking at Sybil Laidlaw now, and sounding reproachful. 'I must have made an awful fool of myself.'

Say it as if you mean it, darling, Madge Innes thought.

'I'm sure Miss Innes must be quite bored with people talking about her all the time,' Sybil Laidlaw said.

'Not at all. I haven't been bored with myself as a subject since I was seventeen years old.'

The Arnott thought she was being clever again, and Sybil Laidlaw chose to think so. They went back to talking babies, and she studied the green and golden liquid swirling sluggishly in the glass. All she knew about babies was how to avoid them, and since the pill there was very little effort involved in that. So she was out of it, which was what they wanted, and her too. She wanted time to look back, before the Laidlaw remembered her manners and tried to be social. For Sybil wasn't a thicky, that was obvious. And she'd know her way around in bed too: couldn't miss, with that cute little body and Tommy Laidlaw for a teacher. But Tommy came later. First was the fact that one day she was beautiful, like a butterfly out of a chrysalis, a duckling turned into a swan. And by and large she'd lived happily ever after, too, and tonight it would be more so.

At first it had been enough just to look the way she did, to examine her skin in the mirror, thick, smooth as cream, and not a bloody pustule in sight: to sneak her mirror into the bathroom, and, with the help of the steamed-up glass in the bathroom cabinet, to look at her body's flawless generosity, to reassure herself, day by day, of its flow, its firmness, the comforting fact that however much she curved she never bulged. From the beginning she knew that she had, and in exact abundance, what any man would want: an opinion increased by the sight of the pin-ups in *Reveille*, and *Lilliput*, and *Men Only*. What she hadn't recognized—was at first too scared to face up to—was her own need for men. As Fatty Innes it hadn't been a problem except in her own private fantasies—but as the pounds melted the problem grew. She could have a man, that was apparent, but a man meant marriage and babies, which would have suited her mother down to the ground, but wouldn't do for Madge. Cooking and suckling were all right if that was what you wanted, but they were a hell of an impediment to Sallust and *Phèdre* and the Treaty of Utrecht: to all the things that would get her away from Wreckenton Street and the shop and Mother, and into an acceptable university. So at first she'd lived like a nun, and if nuns took cold baths when they had to, she quite understood why. It was only later that she realized that what she needed was not a man, but men. That there could be, quite literally, safety in numbers.

At first she'd made do with the admiration of other girls. Her mother, it seemed then—Jesus, it seemed *now*—never even looked at her, or when she did saw only adolescent Madge with her podgy hand trapped in a sweet-jar. Early in life Mrs Innes had decided her daughter was clever, and, like Susan Arnott, saw only cause for regret in the fact, but once the terror of glands was removed she accepted it

33

as something you could do nothing about, like a technical hitch on the telly. No—that's wrong. Unlike a technical hitch, it wasn't something a man could come and fix. Mrs Innes, a widow whose happiness had begun with her widowhood, had nevertheless looked forward to herself bawling in church and her daughter cutting a cake, and the opportunity to help wash nappies whiter than white. When Madge was twelve, her mother accepted, once and for all, that those things would be denied her, and took to being ill instead. Once she'd sold out the shop to a supermarket, she was able to make quite a hobby of it.

But the girls in the grammar school, they'd known about it all right. Spotted it as soon as it happened, trying to get close to her, as if there really were such a thing as sympathetic magic, and to be close to Madge would erase their spots, inflate their breasts. She'd liked that. It had been good to be admired and pampered, instead of laughed at. Oh, yes—she was pampered too—presents at Christmas, invitations to parties—what magic symbol isn't? But you had to be careful. It was at school that she met her first dyke, who joined the Wrens the day Madge accepted a place at Manchester University, and also lived happily ever after. Then there were the mistresses: some of them, the younger ones especially, the ones with a bit of hope left, were also disposed to pet and pamper, but the older ones, the ones who'd lost it or never even had it, poor bitches—they hadn't liked her at all. But her work took care of that. She'd slogged on like a maniac, beautiful or not, and got herself a place at Manchester. Oxford and Cambridge had regretted, London wasn't quite sure, but Manchester came across almost by return of post. At the time she'd wept—she'd had hopes of the big three—but in the end she was glad of it. It so exactly suited her image.

And anyway, it was good to get away, she thought, from Mother, who was flirting delicately with heart-trouble, from les girls at school, who wept and gave their addresses and made me promise to keep in touch—(what was the *point* for God's sake?)—and the parties. The parties were really bugging me. This was 1952, remember, and parents still hadn't learned that their only occupations in life were (a) to provide their adolescent offspring with money, and (b) to keep out of their way. At least, not up our way they hadn't. But parents did go away sometimes, and when they did we had parties: sandwiches and Glenn Miller at 78 r.p.m. and gin-and-orange—it would make me vomit for a week now, but then I developed quite a head for it. I had to. Adolescents' parties are all alike: built on the unshakeable theory that sooner or later you're going to do it anyway, but it won't be so bad if you do it in company. By 'it' I don't mean *it*, except in extreme cases, but practically any near-substitute you can imagine was

34

acceptable, and since boys take to this idea more easily than girls, the gin-and-orange was what you might call a *sine qua non*.

My trouble was that I took to the whole thing like a duck to water: more easily than I dared let anyone suspect, what with all those babies in the background, not to mention The Voice That Breathed O'er Eden and the three-piece suite from G Plan. The boys at the parties were most of them our contemporaries from the boys' grammar school, clumsily and single-mindedly urgent for the most part, but two or three of them did have a talent for it. As people they ranged from average to unbelievable, but let them get their hands or their mouths on me and I didn't even care. Except for the babies. It was a trick I learned early on—had to, or I'd have been a grand-mother by now. All I had to do was think about the babies and I went frigid, every time, no matter what they were doing. How I never collected a black eye I don't know—it was the only thing that might have got me started. But all that yielding and stiffening was taking its toll. I was bloody glad to get to Manchester. . . .

The habit of work was one she found easy enough to sustain: and the course, in history, sociology and politics, was stimulating in itself as well as invaluable to the career she had already chosen. The decision had been made instantaneously, without effort, when she watched the coronation of Queen Elizabeth II on her mother's tele-vision set, heard the voices of the commentators, Dimbleby's in par-ticular: deft, professional, utterly assured, belonging in the abbey as of right, every bit as much as the rather gauche young woman round whom the old men fidgeted and fussed with their vestments and crowns and oil. It was the voices of the commentators that trans-formed into sound the vaulted ceilings, the massed ranks of the choir, the anachronistic glitter of Life Guards and Blues. They belonged, they were part of the things but they were also a part of her times. Why, even her mother forgot her symptoms when Gilbert Harding was on, though she abominated Bilko. Madge Innes knew her desti-nation from the beginning: the route was her only problem. Almost at once she decided that it would be journalism. She had a quick skill with words, and a mind the university could train. Ideas she could get from other people. . . .

It took her some time to realize how much her body was also an ally. As a first-year student she lived in a hostel, and in many ways it was the grammar school all over again, sympathetic magic, dykes and all. There were differences of course—welcome ones: the clubs, the Hall, the Library Theatre. She discovered she had a passion for the theatre, and could learn from it too. Learn to move, to laugh, to modulate her voice, pitch it lower. Men liked that. At one time she'd considered getting rid of her Tyneside accent, too, but in the end she decided against it. It was the age of Osborne and Amis, and regional accents were in. If they ever started to go out she could hire herself a Professor Higgins. So far she'd never been obliged to do so. . . .

Sybil Laidlaw said, 'How boring you must find us.'

Madge, lost in memory, took a second too long to recover. The lost look she gave was a very effective insult, and the little woman winced at it, but went on trying.

'We've gossiped about nothing but the children,' she said. 'I don't want you to think that that's all I know—all *we* know, I should say.'

I'm bloody sure it's not, thought Madge.

'I'm sure it's not,' she said aloud, 'but other people's shop is always so interesting to a journalist. Do go on.' She searched her memory, trying to disentangle the haze of sounds that had flown by her. 'That party dress of Jane's—it sounds enchanting.'

Poor idiot Susan actually looked flattered, but the pitying look was still there.

'Well, honestly, I believe it was. I bought it at Harrods when I went down to see Daddy. He does suffer so. He commanded a destroyer on D-Day, and he was wounded quite dreadfully, poor darling.'

So we know what class you belong to. Get to your little brat's dress.

'. . . such a sweet affair. Cherry velvet—Jane's a brunette, you know. Trimmed with white fur. And with white stocking tights. Really they make children so mature these days . . .'

Larry had been wounded on D-Day plus two. He'd been a sergeant then, and a machine-gun bullet had gone through the calf of his leg. A Schmeisser, he'd hoped, but it might have been a Bren. At that point in time everybody had been firing at everybody. But he'd recovered and gone on to OCTU, just in time to catch a posting to Korea, and been wounded again in a dirty little village near the Imjin River. That time it had been a thing called a burp gun—really men used words in the oddest way—and he'd killed the gook who'd fired at him in the same moment that the gook got him. Just as well because otherwise he'd have been dead, and she'd have been a virgin still, or at least, she thought, her defloration wouldn't have been nearly so easy. Larry had lost half a lung in Korea and all his ideals, but not his aptitude for women. Thank God.

Larry had by the time she met him come to his senses. That was the way he put it. It meant that he had put aside all ideas that were not conducive to his own comfort or pleasure. Instead of going to university, as he'd been advised to do, he'd taken his discharge grant and gone into the used-car business, and done very well. Madge suspected that he was in on other things too, even more dishonest than used cars, but she never asked him about it: it was no concern of hers. Where deals were concerned he used the same kind of brutal ruthlessness that had served him as a combat officer; he had an infantryman's skill in unarmed combat, and used that too when occasion arose. It more than compensated for the loss of half a lung. He had a gun, too, an American Colt .45 semi-automatic that he'd 'won' from a U.S. Marine, and Madge had no doubt that he would use that too if the need arose, and that he would be the judge of that need. And he enjoyed it all: the risks, the deals, the unhesitating attack on opposition, just as he enjoyed women and food and wine.

She'd met him in a theatre bar. Peter Knowles had taken her to see a *pièce rose* of Camus, and the play had delighted her so much she knew she must be looking her best. Peter Knowles had been a dramatic critic then, on the *Evening News* still, but with hopes of the *Guardian*, and Madge had no doubt of the help he could offer, if his career developed as she was sure it would. And he wanted her desperately, wanted to marry her. And that was the problem. Sooner or later he would settle for having her as his mistress, but the thought of the hurt he might do her frightened her: to become a woman involved pain, and she was willing to accept it, but the subsequent revulsion might harm a relationship from which she hoped for so much. Besides, she had little doubt that he was clumsy, so she'd held him off by making him aware of what a nice girl she was, and then they'd met Larry.

Peter had bought a car from him, and it had gone much better than Larry's cars usually did. He'd insisted on buying Larry a drink, and when he'd gone off to fetch it he'd asked her for a date, sublimely unconcerned by all the old boy rugger club rules about poaching another chap's girl. He'd been so sure of himself, and she'd accepted at once, then gone back to the second half of Camus feeling very much a *pièce rose* herself. Even the obligatory wrestle in the car with Peter afterwards had had its relevance, like an athlete's warm-up before the big event. . . .

Larry took her to a restaurant, listened to a recital of her likes and dislikes, and ordered the food himself, and the wine. She found she liked both amazingly. Throughout the meal he talked about the fun he got out of life. With the sweet he told her that she was beautiful, with the apologetic air of an intelligent man stating the obvious. Over coffee he asked her to go to bed with him. She had never known a proposition so matter-of-fact: no love speeches, no flowers, no delicate hints, but its very briskness was pleasing to her, like drying one's body on a rough towel.

'But why on earth should I?' she asked, and instantly felt a fool.

37

The answer delighted him.

'Idiot,' he said. 'Because you'd enjoy it—and so would I.'

'I think I should tell you—I'm a virgin,' she said.

'You've no need to tell me. It's written all over you. You'd still enjoy it.' He leaned forward and tapped her gently on the lips. 'That mouth,' he said. 'It's a dead giveaway.'

'I have to be back in the hostel by ten,' she said.

He looked at his watch. It was nine forty-five.

'I can't deflower a virgin in fifteen minutes,' he said. 'Particularly in the back of a car.'

She blushed then, and he signalled a waiter, paid the bill, generously overtipping. She learned later that that was a pleasure too.

That night he drove her back to the hostel in a noisy and aggressive Morgan two-seater. She wanted to be as briskly matter-of-fact as he was, but the words were hard to form. At last he pulled up in a pool of shadow near the hostel door, and kissed her on the mouth. It was a friendly kiss, but it demanded an answer. She had three minutes.

'I haven't said I would,' she said.

'You haven't said you won't. Look—if you should decide to give it a whirl, I'll be waiting here Sunday morning. Ten-thirty. You'll know me by the gleam in my eye.'

'Sunday?' She wanted to tell him that she had a date for Sunday, but his laughter reduced her to silence.

'The better the day the better the deed,' he said. 'Don't worry. It'll all be fine.' He squinted at the dashboard clock, then leaned over to open her door. 'Off you go,' he said. 'You don't want to get yourself gated.'

She hurried off then up the road, not looking back, and as she waited for the porter to mark her name off the list (Miss M. Innes—returned 9.59) she heard the blatant roar of the Morgan. The whole thing's ridiculous, she thought. I've only known him three hours. But in bed she remembered the sureness of his hands, the sharp, masculine taste of Cognac on his mouth. Maybe it was the answer. Maybe. Though if it were she hoped he'd find a better place than this cubicle she was in now. Iron-framed cot, bookshelves and dressing-table, and matchboard separating her from Rhoda Jervis (Physics and Chemistry) who snored. But until she made her mind up there was no point in getting herself all excited, and she'd better remember to do extra work tomorrow to make up for Sunday; remember also to be specially nice to Peter Knowles—whose date she might have to break. . . .

'How interesting,' Madge Innes said. 'And what did Andrew say?'

38

'Well of course, he's only five but he is my son—so perhaps I really shouldn't——'

'Oh, please. Do tell,' said Madge.

'Well he looked at that wretched little shopgirl as large as life and said, "If you breathe through your mouth like that it means you've got paranoids." Really children these days are absolutely too much.'

She'd gone, of course. She'd put it off till ten forty-five, but she'd gone—hair washed the night before, new nylons, new panties, nearly new girdle and bra, and a dress and coat she'd never worn in Manchester, saving them for a special occasion. Well, what could be more special than this? And when she'd got on to the road there'd been no sign of a Morgan—just a lordly bloody Bentley slap where he should have been. She'd started to turn back when the Bentley tooted at her, and when she turned again she saw Larry behind its wheel. She'd already started running before she realized she'd been about to cry.

He got out and opened the door for her, bowing like a chauffeur.

'How very grand,' she said.

'It goes to a customer tomorrow,' he said. 'But till then it's ours. I thought we should to the thing in style.'

And that was precisely how they had done it. In a cottage in Derbyshire, at the end of a deserted dale: all truly rural outside, but the inside all mod con: refrigerator, drinks cupboard, a vast and accommodating bed. Not his, of course—Larry was far too wary to lumber himself with possessions—and in any case why should he, when he could so easily borrow other people's? He'd made her a drink and cooked her a meal and listened patiently to her gabbling nervousness. Towards the end it had been mostly about the babies, and her distaste for having them, and only then had he answered her sharply.

'My dear girl,' he said. 'Don't be ridiculous. Babies to you is affiliation orders to me. I don't want bastards either. Come here.'

After that he'd taken her with a skill and sympathy which were a kind of ultimate selfishness: her response was essential to him. He couldn't stand passive women. But then she hadn't been passive: in fact her capacity for sexual pleasure had first frightened then delighted her. At first it had been just like the parties: the kisses, the yielding, the questing, exploring hands. But then he had started to take her clothes off, and after that it wasn't like the parties at all. At first she'd panicked, and wanted to stop him, but that was ridiculous. It was what she'd come for after all, and anyway how could she stop him? They were alone, weren't they—nineteen miles from nowhere? So she willed herself to be still as he stripped her, blushed and tried to hide herself, and failed.

39

'Well, well, well,' Larry said, and his coaxing fingers moved about her so gently, so surely.

'What's wrong?' she asked. He kissed her mouth.

'Nothing's wrong. Everything's right. Every ounce of you. Come on. Up you get. It's time we went to bed.'

The shyness came to her then: the consciousness of the way her breasts swung as she moved, the very fact of her pubic hair seen by a man, and with it the fear: a fear intensified when she saw herself flushed, dishevelled by passion, became aware of the towel on the bed. In silence, he took off his own clothes, and the sight of him increased her fear. She wanted to run, but he was between her and the door.

'Idiot,' he said. 'I've never raped anyone in my life. Now come and lie down and behave.'

He took her in his arms then, kissed her, deftly tripped her on to the bed, and she'd struggled hard as he held her, his hands moved over her again, moved and moved till her struggles ceased, and she lay passive still, but open to him at last, until, 'Oh, no,' she said. 'You mustn't really.'

'No, of course not,' he'd answered, and gone on doing it until what happened wasn't just inevitable, it was essential, pain or no pain, and when they'd done and she'd rested, he'd taken her again, coaxing and teasing her back to the same vulnerable passivity, and she'd adored it all, not just the love-making, but simply being naked in front of him. There was a strong streak of narcissism in her, maybe because beauty came to her so late and his admiration of her was pleasing in itself; pleasing too was the power her body gave her over him, the power she was learning to use even as he delighted her. It had been a bore to get dressed again, a bigger bore to go back to that bloody hostel, and Jesus how sore she'd been that night, but she'd met him every day that week at his flat, and it had got better every time, especially after he'd sent her to that obstetrician pal of his and had her fitted. After that she hadn't a care in the world, and it showed.

'What a generous girl you are,' he said to her.

She was making tea for them stark naked, wary of the kettle, and put it down carefully before she turned to face him.

'I try to be,' she said, and went up to him, sat beside him on the bed, fondled him as he had taught her. His response was immediate, and gratifying, and he lay still for a moment, lazily enjoying what she did.

'You succeed, Madge,' he said, then: 'Madge. That's a bloody silly name for you.'

Her hand stopped. 'Why?' she asked.

'Go on with your work and I'll tell you.'

Her fingers moved again, and he said, 'It's silly because it doesn't fit you. Madge Innes. The words are all angles, whereas you ...' His hands reached out to her, spanned her waist, explored the curves of her belly and hips, then moved up to support her breasts, coaxing the nipples erect.

'It's the name I'm going to keep,' she said.

'Why?'

'Maybe because it's inappropriate. That means people won't forget me.'

She bent closer to him.

'My God, I certainly won't,' he said. ...

Really, this is too absurd, Madge Innes thought. If I go on like this I'll wet myself. She turned to Sybil Laidlaw.

'Tell me,' she said carefully, 'how you cope with the servant problem.'

'Oh, easy,' the little woman said. 'We import them. Spain mostly. They stay for a few years, save their money and go home.'

'Do they like it here?'

'They like us. Tom says it's because they think they're robbing us—whereas actually we think we're robbing them. It does lead to a certain emotional interdependence.'

Clever Tom, clever, clever Tom, Madge thought. Even when he's acting like a bastard he still seems whimsically charming.

The Arnott was looking puzzled again. Time for her to be spiteful.

'Our men seem to be taking a long time over their wine,' she said.

'Such delicious wine it was,' said Madge.

'I'm not really much of a connoisseur.' Really she made connoisseurship sound like exposing oneself in public. 'But Robert is driving, you know.'

'So am I,' said Madge. Please let her get on to what sods the police are—that'll keep her going for hours.

'And really, the police these days aren't understanding at all. These *stup*id breathalysers. D'you know, a friend of mine ...'

Thank God she's off.

Writing her weekly duty letter to mother that term had seemed like an exercise in applied lunacy. Her life had changed so much her mother seemed unreal to her, like a character in a play, who existed only when you watched her. Just because you'd learned to open your legs, she thought. But it wasn't that. Learning to fuck was an end, not a beginning. It was the result of the change in her life she was achieving: the application of her brain as well as her body—her whole self, in fact, towards the final goal of herself on T.V. In that context mother had only one rôle to perform: she was, could only be, a viewer. Whereas Larry ... silly bitch, she thought. Forget about Larry. It's Tom you should be thinking about. Tom and Jim Moulton there. Professor James George Moulton, D.S.O., M.A., PH.D. They're only fifteen feet away from you, Madge darling, and tonight is going to be just marvellous.

LEARNING THE KNACK

Jim said, 'I don't want to be grateful to either of you.' He paused, taking his time. 'What I mean is I don't think either of you want my gratitude.'

'What do you think we want?' Laidlaw asked.

'A fair day's work for a fair day's pay,' said Jim. 'That means as much sweat as you can get out of me for as much cash as I can get out of you.'

'My dear man,' said Laidlaw, 'you don't suppose for a moment that we're thinking of employing you ourselves?'

'Aren't you?'

'You forget what a very involuted specialist you are.' He turned to me then. 'Involuted—that *is* the word, isn't it?'

'It could be,' I said.

'Bob here's an expert,' he said to Jim. 'He scribbles a bit, you know.'

'I know,' said Jim.

He had a right to: I'd shown him quite a bit of my stuff. But how Laidlaw knew was another matter: I'd never said a word of it to him. It was the first intimation I had that I too was menaced.

'You wouldn't fit into anything I own,' he said to Jim. 'And quite honestly I don't see you on the telly, either. You're a little too rich for the viewers' blood. My viewers anyway.'

'You own a T.V. company?' Jim asked.

'I'm part of the consortium up here. How grand that sounds. So's Madge, incidentally. A licence to print your own money, as that all too honest Canadian said. But not yours, alas. For you we'll have to look elsewhere.'

'Where exactly?' asked Jim.

'Where had you in mind?'

'My field is theoretical physics,' Jim said. 'Certain aspects of the quantum theory. There's a Hungarian, four Americans, two Russians and a Japanese who have some idea of what I'm trying to do. Would you like me to explain it to you? It would take about nine years.'

Careful, boy, I thought, take it easy. But Laidlaw looked delighted.

'You had me back in the Sixth there for a minute,' he said. 'Sitting in the prefects' room. Fiddling with a slide-rule and shouting out the answers to some impossible equation while I wrestled in an obscure

43

corner with Adam Smith. Funny—I always remembered your voice as much louder than it actually is. "Certain aspects of the quantum theory." Do you think there's much scope for that sort of endeavour up here?'

'It's all I want to do,' said Jim. 'It's all I can do—except fight.'

'Fight?' Laidlaw was delighted. 'D'you mean you're willing to become a mercenary?'

'It's something you don't lose the knack of—and I had four years of it.'

'I had rather more,' I said, 'and I know that what you say is true. But surely you're not serious?'

'I nearly did—a few years back,' Jim said. 'I was going out to join Che Guevara—but he was killed before I was ready to go.'

'That tatty little pop idol?' said Laidlaw. 'I'm so glad you didn't manage it. What a waste—to be shot among a heap of Marxist cigar manufacturers by the C.I.A.'

Jim said, 'Excuse me. It's getting a bit hot in here.'

He took off his coat, hung it carefully over the back of his chair, and returned to Laidlaw.

'It's the only good coat I've got left,' he said casually, 'and I don't want it torn if I have to dot you one, Goofy. . . .'

BRUISED APPLES, BRASS BANDS,
THE POET SHELLEY

THE knack of soldiering had come to him early, though he didn't apply it till 1941. Before that his life had been all school and Matt Bohill. His father he scarcely saw even when he was there, and his mother had dwindled, early in his life, from a bosomy, cheerful provider of treats to an apologetic wraith who lay in bed and coughed and said, 'Excuse me,' till old Silverstein got her at last into Poole Sanatorium where she promptly died, apologizing to the last for the trouble she must be causing. After that his father's sister Sarah had come to keep house for them, and Sarah wouldn't put up with anybody's Old Buck, not even his da's. He didn't get so many sweets then, but he didn't get belted so much either. And anyway, he got on fine with Aunty Sarah. She'd been hauled out of school when she was twelve, to be a scullery maid in a house long since demolished, but she had a mind, and liked to use it, and liked to see him use his. If she hadn't he'd never have got to the grammar school. That was all Sarah's doing, hers and Matt Bohill's. His father had written it off as insanity—any attempt to rise above your station in life was insanity, according to his father—from the moment he'd first seen his son's school cap.

But Matt and Aunty Sarah were different. They understood. Matt was a hewer, like his da, but there the resemblance ended. Their bodies might look alike—how could they not, crouched in the dark, hewing at a three-foot-six face of coal for eight hours a day, their piece-work per ton measured in pennies? They all looked alike: stocky, big-chested, thigh muscles like a horseman's because of their eternal squatting—but in mind they were chalk and cheese. Matt was a thinker too: he'd begun the habit in the years 1915–18, as a member of a D.L.I. battalion in Flanders, during the intervals of being shot at, and it had never left him. Thought, a quick dose of gas and a shrapnel wound had convinced him (a) that the First World War was a bosses' war; (b) that Capitalism was invariably wrong; (c) that Socialism was quite often right. Matt's one quarrel with the Communists was that they claimed to be invariably right. (Three years at the mercy of a General Staff, who made similar claims, were more than enough to convince Matt that that was impossible.) The miners' strike of 1925 and the General Strike of 1926 only served to underline points (b) and (c) of Matt's thesis. About (a) he needed no such re-assurance.

Matt's relationship with his father was just about as perfect as it could be. He'd given the old bugger a belting for threatening to blackleg when they came out in 1925, and he'd been scared of Matt ever since. And that was important, because Matt was a leader in the lodge, an activist. It was his business to see that the men stuck together, and if he couldn't do it with his tongue he did it with his boot. Pit boots they were, steel toecaps. His da had never been any trouble after that one time. Mind you, they'd starved for it, and a lot of the women hated Matt for what happened: Means Tests and Board of Guardians and soup kitchens; kids with rickets, wives with T.B. They blamed the bosses all right, but it was Matt Bohill they hated. Poor bitches. He'd hated *them* for it at the time, but now he understood. It was all ignorance. They knew nowt because they were too close to it, casualties in the class struggle, and what poor bloody swaddy ever understood what his general was doing?

The analogy was apt enough. The class war was the first one he'd taken part in, and miners and their families were the corps d'élite of the Left. Discipline, intelligence, tactics, strategy, they knew them all—aye, and used them sometimes. Like the Salt Pans Riot in 1933. That was a day to remember. The pitmen of the four collieries had held a mass meeting there—though his father had missed it. He'd had five bob on a dog that came in at a hundred to seven, and was missing for three days. When he came back he was penniless and drunk, and Matt was in Durham Gaol. But Matt too had lived in the interim.

The meeting was held on a Saturday and Aunty Sarah had taken him to see it. His mother was still alive then, but ailing, coughing and apologizing on her bed, and Aunty Sarah had said it would be good for him to get away. They'd turned the outing into a picnic, bread and margarine and sugar sandwiches, bruised apples for twopence, a bottle of water, and walked the mile and a half to the Salt Pans because the five bob da had invested on the dog had been all the money they had—when he got back Aunty Sarah had gone for him with a broomstick—and the tram fare for two was three halfpence each way. But anyway he hadn't minded walking. The streets were alive with hurrying miners, face men and surface men, walking quickly, talking as they walked, deaf to the women calling after them in warning. Even then he'd responded to the excitement, sensing the violence and the danger behind it, waiting to be unleashed. They'd walked across the cobbles of Eda Place to Cobden Street, and everywhere the miners came out hurrying, heavy boots, suits of badly fitting serge, white scarves knotted like ties and clumsy caps. Like a bloody uniform in those days. Poverty's Own. Down Shire Street then, and along Sea Road, and everywhere hurrying miners, some of them with their women, the good ones, the right sort, who stood by their menfolk and when they were hit hit back. But now there were policemen too, on the street corners, by the doors of the pubs with their morning sour beer smell. More policemen than he'd ever seen before, in twos and fours, and then a car passed him full of coppers, and one so resplendent in black and silver he thought it must be a general at least till his Aunty Sarah told him, with a certain bitter satisfaction, that it was only the Chief Constable.

They passed the Alhambra Cinema (Now Showing: *The Cat and the Canary* with Laura La Plante) and on the waste ground behind it were parked two buses and five ambulances. The buses were full of policemen.

'Aye,' his aunty said, 'this'll be a day we'll none of us forget in a hurry.'

They walked on, and came to the sea, steely grey and glittering in the fitful October sunshine, its hammering whitecaps another hurrying violence, another excitement. Then past the Sailors' Memorial and the tram terminus, till their footfalls were softened by sand, and they reached a stretch of coarse bent-grass, the only thing that would grow there, that was still called the Salt Pans, though sea-water hadn't been boiled there for two hundred years.

And more miners, all the miners in the world it seemed to him then, not just the four collieries' men but delegates from all over Durham and Northumberland, even from Yorkshire. Demonstration of Solidarity, Aunty Sarah said. There were lodge banners too, vast and intricately patterned—it took two men to carry them—with their symbolic pictures of Freedom, Socialism, the Union Movement, holding out their hands in welcome to a fighting miner. Round each banner the men of its lodge were assembled, but here and there were men who carried red flags, or wore red shirts, and they had their followers too. But best of all there was a band, the Maydon Colliery Prize Silver Band, three times winners of the *Daily Herald* Brass Band Contest, in the glory of scarlet and glittering brass, thumping out 'Poet and Peasant' and prodigally sweating.

Aunty Sarah looked at the mass of men and moved to a far-off sandhill. The boy protested that it was too far from the excitement, but she was adamant.

'You can see all right from here,' she said, 'and it's near enough if there's trouble—and there will be, if Matt Bohill's speaking.' She groped in a battered straw bag and gave the boy a sugar sandwich.

'Now listen, Jim—today's important and I want you to watch. You're not too old to start learning. But when the fighting starts—you stay close to me. Promise.'

47

His mouth was full, so he just nodded, but his eyes blazed with excitement. He was six and a half years old.

It seemed to him an awful long time before the fighting started. Before that there had to be talking—a lot of talking, by a fat man who mumbled and a thin man who whinnied. They got up on a rostrum made, precariously enough, of unshaven planks, the band struck a chord for silence, and they started, first one, then the other, their voices competing unsuccessfully against the soft crash of the sea, the rustle of bent-grass in the brusque October wind. But the men were patient, listening with great care and attention. When the one who whinnied asked them to pray, quite a lot of them knelt down. (In those days there were religious miners, as well as political ones and a lot who were just plain boozers. But that day even some of the boozers knelt: as Aunty Sarah had said, that day was important.) The words went on, and Aunty Sarah said it was all about presenting a petition. The boy thought it must have something to do with Christmas.

Then it was Matt Bohill's turn, and the noise of the sea and wind ceased to be a problem, rather they became a counterpoint to the brazen force of his voice: two other natural forces joining their power to his, for the dark strength of the sea and the sting of the wind were in every word he said. He spoke simply, and there was much in his words that even an intelligent child could understand. They were going to ask for work. Not charity; not hand-outs. Work. And God knew that wasn't much to ask. Going down to cut coal in three and a half foot of wet darkness with the chance of an explosion to make it interesting—it wasn't exactly a holiday in Monte Carlo—it was work and bloody hard work at that. But it was also their dignity, their independence. It was the only thing that made them free of the pawnbroker and the Means Test man and they were going to have it. By God, it was their right to have it.

Nobody was saying the miner was perfect. (From up there on the rostrum Matt Bohill could look down into the crowd, see the man who'd cracked two of his wife's ribs the week before, the man who drank eight pints of beer every Saturday, work or no work, and topped it off with rum, the man whose children went hungry while his whippet was fed)—no miner was perfect. No man was. But they were men. They asked only for the rights that other men—the bosses—took for granted. The right to work to support their wives and children. That was all they asked. No. Not asked. Hell no. That was what they demanded.

The last word was a wild yell like the sting of the wind, and the dark mass of men beneath him heaved and shifted and growled like the sea. Then Matt Bohill held up his hand and they were silent as

48

he told them that a poet had said it all better than he ever could more than a hundred years before. The poet's name was Shelley, and he began to recite: Men of England, wherefore plough; and the silence as they heard him was absolute. Then his mood changed again, and he hurled his words at them like weapons, and they caught them and brandished them, words like rights, and demands, and dignity, till the boy thought his heart would burst, for there was nothing in the world like this: so brave, so splendid, so important.

And only then did he see what his aunt had been aware of for minutes past, a great phalanx of police, the Chief Constable at their head, pushing slowly into the crowd, heading for the platform. Their progress was slow at first for the men resisted their pressure, but in the end Matt Bohill held up his hand once more, and the crowd yielded. The Chief Constable snapped an order to his men, and moved forward alone in his glory of broadcloth and silver and ebony cane. He was alone, and so far as the boy could see quite unafraid, but the child had no admiration to spare for his courage, knew only hatred for all the silver buttons stood for. The Chief Constable stood below the rostrum and looked up to Matt, but the wind whipped away his words.

'Come on up, Mr Henderson,' said Matt. 'Come on up and let us all hear you. We're all friends here.'

The crowd laughed then, and there was menace in their laughter, but Chief Constable Henderson climbed up steadily, alone, and it seemed still unafraid, and spoke to them in a high, piercing voice, a Lanarkshire voice that could never unite with the sea and wind, like Matt's, but that day at least defeated them.

'You men can have your meeting here,' he began, and the crowd roared in a mockery of gratitude, 'but there's to be no parade through the streets, and no presenting a petition. Now I want that quite clear.' He paused then, and looked about him. Fourteen years later the boy was to see a similar look on the face of a famous general. It was the look of authority, that knows it must be obeyed. 'The magistrates have refused sanction, and a march would constitute unlawful assembly. There will be no march.'

He moved off the platform then, and the boy heard Matt Bohill's voice say, 'Let him through,' and in it was the same authority. He was obeyed at once, and the Chief Constable moved erect and slow to where the phalanx of police stood waiting. Matt climbed back on to the rostrum.

'Well,' he said. 'You've heard the man. We can't go and present our petition—so he says. Now then—what do *ye* say?'

The answer was spontaneous and immediate: a fierce, even joyful

49

yell as the pitmen responded to their own power, but Bohill's arms went up, conjuring silence.

'Wisht, lads,' he said. 'We can't do it like that. What are you thinking of? Where's your manners? And the Chief Constable watching an' all. Now then, let's do it the democratic way. Show of hands. Those in favour—let's see you now.'

The arms went up at once, and suddenly the boy was back in school—Please, miss, I know, honest. Please, miss—ask me.

'That's very encouraging,' Matt Bohill said. 'Now then—those against?'

The police were extending now, across the path that led back to Sea Road and Shire Street, and the Town Hall, where the mayor lived and wore a robe and a cocked hat and a chain. The boy knew this, because he'd seen him. He looked back to the pitmen, and not a hand was raised.

'Looks to me as if the motion's carried,' Matt Bohill said.

Later Matt was to tell him all the preparations that had been made for that day. The activists in the front, pick-handles hidden under their coats—a lot of red shirts among them; women in the rear encircled by a mass of older men; and off to one side the band, serious now, playing a tune that he was hearing for the first of many hundred times, a tune with words that the men sang as they marched, Matt Bohill at their head, up to the police column. ('It's called "The Red Flag",' Aunty Sarah said.) In the middle of the policemen was a posh feller—bowler hat, dark suit. He was holding a bit of paper and reading aloud, his voice obliterated by the crash of brass, the men's strong voices.

'That's Alderman Jameson,' Aunty Sarah said. 'A J.P. *he* is. He'll be reading the Riot Act.' She said it in tones of immense satisfaction, but the boy was puzzled. To him reading the Riot Act was what his mother said when he was late in from school or he'd forgotten to buy something when she'd sent him out on a message; and what it meant was a belting from your da. But not this time.

The men reached the waiting lines of police and Matt Bohill was yelling something about the rights of the free people in a democratic society, and the Chief Constable was yelling back about law and order being upheld, and the men stood facing the police waiting, and their voices sang:

'Let cowards flinch and tyrants sneer,
We'll keep the Red Flag flying here!'

There was anger and courage in the voices—and not a little despair. Then their voices died, the band ceased, and the only sounds were the whisper of the wind to the grass, the steady bump-bump of the drum like the pulse of blood, and the intonation of Alderman Jameson, who read the Riot Act as if it were the Bible. But even he stopped at last, and the rear police rank opened to let him through to a car, then re-formed at once.

'For the last time—no procession, no petition,' the Chief Constable said.

'Henderson—you're between us and our rights. Out of the way,' said Matt Bohill.

The Chief Constable yelled an order, and the police drew their batons, and at once the pick-handles appeared. And the boy knew then that these men—these giants who could pick him up one-handed and sling him on their shoulders the way miners love to do—were going to hurt each other. Not just pretend like he did. Really hurt. Hit each other with sticks.

'Come on,' said Matt, and the miners charged.

It was the beginning of the Battle of the Salt Pans, and it was famous enough in its day. All the English national newspapers had it. 'Miners Unleash Mob Rule in North-East,' 'Savage Attacks on Police,' 'M.P. Condemns Unauthorized Demonstration.' (Their own M.P. at that—with an eye on a junior ministry in the next Coalition Government.) The left-wing Press called it the D.L.I.'s last battle—and there was some truth in that one. Of the men over thirty engaged, more than sixty per cent had served in the Army of the First World War. The foreign Press made a fuss about it too: in Russia they were heroes, the Nazi and Fascist Press of Germany and Italy was at once aware that they were villains, and in the United States they had their own problems and were if anything delighted to find that those of Great Britain were similar in content and solution. . . .

The pitmen won the first battle. To the boy it was just as if a black wave slowly, inevitably uncoiled and engulfed a black rock. There was too much to see that was horrible for the visual horror to register, but the sounds it made would stay with him for ever: the sound heavy wood makes when it breaks a man's face and bones, the blasphemies and cheers and prayers, the way a man shrieks just like a boy shrieks, when he's hurt, feels pain—no, agony; the boy heard all this and wanted to be sick, to spew on the grass, but he dared not. What was happening was so important.

Then the wave flowed through, and the miners dashed on for Sea Road, for Shire Street, and now the boy could see the horror as well as hear it. Men lying, bleeding, ribs smashed, noses spouting blood, faces transformed into the grotesque masks of clowns by one jab from a truncheon. There were police lying everywhere too, but he had no eyes for them—not for the ones who were hurt. But there were others ranged in an unbroken circle round the Chief Constable, and as he watched they formed up, marched after the miners. Some of them kicked wounded pitmen as they passed, and the boy hated them for it.

'Don't be daft,' Aunty Sarah said. 'They're fighting to win, Jimmy lad. And so are we. Come on. We'll get down to the beach and have our picnic.'

'Can't we go on and see some more?'

'Too dangerous,' his aunty said.

'But we're winning.'

'So far,' she said. 'There'll be a lot more battles before we've won.'

'Will I fight too?' he asked.

'By God,' his aunty said, and that surprised him, his aunty never said words like God. 'By God, you'd better.'

The pitmen lost, of course. They'd got as far as Sea Road—some of them even pushed round the corner into Shire Street, but the Mayor in his red robes and chain and cocked hat stayed inviolate in his palace. The police too had sent for fraternal delegates: from all the neighbouring boroughs. There had been a hundred and seventy-eight arrests, eleven of them women. Thirty-four police and sixty-five miners were in hospital. And the war continued.

That night his aunty had borrowed a shilling from a money-lender (pay back twopence a week for ten weeks) and sent him out for fish and chips. On his way home, running, greasy newspaper wrappings burning his fingers, a policeman had stopped him, grabbing him by the shoulder, asking what his da did, and when he said his da was a miner the grip tightened, hurting him, and the policeman told him to take him to his house. When the boy hesitated, he clipped him with the gloves he carried, clipped him hard enough to hurt. They went to his home then, but his da was away drinking, and his mam was poorly. There was only Aunty Sarah to defend him.

'You're out of luck this time,' she said. 'There's only two women and a bairn to pick on.' She looked at the red welt across the boy's face. 'Or mebbe that's what you prefer,' she said. She moved across to the breadboard then, and when she turned round the breadknife was in her hand.

'Out,' she said.

'He says his da's a pitman,' said the policeman.

'He is.'

'I want to talk to him.'

'So do I. So do a lot of people. You don't think he was one of the villains, do you? He won a few bob on a dog two days ago. We haven't seen him since. We will soon though—when the money's gone.'

The policeman hesitated.

'What's the matter?' his aunty asked. 'Want to search the place? It won't take long. There's only his mam upstairs. Her and her T.B. germs for company. Or maybe you want to take me upstairs—is that it?' She put the knife down, but her hand stayed very near it. 'Come on, me bold hero. You're welcome to try.'

The policeman left then, and aunty sent him into the kitchen to put cold water on his face where the policeman had hit it. When he came back, she was sharing out the fish and chips, and crying as she did it.

THE GREAT GOD MATT

THAT had been his first lesson: Matt Bohill his first—and only—hero. Matt had got six months in Durham Gaol for, among other things, inciting a riot, assaulting a variety of policemen, obstructing the police in the performance of their duty, and larceny of planks—the planks he had used as an improvised rostrum. The last charge was the only one that had annoyed him: he had always insisted that he had only borrowed them from a building-site, and had meant to return them as soon as the petition had been presented, but the magistrates wouldn't listen. They found him guilty of that too, and Matt resented it far more than the belting the police gave him in his cell before the trial: that he expected, but to be branded as a thief was unfair in a way that differed from all the other unfairness of life.

He did his six months stolidly, without fuss, the way his followers did their twenty-eight or fourteen days. In a way he was lucky. He was at least as well fed as he was at home, he had time to think, and anyway six months was less than he had expected. The power-wielding Left had backed him: not just the *Daily Worker* and the *Daily Herald* but the National Union of Mineworkers and a handful of noisy and popular M.P.s: enough noise in fact for the magistrates to listen to before they told him how lenient they were going to be; enough noise for the creation of a fighting fund to hire him a fellow-traveller K.C. and see the wives and bairns of the prisoners were fed while they were inside. Enough noise to make Matt Bohill think it maybe hadn't been such a defeat after all, but not enough noise to make him chance it again. Not nearly enough.

While Matt was inside somebody had to look after his widowed mother, who kept house for her son—Matt was a bachelor—and had broken her leg three weeks before the riot, and missed it. Mrs Bohill never forgave Providence for making her miss the riot. It was Aunty Sarah who looked after her mostly, and often enough she took the boy along. Mrs Bohill fascinated Jim. It wasn't just that she wore a man's cap under her shawl and smoked a clay pipe: there were plenty of old women who did both. What fascinated him was that she could play the violin: sit up in bed and scrape away for hours, bowing badly, fingering all wrong, but producing even so in a small, true sound an unending variety of tunes that found their way from memory to fingers: old music-hall songs, folk-songs, scraps of light opera from concerts, Salvation Army hymn tunes, ragtime, one flowing into the other. She would sit up in bed in the kitchen that was also her bedroom, burnished and polished oven, tea always on the hob, fire burning winter and summer, and play. (Like all pitmen, Matt couldn't stand the idea of a dead grate. It was as if the thought of risking his life in the dark had to have some relevant point that they could see when they came up again, and that point was the hearth fire that must never go out, so that when there was no work, and no concessionary coal, Matt like all the rest would spend hours on the slag-heaps with a sack, picking over, searching for anything that would burn; and in the good times, when there was work, fling a whole bucketful of coal to the back of the fire, raking it forward as the flames dwindled. Money to burn.)

Mrs Bohill lay on her bed like a queen: leg out-thrust, using each day a clean work shirt of Matt's as a nightgown, a bottle-green shawl wrapped over her cap and pinned across her chest. She didn't bathe much, he thought later—they none of them did. A bath was a major undertaking in a two-roomed house which as often as not had five people in it, and anyway, heating water cost money—but the place was clean. They mostly were: fanatics for cleanliness, miners' wives; holystoning doorsteps, polishing ovens, attacking a pile of washing every Monday morning as if it were the Means Test man, immersing the clothes in a vast wooden tub, pounding them with a wooden club called a poss-stick as if they were the face of the pawn-broker. So Mrs Bohill's house was clean, and she herself presentable, according to her lights.

Once, years later, he'd told his wife about Mrs Bohill. They'd taken a suite at the Plaza in New York, and he'd been angry because her money had paid for it, or rather her father's money. Her father's money had been the beginning of most of their quarrels . . . but their bodies' needs had been demanding, imperious. In the beginning at any rate their quarrels had never lasted long. They had made love all one long afternoon, and as always he had marvelled that her slight body could engulf his male strength, suck him into her yielding moisture until there was nothing left; as always he'd marvelled, and as always, in a sealed-off corner of his mind, resented too. But that day at least the resentment had seeped in, unnoticed.

They had lain on the bed, while the air-conditioning had murmured away New York's appalling summer heat, and below them Central Park, not yet restricted to gangs and fags and junkies, was alive with young men in white shirts, young women dressed like Marie Antoinette's concept of a milkmaid, for this was the year of the New Look: long-skirted dresses that made much of breasts and buttocks and hips, for the war was over now, London and Berlin crippled, Hiroshima smashed, and Korea no more than a gleam in

Stalin's and Truman's eyes. The war was over and the girls had their men back, and set out to remind them that they were girls, feminine and frilly, emancipated at last from overalls and headscarves.

He had needed no such reminder. Tracy lay beside him, and they were both naked on the broad, hard-sprung bed, its sheets as white as the frosting on a cake. As always after love he was drowsy, and as always she was wide awake, bright-eyed, already groping for a cigarette, eager for talk, since his body could then give her nothing else. He'd looked at her, and the slightness of her body had moved him deeply: first because of its very perfection. It flowed so easily, curve merging into curve as she groped for the lighter on the bedside table. The flow of her body was immensely satisfying; satisfying, too, the slightness of her breasts, the nipples dark, erect with love, the small curve of her belly and her tight little haunches: satisfying in a fulfilled, objective way, because his sexual drive was spent. Sex came second, with the thought of how easily he could hurt her, not with his tongue—she could match him at any time in spite—but with his hands, the way he had been taught. There. Or there. Or there. And Tracy Moulton crippled. Tracy Moulton dead. The unbidden thought first fascinated then revolted him, and he began to talk quickly, grabbing ideas out of the air, not even thinking that the subject he chose—his childhood—was the one that would please her most; concerned only to get rid of the unbidden idea.

He'd told her about Mrs Bohill, and Tracy had been delighted. What did she play, and what did she look like? Did she lie like this or like this?—and her body flowed and posed on the white bed, demanding an answer, until he'd propped her up against the pillows, pushed one leg out rigid in front of her.

'Madame Récamier,' said Tracy, and there'd been some truth in that. Mrs Bohill had presided over her salons, too: dark tea and stotty cake, and marge if you were lucky, and the fellow-travelling K.C. had come to see her, and the Newcastle correspondent of the *Daily Herald*, to be met with the same rigid standard of behaviour she'd show to miners and their wives and children. Tracy had enjoyed that, then like a fool he'd told her about the clay pipe.

'But that's ridiculous,' she said.

'I don't understand you.'

'I mean it's overdoing it. Come on, now. Nobody smokes a clay pipe. Not even Southern mammies, darling. Not even *squaws*.'

Then they'd gone back to quarrelling again, but the portrait of Mrs Bohill had stayed with her as so many of his childhood memories did. Her own childhood in Santa Monica had been rich in many things: money, possessions, achievement. But not in people. For people she had turned to him.

56

He saw Mrs Bohill every week until he went to war, in 1941, and when he came back she was dead. Every time he saw her, he admired her: the rock-like strength of a character that opposed poverty head on, and never conceded defeat, her devotion to her son and his cause, her joy in music, even the pleasure her pipe gave her—her one extravagance, but an extravagance used in such a way as to prove that extravagance too is a necessary and proper part of a human life, when kept in its necessary and proper perspective. He'd enjoyed going to see her, and sat quiet always, on his best behaviour, while Aunty Sarah and Mrs Bohill talked the way women always did talk, and Aunty Sarah moved deft-handed, the kitchen her work-bench, till Mrs Bohill grew quiet at last, and picked up her violin, and Aunty Sarah sang. Then Matt came home and it was better than ever. Matt was a hero, and the band turned out for him. (They'd been clever about that. Henderson had said no demonstrations, but the band had permission to march to rehearsals anyway, and the way to the drill hall led right past Matt Bohill's door. Was it their fault that Matt just happened to be walking home from the station as they marched off to practise?)

So the first time the boy saw Matt close to he was laughing—with pride and pleasure for his musical reception, with joy to be back home—and his eyes darted from one object to another: the handful of marigolds in a jam-jar on the window-sill, the clippie mat on the flagged floor, the patchwork quilt that covered his mother's sagging bed. He went up to her, stood close, but made no move to touch her, nor she him.

'You're back then,' said his mother.

'Aye,' he said. 'I'm back.'

'How was it?'

He chuckled then, a deep and zestful noise that warmed the boy like sunshine.

'Better than the Somme,' he said.

'Jokes,' said Mrs Bohill. 'Back two minutes and he's making jokes. Give us a kiss and say hallo to Sarah Moulton.'

He bent then, his lips just touched his mother's brow, and her hand reached out to touch him, fiercely protective, then dropped. What hand could protect him now, compact in power, ready to take on the world again and again, and ready to pay the price too, if he failed.

'You remember Sarah,' Mrs Bohill said. 'She's been looking after me.'

'I won't forget it,' Matt Bohill said.

'And the little un's Jim Moulton. Sarah's brother's boy.'

'Hallo, Jim,' said Matt. 'I know your da. We worked on the same seam—when we did work.'

'Jim's different,' Sarah said quickly.

'How are you different, Jim?' asked Matt.

'Well for one thing he was at the Salt Pans,' Sarah said, her voice tart.

'Were you?' Matt said. 'Were you there, bonny lad?'

He nodded, too shy to speak.

'And what did you think of it?'

He could remember again the importance of it in the hammering of his heart, but again the shyness was too strong.

'What's the matter?' said Aunty Sarah, tart still. 'Cat got your tongue?'

Blushing scarlet, pushing out the words, he said at last, 'We should have won.'

Matt Bohill yelled his delight, picked him up, swung him on his shoulder so that he ducked just in time to miss the gas mantle.

'You hear that, ma, Sarah?' he shouted. '*We* should have won. Not *you*—not the pitmen. *We*. You know what I think? I think I've got a disciple.'

In the years that followed, he thought so too, because that is what he was, from the beginning. From the first Matt had been impressed by his capacity to learn, his quickness with letters and figures, and every week he would make him read with him, do sums, until he could read far more easily than Matt, work out problems in his head that took Matt pages of calculation more hopeful than accurate: and yet he never lost his admiration for Matt, as thinker or as leader. Early in life Jim Moulton had learned to regard his alphabetic and numerical skills as little more than luckily developed muscles. It was Matt's habit of thought that he wanted; that and the ability to lead as Matt had led. In a colliery community there are few secrets, and Jim had soon discovered that Matt had once given his own da a belting. It didn't worry him: he despised his da anyway, as Matt despised him, as Aunty Sarah despised him, but it led to emulation: to the use of his fists not for achievement alone, but for discipline, adherence to the party line on teachers, parents, rival gangs. His father was scarcely aware it was happening, and his aunt and Matt, who were, never tried to stop it. Why should they? For them, to fight was to survive, and without the survival of boys like Jim, what hope was there for pitmen and their families?

Looking back, it seemed that Matt Bohill was always there, exhorting, encouraging, advising: the father he wanted, the father he should have had. After Goofy Laidlaw's granda had clouted him, Matt had gone round in a fury to the *Lord Nelson* to have it out with him. The rich, it seemed, were again picking on the poor. The boy had waited in terror for what would happen, and Matt had come back hours later, mellow with beer.

'Did you hit him?' Jim asked.

'No,' said Matt, and chuckled as the boy's face showed its disappointment. 'We had a bit of a crack, Jim boy. You didn't tell me you'd been hitting his grandson.'

'He's wet,' said Jim. 'One of them posh kids.'

'That's his parents' fault, not his granda's,' Matt said. 'And he wears glasses. You did wrong, Jim.'

That was the one thing he never understood about Matt: his obsession with fairness, in a world where nothing was fair.

'His granda's a boss,' said Jim, and Matt chuckled again.

'I'll lose you to the Communists yet,' he said. 'And anyway you're wrong. Old Laidlaw isn't a boss—he's a what d'you call it?—a border reiver.' The boy looked puzzled, and he added: 'They had them in the old days up the Tyne Valley. Sort of land pirates. Just men in their way—they robbed everybody, and treated them they liked. That's old Laidlaw. He treated me three pints. Come the revolution he'll have to go, but meantime he's better company than the J.P.s and Sunday-school teachers we work for. We might as well enjoy him.'

'The posh kid wears a suit and . . . and shoes,' said Jim, 'Not boots—shoes.'

'One of these days we all will,' said Matt.

He asked Jim frequently about Goofy Laidlaw, particularly after he'd finally cursed and cajoled Jim's father into sending him to the grammar school. The possession of wealth fascinated him, even the very modest wealth that Goofy's parents had somehow managed to cling to, throughout the depression, as a known but never-glimpsed species fascinates a naturalist. It was perhaps his habit of thought that led him early to believe that Goofy was an enemy to reckon with, and he told him so. Jim promised to be careful, and never moderated his attitude in the slightest. What Matt said was always important—but Goofy! You'd only got to look at him to know what he was—wet. About Bob Arnott Matt had no reservations at all. A good lad, a good marrer. 'Marrer' meant friend, and something more than friend; comrade-in-arms, almost. Bob was all right, he was sure, though it was a pity his father wasn't a pitman.

'Treat him fair, Jim,' Matt said. 'One of these days you might be glad of a friend like that.'

And Jim had promised, because he liked Bob, not because he needed him. He needed nobody: he'd got to the grammar school. If you could do that, with a boozy pitman for a father, you could take on the world.

SUSAN AND THE LILY

SUSAN ARNOTT thought what a pleasant room it was: the kind of judicious blending of old and new that she had promised herself if Bob ever made the kind of money that ... she looked about her again: the masses of hothouse roses, the Georgian sofa table, the Waterford crystal glass in her hands. Better forget it. Bob would never make that kind of money. This was six-figure stuff, and one day, and that day soon, it would be seven. Doctors didn't earn like that: not G.P.s, anyway, and that was all Bob was, would ever be: a G.P. with a large practice and an insane assistant who would one day take off and be a specialist in psychiatric medicine and make pots of money to buy the sofa tables *she* should have had.

People like Arthur Harkness bothered her, and she couldn't help it. Clever people always had bothered her, like that big bitch swilling that B and B stuff, and pretending she wasn't being patronizing. Like mummy doing *The Times* crossword puzzle. Clever people who made a thing out of being clever. That awful Moulton man with his Ph.D. and Cambridge and M.I.T., whatever *that* was, and his rough accent and awful manners. Look at Bob—he was clever too, but he didn't go on about it. Jolly clever. And a gentleman too. You weren't supposed to use that word these days, but that was what Bob was, and Tom Laidlaw too. She'd never felt uncomfortable, married to Bob. She'd belonged with him. He'd made her come up to this awful North-East, but even that was bearable. Doctors did well up here, but that wasn't all of it. Bob cared for her. It didn't bother him that she was ... like Daddy. It *couldn't*.

Daddy was ... not bright. Or Daddy meant well. Or Daddy was stupid. It all depended on your point of view. Daddy was an ex-lieutenant-commander R.N. Daddy was a gentleman. All his family had been gentlemen since the days of his great-great-grandfather, who had made a fortune in the East India Company. Susan had never understood why Mummy mentioned Daddy's great-great-grandfather whenever Daddy talked of his gentility. He was a good-looking man: yellow-haired, pink-cheeked (Mummy had another joke about how gin and angostura bitters were good for a sailor's image), eyes of palest blue fading almost but not quite to grey. After the war Daddy lived in the house outside Reading which was about all that was left of the East India Company fortune, and Mummy went up to London on weekdays and wrote something called copy.

When she was a child she loved the weekdays, because then she had Daddy all to herself: and the radio played nice music, not loud, not difficult, but pretty, cheerful tunes, the kind one liked, and Daddy taught her which knives and forks to use and told her such lovely stories, about the China Station, and the Governor-General's ball in Gibraltar, and Uncle Reggie in Malaya, and Uncle Dennis in the Blues: all the lovely, faraway things in the super time, the Golden Age, the days before the war.

At weekends it was different, when Mummy was home, and the whole house bustled, washing-machine thumping, dishes clattering, Daddy pushing the lawnmower. At weekends Mummy told her stories, but they weren't nice, like Daddy's. They were stories out of books: all goose-girls, and witches in gingerbread houses, and princes turned into frogs. She tried her very best to like them, because Mummy said all children did, but they only made her cry. It was wrong, it was downright wicked to cry at one's Mummy. She knew that. But she couldn't help it. Mummy wanted her to learn to count, and read, and write, but Susan couldn't, even when Mummy tried to teach her herself. She would try and try, and then she'd weep, and Daddy would come and pick her up and say, 'Never mind, Susan darling. Don't cry. We can't all be clever. Look at me. I was always a juggins at school.' Then she'd feel better, because 'juggins' was a very special word to her and Daddy, and she'd cling to him and look down at Mummy, and Mummy wouldn't say a thing: just look at her.

One summer they'd given a party; drawing-room open to the garden, dusk smelling of roses, and Daddy had said she could stay up. Lovely, tiny sandwiches, and a peach Daddy peeled for her, and lemonade in a special glass. She'd gone to the breakfast-room to find Daddy's lighter, and Mummy was with a man from London, the sort Daddy couldn't stand, one of those clever fellers. Business chappies. He looked very red, but Mummy didn't. Just cool and clever, like always.

'What is it, Susan?' she asked.

'Daddy sent me to find his lighter,' she said.

'I thought perhaps Daddy might,' said Mummy.

Susan didn't understand.

'He said it was here,' she said.

Mummy took a box of matches out of her bag.

'Give him these. Tell him it's the best I can do,' she said.

The clever man turned redder than ever.

'She's awfully pretty,' he said.

It was nice when they said that, and she lingered.

'Run along, Susan,' said Mummy, and turned back to the clever feller.

'Yes, she is, isn't she?' said Mummy. 'But then so's Rupert.'

But Susan knew she'd got *that* wrong: Rupert was Daddy's name.

That night she heard them shouting. She'd been asleep and when she woke up the party was over, and it was very dark and there should have been no noise at all, but there was: first Daddy's voice, then Mummy's. Daddy's was about clever bitches and making him look a fool, and Mummy's was all how she was sick and tired and what was the use; and at first she'd thought they were quarrelling, but that was *silly*. Mummy and Daddy *never* quarrelled. She reached out in the dark and found her dolly, a beautiful new dolly called Elvira. As she cuddled it she realized that Mummy and Daddy were—playing a game, and went back to sleep.

When she was twelve she went away to school. Mummy had stopped writing this copy stuff then, and gone to work for a magazine and that was super because it meant she could have a pony, so at first she'd cried when she had to go away to school and leave Rob Roy, but it hadn't been so bad, not really, because even if she hadn't been very bright the nuns didn't go on at her as if it were all her fault, like Mummy did, and anyway she'd learned shorthand and typing, and she cooked jolly well and always won the prize for flower arranging, and Mother Beatrice said in her report she was sure Susan would do well, because she was such a kind and considerate girl.

'Not perhaps the most fortunate choice of adjectives,' said Mummy. 'Really, these nuns.'

'I don't understand,' said Daddy. Susan didn't either. Mummy sighed.

'Where are we going to find an outlet for all this kindness and consideration?' she asked. She looked from handsome, baffled husband to lovely, bewildered daughter. 'What are you going to do?' she asked.

'Do? Why should she do anything?' Daddy said. 'She's got her friends, there's the house to look after, one of these days she'll be getting ma——'

'Oh, no, Rupert,' said Mummy. 'Oh, no you don't.' She turned once more to Susan. 'Darling,' she said, 'what would *you* like to do?'

It was not an unexpected question—she and her friends had lived with it all their final year: university, acting, modelling, painting—but it was a question to which she could find no answer.

'I don't know,' she said, then, as Mummy's face began to close: 'Can't I just stay here and look after Daddy?'

'Can't she?' Daddy said, and, as so often these days, his voice was pleading.

'Mrs Drew looks after Daddy,' Mummy said, 'and Mrs Girtin does the rough, and Joe Philbin does the garden and his son helps him with the digging. That's three all day and one part-time. How much more help do you think Daddy needs?'

It was a voice Mummy used often: thin, piercing, clever. Susan hated it, and feared it, for if it went on it would end in defeat for Daddy, for herself. It always did.

Miserably she said, 'I don't know what I can do.'

Her mother said, 'Do you know who paid to find out how kind and considerate you are?'

'Of course I do,' said Susan. 'Daddy.'

'Not quite, darling,' her mother said. 'But you're getting warm.'

'For heaven's sake,' said her father. 'What on earth is the point of all this?'

'Get yourself a drink,' said her mother. 'It's after six o'clock.' He didn't move, and she said again, 'Get yourself a drink,' not angry, not even loud, and this time he went. 'All in all,' said her mother, 'you've cost me a shade over two thousand pounds. I don't suppose you'd like to pay it back?'

'I can't,' she said. 'You know I can't.'

'Precisely.' Her mother paused, and Susan could sense a struggle going on inside her, as if she were willing herself to be kind, and not finding it at all easy. At last she said, 'I don't have to pay for you any more, darling, but there are other things. Mrs Drew and Mrs Girtin and Joe Philbin and Joe Philbin's boy in the autumn, and the car and the radio and the television and the grocer and the butcher and Rob Roy's new shoes and my season ticket and the dog licence and Daddy's gin.' She paused. 'Would you like me to go on?' she asked at last. 'Wine when we have guests; the new vacuum cleaner, the rates, the chimney-sweep, Daddy's club?'

'We must be . . . very expensive,' Susan said 'I didn't realize.' She hesitated then. 'Doesn't Daddy——'

'What, darling?'

'Have money too? I mean. I always thought——'

'Consider the lilies of the field,' said her mother, then added quickly, 'No, forget that. It's meretricious, and not really relevant.'

To ask what 'meretricious' meant would wreck an evening already disaster-prone.

'The point is, darling, I can't afford all this—and pocket-money for you both. It would be a big help if you could get a job.'

'But what could I *do*?' she asked.

'We must think where girls can be kind and considerate for money,' said her mother gravely, 'and still remain perfect young ladies.' She looked hard at her daughter. 'You really are very lovely,' she said. 'And sort of soothing. I think you'd make a good doctor's receptionist.'

Susan considered the idea. As she remembered it, white coats were involved, and a little desk with flowers on it. Receptionists were bossy too.

'I think I'd like that, Mummy,' she said, 'if you think I can do it.'

'Of course you can,' said her mother. 'Just remember to write everything down.'

Then her father came back, and he brought the gin-bottle with him, ice-cubes and angostura and water.

'Settled it all between you?' he asked.

'She's going to be a receptionist,' her mother said.

'Jolly good idea. Where?' he asked, and Susan blushed. She hadn't even thought to ask.

'That new outfit of Bellerby's,' her mother said.

'Bellerby? Dr Bellerby? Isn't he dining with us next week?'

'Tuesday,' said her mother. 'We'll ask him then.'

'Can we do that? When he's a guest, I mean?'

'Of course,' said her mother. 'Why do you suppose he was invited, anyway?'

That horrified her father, and Susan too a little, but she consoled herself with the thought that Mummy would know, because Mummy always did. That night Daddy had brandy with his coffee while he watched Gilbert Harding, and Susan borrowed her mother's dictionary of quotations.

Consider the lilies of the field, how they grow; they toil not, neither do they spin. And yet I say unto you, that even Solomon in all his glory was not arrayed like one of these.

Saint Matthew, Chapter 6, verse 28. It sounded like what the nuns called King James's Version. She giggled. So *silly* to call Daddy a lily. And then the giggle died. It was like poetry really. So often what Mummy said was like poetry, and if you thought of it that way it made jolly good sense. Daddy had neither toiled nor spun since 1945. Not that it mattered. Mummy toiled and spun all the time. She put the book back, went to her room and stared in the mirror, and the idea when it came made her giggle again. If Daddy was a lily what kind of flower was she? Mummy was easy. Mummy wasn't a flower at all: Mummy was a difficult but rewarding vegetable. Asparagus say, or Jerusalem artichoke. But she . . . she was very lovely. Mummy had said so. Usually that meant roses, but privately she was fed up with roses. Susan decided that she was a gardenia—only she didn't remember what they looked like.

Mummy got her the job, and it worked out just beautifully. Bellerby was part of something called a 'unit': five doctors and two midwives and a combined surgery like a miniature hospital. There were always two nurses on duty, as well as the receptionist, so that was all right. Her only nightmare about the job was that people might start having babies, or bleeding or something, and she'd be the only one there. But there were always doctors and nurses about, and all she did was answer the telephone, and make appointments, and keep the card index up to date, and really Mummy was absolutely right. So long as you remembered to write everything down being a receptionist was no trouble at all.

Old Bellerby had a son, too, Henry Edward Bellerby, known as Hank. Hank was up at Cambridge reading medicine, and when he qualified he too would be part of the unit. He was an elegantly saturnine boy who could play the guitar and sing like Elvis Presley, and during the long vac they reached the semi-final of the mixed doubles, and they kissed a goodish bit and she had to do a fair amount of wriggling to keep him from putting his hands where they weren't wanted—or at least not wanted enough to start taking any chances. Not yet anyway. It occurred to Susan that Mummy was really very clever indeed, and even Daddy seemed to approve of Hank, or at any rate to be resigned to him, but then Daddy didn't have to wrestle with him in the back row of the three-and-nines.

What Daddy did not approve of was Bob Arnott, but then Daddy was a snob, to the point where he even boasted about it. Daddy disliked West Indians, Pakistanis, Green Line buses and second class on the train. He disliked people who called their lunch their dinner, fish and chips, draught beer, all newspapers except *The Times* and the *Daily Telegraph*, holiday camps and the Labour Party. He considered factory workers necessary but dangerous, like anaesthetics, and was the last person in his district to get a television that could receive I.T.V. His snobbery was as impenetrable as armour, and it made him very happy. He detested Geordies.

The first time she saw Bob Arnott he was in a major's uniform. He was fit and sun-tanned, and his excellent teeth flashed white when he smiled: he had two rows of medal ribbons and a slight but interesting limp. He came into reception while she was chatting to Charlotte, the nurse who was on standby.

'Dr Bellerby's expecting me,' he said. 'My name's Arnott—Major Arnott.'

'Please sit down, Major,' she said. 'I'll tell the doctor you're here.

She smiled then, and he smiled back. 'Thank you, miss,' he said.

Later he told her that he'd known as soon as the smile, and she was certain it was true. There are some things you realize at once, even if you are stupid.

Dr Bellerby came out of his surgery, talking and spluttering as he always did when he was excited. That made the major important, and Susan was glad. She wanted him to be important.

'I wonder what he wants to see the doctor about?' she said.

'He looked fit enough—apart from that limp,' said Charlotte.

'What part of Scotland do you suppose he's from?'

'He isn't,' said Charlotte. 'He's from Tyneside. What they call a Geordie.'

That night she discovered how much her father detested them: rude, boorish, aggressive, Communists to a man.

'But he's got the M.C.,' Susan said.

That meant nothing: probably some obscene blood-letting when he was drunk.

'But he's a doctor,' she said. 'He must be. He's in the R.A.M.C.'

'Guttersnipe,' said her father. 'Probably went to some university nobody ever heard of—and now he's an officer. Officer! I know the type. Want to nationalize everything in sight.'

'Really,' said her mother, 'you make him sound like a herald of the Red Dawn or something.'

'It's all very well to laugh——' her father began.

'Somebody has to, my dear. Unless you'd like to treat us to further excerpts from your memoirs?'

He went out for the brandy.

'What do you mean, Mummy?' Susan asked.

'Mean? I don't mean anything,' said her mother. 'How could I? I'm a magazine editor. Tell me, does Hank still write to you?'

'Yes,' she said.

'Your father will be pleased,' her mother said.

Major Arnott, she learned, was on demob leave, and considering a partnership in the Bellerby unit. It was doing so well that they couldn't wait for Hank to qualify. There was the question of Arnott's gratuity too. It was sizeable enough to buy a partnership and the unit was always hungry for equipment.

('There's the suntan and the white teeth, too,' said Charlotte. 'Not to mention the M.C. That'll pull the mums in all right.')

Her mother appeared to agree, though obliquely. 'There's something agreeably wicked about the rank of major,' she said.

But he wasn't wicked at all: did nothing but work in fact. There were an awful lot of gaps to plug before a combat doctor could call himself a competent G.P., and he worked away at them for more hours than anybody realized: quiet, patient, intent, so that within a year he was the most successful of all the partners, and the most

66

sought after. The suntan faded, and the limp too went at last, but his teeth were as white as ever, and the quiet voice with its flat vowels and sing-song rise and fall could coax obedience, co-operation, tolerance of pain from patients even at their most frightened. He was witty too, in an absorbed kind of way, and just by being near him you realized what a big kick he was getting out of life. It was something she didn't understand. Not then. The only real excitement in her life till then had been in her childhood, playing grown-up pre-war ladies with Daddy like a film director or something, and that had been only Daddy's dreams. Since then her life had been mostly content: the biggest excitements a tennis match or wrestling with Hank; the biggest fear that Mummy would start mocking Daddy in that clever way she didn't understand. No. That was wrong. The biggest fear was that one day she would understand it.

And yet when she did, there was no fear in it at all, only relief. It was that day when she was alone in the reception-room, and the man came in. Not a tall man, but heavy-bodied, deft and strong. He was . . . not poorly dressed exactly, but totally devoid of elegance, as if he'd picked up just sufficient clothes at random because if you went out without them you got arrested. He looked at the name-plaque on her desk.

'Miss Jennings,' he said, 'I'd like to see Dr Arnott.'

'Are you a patient of his?' she asked, and knew very well he was not. This was a man she would never have forgotten: there was a challenge in him, a force, that was utterly memorable.

'Personal matter,' he said.

'I'm afraid the doctor's on his rounds at the moment,' she said. 'He won't be back for half an hour at least.'

'No hurry,' he said, and sat down. Even at rest, the force was still there. The man throbbed like a dynamo.

'Don't let me stop the work,' he said, and took a paperback out of his pocket. It was Chester Wilmot's *The Struggle for Europe*. Within seconds he was completely absorbed. One of the other partners came in, and the duty nurse, but always in the background she was aware of the silent, intensely reading figure. When the phone rang she spoke in a whisper, and yet he ignored her totally, as he'd ignored the partner and the nurse. At last he finished a chapter, put the book back in his pocket and said, 'What time is it?' She looked at his wrist: he had no watch. The fact disturbed her. People didn't just appear without watches.

'Two thirty,' she said.

'That's more than half an hour.'

'The doctor can't always keep to an exact time—not with sick people,' she said.

'Miss Jennings, can I ask you something?' he said.

'Or course,' she said, but she always dreaded it when people said that.

'Why do you call him "the doctor"? Don't you like his name?'

'It's just a habit you get into,' she said and was amazed, delighted at the fluency of her lying. He nodded, and the nod told her both that he was aware of the lie, and that he accepted it. She began to blush.

'Another one, Miss Jennings?' he asked, and she began to hate him now: he was turning it into a game, one that only he could win.

'Are you any relation to a Lieutenant-Commander Jennings?'

'He's my father,' she said.

'I thought he might be.' He said no more: the game, it seemed, was over.

At last she said, 'Do you know my father?'

'In some ways very well,' he said. 'In others not at all. Your mam alive?'

'Of course she is,' said Susan. At nineteen the implication that death can affect those one knows is so shocking as to arouse resentment. More gently, she added, 'My mother works in London. She's a magazine editor.'

'Culture,' he said. 'That's nice. You got culture here too.' He looked round the walls at the pictures: Cézanne, Van Gogh, Matthew Smith. Flowers, difficult flowers, but the frames were pretty.

'Win 'em in a raffle?' he asked.

'Dr Bellerby chose them,' she said coldly.

'Christ Almighty,' he said, and looked at them more closely.

'How many hours a day you work here?' he asked.

'Eight,' she said. 'Look. What business of yours——'

'You need glasses, kidder,' he said. 'That or a new job.'

She turned away, angry, and the door banged. When she looked up he was gone. It was ridiculous, she didn't even know his name.

When Arnott did get back (a tonsillitis, a gallstone and two suspected food poisonings had delayed him) he seemed to take the strange man's behaviour for granted.

'He was very rude,' she said.

'He would be. He doesn't realize it, you know. Not that that's any excuse.'

'And he asked a lot of questions about my father. He said he knew him.'

'You sound as if that's unlikely.'

'He talks like you do,' Susan said.

'You can be rude too—in a different way of course. I expect you don't mean it either,' he said gently.

68

He left her then, and she was very anxious to cry, but how could she? There was no one else on duty.

That evening he was due to leave at five, but it was five thirty when he came out, when she too was ready to leave.

'I'll give you a lift,' he said.

The heroines of her fantasy then were aloof and stately creatures who could freeze with a glance, but she accepted at once. He really had beautiful teeth, and she adored his car, which was big and powerful and glittering clean. Mummy drove a Morris: Hank had an angular and spiteful two-seater; but in Dr Arnott's car you felt you were in a movie or something. He drove well, and talked easily, not referring once to what he had said before.

'I must be taking you miles out of your way,' she said.

'Driving a pretty girl isn't exactly a hardship for me.'

Really that was being so damned nice that she had to accuse herself.

'I was awfully rude this afternoon,' she said.

'It wasn't very polite of me to comment on the fact.' He flicked a glance at her, then looked back once more to the road. 'It would save embarrassment all round if we concentrated on general topics,' he said.

'All right. How do you know where I live?'

'There's a green file in Dr Bellerby's room,' he said. 'It's labelled *Staff*, and it's full of such vital information.'

She giggled then, and it was all very easy, until he pulled up outside the house. It was June, and the sun was tender. Joe Philbin had been good with the roses that year, and the place had never looked better. She'd expected Daddy to be seated on the lawn, dozing over the *Telegraph*, but the garden was empty.

'Would you like to come in?' she asked.

'Very much,' he said, 'but I have to get back.' He saw the hurt on her face. 'That food poisoning,' he said. 'The hospitals should have the samples analysed by now.'

'Some other time then?'

He looked again at the house: sedate, Georgian, correct. The kind they used to use to put maiden aunts out to pasture.

'I'd like to,' he said. 'Very much.'

As she walked up the path she heard his car move off, and turned to admire a spray of roses. It made a pretty picture, the red against her hair's soft gold, but she was too late; he was gone.

The first thing she noticed was Mummy's driving-gloves on the hall table. The next the long trail of garments that led up the stairs: linen coat, nylon shirt, flannel trousers. At first she thought Mrs Drew must have dropped Daddy's things when she took them out to the laundry, but then she noticed the shoes, the Panama hat. Mechanically she began to pick the things up and fold them: they were the things Daddy had been wearing when she'd gone out that morning. The house suddenly seemed very quiet, and Susan was frightened. Then there was a click in the corridor above her. She looked up; her mother was coming out of the bathroom. When she saw Susan, she put a finger to her lips, and ran down the stairs to her, moving lightly, graceful still. She took the clothes from Susan's hand and put them on the table.

'Thank you, darling,' she said.

'Mummy, what's happening?' Susan said.

'Happening?' For once her mother seemed completely devoid of her particular kind of ironic intelligence.

'You're back so soon.'

'Just as well really,' her mother said. 'I brought some proofs home with me. I don't think Mrs Drew could have coped on her own.'

'Is it Daddy?'

'Of course it's Daddy.'

'Is he——?'

'Drunk,' her mother said. 'Stinking.'

'Oh, *no*,' said Susan.

'He appears to have consumed three-quarters of a bottle of gin and several very large brandies.'

'But why?'

'It seems he had a visitor. From Mrs Drew's description I gather he was a Tynesider, and not terribly couth. You're familiar with your father's antipathy to Tynesiders? Today it seems to have taken the form of an all-out attack on bottles containing alcohol.'

'Mummy,' Susan said. 'Please.'

Her mother stopped then, put out a hand, touched her daughter on the cheek.

'You know,' she said, 'sometimes I like to hope there's a little of me in you too.'

'This man,' Susan said. . . . 'Was he sort of squat? Were his clothes funny?'

'Mrs Drew just said he was odd. . . . Have you met him?'

'There was a man came to the unit today. He asked about Daddy. He asked about Dr Arnott too.'

'We'll talk about it later,' her mother said. 'In the meantime, darling, I'm awfully sorry, but I really am going to need your help.'

She saw her daughter's look of bewilderment, and sighed.

'Daddy weighs over fourteen stone,' her mother said. 'At the moment he's got absolutely no ability to help himself, and'—her voice grew shrill—'I'm simply not strong enough to cope by myself.'

'Of course I'll help you,' said Susan.

'He's in the bath,' her mother said. 'He's been there ever since the odd man left. From what Mrs Drew tells me, he's been trying to solve some problem in naval tactics.'

'Where is Mrs Drew?'

'When I last saw her she was having a bout of hysterics and giving notice. By now she'll be in the lounge bar of the Waggoner's Rest telling her adventures to everyone in sight. I think,' her mother said waspishly, 'she enjoyed every minute of it.'

They went up to the bathroom. There was water all over the place, sodden bath-sheets and bath-mats lay entangled on the floor, and once her father had been messily sick. He lay on his back in the bath, from which the water still drained. He wore underpants, one sock, and a uniform jacket he had been unable to fasten. His face was a red so brilliant as to seem artificial, his eyes were tight shut, and he made a high, keening sound with his lips.

'He's slipped again,' said her mother. 'It took me minutes just to prop him up.'

'Why don't we just leave him?' Susan asked.

'It's a question I've asked many times,' her mother said. 'The answer is because we can't. He has to drink this.' She held up a glass on the shelf. 'Mustard and water. If he's sick again he might get rid of some more gin.' She looked down on her husband. 'Home is the sailor, home from the sea,' she said, and turned on the shower's cold tap, twisting it until the water came down with the force of hail.

At first it seemed to them to have absolutely no effect, but at last he stopped making the keening sound: his eyes opened.

'Dirty weather for the Channel,' he said. 'Better batten down.'

Slowly, he turned over on his side, facing them, not moving for a while. Then his face expressed astonishment.

'Cabin's all wet,' he said. 'Rain coming in. Who opened the port-hole?' His voice rose to a roar. 'Who opened the fucking porthole? Steward! Steward!'

Her mother moved forward.

'Get me a drink,' her father said.

'Aye, aye, sir,' said her mother.

'And shut the fucking porthole.'

Her mother held out the glass of mustard and water. As he struggled up to take it, Susan turned off the shower. The water flowed away, and she noticed that the bath contained their tooth-brushes and an ungainly plant pot that bumped against his foot. He too became aware of it, and looked down with satisfaction.

'Beach was right, tide was right,' he said. 'I just proved it.'

He reached out for the drink then, and took a long swallow. As it hit him, he became aware of his wife.

'Bitch,' he said. 'Bloody bitch.'

'Two bitches,' she said. 'Help him up, Susan.'

They got him to the lavatory, and he was agonizingly sick. Between each spasm and the next he looked older, and smaller. After ten minutes he was well enough to ask them to leave him: after half an hour they did so. Susan was not to see her father again for four days.

When they left him, she and her mother went to the kitchen, and cooked omelettes.

'He rammed a landing-craft in 1945,' her mother said. 'A lot of men died. There was an inquiry, of course, but he'd just been recommended for a V.C. the day before. He broke a leg in the crash, and it was suggested—very tactfully—that he retire, so he did. But of course he never got his V.C.'

'That man,' said Susan. 'The man who came here. He must have known.'

'Of course,' said her mother. 'He probably dropped in for a chat about old times.'

'How beastly,' she said.

'Thirty-seven men were lost from that landing-craft,' her mother said. 'Some of them were cut in pieces. Like meat. They were a commando company who'd seen a lot of action. Men like that develop a certain loyalty to each other.

'Poor Daddy,' said Susan.

Her mother said, 'It happens about once a year. Not this bad—I can usually get him into bed. I'm sorry you had to see the worst one first.'

'Bronchitis,' Susan said. 'You called it bronchitis.' For the first time she and her mother exchanged a smile that was all complicity. 'Why didn't you ever tell me?'

'I have a certain arrogance,' said her mother. 'I found it very difficult to explain that my marriage had failed, particularly to my daughter.'

Later Susan said, 'I've just realized—children never question why their parents get married, do they? I mean they're just *there*. But you two—now I have thought about it—you're so unlikely.'

'You have no idea how beautiful your father was,' said her mother. 'But it isn't enough.'

'Hank isn't beautiful,' Susan said.

'I very much doubt if he's stupid, either. Because your father is, you know.'

'I know.'

'And you're not. You're not exactly brilliant, but you have quite enough brains to supplement that face—now you're bothering to use them.'

Susan said carefully, 'I wish you didn't have to be so honest all the time.'

'It is a handicap, isn't it?' said her mother. 'It's kept us apart for twenty years.'

They made coffee then, and talked about Dr Arnott. Susan gathered that it would not be a good idea to bring him to the house just at the moment.

THE SUITORS

Life was easier with her mother after that, and more explicable too. She realized the point of her mother's mockery, her fear that her father would start drinking, her savage need to earn, to keep up a standard, when her father couldn't: only it had all happened too late. They could talk now, *really* talk, be honest with each other, even smile at each other and mean it, but the need to connect wasn't there. The only link between them was her father. He stayed in bed for four days, and refused to see Susan at all. On the fifth day he came down to breakfast, and behaved as if nothing of importance had happened. Since her mother behaved in the same way, Susan accepted it, but it wasn't easy. The pretence sickened her.

What saved her really was the unit, and Hank on vacation. Telephones, tennis and wrestling. There were times when wrestling with Hank seemed a good idea, except that he rushed at her so, and it frightened her. Then she had lunch in town with Jane Prescott. Jane had once been very much her junior: two years at school is an enormous gap—thirteen and eleven, seventeen and fifteen, but she'd had a crush on Susan which dwindled at last into a casual friendship: three phone-calls a month, a lunch or tea when Susan was in London and nothing more exciting offered. She hadn't seen Jane for a year, and was aware at once of a change in her: an intensity of excitement, like a child who knows where the sweets are hidden.

Jane was an actress, and Susan assumed at once that that was it: she'd got a new part. But she was wrong. Jane had been efficiently, even expertly seduced by an account executive after she'd completed a commercial for a new brand of chocolate with nuts inside, and appeared to regard the loss of her virginity much as a galley-slave would regard the loss of his oar. Throughout lunch she told Susan of the happiness she had found, with all the fervour of the new convert, and after lunch, as a very special treat, she allowed Susan to meet him. When they did, Susan finally believed that what Jane had said was true. They were so intensely aware of each other, so very obviously on their way to bed—but that was their own business after all, she thought determinedly, remembering Jane's gospel: only her boyfriend wasn't a boy at all. He was a man, really a man, thirty at least, and Jane was just eighteen.

That night she went to a pub with Hank, and drank gin she didn't want, then on to a party and Hank sang and played the guitar, and everbody loved him so much she thought perhaps that she loved him too, and tried very hard on the cushions in the conservatory, the darkness whispering with lovers. But when he touched her she was afraid, and he knew no antidote to her fear. All he could say was, 'Oh, come on. Oh, come on.' It was all so easy for him, but for her it was impossible. She knew beyond doubt that it hadn't been like this with Jane, all hands and sweat and fear.

He'd taken her home then, far too early, slamming and rasping his gears, his anger the more intense because it seemed to him entirely justified. She'd led him on, she'd made him think, she'd behaved like a bitch. She. She. She.

'But I didn't,' she said.

'You went with me, didn't you? You knew what would happen in the conservatory. You must have done. All the lights out. And the way you kissed me—what sort of a girl are you? Is that how you get your fun?'

'I don't understand,' she said.

'All right. I'll tell you in a way you will understand. You're a prick-teaser.'

But she didn't understand that, either.

'I liked the kissing,' she said. 'Honestly I did.'

'But that's all, is that it? Thus far and no farther?'

'Yes,' she said. 'It is.'

She got out of the car in silence, and it roared off at once, back to the party, she thought bitterly, back to find a girl with more amenable knees than mine. She went in quietly, but her parents were up anyway: her mother reading a manuscript, her father absorbed in a book of somebody's memoirs. Naval or military no doubt. Public School. Sandhurst/Dartmouth. Polo. Pig-sticking. Pink gin.

'I thought there was a party,' her mother said.

'There was,' said Susan. 'I left. I'm sick of parties.'

'Wasn't Hank there?' her father asked. He sounded positively roguish.

'Oh yes,' said Susan. 'He was there.'

'You want to hang on to that young feller,' her father said. 'I like him. Good type. Brainy too.'

'He plays the guitar,' said her mother.

'He isn't going to make his living at it,' said her father with inexorable logic.

Her father it seemed thought very highly of Hank, and spent a lot of time saying so, all of it wasted. It occurred to Susan as she undressed for bed that he was trying to help her, establish her safely beyond the reach of himself, her mother, his house, but that was too

75

late too, and too arbitrary. Boys weren't like toy soldiers—all alike and six to a box. Before she fell asleep she thought of Jane. Lucky Jane, she thought and then—It would serve everybody jolly well right if I let Dr Arnott seduce me.

The thought stayed with her next morning, and she giggled at it: it was at once so childish and so dishonest. What did it matter whether it served everybody right or not? Whether or not she wanted it—and he—that was all that mattered. It was Sunday, and a great day for cooking breakfast, reading papers, listening to *Your Concert Choice* on the radio. Mrs Drew was back with them (terrified she'll miss round two, said her mother) but on Sundays she went to chapel, and Susan's father went to church and read the lesson. She remembered him as a child: dark suit, stiff white collar, discreet tie, feet evenly planted, reading the doings of Jehovah as if they were Admiralty Orders. Nowadays there wouldn't be fifty in the church—thirty if you discounted the Vicar, the Curate, the verger, the choir—but he continued to go. It was his duty to go. Susan hadn't bothered since the fifth form.

Over lunch he talked about Hank, and would have made a thing of it if her mother hadn't taken him off to dry the dishes. Then Hank called anyway, just before tea, to ask if she could dine with the Bellerbys, and of course her idiot father had to practically force him to stay to tea and make her pour out as if she were a duchess with footmen dangling from each elbow. She managed things so that Hank left without getting her alone, but he came back for her later, all neat and tidy but already hot in a suit of too heavy cloth. She on the other hand felt great: new dress of blue and white linen, duster coat, openwork shoes. This time, she was sure, she could cope with Hank. She was wrong.

He said at once, 'Look, I'm sorry.'

'That's all right.' And really it was. Over, finished. Why dwell on it?

'You're sure?' he asked.

'Of course.'

But she was too quick for him. His apology, she gathered, had been prepared. The least she could do was let him work it out.

'You see the trouble is I'd had a bit to drink. Now that's not an excuse or anything, but it is a fact, a physiological fact, I mean. Alcohol in the bloodstream, reaching the brain, getting all the Freudian censors plastered. You know.'

'Yes, Hank,' she said.

'And that's how I did it. How, mind you. Not why.'

'I see,' she said.

'It's the why I really want to talk about.' He hesitated. 'Don't think

76

I'm avoiding the issue or anything, but weren't you surprised when I asked you out to dinner tonight?'

'Yes,' she said. 'I was.'

'My parents were too. When I suggested I ask you, I mean. Not that they minded. I mean they'd love to have you. It's just that . . . you only see Dad at the unit, and you've hardly met my mother at all.'

That was when her confidence began to ebb.

'They're both awfully nice,' she said.

'Would you mind if I pulled up, just for a minute?' he asked. 'No funny business or anything, but I just can't talk to you when I'm driving.'

'All right,' she said.

He pulled up under an elm tree. Before, behind her the fence-lined road bisected fields and pasture. They were utterly alone, but that wasn't why her confidence seeped away.

'I said a pretty beastly thing to you last night,' he said.

'Oh, please—don't let's talk about it.'

'But we must talk about it,' he said, with the first touch of what she feared might be a lifetime's impatience. 'You see . . . you're very beautiful, Susan. I love you very much—and so I want you. And last night I was so sure . . . you've no idea what your rejection did to me. I couldn't sleep.'

'I'm sorry,' she said, 'but——'

'No. Don't be. It was the best thing that could have happened. You see, I worked the whole thing out. You see, it isn't just that I want you—though that's a very important part of it. . . . I love you. You realize what I'm saying, don't you?'

'You . . . you love me?'

Again the barely curbed flash of impatience. 'I want to marry you,' he said.

'Oh!' The exclamation was of fear, but he took it for surprise.

'I suppose we should have both seen it coming,' he said. 'I mean we've been going out for ages, and your father likes me, I'm sure he does—and your mother will come round.'

'You don't think my mother likes you?' There was hope in this at least.

'To tell you the truth, I don't think your mother likes anybody much. But she knows I'll be a pretty competent doctor, and make a bit of money. And anyway, my parents will adore you. . . . Dad already does.'

'You mean you've told them?'

'I dropped a pretty broad hint,' he said. 'Hence the dinner. They want to have a look at you on their home ground.'

He talked as if it was settled. That he'd be getting impatient and sticking his thing in her for the rest of their lives. His father. Her father. Family dinners.

'Shall I tell them it's on?' he asked.

'I don't know,' she said.

'But you must know,' he said. 'I love you.'

The impatience again. The need to take her so he didn't have to talk.

Of course she knew. The answer was no. Not now. Not ever. But the difficulty would be in saying it, not just to him, but to her father, his father, perhaps his mother too. She wished that her mother were there, but to turn to her mother at that point would be to jeopardize the respect her mother had so recently acquired for her.

Carefully she said, 'It's all happening so fast.'

'Oh sir, this is so sudden,' he mocked. 'Come off it, Susan.'

'Well it is,' she said. 'I want to think about it.'

'You mean there's somebody else? There can't be.'

There was horror in his voice at the thought that somebody else might have purchased the toy he had marked down for his own.

'It isn't that,' she said.

'Well then?'

'I want to think about it.'

It was a useful phrase and she stuck to it under the elm tree, and watched Hank sweat until it was time to move on or be late for dinner. It held her secure all the way to his house, though its magic weakened at the end, because he chose to see it at last as maidenly reluctance, a rare virtue, and therefore all the more to be valued in the mid twentieth century. 'I want to think about it,' for Hank was the same as 'I'll answer yes tomorrow'. That it could mean 'no' was clearly impossible.

The Bellerbys lived in a street of early Victorian terrace houses that were big and ugly and expensive to inhabit. Each side of the road was lined with cars, and suddenly Hank said, 'Damn.' Somebody had parked in his place, his *special* place, that everybody knew was his. He eased past the intruder, and swore again.

'Bloody hell,' he said.

'What's wrong?' Susan asked.

'That bastard Arnott's here.'

That was the end. To have to dine with the Bellerbys because Hank had made up his mind to marry her was bad enough: to have to do it with Arnott watching was unbearable. She wondered desperately if she could be ill, but abandoned the idea at once. She was dining with two doctors.

'Don't you like Dr Arnott?' she asked.

'He's all right I suppose,' said Hank. 'But why the hell did he have to come here tonight? We wanted you to ourselves.'

There was comfort of a sort in that, and comfort too in the glimpse of herself the hall mirror gave her. The duster coat didn't look at all bad, and the dress beneath it was positively good: terrific in fact. Susan looked long and carefully at her hair, and decided she'd make a fight of it. They went into the drawing-room.

Bellerby, who was tubby, genial and finically neat, was standing in front of an enormous, empty hearth drinking whisky. In chairs on either side of him sat his wife and Dr Arnott, drinking gin. Mrs Bellerby got up at once as Susan came into the room, but it was Bellerby who came over to her, told her she was welcome and put an arm round her shoulders, squeezing her, then asked what she would like to drink. She asked for sherry, and he poured it for her with a careful skill that reminded her at once of the unit's dispensary. Then it was Mrs Bellerby's turn. Mrs Bellerby was tall, with the kind of features that are sometimes called aristocratic by the charitable, the nose being long, the lips thin. In her own game of Happy Families she was much more the squire's lady than the doctor's wife.

'Susan,' she said. 'You don't mind if I call you Susan, dear? It seems a little late for Miss Jennings.'

Hank, who was pouring himself a whisky, snorted. His mother as *grande dame* appealed to him: an old but well-loved turn. Susan decided she got quite enough of that from her mother, who did it better anyway.

'Susan's fine,' she said. 'Hallo, Dr Arnott.'

'Hallo, Susan,' Arnott said. He seemed so pleased to see her she could have wept.

'Hank, say hallo to Dr Arnott,' Mrs Bellerby said.

'Oh, sorry,' said Hank, and added soda. 'Hallo.'

'Hallo to you too,' said Arnott.

The uneasy pause that followed delighted Susan. Hank asked for it so often, and got it so rarely.

After a while Mrs Bellerby said, 'Hank's doing frightfully well at Cambridge.'

'I'm delighted to hear it,' said Arnott.

'Next term he'll get his college colours for rugger,' said Bellerby.

'Jolly good,' said Arnott.

'Did you ever play rugger?' Mrs Bellerby asked.

'A bit,' said Arnott.

'Who for?'

It was Hank's question, both syllables so weighted with insolence that even his parents looked uneasy.

'The Army,' said Arnott.

Conversation languished.

Arnott sat and sipped gin, Bellerby cleared his throat, Hank fidgeted. It was Mrs Bellerby who talked at last, soothing the sensibility of her wounded males. Her two splendid fox-hounds had tried to bite a tiger, and if it was the tiger's fault that they had failed she offered no reproach. Only it did seem a little unfair that the tiger should insist on a share of their dinner afterwards, particularly when such a toothsome little bitch had been invited. Mrs Bellerby talked of roses, furniture, her last visit to London, but her thoughts were her own. Her thoughts were limited, but intense. One: why had Bellerby forgotten to tell her he'd invited Arnott to dinner? Two: why couldn't Arnott see he wasn't wanted, and go? Instead, he accepted more gin and told her about his last visit to Newcastle, and Mrs Bellerby cried, 'Oh, really? How *interesting*,' while she hated him. Mrs Bellerby at that point thought that Susan had money of her own. Hank fidgeted more than ever, and wondered if Arnott played the guitar, and Bellerby stopped clearing his throat and offered Arnott more gin, which he accepted. Susan thought she had never spent a more ghastly evening.

Then suddenly it wasn't ghastly at all: it was wonderful. Hank fidgeted once too often, and his father sent him to fetch a third bottle of wine. Five was a ghastly number for dinner, Bellerby thought. Two bottles might be enough, but one could never be sure. Better open a third and finish it next day. At least it got rid of Hank for a few minutes. In fact it got rid of him for quite a while. Hank in a bad temper tended to rush at things, and that night he rushed at the stairs leading down to the cellarette, and broke his ankle. When the resulting uproar had subsided and two doctors had done all they could, it was still necessary to go to hospital. His father and mother went with him: dinner was abandoned.

'Poor Susan,' Bellerby said. 'What a wretched evening for you. What will you do?'

'I'll see she gets home all right,' said Arnott.

Bellerby pondered. He was an astute man, and yet he loved his son without reservation, with a love that transcended even his wife's: he at least was aware what Hank was like. All his instincts told him that Arnott was a threat to his son's happiness. He looked at him: courteous, concerned for Hank, resolved it seemed to do no more than help out in a family crisis, and believed none of it.

'That's very good of you,' he said.

He drove her to the end of the road. Suddenly she seemed to be enormously cheerful, perhaps even more than cheerful. The time had come to get out of this mess. Bellerby was senior partner after all, and Bellerby's Hank obviously claimed this one for his own.

'Run you back home?' he suggested.

'But I haven't eaten,' she said. 'I really am rather hungry.'

'Where would you like to go? Trouble is it's Sunday. Most of the good places are closed.'

'It doesn't matter,' she said. 'Somewhere quiet. There's something I want to talk to you about.'

They ate steaks and drank lager in a pub near the river, and she told him about Hank. And really it amazed her, there was such an awful lot to tell: not just about Hank of course, but about herself, and Mummy and Daddy, so much that once he tried to stop her, but in the end he made her go on, listening in silence, smiling sometimes, till the steaks and lager were finished. She looked at the clock on the wall: ten past nine.

'Please,' she said. 'We don't have to finish just yet, do we?'

'Where would you like to go?' he asked.

'Anywhere,' she said. 'Just so we can talk.'

He took her to his flat, the ground floor of a converted Victorian barrack. No nosy neighbours, no landlady, no *fuss*. He made coffee, and she went on talking, pouring it all out: despair at the boredom that was all life offered, the terrible, unfulfilled need for some kind of excitement that would offend Hank, outrage her father.

'You're just twenty,' he said.

'I'll be twenty-one in October.'

'I'm thirty-four,' he said, and she winced.

'I wasn't talking about you,' she said.

'Weren't you?'

'You're not being *fair*,' she said.

'Oh, yes, I was,' said Arnott. 'I wasn't being kind but I was terribly fair.'

She thought about it, accepted it and said at last, 'It's all up to you really.'

He came over to her then, and kissed her, and in a crazy kind of way it was like being back at school. He taught, she learned, and the dialogue they achieved was so perfect it sustained her even through the pain. She had heard a great deal about the pain, and it was real enough, but even the pain had its compensations. He must be, she realized, a very skilful lover, and the thought at the time was one of relief. Jealousy didn't come into it. Not then.

Later he made more coffee, and cleaned her up. She realized, with surprise, that she'd bled in some quantity, but his hands were gentle, the water soothing: he was as naked as she, and suddenly she reached out, caressed his maleness.

'Less of it,' he said. 'You've had enough for one night.'

'Will it hurt so much next time?' she asked, still holding him.

'There's to be a next time, then?'

She looked at her hand, and began to giggle. Really it was funny: men could never have any secrets. He drew her wrist away, kissed her mouth and went out for the coffee. When he came back she was seated in front of the mirror, making up her face. She seemed completely relaxed; not unaware of her nakedness, but at ease with it, perhaps more than at ease.

'Smug,' he said.

'I beg your pardon?'

'That's how you're looking. Smug.' Her face darkened. 'Endearingly smug.'

She brightened at once. 'Why do you say that?'

'Because it's true. You know precisely how beautiful you are.'

'Oh, so I'm beautiful, am I?'

'All the way from the mammary glands to the nates,' he said.

She looked in the mirror with satisfaction. No one could call her plump, but then no one could call her skinny either. All in all she balanced out very nicely. He poured out coffee, brought a cup to her, stood beside her, and she put an arm round his waist. His hand stroked her shoulder, then cupped a breast, and she sensed the friendship in his touch as well as its sensuality.

'We *will* do it again?' she asked.

'I'd take it very kindly.'

'No,' she said. 'Don't joke. Look. Please don't let's talk about love and all that.'

'Isn't it customary? At this point I mean? A priest might say we'd left it rather late.'

'Don't *joke*,' she said, and realized, in a kind of horrified delight, that she'd spoken sharply to him and that it was O.K. Absolutely. That that kind of teasing was meant to provoke just that kind of sharpness.

'Darling,' she said—and that was O.K. too—'when I said love, I'm talking about all this Hank nonsense.'

'So that's nonsense, is it?' She nodded. 'And you'll treat it as nonsense?'

'Well, of course I will,' she said. 'After what we've had ...' She hesitated. 'This could make things a bit tricky for you at the unit.'

'Extremely tricky,' he said.

'Then we'll have to be jolly careful,' she said. 'Take care nobody finds out, I mean. When we're at the unit we'll have to be just like we used to——' She broke off. Arnott was laughing. 'Why do you have to laugh at me?' she asked.

'Who's laughing at you? I'm not laughing *at* anybody. I'm laughing because I'm happy.'

'Are you?' she asked, suspicious.

'Extremely happy,' he said. 'I just discovered you're even more adorable than I thought.'

'That's all right then,' she said, and smiled at him. 'But that's as far as it goes, mind. We're lovers, and that's all. I don't want you to think I'm trying to force you into something.'

'Nobody shall ever say that you took advantage of my innocence,' he said gravely.

She struck out at him then, and he yelled, picked her up and slapped her. She kissed him fiercely, then shut herself to him, all knees and elbows.

'I have to go,' she said. 'Honestly I have.'

It was midnight, and more than time to leave. He sipped his coffee, watching her dress, then reached reluctantly for his shirt. She noticed then a long scar, faded now, that ran from the middle of his back to his hip. Another climbed his leg from behind the kneecap to his thigh.

'My God,' she said. 'What on earth did you do to yourself?'

'This was done to me,' Arnott said. 'In a place called Kuala Kudu. Malaya.'

'You were wounded? Oh yes. Of course you were. You limped, didn't you?'

'I don't limp now,' he said. 'I'm strong and fit. I have to be. . . . Come on, we're late.'

They drove back quickly, and she worried about what to say, and tried not to show it, but already he knew her too well for that.

'Truth or story, my darling?' he asked.

'Story, of course,' Susan said. 'The trouble is I'm not awfully good at them.'

'Hank broke his ankle and you went to a party,' he said.

'But it sounds so callous.'

'It's what happened,' he said, and she laughed.

'I suppose it is. Anyway, it's got Hank out of the way for a bit. Daddy'll hate that.'

'He'll hate me too.'

'You won't meet him,' she said, so maternally protective that this time he didn't laugh.

'Just as well,' he said. 'What with me being a Geordie.'

'That's that awful man's fault. The one who came to see you. Tell me about him.'

'Maybe I will one day,' he said, 'if we go on.'

And that had begun her career as a liar. She had, so she discovered, a natural aptitude for it. (Later on, when it all came out, 'liar' was her father's word for it. Her mother called it a natural though hitherto latent gift for subterfuge.) It was all much simpler than she would ever have believed possible. Hank was in hospital, so of course she had to spend her free time as best she could—and that meant with Hank's friends and hers: a group so amorphous that tracking them down was impossible. Then there was Jane—jolly useful for Saturdays, and now and again a whole weekend in town. The Jane idea was absolutely perfect, because quite often Jane needed an alibi too. So she could really see Bob pretty often: at least twice during the week and on Saturday, sometimes Sunday too. Of course the thing had its drawbacks, principally Hank. She did have to visit him sometimes, and really, the way he went on about that ankle of his, you'd have thought he'd broken it in the Olympics or something. And he still wanted to marry her. Sometimes he talked as though he thought she had to marry him because he'd broken his ankle, as if she were a prize for suffering, but she'd learned how to be firm about things like that. She said they were both too young, and ought to wait till he qualified, and see less of each other in the meantime. Mrs Bellerby did some more squire's lady over that one, at first, but Susan said she was thinking of Hank too, and Mrs Bellerby became quite human. Dr Bellerby was different, a lot shrewder, suspicious too; and besides, she liked him. But not as she liked Bob. (Love was still a forbidden word: love was Hank, and all he stood for.) So she deceived Bellerby, and was quite good at it, and went on being Bob's mistress.

Her body had an aptitude for sex that surprised her. Once the pain had gone she showed him a curiosity and a skill he found both frightening and delightful. 'Show me,' she would say, and, 'What else? What else?' Greedy as a child is greedy, always asking one more treat. She learned quickly how to arouse him, learned also to use the moments of rest to question him, to learn. The wounds for instance. The story of the wounds had fascinated her. He was the only man she knew who had been hurt grievously by other men. (Daddy's broken leg didn't count at all. It was an accident, no more important than Hank's.) But Bob had been shot and stabbed, and nearly bled to death. He had also killed one of the men who had done it. It made him, to her, a special person. There was something deliciously terrifying in opening her body like that to a man who had killed. Not that the story came easily. It took a really special assault of her ardour and skill to get it out of him. But in the end he had told her: a great victory for Susan. A special part of his life that he would tell to no one else.

There'd been a patrol of British infantry shot up in a rubber plantation, and three of them were badly hurt. He'd gone out to them in a jeep with a Gurkha escort, four tiny, chattering men who were the most professional soldiers he'd ever seen. They reached the patrol, a section of eighteen-year-old conscripts commanded by a sergeant, a veteran of the Second World War. The sergeant had three bullets in his stomach—a burst from a burp gun—and died as Arnott examined him. That left two boys with localized wounds, and four unwounded. As he bandaged the wounded, the others clung to him too, seeking the protection of his authority, his officer status, while the Gurkhas scouted the area. Arnott knew there was no point in trying to explain that he knew even less about jungle fighting than they did. They were good enough boys, but the ambush had unnerved them, and they were terrifyingly short of experience. It was their first patrol: three weeks before they'd been in England.

He waited till the Gurkha *jebadar* came back from his scouting, and talked it over with him. It was evening, and the tropical night was swift. Their best chance was to get back to Company H.Q. at once, and he told the W/T operator to radio back to say so, and ask for reinforcements. The W/T operator tried and failed. The set, which looked perfect, obstinately refused to communicate. They set off anyway, the two wounded men and the dead sergeant in the jeep, one Gurkha driving, a second manning the mounted Bren gun. The jebadar, the fourth Gurkha and the fit men walked. So did Arnott, carrying the dead sergeant's Sten. The walk was a nightmare of bad tracks, clinging lianas, leeches, dangerous shadows. To go on was dangerous in the extreme; to stop, if the Chinese were still trailing them, would be fatal. They went on.

If they hadn't had the Gurkhas, Arnott said, they'd have been killed to a man—the ambush was that good. The Chinese let the men in front of the jeep go past, lobbed grenades at it and opened fire on the marching men. The two wounded men and the driver were killed at once, but the gunner, hideously wounded, still hung on to the Bren and sprayed at the gouts of flame in the undergrowth till he died. The two Gurkhas and Arnott dropped at once, but the boys, bewildered by fire, hesitated too long, and three of them fell. Arnott as he loosed off the Sten was conscious of an appalling pain in his back, as if he'd been flogged, but his terror and rage were so intense that he was aware of being able, quite deliberately, to ignore it (adrenalin's pretty remarkable stuff, he said), and go on firing. The Chinese threw their last grenade, and rushed the survivors. Unfortunately for the Chinese, the surviving Gurkha private got back in the jeep and loosed off one more burst before he too was shot dead. What was left of the Chinese kept on coming and Arnott killed one of them at a range of four feet. As he did so, the jebadar leaped over him, swinging his kukri, and Arnott became aware of a second pain, this time in the leg. He swung round to see a dead Chinese beside him, a long knife in his hand. The knife had scored a deep groove down

85

Arnott's thigh, just before the jebadar had beheaded the Chinese.

'Then what happened?' Susan asked.

'I fainted. Not much of a solution to the problem but the best I could do.' He hesitated. She was looking at him as if he had betrayed her. 'And I'd lost a fair bit of blood. When I came to the jebadar had bandaged me up—not a bad job either—and he was feeding me palm toddy out of his canteen. Not the right prescription of course, but it was the best *he* could do. Set the adrenalin off again while I bandaged up the survivors. We were down to five little niggers by then.'

'And then what happened?'

'The jebadar fiddled with the W/T—the operator was dead—and it worked first time. They sent a tank for us, and two platoons. We had seven Chinese dead for them—and two prisoners. Both wounded. One of them was a woman. About your age,' he said, then added: 'So were two of the dead.'

'Did you kill them?' she asked.

'You're asking a hell of a lot.'

'I know,' she said.

'Maybe. The one I got for certain was a man. We all just loosed off at anything we saw.'

'Would it bother you?' she asked. 'If you *knew* I mean.'

'It all happened so fast,' he said. 'All I could think about was not being killed.'

'It was lucky you had those Gurkhas with you.'

'For me,' he said. 'Not for them. The jebadar got a D.S.O. as well.'

'He must have felt pretty rotten—his men being killed like that.'

'They expect to die,' he said. 'If they kill a few of the others as they go—they don't feel so bad.' He paused. 'He was a good lad—that jebadar. He'd been with a bunch of the Parachute Regiment before he met us. They understood each other. But that bunch of boys had him baffled. "They just don't know *how* to kill, Sahib," he said. Not that they were cowards—he didn't mean that. They stayed where they were, and they even managed to fire a few rounds. But they did it all wrong, he said. They didn't know *how*.'

'And you did?'

'I was twice their age,' he said, 'and brought up a lot harder. I didn't think about it. They did. A clerk in a bank, two factory hands, a shoe salesman, a boy straight out of grammar school. They didn't run away—and they thought about what they were doing. I couldn't be like that—but I'm glad they are. You should be like that too.'

'It's nice to know you were brave,' she said.

'Not brave,' he said. 'Mad.'

'That's what my father said about you,' she said. 'It can't be true.'

'Because your father said it? Look,' he said. 'We'd killed ten of them—mostly with two bursts from the Bren. They were small people—Cantonese—about the same size as the Gurkhas. They wore blue boiler-suit sort of clothes and they were all ill before they died. Dysentery, vitamin deficiency. One poor bugger had rickets. I didn't feel a hero. Not then, not now. I just wished—they hadn't tried to kill me. Those boys felt the same. When they saw the one the jebadar beheaded, they vomited.'

'Did you?'

'Not then,' he said. 'I had to make the jebadar go on respecting me till the relief arrived, otherwise the whole group would have fallen apart. Then they gave me an injection. I couldn't be sick till two days later. When I was, they blamed the toddy.'

He lay back on the bed and she got up, mixed him a Scotch and water the way he liked it—lots of ice—then lay down beside him, and began, softly, craftily, to tease him with love.

'What a clever little whore you are,' he said, and already it was a joke between them, the tribute her body demanded from his before they enjoyed each other.

'I know,' she said. 'Self-taught too. You know that.'

He smiled then. 'Only I know,' he said. 'It's a bit worrying.'

'You don't have to worry about me,' she said.

'Suppose I ran out of secrets?'

Her hands, her mouth, continued to please him. 'Am I the best?' she asked.

'Yes,' he said. 'You know you are.'

'The best ever? Honest?'

'Cross my heart and hope to die,' he said, and reached for her. She wriggled away.

'No, wait,' she said. 'I haven't finished.'

It was strange that those others never bothered her. She had known him for so little time, his past was so sealed off from her, that they bothered her not at all.

'I bet you had nice ones,' she said.

'I had what I could get,' he said, 'like everybody else.'

'Didn't you love *any* of them?'

The more expensive kind of South Korean whore, Malays as alike as cigarettes in a pack, a Tamil nurse, black and quite startlingly beautiful, a shrill Chinese with a tendency to bossiness.

'Love didn't come into it,' he said. 'I hope I was grateful.'

'I hope so too,' she said, and opened to him then, opened and

87

flowered, and it was beautiful. He looked down into her eyes, and she saw how serious he was.

'Susan,' he said, but she covered his mouth.

'Please,' she said. 'Please. Don't say anything. Don't spoil it.'

That was how their best time began. His secrets, and the clamouring strength of their love-making, and the way she hid them both from Mummy and Daddy, and Hank and Dr Bellerby. Perhaps she needed secrecy to give a spice to her love. She had been shameless then because there hadn't been any shame, there couldn't be, not in that secret room of his, where she could come and go and no one could see. Besides he'd been so good to her from the first, patient and understanding, and so proud of her too. And he'd loved her, she realized, almost from the first. Loved her enough to want to marry her, just like Hank. It had taken all her skill to keep that one at bay. She had not realized then that she had succeeded because of her body's new-learned skill; nor that her body's responses to his skill grew daily less important to her delight in making love.

'I thought you'd got what every man wanted,' she would say. 'A willing mistress.' Or, borrowing a line of attack from Hank: 'I don't want to be made an honest woman of.' But he did want it. He loved her so much that it was only when he saw how much it distressed her that he stopped talking about marriage, and when he did she made love to him more fervently than ever, and went on fooling Hank and the Bellerbys and Daddy, and even Mummy; and, much as she liked her mother then, that was the biggest triumph of all.

She kept it up for ten weeks: till Hank had gone back to Cambridge, limping and sulky because she wouldn't see him off. There had been two fabulous weeks when Mummy and Daddy went off fishing in Ireland, and Mrs Drew and the rest of them had their holidays too, leaving Susan to do whatever she liked. That had been absolutely super: though there'd been a bit of a fuss about her own holidays, as she'd put them back to late October, when Bob Arnott had his. All the same, it had all been perfect, until the day she forgot to ring Jane.

It had been a marvellous Saturday. They'd driven up to Oxford and had lunch at the Mitre and looked at the Magdalen swans. They'd driven back to his flat, and she'd made tea for him and loved him, and they'd lain on the bed very close, making plans about how to meet during the holiday. It involved going away with Jane somewhere, and hiring a place where no one knew them, and it would be perfect, she knew, so perfect that he would tell her the biggest secret of all, the one he'd always wriggled out of so far, about the strange man who made Daddy get so drunk. She'd been talking about Jane all evening, but she'd forgotten to ring her, and Jane, the idiot, had called *her*, just because she and the boy-friend had had a row, so that when she got home there they both were, waiting for her, like a couple of prosecuting counsel or something. Well, not Mummy perhaps. Mummy hadn't been so bad, and anyway Susan had a feeling that she could cope with her mother, brains or no brains, but her father had just about run amok. And all the time he drank pink gin and got more and more energetic, as she grew more and more drowsy with love.

It was, he said, the deception that bothered him most. Why should she say she was going to be with Jane if she wasn't? Obviously there was no answer to that that wouldn't bring the ceiling down, so she said nothing.

'Well?' her father said. 'I'm waiting.'

She struggled with her body's pleasant languor.

'I wanted to be by myself for a bit,' she said.

'By yourself?' said her father. 'Rubbish. You wouldn't have to start telling all those lies if you wanted to be by yourself.'

It was strange, she thought. She'd never noticed before how *noisy* her father was.

'You've been with some man,' said her father, 'and I'll bet it wasn't the first time.' She said nothing. 'Susan I want an answer.'

'Did Jane say that?' she asked.

'Jane rang off,' her father said. 'If you ask me Jane's as big a liar as you are.'

Nobody *is* asking you, you stupid idiot. And don't shout.

Her mother said, 'Maybe I ought to talk to Susan on her own. We're getting nowhere like this.'

'Oh, no you don't,' said her father. 'This is something that concerns us all, and I'm going to be in on it.' He turned to his daughter. 'Susan, you're going to tell us who the feller is if we have to sit here all night.'

It was at this point that Susan yawned, and her father rose to hit her. Nobody had ever hit Susan, and as he lumbered across to her, she wondered if she could bear it, but made no move to avoid him. He was not particularly steady on his feet, and his eyes were red. Susan realized that he was not only noisy, he was extremely strong, yet even so she made no move to avoid him. There was no trace of the queenly dignity of her fictional heroines. The only thought in Susan's head was that it would be too absurd to start dodging round the room with Daddy stumbling after. Even as he swung his hand back she wanted to giggle, and had to fight hard to suppress it. Then his hand dropped, and he began to cry.

'I do hope,' said her mother, 'we're not going to turn into one of those Russian families—all tantrums and uproar.'

'How could you do this?' said her father. Then again, more accurately, 'How could you do this to me?'

Still crying, he went back to his gin. It took another hour for him to drink himself unconscious, and by that time Susan was almost out on her feet. Her mother took her into the kitchen, poured milk into a saucepan, began to heat it.

'I wish you had considered the side-effects of this amour of yours,' she said. 'Your poor father will be stoned for the next week.'

'Do you mind?' Susan asked. 'That I did it I mean?'

'I honestly don't know,' her mother said. 'You see, I never did, and that does make a difference.' She turned away to look at the milk and said, 'I'm talking about before I married Daddy.'

'You really do have to be honest, don't you?' said Susan, and her mother turned then, ready to meet the bitterness in her voice.

'Darling, I hope you have to be honest too,' she said.

'All right,' said Susan. 'I've been seeing a man. I've been sleeping with him.'

'A man?'

'I haven't turned into a whore yet, Mother,' she said. 'Though it seems I have a talent for it.'

'The man told you so?'

'Yes he did. It's a joke we have between us. Maybe not a very nice joke——'

'You don't have to say that,' said her mother. 'Under certain circumstances it could be a very nice joke indeed.'

Susan said, 'I like him very much. I like what we do. So it is a nice joke.' She hesitated, then added, 'You said you wanted me to be honest.'

'I think that's all we have left,' said her mother. 'Are you going to tell me who he is?'

'No,' said Susan.

'I could find out.'

'Please don't make me hate you,' Susan said.

Her mother took the milk from the stove, and poured it out steadily.

'What an odd conversation this is,' she said. 'I should be screaming at you to denounce the man who brought about your dishonour.'

'Daddy's doing that,' said Susan.

'You *have* changed, darling, and altogether for the better. D'you want to marry this man?'

'No,' said Susan. 'It's absolutely super the way it is.'

'Suppose you got pregnant?'

'Maybe then,' said Susan. 'I don't know. But I hope it doesn't happen for years and years. What we've got is perfect, Mummy. Please don't make me change it.'

Her mother sipped her milk.

'I suppose I should apologize,' she said at last, 'for not interfering years ago. But you're very happy—that's obvious, and why should anyone apologize for that? But it's over now, you know.' She hurried on before Susan could interrupt her. 'I'm sorry, darling, but it is. Rupert knows.'

'D'you think I care about what Daddy says?'

'I think you will care,' said her mother. 'Because he'll make you.'

'But how could he?'

Her mother sighed. 'He'll shout at you and drink at you and cry at you. On and on and on. His technique doesn't need brains, you know. Just stamina. And he's got enough of that for the two of us. Believe me, Susan, I know.'

Susan said, 'I'm sorry, Mummy. But I'm going to keep what I've got. I like it—being alone together, nobody knowing. We don't *want* anybody else.'

'You're talking about a honeymoon,' her mother said.

'It's lasted ten weeks,' said Susan, 'and it's gone on getting better.'

She held out for fifteen days, a nightmare of her father drunk, her father angry, her father in tears; no meetings with Bob—her father escorted her to and from the unit every day—only quick and ineffectual whispering. On the fifteenth day he told her she was looking unwell and called her into his surgery. She wanted him to make love to her there and then, and for the first time ran into a hardness in him, the hardness of his wounds, his killing, that demanded explanations, demanded facts. By then she was worn out and told him everything. In five minutes he had persuaded her that the only solution was marriage, and she agreed. Marriage with Bob was the only way to get any peace. That night he came to her house, and told Daddy everything. Then there were tantrums and uproar if you like.

THE NEED FOR A GOOD CAUSE

I WAITED while Laidlaw made up his mind what to do. Jim, in his shirtsleeves, picked up an apple and crunched into it, his coat dangling awkwardly from the back of his chair. At last Laidlaw got up, hung the coat neatly over the back of an empty chair, and sat down again. I got the impression that he couldnt've have gone on until Jim's coat was hanging straight.

'Violence,' he said at last. 'You always had a talent for it.'

'Just as well,' Jim said. 'We live in a violent world.'

'Correct me if I'm wrong,' said Laidlaw, 'but didn't you people once have the custom of confessing your weaknesses to each other?'

'That was the Communists,' said Jim.

'You mean you weren't one?'

'Come off it—I've been to America three times. I got a work permit when McCarthy was the biggest hit on television. I was what you call a fellow-traveller.'

'And as such ... you never confessed your weaknesses?' Laidlaw paused. 'I was going to suggest you did so now—this weakness for violence. It would help me enormously if you were purged of it—help in finding you a job, I mean.'

Jim bit again into the apple, and looked round for the decanter. Laidlaw pushed it to him and he filled his glass and pushed the decanter on to me, as happy as a visiting colonel in a good mess.

'Purge,' he said. 'I like that word. Where d'you get it—Chairman Mao or M.R.A.? Not that it matters, does it? You're after a little innocent fun out of Peter Pan Moulton, aren't you?'

'Peter Pan?' said Laidlaw. 'I've thought of you as a lot of things, I admit, but never as something out of Barrie.'

'The boy who never grew up,' said Jim. 'The smasher. The clogger. The lad who still uses his fists to give his brains a rest. Well, I'll tell you. We live in a violent bloody world, old lad. I've known it since I've known anything—and so would you if you'd kept your eyes open. Theoretically it's wrong—and we all know it—but practically it's a necessity, and we admit it—those of us who have any honesty.' He looked at me then. 'Right, Bob?'

I said, 'I'm pleading exemption. Doctors haven't got time to be violent, they're too busy patching up the end product.'

'Not always, Bob,' Laidlaw said. 'Take you for instance—you were violent enough when you won that M.C.' He turned to Jim. 'You heard about that?'

'Yes,' Jim said. 'I heard about it.' It hadn't made him happy.

'Bob shot and killed a Chinese Communist guerrilla in Malaya,' Laidlaw went on unheeding. 'He was in charge of a patrol at the time. They killed ten Chinks and took two prisoners—both wounded.'

'How the hell did you know about that?' I asked.

'When you hear an old acquaintance has done well, naturally you make a note of it,' said Laidlaw; then to Jim: 'I'm glad you heard about it too.'

'I didn't hear about the ten dead,' Jim said.

'A couple of Gurkhas got most of them with a Bren,' I said. 'They were both killed too.'

'There was a Gurkha with a kukri too, wasn't there?' Laidlaw asked. 'Didn't he chop a woman's head off?'

'A man's,' I said. 'He was sticking a knife in me at the time.'

'But surely there were women there?'

'Three. Two were shot dead. The third was shot in the neck. We took her prisoner. She died later.'

'Under interrogation?'

'I believe so,' I said. 'Where did you hear all this?'

'A chap called Watson,' Laidlaw said. 'He manages one of my supermarkets. He was one of that patrol—one of those helpless boys whose lives you saved. He . . . admires you, Bob.'

Jim said to me, 'Is that the way you look at it?'

'No,' I said. 'It's not. It was all bloody waste. But I'd do it again now if it was them or me.'

He sighed then. 'Aye,' he said. 'All right. But Bob's violence is something we can take up later.'

'You mean you'll excuse a man who's responsible for the death of eleven party members?'

'No. I won't,' Jim snapped. 'He should never have been there in the first place. But that can keep. It's *my* violence you were on about.'

'It's caused quite a stir from time to time,' said Tom.

'I got the D.S.O. for it,' said Jim.

'You also got the sack for it.'

'Twice,' said Jim. 'I assaulted a copper on a peace march and had to resign my fellowship. Would you say there was irony in that?'

'I would,' I said.

'The other one was better,' he said. 'It was when I was an associate professor in London. I'd gone to help break up a meeting of so-called Socialists who were voting in favour of Yankee policy in the Far East. One of the ushers was a parson. He asked me to leave quietly and I dotted him one—irrespective of race, colour or creed, you see, Goofy, that's what I stand for. It turned out he'd been a heavyweight boxer in the Navy. Put me down with the sweetest left hook I ever felt. I didn't blame him for that, but he came round to apologize to me next day while I was writing my letter of resignation. Now that really is irony.'

'Do you ever regret it?' Laidlaw asked.

'I regret having to use it,' said Jim, 'but that's just regretting the world's imperfections.'

'So you intend to go on being violent?'

This prosecuting counsel stuff was going too far for me, but Jim wouldn't see it.

'Let him go on, Bob,' he said. 'Goofy reckons he's purging me. I reckon he's swallowing a few senna pods himself, an' all.' He turned back to Laidlaw. 'Yes, I'd go on being violent,' he said. 'If I had to, and there was a good cause left.'

'Was my cause good?' Laidlaw asked.

'How d'you mean?'

Laidlaw sat back in his chair. He looked completely relaxed, and his voice was calm.

'You beat me, bullied me, kicked me at least twice a week for seven years,' he said. 'Was that in a good cause too?'

'Why, the best,' said Jim. 'I was trying to save you, lad. Trouble is I didn't kick you enough. I failed.'

'Save me?' Laidlaw asked. 'From myself perhaps?'

'For yourself,' said Jim. 'Your real self. Not the one Old Bickersley and your parents made for you.'

'And what was my real self? An infants' school Marxist-Leninist?'

'No,' Jim said. 'You weren't ready for that. Your real self was something like your granda—but it got away.'

'And you achieved this analysis at the age of nine, and applied your shoeless children's fund boot therapy more in sorrow than in anger?'

'I couldn't verbalize it then,' said Jim. 'But I felt it. I knew it was there.'

'At nine years of age?'

'At nine years of age.'

'And it gave you no pleasure?' Laidlaw asked.

'I didn't say that. Fighting often gave me pleasure. Too often.'

'What you did to me could hardly be called a fight.'

'But it should have been,' said Jim. 'Christ almighty, man, why on earth couldn't you just hit back instead of storing it all up?'

'I think that's one of the things we're about to find out,' said Laidlaw.

SIX-FIGURE MAN

IT was perfectly possible for physical cowardice to be an acquired characteristic; in fact it was perfectly possible for physical cowardice to be a sort of conditioned reflex triggered off by one other human being. Every time he had met Moulton, Moulton had reduced him to cowardice, and it was vital to know if the condition still persisted. The hell of it was that he was still not sure: the only thing he knew with certainty was that he wasn't a coward, physical or mental, when Moulton wasn't there. It had taken nerve of a sort to fool Old Bickersley with his high-church aspirations, and a great deal of nerve to take those flyers in supermarkets and cheap nightclubs. There'd been physical danger too. He'd missed the forces because of his eyesight, but he'd served in an A.R.P. unit as a volunteer when he was an undergraduate at the London School of Economics, from 1940 until 1943. There had been plenty of opportunities for cowardice then, and of course he'd had his share of it, but he'd always had it under control. The fizzing incendiary bomb waiting to explode as you crept up on it with a sackful of sand; the warehouse wall, bulging with heat as you scrabbled for survivors at the periphery of the fire; the smell of leaking gas when you dug down for an old girl in a basement who you knew *had* to be dead, and yet you went on digging: he'd faced them all, and conquered them. He'd never conquered Moulton.

There had been other times too. In 1943 he'd got his degree in economics, and gone at once to the Ministry of Economic Warfare. He'd been exactly what they were looking for: audacious, knowledgeable, imaginative and ruthless. A damn sight too ruthless for the pillars of the Treasury who ran the show, but that hadn't mattered at the time. He'd never dreamed of a Civil Service career. But to be known as a sort of scholarly pirate did him no harm at all among the businessmen temporaries, and after the war they would be once more the ones who counted. Even so, it had taken a lot of cold nerve to put across some of the deals he'd made then—when he'd been twenty-two years old, and Moulton thousands of miles away. In 1944 and 1945 there'd been buzz bombs too, V.1s tuff-tuffing across the sky while you waited in agony for the silence that meant they were falling, maybe close by, maybe too close: the roar, the fountain of laths, broken furniture, brick, and, underneath, the bodies. And then after that, the V.2s. The rockets. The deadly little prototypes of moonshots. No warning at all with them. Explosion and death erupting out of silence. He'd faced them both, and learned to live with them. Of course by then he'd been too important to go back into the A.R.P., but the old skill was still there, and once he'd helped to dig out a cinema that a V.2 had hit. He'd been wearing a new suit he'd bought that morning, paid for with cash and carefully hoarded clothing-coupons. It had been ripped to bits in minutes, and he'd had to wait weeks for authorization to buy another. A Saturday morning, he remembered. Springtime, blue sky, high, pure clouds. The dead were all children. Laurel and Hardy, Flash Gordon, Joel McCrea—and death. A bad one. The shaft they had dug down slipping all the time, always just not coming down on top of them, burying them alive. But he'd stuck at it. He'd helped get them out, some of them still breathing. But not very many. He'd hated the Germans then. Just as they'd hated the British, and for the same reasons. It had only taken two visits to Germany to get rid of all that nonsense. But surely it had taken guts to say so out loud, in the early 1950s?

Then there was Charlie Dodds. It had taken guts to get involved with Charlie, too. Even now he could remember the amazement of those Treasury blokes when he said he was going to work with Charlie Dodds. No, amazement was too gentle a word. Horror. They couldn't, wouldn't believe it. It was as if he'd said he was setting up as a pimp. And all because Charlie was a junk man—but a junk man of genius. Rag-and-bone man to the nation. All he knew was scrap, but that he knew as comprehensively as Mozart knew music, and there'd been a fortune in scrap just after the war. They'd had lunch in a famous restaurant, but in a room at the back, a room for a dozen people, no more, and the maître d'hotel had served them with his own hands. Scotch salmon, fillet steaks, strawberries and cream, coffee. Real coffee. Scotch before the meal, Clos de Vougeot with it, brandy with the coffee. And afterwards, Charlie had produced Havana cigars. It was the first time he'd ever tasted Scotch salmon, fillet steak, Clos de Vougeot, V.S.O.P. Cognac, Carl Uppmanns. He'd enjoyed them all, and he'd had the sense to say so. Charlie Dodds wasn't an easy man to fool....

'How many laws d'you reckon we've broken?' Dodds asked.

'Enough,' he said.

'We better scarper.'

Dodds reached for his hip pocket, took out a wad of money, and detached two large pieces of white paper: beautiful paper that crinkled to the touch, the engraved letters bold yet exquisite. Old-fashioned fivers. Dodds held them out to him.

'Want some?' he asked, then his fat, strong hand moved, crumpling the notes, and he dropped them on the table.

'Time to go,' he said.

Outside a Rolls-Royce was waiting. Three weeks before, Charlie said, it had belonged to a dowager marchioness, but she couldn't afford it. Laidlaw knew at once that, rationing or no rationing, Charlie had unlimited petrol, and that the police couldn't touch him for it. They'd driven back to Charlie's place then, a twelve-room penthouse in a Mayfair block of such startling ugliness that it might have been built as a setting for Charlie; who was noisy, obese, pock-marked and all too obviously cunning. The whole place was fur-nished with what he could only describe as expensive junk: overstuffed monsters of mahogany or tubular steel and silk that should never have been made in the first place. The kitchen was like a warehouse: crates of wine, whisky, gin, liqueurs, and the first deep-freeze Laidlaw had ever seen, a U.S. Army surplus monster crammed with steaks, sirloins, chops.

The flat was also crammed with a continuously shifting popu-lation: young women of varying degrees of attraction and men with something to buy or sell. Throughout his association with Charlie, they were the only kinds of people he ever saw. To talk in private, they had to go to Charlie's bedroom, the only room in the flat that was sacrosanct. It was enormous, with mirrors all over the place, and a bed that was inevitably canopied. There was a mirror in the canopy too. Charlie kicked off his shoes and bounced happily on the bed's springs.

'Bit of a change is this,' he said.

'Indeed?' said Laidlaw.

'Indeed is right,' said Charlie. 'I were in t'Army up till fourteen months ago. Pioneers. Up to me bloody ears in mud most of time. Then I had a bit of luck. I got hit by a jeep. Honourable discharge. Disability pension. Look.'

He pulled up his right trouser leg. The shin had been compre-hensively broken. Small wonder Charlie limped.

'They thought I would lose it,' Charlie said. 'But I made up my mind I wouldn't. I got out of hospital six months ago—just in time. Three more months and I'd have missed it.'

'Missed what?'

'Scrap,' said Charlie. 'Bloody mountains of it. I read somewhere some old general said war is hell. Happen he's right. But it's also waste, lad. Scrap. Stuff nobody wants when it's over because they think it's too much trouble. Only I know better. D'you want to be a junk man, lad?'

'What do I do?'

'Work it out for me,' said Charlie. 'Books and that. Buyers and sellers. Marketing. Talk to customers. Get abroad. There's a bloody fortune rusting away in the Ardennes alone. Oh aye—and keep your mouth shut.'

97

'You're sure I can?'

'I'll fix it so you have to,' said Charlie.

'How much?'

'Fifty a week off the top—for a start. And there'll be opportunities if you've got the guts to take them. Now then. Here's the way I see it.'

He began to talk then, and Laidlaw took out a notebook, made notes and listened. Time went on, Dodds rang a bell, and a girl brought in meat-paste sandwiches and Champagne. The meat paste was delicious. Later he discovered it was called pâté de foie gras. When it was his turn to talk he summarized what Charlie had told him, then advised him on which schemes were feasible, which were not. Charlie hung on to one like a terrier until Laidlaw told him it constituted conspiracy to defraud and could get him six months, then he dropped it at once. When they reached agreement at last, Laidlaw tore his notes from the book, set fire to them in an ash-tray, then flushed the charred scraps down the toilet. Charlie chuckled.

'I like a careful lad,' he said. 'You're from up north, aren't you?'

'Tyneside,' Laidlaw said.

'Good stuff up north,' said Charlie. 'I'm Yorkshire meself.'

'When do I start?' Laidlaw asked.

'You started at lunch,' said Charlie. 'Here.'

He rolled over on the bed, dug the wad of money from his hip, counted out ten white pieces of paper.

'Week in advance,' he said. Laidlaw put them carefully into his wallet, and Charlie chuckled again. 'You'll soon get used to it,' he said.

'What about income-tax?'

'I got accountants,' said Charlie unhappily. It was as if he'd said, 'I got halitosis.'

'Just as well,' said Laidlaw. 'You'd have been nicked weeks ago.'

'And now I got you. They worry about the tax. I pay you direct—and you figure how I can hang on to some of my money. All right?' He looked hard at Laidlaw. 'Do I frighten you, son?'

'You don't,' said Laidlaw. 'One of these days I might frighten you.'

'Bloody Geordie,' said Charlie. 'Let's go into drawing-room and have a bit of fun.'

The drawing-room contained the same shifting mass of men, all exhibiting a kind of wary greed, and young or youngish women. Some of the men and women danced, and there were two poker schools, one stud, the other strip. All of them were drinking, and all of them were glad to see Charlie—and Laidlaw too. He'd spent so much time alone with Charlie he had to be important.

It was apparent at once that among the fringe benefits of working for Charlie was Charlie's private brothel—if you were important enough. There was a plump young man called Lardy Rigg, for example. That night Lardy could just wade in and help himself, because Lardy had just bought a consignment of unused 500 c.c. Norton motor-bikes at three quid a piece. Lardy was a hero. Booker was not. Booker, over-tense and middle-aged, had failed to get a consignment of unused Army blankets. He could play poker, he could drink, he could dance, but when he tried to slip off with a girl Charlie said, 'No, Booker.' And Booker stayed. It wasn't just the deprivation of sexual need, Laidlaw learned. Receiving a girl from Charlie was like receiving a medal from Montgomery. ('Even Pretty Flynn wants one,' Charlie said later. 'Though Christ knows what he'd do with her. Pretty's so queer he goes to the Ladies'.')

Charlie, it appeared, was not. He drank and played poker till midnight, won forty quid, and reeled off to the door with a couple of girls. At the door he turned, and shouted, 'Help yourself, Tom. Anything you want. I kept the guest room for you.' Then he staggered off to bed, the girls buckling under his weight. Laidlaw found that he had never been so important in his life, learned too how pleasant power can be. Next day he took a taxi to the Ministry, asked to see the deputy chief and resigned in thirty minutes. The war was over, there was urgent need that skilled men should take up civilian occupations, and the deputy chief was delighted to see him go. Yet even so, when Laidlaw said Charlie Dodds, he hesitated.

'But the man's a sort of bandit,' he said.

'And I've made a reputation as a pirate with brains,' said Laidlaw. 'We'll get along.'

'Do you honestly consider that what he's doing is legal?' the deputy chief asked.

'It has to be,' said Laidlaw.

'Ethical then?'

'I haven't done anything ethical since I left L.S.E.,' said Laidlaw.

'You may leave at once,' said the deputy chief.

It was the same with all the Administrative Officers and Executive Officers. They wanted to be out, they wanted to make money. What they did not want was Charlie Dodds. Even his typist was stunned. It seemed to Laidlaw illogical. Dodds was noisy, vulgar and as dishonest as he could safely be, but then so were many other tycoons. What horrified the A.O.s and E.O.s, whether they had met him or not, was that he was making money out of the machinery of war, that in some of that machinery, men had suffered, sometimes died, and that all of it had been produced at an enormous, even crippling cost of money and labour. They acted as if Charlie had cut up El Alamein into little pieces and sold it in Woolworth's at sixpence a time. It seemed to Laidlaw very great nonsense. The stuff was there, and the Government wanted to get rid of it. If the prices they were beaten down to were derisory, why blame Charlie? He was to see the same utter lack of logicality when he first sold scrap steel to Japan, first bought typewriters from Germany. Most people, he discovered, actually prefer to live in the past: they have no aptitude for the present.

The present, then, was Charlie. Laidlaw spent almost the whole of his time, waking and sleeping, in the ugly Mayfair block, drinking, dealing, taking a girl so that he could relax enough to sleep, as if she were a sleeping-pill. Once he caught a dose and Charlie hired a room in the most expensive clinic in Mayfair, but the work kept coming in all through the treatment. Not that he minded. The work was the whole bloody point of it all. Inside information, rigged auctions, rings, and bribery of almost insane proportions that took all his skill to remain on the right side of lunacy. The booze was good, and the food, and the women were marvellous—an aspect of his education he'd neglected for far too long—but the work was the only thing that really mattered. Sometimes he went on trips: Normandy, Belgium, the United States; once to Australia in a converted Lancaster bomber, then on to Midway Island to bribe Americans: for always it was work, fourteen, fifteen hours a day, while Charlie prospered, and he prospered too. The fifty a week jumped to a hundred, a hundred and fifty, two hundred and the opportunities were there too: especially in small-arms. It was heartrending to see how soon people started to kill each other again once the big one was over—but there was money in it, especially in Algeria, though Indonesia had turned out very nicely too.

He and Charlie got along just fine: age and youth, intelligence and instinct, adjusting to each other to form a formidable weapon. Charlie made a far better father-figure than his own father, stuck in the North-East denouncing the sweet-ration. Charlie and he were like a self-taught speculative builder and his architect son. It was the kind of relationship he'd longed for, and never achieved, with Granda Laidlaw. They got on, and they made money. By the end Charlie had topped the million mark, and Laidlaw had run his share into six figures. And so what? Where was the bloody harm? They'd made money when half the world thought it was a nastier crime than incest, but they'd made money for the country too. Millions of it. Dollars. Where Charlie went it snowed dollars—Detroit eats scrap steel. But there were no K.C.V.O.s for Charlie, no O.B.E.s for him. Not that he cared. When it finished he was downright miserable, even though he knew it was time to move on.

Long before the end, Charlie had begun to slip. It had all got too easy for him: it was a middleman's paradise. The sellers all wanted to sell, and the buyers all wanted to buy. His only problem was the sheer volume of stuff coming in, and for that he had Laidlaw. There was no need of flair: Laidlaw's efficiency, his capacity for work took care of everything. Charlie took his flair and went racing with it, ending up with a filly that won the Oaks; he bought a half share in a middleweight who won the European championship and went the distance with Sugar Ray Robinson; he backed three shows and one of them ran for two years. Charlie couldn't help making money, and Laidlaw was pleased to see his flair still working. The trouble was that Charlie got bored. Horses don't race in the winter, boxers relax between fights, once a show starts to run and the coach parties come in, all you can do is count the money. Scrap was different: scrap meant action. With scrap you were always too busy to be bored. Charlie began to interfere.

By that time Laidlaw had moved out of the Mayfair block, and bought a mews house in Belgravia. The two ground-floor rooms were his office, and above he had a bedroom, sitting-room and kitchen. No maid, no secretary, no accounts except those he kept in a series of little notebooks in cipher, then burned as each one was filled. The accounts were made up twice a week in sessions with Charlie's accountant. They were honest, law-abiding accounts, open to inspection by His Majesty's Inspector of Taxes at any time: tax on profits paid immediately on demand. They represented ninety-five per cent of everything earned: of the remaining five, Charlie got three and Laidlaw two. There was simply no point in being too dishonest. . . . From time to time, he kept a girl in the house. Women relaxed him, and he liked their company, over limited periods. He always insisted on one who could cook: he had no talent for it himself, and he was sick of restaurant meals. They were European girls mostly: there was an organization in Brussels who fixed that sort of thing up for you without fuss: Italian and French girls from different regions gave a kind of gastronomic bonus to the whole thing. Besides, they were admirable teachers of language. Teaching gave them something to do when they weren't busy, and they were grateful for it.

When Charlie first came to see him he was living with a Spanish girl, Asunción. She came from Gallicia: small, busy, black-haired. Her stories of her family's unrelieved poverty bored him, but she cooked well and was expert in bed. Her accent, he knew, was far from good, but that didn't bother him. All he needed was fluency, and that she gave him. She chattered incessantly. Charlie arrived one night after dinner. They had eaten well, and drunk a bottle of red wine called Valdepeñas. Asunción adored it. As they finished it he talked to her in Spanish, and she corrected his grammar. It was a hot, sticky June night, and they had both undressed, he to his underpants, she to bra and panties. He had decided that he would take her to bed as soon as he got one sentence right, and had just achieved it, sat back triumphant. She came to him, sat on his lap, moving as he liked her to move, and his hands pulled down her bra straps. The bell rang. He swore, using one of the very few words of English which is truly international, and she giggled.

'*No lo podemos ahora,*' she said. The bell rang again, and she fetched his robe, and her own, then he went to the window and looked out. The vast Rolls straddled the street, and he went down to let Charlie in. Charlie had dined well, and it took the combined efforts of the chauffeur and Laidlaw to get him up the stairs. The chauffeur left him at the living-room door, and Laidlaw heaved him inside, settled him in a chair. Charlie looked round the room, tasting it, absorbing it, then looked at Asunción.

'Get me some brandy, lass,' he said. She went off at once. 'You fancy them small, don't you, Tom?' he said.

'Sometimes,' said Laidlaw.

'Remember that one from Richmond? She weren't much more than a midget.'

'Oh, yes, she was,' said Laidlaw, and Charlie wheezed his laughter. Asunción came back with a decanter and glasses.

'Fill 'em up,' said Charlie. 'And have one yourself.'

She looked at Laidlaw, and he nodded, smiling. It was nice to see Charlie again. He'd been neglecting him lately, and that was a mistake. It was always a mistake to neglect the kind of relationship he had with Charlie. Asunción poured out three brandies and took one to Charlie. As she bent over him he put his hands round her hips, pulled her to him.

'Give us a kiss, lass,' he said.

Laidlaw said, 'No, Charlie,' and the girl pulled away. She was flustered, and a little angry. The contract hadn't said anything about Laidlaw's friends. If it had, she wouldn't have taken it. That kind of promiscuity was vulgar.

'Doesn't have much to say for herself, does she?' Charlie said.

'She's Spanish,' said Laidlaw. 'She can't say much.'

'Too good for old Charlie?'

'Don't talk daft,' said Laidlaw. 'She's one of Cleef's. If you want one go over and see him.'

'Too much fuss,' Charlie said. 'Too la-di-da. I'm happy the way I am.'

Asunción pulled her robe closer about her.

'She practising to be a nun or something?' Charlie asked.

'She's got her pride, Charlie,' Laidlaw said. 'Let her keep it.'

'Aye,' said Charlie. 'Happen you're right. Here, love.'

He wriggled in his seat, came up with the wad of notes, and detached a handful. Asunción watched him, wary.

'Come on,' Charlie said. 'I won't bite you. I just want to show you I'm sorry I hurt your feelings.'

Warily she moved to him. The money hypnotized her. When she stood by the chair Charlie crumpled the notes in his hand with a gesture Laidlaw still remembered, then very slowly he reached up, pushed the notes down into the cleft between her breasts. It took him a long time, and she stood quite still.

'All right, lass, hop it,' he said at last. She went at once to Laidlaw, and sat, curled up, at his feet.

'Pride,' Charlie said. 'You and me—we're experts on pride. We're in the junk business.'

'I'm sorry we hurt your feelings,' said Laidlaw.

'Tom, Tom. Don't talk like that,' Charlie said. 'I've been drinking. You know what I'm like when I've been drinking.'

'You want to watch it,' Laidlaw said. It was no good. Once you started to like the old bastard, you couldn't help worrying about him.

'Can't help it, lad,' said Charlie. 'I'm lonely.'

'No birds?'

'Birds,' said Charlie. 'Birds and booze and musicals and horses and fighters. What's the good of that? I tell you I'm lonely. For the business.'

Laidlaw looked down at Asunción, and Charlie said, 'Let her stay. For now, anyway. You look nice together.'

Laidlaw put out one hand, and rubbed the back of the girl's neck. At once she relaxed, and snuggled closer against him. The money crackled between her breasts. Charlie grinned.

'You're getting posh, Tom,' he said, 'and I won't say it doesn't suit you. But you won't forget where you came from, will you?'

'Charlie, what's wrong?' Laidlaw asked.

'What I said. I miss the business. You know . . . when I hired you, I never thought it would end up like this.'

'Like what, for Christ's sake?'

'When I hired you I thought you would be helping me. The way it's turned out, I'm not even allowed to help you.'

'Charlie, believe me, I'm not trying to take the business off you.'

'Not the business. No,' said Charlie. 'I know you wouldn't do that. But you've taken the bloody work off me. And I want it back.'

'Do you, Charlie? Do you really?'

'Some of it, anyway,' Charlie said. 'I'm fed up.'

'All right,' said Laidlaw. 'What d'you want? The W.D. surplus auction ring? The Italian contract? The store sales? The garages?'

'No,' said Charlie. 'You're doing all right with them.'

'There isn't much left,' said Laidlaw. 'Surplus shops, electronic equipment, paper——'

'You can have 'em,' Charlie said. 'I got a new idea.'

Laidlaw's hand stopped moving, and she looked up at him.

'*Anda a la cama,*' he said.

She got up at once.

'Good night, Tom,' she said, and turned to Charlie. 'Good night, sir,' she said, and left.

'You said that beautiful,' said Charlie. 'Whatever it was. But what did you want to send her away for?'

'You know what for, you old bastard.'

'Happen I do,' said Charlie, 'but dammit, Tom, we can't be honest all the time.'

'No, Charlie,' said Laidlaw.

'Look,' Charlie said. 'I know this chap. Dutchman. Name of de Groot. He wants a line of electronic stuff. They're crying out for it.'

'Who are?'

'The Chinese.'

'Charlie, that's classified war material. There's an embargo. You *know* that.'

'It's all right,' Charlie said. 'It doesn't go to China.'

'Where then?'

'Burma,' Charlie said. 'The Chinks pick it up from there.'

'You're kidding,' said Laidlaw. 'You have to be. The British Government'll eat you alive. Especially this Government.'

'If they find out.'

'They'll find out.'

'How? Will you tell them?'

Laidlaw sighed. 'No, Charlie. I won't tell them. Look ... You brought me out of the Ministry of Economic Warfare. That doesn't mean I've forgotten what they taught me. All right, World War Two's over, and the Ministry's closed down, but the techniques haven't. They just practise them in other buildings, that's all. There are spies in Rangoon, Charlie. Economic spies. Cargo checkers and shipping clerks and Customs officers. And they'll shop you. You'll be lucky if you get ten years.'

'They'll pay me in anything I want. Even gold,' said Charlie.

'Forget it.'

'No,' Charlie said. 'I won't forget it. I can't. *I have to have something to do.*' He looked at the door leading to the bedroom, and lowered his voice. 'Our end's a quarter of a million.'

Laidlaw said, 'I'm sorry, Charlie.'

'Suppose I said I'd do it anyway?'

'Then you'd go ahead and do it—and I'd resign.'

Charlie sighed, and sucked down what was left of his brandy. Laidlaw rose at once, and poured him another.

'You mean it, don't you?' Laidlaw nodded. 'I taught you good, all right.'

Laidlaw said, 'It isn't personal, Charlie.'

'No,' Charlie said. 'I realize that. We can still get on.' He rolled over, fought his way to his hip pocket, and came out with a handful of pieces of paper. Carefully he detached one and handed it to Laidlaw.

'Here,' he said. 'Give your lass a night out.'

It was a complimentary ticket to his show, for two.

After that they talked for a long time, and the talk was a desperate attempt to sustain a relationship each knew was over. Laidlaw had shown by his refusal that he believed Charlie's flair had left him. The mutual respect they had felt had suddenly become one way. But they talked on, because the respect had been real, and important to both of them. They talked of the early days, of Lardy and Booker and Pretty Flynn and Charlie's girls. Charlie told him about the National Sporting Club and dress calls and the Royal Enclosure at Ascot, and he told Charlie how much they had made that week. He drank a little brandy, Charlie a lot, and in the end, Charlie had regained enough dignity to go back to the Rolls. He walked down the stairs without help, but Laidlaw went with him anyway. On the doorstep Charlie turned.

'You shouldn't have bothered seeing me out,' he said.

'No trouble,' said Laidlaw.

'Aye,' Charlie said. 'You really do like me. I'm glad. There were times I thought I didn't need anybody. That's daft. Only you've got to keep on going, Tom. You've got to keep on going.'

The chauffeur guided him into the Rolls then, and it moved softly away, merging into the warm darkness. He locked up, and went back upstairs. Asunción was waiting for him. He noticed without surprise that she had been crying. Of the money Charlie had given her there was no sign.

The second time Charlie came to see him he was alone.

'I'm sorry to see that,' he said. 'It's nice to see a bit of young stuff about the place.'

'I sent her back,' Laidlaw said. 'We were getting too fond of each other.'

'You're a hard one all right,' Charlie said. 'Not that you don't make sense.'

Laidlaw waited. There was bound to be more.

'I haven't had a drink for two days,' Charlie said. 'Surprises you, eh?'

'Can I get you something?'

'Like hell you can. I'm working, Tom. Got to keep my head clear.'

'Got a new scheme on?'

'No,' Charlie said. 'It's the same one. I've got it all worked out.'

'Charlie—I meant what I said.'

'Course you did, lad. Course you did. I've come here to make a deal.' He hurried on as Laidlaw tried to interrupt. 'Wait. Always hear a deal out before you turn it down. Surely I taught you that much? The deal's this. You get nowt and the company gets nowt. You're not involved. But you go on just like before. All right?'

'You don't use company money, and you don't draw company cheques, and whatever electronic stuff of ours you take is paid for.'

'That's the idea,' said Charlie.

'But *you* don't pay for it.'

'I'm not that daft,' said Charlie. 'De Groot'll handle that end.'

'All right,' said Laidlaw.

'That's all right then,' said Charlie. 'All you have to do is keep your mouth shut.'

'I've been doing that for years,' Laidlaw said.

'These spies of yours,' Charlie said. 'Any chance of finding out who they are?'

'Not that I know of,' said Laidlaw.

He said it at once, without hesitating. There was a way. He still had contacts, and they could have given him some kind of a lead at least. If they were handled right they wouldn't even know they'd done it, and he'd make sure they were handled right. But this scheme was madness. It would destroy him.

'I wouldn't know where to start asking,' he said.

'I thought you would say that,' said Charlie. 'I reckon we'll have to leave it up to the Chinks. De Groot reckons they can handle it.'

'Charlie, for God's sake,' he said. 'Why don't you wait a bit—try something else?'

'No,' said Charlie. 'This'll do me. You're going to be sorry you didn't trust me, lad. A quarter of a million quid's worth.'

He'd gone up north then, the next morning. He'd seen the way things were moving in the States, and knew it wouldn't be long before Great Britain followed. The thing was to get in quick, before the big boys started, and that meant sites. He bought options on seven in four frantic days, and came back to London on the night sleeper, his brain grappling with the problems of suppliers, outlets, training personnel, deep-freeze equipment. He would have to go back to the U.S.A., of course, but before that he'd have to get away from Charlie, and winding up would take a month at least. Then there was the question of a successor. He phoned the Mayfair flat. Charlie was away, and nobody knew where he was, nobody knew when he'd be back. It didn't seem as if anybody cared very much, either. Harries, the Midlands manager, was the best of the bunch, he thought. By far the best: and he'd had a grounding in economics too. He phoned him, and told him to come to London as soon as he could, leave his assistant in charge. He hinted a lot, and Harries at once became frantic with eagerness. It would take him three days, he said. Laidlaw didn't mind. It would take him three days to work out how much Harries needed to know. When he put the phone down, he realized that his hands were trembling. It occurred to him that he hadn't slept more than six hours in the last four days. He picked up the phone again, and asked for a line to Brussels: what was to be his last call to Cleef's organization.

There was something very pleasant in waiting for a girl to arrive. You were never quite sure what she would be like, but you knew she would be good: it was de Groot's business to see that she was. So you waited, and stood exactly where she had been told to find you, the red carnation in your buttonhole, holding your bunch of roses and your bottle of Chanel, and watched the passengers pouring out, at peace with the world. The economics of the arrangement all taken care of, all you had to do was be nice to her, and release to the flow of femaleness that never failed to engulf him so soothingly, so drowsily. He watched the crowd more intently. A hell of a lot of them were carrying paperbacks. If he could find the right outlet, there might be money in that. And television. It wasn't so long since they'd crowned Elizabeth Queen, and television had scooped the pool over that one. Hundreds of thousands of sets bought to see that young woman crowned. Millions of watchers—viewers, they called them—and already the movie people were yelling. He'd heard rumours that some day there'd be commercial television too. He'd have to watch out for that. It would affect his advertising.

There was a woman standing in front of him. She too had a red carnation pinned to her lapel. A yellow-haired woman, with a wide, slightly feline face. If he were right, she was Hungarian.

'Dagmar?' he asked.

'Tom, darling,' she said, and embraced him, kissed him lightly on the cheek. 'Have I kept you waiting? Oh dear, how sorry I am.'

She walked out with him, exclaiming over her presents, looked at the Daimler he had hired, and cried out in delight.

'I am sure,' she said, 'that I shall have a lovely time in England, and I rather think you will too, darling.'

That night he slept for nine hours.

After that it was easy. Harries arrived and learned fast, but not too fast. The undeclared five per cent remained Laidlaw's secret, and Charlie's. Soon it would be Charlie's alone. But otherwise Harries knew what he was doing. It became possible for him to take Dagmar out to lunch, or better still, to lie in bed with her in the morning and know that what was happening downstairs was less and less his business. He had become fond of Dagmar. She was the only one who couldn't cook, but against that she made love with a more than professional competence, and her conversation was enchanting: witty and clever, yet anchored always with the refugee's uncompromising realism. Life suddenly became very pleasant.

And then Charlie came back, and he played the scene with Asunción all over again, but this time the interpretation was very different. It was Sunday, and they had drunk beer in a pub, eaten a brunch that he had cooked, then gone to bed. By the time Charlie arrived, Dagmar was giggling helplessly over the middle pages of the *News of the World*.

'Tell me,' she said, 'this "insulting behaviour". How can it be insulting? Surely it is a very great compliment. And in any case, why do they say *insulting*? Why do they not say what it is? Maybe it is because the English are all romantics, eh, darling? The most exciting things exist only in the imagination.'

'Is that the way I am?'

'No . . . you are the exception, I think. A realist. That is why I like you.'

She put the paper down then, and embraced him. The bell rang.

'It would be better if you do not answer it,' she said.

'Much better,' said Laidlaw, and got out of bed.

Once again he and the chauffeur hauled and heaved Charlie Dodds up the stairs, embedded him in the vast, overstuffed chair, then the chauffeur went back to the Rolls and the B.B.C. Light Programme. Charlie looked at the dressing-gown.

'Having a kip?' he said.

'That's right,' said Laidlaw.

'Not on your own,' said Charlie. 'Fetch her out, lad. Let her get me a drink.'

'You sure you want one?' Laidlaw asked.

'Positive,' said Charlie. 'I'm not working now.'

'She's sleeping,' said Laidlaw.

'Wake her up,' Charlie said. 'I'm not leaving till I've seen her.'

'You've seen dozens,' said Laidlaw.

'Not like yours lad. Fetch her out.'

Laidlaw sighed, and fetched out Dagmar in a blue silk kimono that was the least revealing garment she owned. She smiled and said hallo and went at once to fetch the brandy.

'Cleef looks after you,' said Charlie.

'This one's a friend,' said Laidlaw. 'She never heard of de Groot.'

'You mean you're not paying her?' Charlie asked.

'Of course I'm not paying her.'

'Well I'll go to France,' Charlie said.

She brought in the brandy then, and he insisted that she too take a glass.

'It's a toast,' he said. 'To me. To my successful bit of business.' They drank. 'And it was successful, Tom lad. The Chinks took care of everything. I made a packet. And you don't get a penny of it. Not a tosser.'

'No hard feelings, Charlie,' said Laidlaw.

'Not on my side,' said Charlie. 'I'm coining money. I'm only sorry you don't get a bit. How about me cutting you in on the next one?'

Dagmar said, 'Excuse me, Mr Dodds. I just remembered I have to do the washing-up,' and left.

'Sensible lass,' said Charlie. 'How about it Tom?'

'The Chinese again?'

'Why not? Their money's good—and we know who to bribe now. It can't miss.'

'I think it can,' said Laidlaw. 'I'm getting out.'

'Leaving?' said Charlie. 'Don't talk daft, man. Just because I guessed right and you didn't.'

'No,' said Laidlaw. 'It isn't that—and you know it isn't. I'm glad you brought it off.'

'What then?'

'Scrap's over, Charlie. Finished. And so are deals like yours. We don't have to take chances any more. The money's there to make without that.'

'Scrap's all I know,' said Charlie. 'Scrap and deals. And what do you mean, it's over? We made a quarter of a million quid.'

'They'll nick you next time.'

'Tom lad,' Charlie said. 'Don't talk like that. I need you here.'

'It's no good, Charlie,' Laidlaw said.

They talked for three hours, and after that Laidlaw knew that it would be days before Charlie would accept it. But no matter how often they talked he knew he was right. He was getting out. In the end he heaved Charlie down the stairs and went back up. He noticed without surprise that he was trembling.

She lay on the bed and he took off his robe and lay beside her.

'I heard you tell him that I did not come from de Groot. That is the only real compliment I have had in a very long time,' she said.

'I meant it,' he said.

'That is how I know it was real.' She hesitated. 'Did that randy old Silenus——'

'That who?' he asked.

'Silenus was a fat old sot. The companion of Bacchus.'

'I know that.'

'And you are surprised that I do?'

'Not surprised. Delighted. It fits him beautifully.'

'Thank you. Did he mean it when he said that you had lost a lot of money?'

'In the first place I like old Charlie,' said Laidlaw.

'And that is important?'

'Yes. In the second place I didn't like his deal. So I didn't go into it. So I don't get a share. That isn't losing money.'

'You are still rich then?'

'What's rich?'

'You can still afford me?' She turned to face him, and he nodded. 'I'm glad,' she said.

It was then that he decided to keep her with him till he got back from America, at least.

'I'm not really a coward,' said Laidlaw. 'I'm afraid you'll have to take my word for it.'

'How could you be?' said Jim. 'You don't make your kind of money unless you've got nerve.' He spoke objectively, without irony. 'And yet you've always been afraid of me.'

Laidlaw reached for the decanter, filled his glass, shoved it along.

'Always,' he said.

'I was bigger than you,' said Jim, 'and I learned how to hit by the time I was nine. But even so—you could have hit me back. You should have done.'

'I think perhaps you're right,' said Laidlaw. 'The alternative isn't very nice, is it?'

'What alternative?' I asked.

'Waiting,' Laidlaw said.

'Waiting for what, man?' asked Jim, his voice impatient now. He had no sympathy for those who waited: immediate action solved everything, so why hang about?

'It's a woman's trick really,' Laidlaw said. 'Madge Innes does it beautifully.'

'You're talking daft,' said Jim.

'No, no.' Suddenly Laidlaw became didactic, schoolmasterly. It was important that Jim understood completely what he was about to say. Then he looked at me, and I realized it was important that I understand it too.

'Waiting isn't just sitting about, you know. At least not the way I'm using the word.'

' "When I use a word," said Humpty Dumpty, "it means exactly what I want it to mean," ' I said.

'Well, it does, you know,' said Laidlaw, 'otherwise you really are in Wonderland.'

And I saw Jim nod agreement to that one: saw for the first time how alike they were in their need to impose their own order, their own discipline on a fuzzy and muddle-headed world.

'Waiting isn't a passive thing. Not really,' said Laidlaw. 'It's all tied up with remembering too. Total recall—all that. Remembering colours and shapes and smells of things—not just incidents. Tones of voice, the feel of an object, even the way a room was lit. That's waiting.'

'It's insanity,' said Jim.

'It's very rewarding,' Laidlaw said.

'What you're saying is that you can remember details about me,' said Jim.

'Principally about you. Of course Bob came into it too, but then he always did—didn't he? Bob was your Merry Man, so to speak. A very coveted position, as I remember.'

'Bob was a good friend. He still is,' said Jim.

'Loyal, certainly,' said Laidlaw. 'But hardly good. Unless loyalty in itself may be taken to constitute goodness.'

Martinis and Burgundy were getting to him now, accentuating the trick of pedantry he sometimes affected in his speech, but his hand on his glass was quite steady.

'But I expect you would,' he said. 'Authoritarians usually do.' He went on quickly, before Jim could speak. 'Let me give you an example,' he said.

'All right,' said Jim, and poured more wine. Unconsciously he was going drink for drink with Laidlaw.

'The spring of 1942,' Laidlaw said. 'March it must have been. Before Easter anyway. I'd come up from L.S.E. for the vacation. You were on leave—embarkation leave, was it?'

'It was,' said Jim.

'And Bob was still at university—travelling in every day. They had longer terms than we did. The night I'm thinking of, Bob wasn't home. It was his turn for fire-watching. All students had to do it, you know. They got a subsistence allowance. Mostly they spent it on beer. I expect Bob did too.'

'I don't want you to go on with this,' I said, and turned to Jim. But this time loyalty wasn't enough.

'Sooner or later he's going to say it anyway,' he said. 'Best to get it over with.'

It's easy enough for you, I thought. It wasn't your heartbreak. But there I wronged him. His own or anybody else's, Jim would have faced it head on, as he did now.

'My father was an A.R.P. warden,' Laidlaw said. 'Granda wanted to be one too, but they wouldn't have him—said he was too old. Ironic that—Granda was seventy and still running his pub, and heaving barrels about that would have crushed my father. Drunks too, come to that. Anyway Granda used to turn out when there was a raid—sort of acting unpaid assistant—and so did I in vacation time. They were glad to see me—I'd had London training. The night I'm thinking of—there was a raid. You were in Granda's pub with Matt Bohill, telling everybody we should start a second front now and help the poor Russians.'

'So we should have done,' said Jim.

'Matt was wearing grey flannel trousers and a Fair Isle sweater,' Laidlaw said. 'You were in D.L.I. uniform. You had a boil forming on your neck—just below your left ear. Otherwise you looked every inch the virile young warrior.'

'Funny,' said Jim. 'I can't remember you there.'

'I was pulling pints in the Snug,' said Laidlaw. 'I could see you through the hatch—and I could hear you perfectly. Your voice always carried—almost as much as Bohill's. I.T.M.A. never had a chance. You remember that show? It was on that night. All catch phrases and funny accents and anti-German jokes. And you remember the pub, don't you? Clean sawdust on the floor every day, and gas-lamps converted for electricity, and smelly blackout curtains and a terrible Gents.'

'And the pump handles were mahogany and brass,' Jim said. 'I remember how they glowed.'

More than ever I wanted him to stop. This delight in memory was exactly what Laidlaw wanted, for now Jim was on his side; he was betraying *me*, and I knew no way to stop him.

'They were polished every day,' Laidlaw said. 'Granda loved the place. Anyway, you and Bohill were on your fourth pint—and Granda let you have a double rum apiece——'

'I'd forgotten how hard it was to get spirits. There was never any whisky, and rum was pretty scarce——'

'Unless Granda liked you. And he did. He liked both of you. So that by the time the siren went you were both fairly drunk, but not objectionable. Granda wouldn't have stood for that. I wonder, Bob—were you drunk too? It was about nine forty I remember—twenty minutes off closing time. Where were you, Bob—sitting in the lounge bar of the Green Man, drinking your fire-watching allowance, all scholarly in your medical school scarf while you tried to sneak a look up the tarts' skirts and wished you could afford one—and had another pint instead?' He waited, but I said nothing, so he probed a little deeper.

'You do remember the night I'm referring to?'

'Very well,' I said. 'But it's none of your bloody business.'

'You're wrong, you know,' Laidlaw said. 'Of course I don't deny it was very much your business too, but I can assure you I was involved.'

I had been drunk that night, as drunk as only a nineteen-year-old can get. My father had had a win in the monthly sweep of the shipyard where he worked and he'd given me a quid. There had been a time when I'd thought of investing it in one of the Green Man's tarts Laidlaw had mentioned, but two things had prevented me. One had been the thought that my father would think poorly of such expenditure, if ever he found out, and the other, not to put too fine a point on it, was cowardice. The Green Man's daughters of joy were a pretty terrifying bunch. So I drank a lot of beer instead, in the company of other fire-watchers who drank very much less, and moped about my virginity and the apparently insoluble problem of losing it, and, in the fullness of time, got drunk. I neither sang nor fought nor vomited: I became sodden. Surly too, I suppose. My fellow-watchers helped me over to the Physics building where we slept, but they were none too gentle about it. Most of the surliness had been expended on them.

The trouble had started at home. Usually I was happy there. My father and mother were the kind of people it's very easy to be happy with. He was a shipyard fitter and she, until her marriage, had been in service, and both were warm yet gentle people. (The day when father hit Mr Futters on the head with his fist had bewildered them both.) Throughout their lives they loved each other, deeply and with passion, and the happiness this engendered had somehow rubbed off on to their children, myself and my sister Freda, now married to an insurance agent in Fulham, but in 1942 an A.T.S. corporal. Both my father and my mother had a deep, uncritical respect for academic ability, and the day I got into grammar school was the high spot of their lives, until the day I matriculated into university and became a medical student.

I'd been a pretty good kid, I suppose: healthy, bright, and happy because I was loved. There'd been a lot of fights—anybody who got involved with Jim copped more than his share of them—but they expected that, and I hadn't turned delinquent. Anyway I made up for them with my school reports—Very Good, sometimes V.G.I. (Very Good Indeed) and even—occasionally—E for Excellent. Three times a year my father would read them aloud to my mother, and we would all three sit and look at each other, delighted and yet vaguely surprised that such superlatives should be heard in a Bright Street kitchen. School days were fine—and so was university, until the time came when I wanted to get a job. We were so often hard up. Father was in work of course—shipyard fitters always are when there's a war on—but all I had was my grant, and that was just—and only just—enough. Out of it I had to buy medical books and instruments, ghastly college meals, transport every day. The grant just about stretched to that. It didn't run to the extra food I yearned for at a time when I was filling out almost visibly, and always hungry; it didn't run to books about other subjects than medicine, or gramophone records (Miller, Dorsey, Artie Shaw's Gramercy Five—let alone Beecham's Mozart and Delius at 78 r.p.m.) or Youth Hostel holidays (suppose I picked up a girl?) or the kind of clothes that set one apart as a dandy, even in wartime.

The solution was a job—and there was plenty of scope for casual labour in 1942, with its desperate shortage of manpower. Laidlaw's father I knew wanted somebody to help him in his shop, and with evenings and weekends it would run to a couple of quid a week at least. And that was money. Big money. The trouble was, my father wouldn't hear of it. I'd been sent to university to study, to be a doctor, a *real* doctor. (Made-to-measure suit bought in Newcastle, Wolseley car, a maid to answer the door.) And if I was going to be a doctor, I had no time to spare serving behind the counter in Laidlaw's shop. I had no time to spare at all; not when I should be studying. And in 1942, if your father said so that was it—even if I was nineteen years old. It was either accept or leave home—and I couldn't afford to leave home, that was the whole *point*—and in any case, I loved them both too much. But the refusal made me angry, and I quarrelled with my father, and with my mother too, when she took his side. The quid he gave me was a peace-offering, and I rejected it, but he tucked it into my pocket when he went off to work—half past six, and a sky as grey and cold as the ships he worked on—and I found it there on the bus, when I reached for my ticket, and resolved to spend it on beer. It was some consolation later that I decided against the Green Man's tarts.

'They picked a good night for it,' Laidlaw said. 'Not much moon—but enough, and plenty of cloud. It's always surprised me that they weren't more accurate.'

'A shipyard's a big enough target,' said Jim. 'But they were greedy—as usual. They wanted to scare us as well.'

He spoke the last sentence as if its content were unthinkable: as if it were impossible to scare Jim Moulton and his like. Somewhere at the back of my mind I began to hate him for it. My thoughts were all with the night of the raid.

When you're nineteen and you've drunk a gallon of beer, you're either sick or sodden, and that time I was sodden. The air-raid siren failed even to brush my dreams, and the Fire Watchers' Alert Bell that clattered where we slept was no more than a vague irritant. It was the others, disliking me still, who slapped and pummelled me awake, prodded me, still in my clothes, out of bed. I went to the lavatory then crawled after them up an apparently unending staircase to the top of the building, through a fanlight and out on to the roof. It was as good a way as any of getting rid of drunkenness, and the view was breathtaking. The university is built on a hill, and the Physics Building was its tallest tower: from where I stood I could see the dark mass of the city, and threading it the great curves of the river, like tarnished silver as the moonlight touched it, broadening at last to the east to meet the challenge of the sea.

The city itself was quiet. There were no H.E. bombs for us that night, no hissing patter of incendiaries. The activity was all to the east, and we could see it very clearly. First the searchlights that were still very tentative, anaemic looking, then the sudden, staccato flash of gunfire. In the still air the sound of the guns carried clearly too, a hoarse bellow like the voice of an overworked N.C.O. We were too far away to see or hear the planes—Heinkels would they be? or Dorniers?—but we knew they were there in quantity. The gunfire told us that. Prodigal the gunfire, and the shell-bursts opened and bloomed across the sky, on and on, but no plane was hit. The searchlights and guns probed and blasted as ineffectually as a child pounding its high chair before the meal is ready. It seemed an eternity before the planes took any action at all.

Then the incendiaries came. First one, then another, red pinpoints of light, like cigarettes furtively dragged on—then suddenly a whole scattering of them, as the first squadron responded to its leader. Seven miles away a whole town suddenly twinkled, as cheery as Christmas, then came the first upsurge of flame. My town had always had a good A.R.P. service, and they did wonders that night. As we watched, many of the little red dots died—fag-ends flicked into a puddle—but the flames here and there managed to reach upward.

The chap next to me said, 'They're copping it badly over there.' His accent was strange, southern maybe or south-western. That night an alien, unbelievable intrusion.

'That's right,' I said.

'Where is it? Do you know?'

'It's where I live,' I said.

He moved away then, as if my bad luck were contagious, and I felt suddenly, overwhelmingly sick, beer and anxiety combining to assault my stomach, and maybe premonition too. I leaned over the guard-rail, my body emptied and purged itself, and within minutes I could look again, my senses cleansed, and even more frighteningly aware, now that the beer had gone.

The little red dots had done their work, and the crews who dropped them were no doubt on their way home, back to interrogation officers and knackwurst and schnapps, and the adulation of blonde, muscular girls. The town now was pitted with fires, leprous against the dark, and in the centre one rigid pillar of blue, where a gas main had burst. Then came the high explosive, and here and there a dark patch would fragment for a moment, as if caught in a more concentrated moonlight, then dissolve into yellow and red—or back for ever into darkness. The noise became more terrible too, I remember. The sound of the bombs exploding was the sound of enormous and effective force, against which the guns' yap-yapping was a heart-breaking futility. . . .

'Of course, the ack-ack may have been better than we think,' said Jim.

'They didn't hit a bloody thing,' I said.

'It's possible they kept the bombers away from the river and saved the shipyards.'

'In which case the crews simply bombed the town,' said Laidlaw. 'Some officer—a colonel or a brigadier perhaps—would have to make a decision about that.'

'Not really a decision,' said Jim. 'Not in a total war. He wouldn't even think about it.'

'Perhaps he thinks about it now,' Laidlaw said.

'I doubt it,' said Jim. 'The odds are he doesn't even know it happened.'

The bombers went on playing hide-and-seek through the clouds: first wave—second wave—third wave—and then, suddenly, there were no more explosions, the gunfire faded in a slow diminuendo. I huddled in my clothes and watched the town. The night was bitter cold, and I suppose I must have been shivering, though I have no memory of it. Someone gave me a cigarette and I crouched behind the parapet to light it, shielded its tip with my hand—the purely reflex actions of 'total war'—then went back to watching the town. The fires were diminishing now, but very slowly. Fighting them were men like my father, and Matt Bohill, and Goofy Laidlaw's da: tenacious men with deft, practical hands, but the fires were so numerous, and so very big. It seemed as if half the town must be destroyed. And then, at last, the All Clear went, a thin unwavering harmony that was meant, I suppose, for reassurance, but which to me has always meant despair, because of what has happened before the All Clear can blow. Someone tapped me on the shoulder, and I went down the stairs at last, and the rhythm of walking made me start functioning again. I became aware of how cold I was, and pulled my coat closer around me. I also became aware of what I must do.

The Chief Fire Watcher that night was a man called Rossington, Lady Spenser's Reader in Geriatrics. He was a fleshy, handsome fifty-year-old, possessed of an unbelievable vitality, particularly when surrounded by the elderly infirm who were, so to speak, his raw material. He looked at me when I went into his office with disfavour. As I went closer he sniffed.

'You stink of beer,' he said.

'Yes, sir,' I said. 'I have to go home.'

'You're Arnott, aren't you?' I nodded. 'Look, Arnott, you're on duty. I can overlook the fact that you've been drinking—especially as you seem sober now—but your place is here.'

'You don't understand,' I said. 'I *have* to go home.'

He looked at me more objectively then: the doctor's look I've used a thousand times, and I've no doubt it was all written pretty clearly on me: booze, reaction, the beginnings of shock.

'Where is your home?' he asked, and I told him.

He said, 'I see. How do you propose to get there?'

'There's a last bus in twenty minutes,' I said.

'My dear man,' said Rossington, 'it won't be running tonight. Take a taxi.'

Even at that moment his words shocked me. To take a taxi anywhere would have been an extravagance to my parents: to take one for a seven-mile journey ranked as an unbelievable frivolity.

'I don't have the money,' I said.

Rossington's hand dived to an inside pocket, and came out with a handful of pound notes. He handed me two.

'Will that be enough?' he asked.

I hope I remembered to thank him.

The one driver who agreed to take me was taciturn, suspicious, and almost as drunk as I had been earlier that night. His taxi was ten years old at least, and smelt, unaccountably, of hens, but even so he wouldn't agree to take me until I had shown him Rossington's two pounds. After that he said at once, 'Fifteen bob the trip,' and drove me off before I could change my mind. From then on he said nothing, which was an ideal situation: I had nothing to say to anybody until I had seen my mother and father. But drunk or not, he drove with ease through the blacked-out streets. I suppose the moonlight helped, but to me his progress seemed cruelly inevitable: I had to get home, but I was already scared of doing so. We passed the shut-down pubs, the static water-tanks, the row upon row of houses from which no chink of light showed, till the city was left behind, the bridge crossed, and the little riverside towns flowed one into the other. More houses, more moonlight, more dead, deserted pubs; and then the last remnant of countryside before my own town: trees still, and pastureland, and scurrying sheep resentful of a disturbed night. It's all gone now: a trading-estate has squared off the meadows, but then it used to be beautiful: austere downland, and the bitter tang of the sea. But not that night. That night there was no sea tang: only the smell of smoke and seared metal from two miles beyond the town. And all the way we had passed nothing, and nothing had passed us except two ambulances going the other way, flat out for the city and the Albert Edward Hospital. We left the meadows behind, and past the Staithes and River Road, Gatton's Shipyard and the Neptune

Dock, and I spoke for the first time, told the driver to turn off into Cobden Road. We were near to Bright Street now, and the burning smell was intensifying.

He stopped, and I wanted to swear at him, but he had to stop. There was a policeman holding up his hand. He came up to us, middle-aged, not hurrying. When he got nearer I saw that he was filthy and exhausted. I got out of the cab.

'Where you off to?' he asked.

'Bright Street,' I said.

He looked at me, taking his time. 'Why d'you want to go there?' he asked. 'The road's up.'

'I live there,' I said.

Suddenly his voice became gentle, much too gentle.

'What number, son?' he asked.

'Seventy-three.'

The driver came out then, and demanded money, since he couldn't go on. I gave him Rossington's pound, and he groped in his pockets, found two half-crowns. Dimly I remembered there were such things as tips, and gave him half a crown back. He thanked me then and would have gone back to his cab, but the policeman reached out and held him.

'Come from the city?' he asked me, and I said yes. 'The fare's ten bob,' the policeman said, 'including tip.'

The taxi-driver wanted to argue, but the policeman looked at him, and he stopped. In his look there was despair, and a longing, almost a need, for raging violence.

'Don't argue,' he said. 'Not to me. . . . Not tonight.'

The taxi-driver gave me more money, and left at once.

'Number seventy-three,' said the policeman.

'Mr and Mrs Arnott,' I said. 'Me mam and dad. They're all right, aren't they?'

'I think we'd better go to the rescue station,' the policeman said. 'It's just round the corner.' He walked off, and I followed him in terror.

It was built like a fort, concreted, sand-bagged, gas curtains ready behind steel doors, but inside it was a miniature hospital ward, with trestle beds and cherry-red blankets and the familiar iodoform smell. The beds were all empty, though some of them had been used. At one end of the room, an exhausted group drank tea.

The policeman said, 'Sit down, lad,' and his hand pressed me down on to a bed. He walked into an office marked *Controller*, and I waited. A fat woman brought me a mug of tea, strong and dark and sweet, more sugar in it than I used in three days. But it was good for me, and I sipped it, until the door opened and a man in dark blue battledress came out, and behind him old Silverstein, the doctor my mother made my father go to see when his chest was bad: the man who had told her it was perfectly possible that I too could be a doctor. He took one look at me, said, 'I'll handle this,' and the man in dark blue went back to his office.

As I watched him come closer, I was conscious of surprise. Silverstein's face for as long as I could remember had had a quality of salacious yet benevolent slyness I had never seen on the face of another human being; he was also glittering clean, always. But that night he was dirty: mud-splashed, smoke-grimed, blood on his suit and the breast of his shirt, and his face, that one, terrible time, was innocent.

'Bob,' he said. 'My God, boy—where have you been?'

'I was fire-watching,' I said. 'At the university. I could see what was happening—so I got excused. I took a cab.' I looked round the station. 'Where did they take them?' I asked. He looked at me with that same strange, terrifying innocence, and I said, 'They're hurt aren't they? That's why the copper brought me here.'

They were dead. When the siren went they'd crawled under their table shelter, just as the instructions advised, and listened to the guns and the patter of incendiaries, and felt glad of the boiler plate that protected them. Then a land mine came down right on the doorstep and the blast wave killed them so quickly they were dead even before the other terrible things happened to them. They must have been dead. They had to be. . . . Old Silverstein was kind—he always was —but that night there was a greatness in him too that kept me functioning and sane till he got me to my Aunt Bet's, my mother's sister, and more hot tea, and a sedative, and bed. That night was the first time I realized how much I had loved my parents: how alone I was going to be. . . .

'Yes,' Laidlaw said. 'Bob remembers that night all right.'

'I had cause,' I said.

'And I don't?' Laidlaw smiled, and for once the smile was friendly, even compassionate. 'Granda and I went down with the Heavy Rescue Squad to Bright Street. I was the one who dug down to them, old son.'

I looked at him: there could be no possible doubt that he was telling the truth.

'And you never told me,' I said.

'It didn't seem relevant,' said Laidlaw. 'I'm afraid it still doesn't.'

'And where were you?' I said to Jim.

'What a very unfair question,' Laidlaw said.

'Me and Matt—we stayed where the rum was,' said Jim. 'We were both pissed, Bob—and anyway, what could we have done?'

The raid that night destroyed seventeen houses, a church and a garage. More than two hundred houses were damaged, and a school lost its gymnasium. Forty-three people were severely injured, and some died later: over a hundred and fifty had minor injuries. But that night there were only two dead: Alfred and Freda Arnott. I think my life was different from the moment old Silverstein told me.

MIXING WITH THE NOBS

SYBIL LAIDLAW thought that Arnott had done all right for himself. There was a very soothing quality about Susan Arnott: her beauty was soothing, her voice was soothing, her very dullness was soothing. Arnott himself was anything but soothing: his kind of dedicated and highly intelligent hard work never was, so with Susan he had got exactly what he lacked—and she, it seemed, from him. They were happy enough, she thought, as if happiness were so much a part of their life's routine as to be slightly boring. Madge Innes, she thought, had never achieved that kind of boredom. Madge was beautiful, and greedy, and immensely attractive. She herself had responded to the attraction from the moment she had seen her. That she and Tom had slept together was not in doubt, and yet the fact failed to move her. The Tom who had embraced Madge Innes was not her husband: that Tom, randy, mischievous, greedy as Madge herself, had ceased to exist on the day they married. Daddy had taken care of that. . . .

Tom had come back from America to the North-East. He'd made a lot of money, and was in a hurry to make more, a rather obvious hurry, if you watched closely, and she'd watched from the moment she first danced with him, at one of those ghastly Rotarian do's. He was in everything: Rotarians, Masons, Charity Committees, and he attended every dance and banquet that came his way, talked earnestly and long with all the people, boring, well-meaning, influential people, who wielded what was left of the money and power of a provincial community: talked as if they absorbed him totally, which in a sense they did: their power and money were what he wanted. Daddy's for instance. Daddy had money, and power too: the power of a magistrate, an alderman, a former mayor, a member of the Watch Committee. Daddy was an unabashed Tory in a town which had been solidly Labour ever since she could remember; that had only once in fifty years failed to return a left-wing majority, and on that one occasion had drawn her father, Dick Jameson, for mayor, and a brief period of right-wing reaction that had culminated in riots in pubs and a fist-fight in the council chamber. Her father loved to talk about it, and Tom had set himself to listen: so he dined with them often, and never seemed to care whether she, Sybil, was there or not.

There had been a woman in the States, that was obvious, and she had left him. In a way that was lucky: all the energy and drive he would have devoted to her were channelled into contacts, business. Tom was very obviously achieving what he had set out to achieve, but the sheer ferocity of it was frightening. He must have adored that woman, to work so hard. And it was the work that convinced Daddy. Lots of young men listened to his reminiscences, and Daddy simply used them and threw them away, but Tom he listened to; Tom he encouraged. He'd even told her he wanted Tom to marry her—and there'd been times, after Mother died, when she doubted if Daddy would let her marry anybody. She'd thought she had no chance at all, but Daddy had known better – and worked at it too. Clothes from Hartnell, a couple of times from Dior, invitations to the great houses that still survive in Northumberland, and trips to London for the coming-out balls of the great houses' daughters. (Daddy was so very Tory, and his stock-market tips so accurate: the great houses loved him. Besides, he never expected to go himself.) So that Tom found himself a socialite, and went shooting with a duke and a viscount, and danced with their daughters—and loved it, as Daddy had known he would. And because he had loved it, he had danced with her—after all, he could hardly dance with Daddy—and she'd begun to look really good about then, tiny, but quite delicious, and much better dressed than the Lady Sarahs and Honourable Emmas. She dressed moreover to assert her femaleness, not to hide it, and Tom had realized it, just as he'd realized he'd never be allowed to marry an Emma or Sarah anyway; just as he'd realized at last exactly how much money and power her father had. It had been enough, and he'd asked her to marry him, and she could hardly believe her luck. From the moment she met him, he had been the one she wanted.

Daddy had been marvellous about it: marvellous as he always was with her. The people who hated him didn't understand there was another, wonderful side of Daddy. Even Bob Arnott, for instance: sweet and happy as he was, Sybil bet he loathed Daddy, because he'd sent Bob's father to prison all those years ago. Daddy had told her all about it: there was nothing he wouldn't share with her—and what Bob didn't realize was that Daddy had his point of view too. The town had been full of a reckless violence then—look at the Salt Pan Riots, for instance—and it was people like Daddy who had held it in check, preserved order and calm, and made money too. Why not? Everybody wanted to make money if they could: even workmen. But Daddy had made his money work for her happiness, tied it up tight in her name, so that Tom could use it if he wanted to, but never possess it. Not like her. He could use her whenever he wished, and possess her too, but the money stayed inviolate, the maidenhead he could never pierce. And Tom had accepted it: and gone on using her, possessing her, ever since their honeymoon, and it was absolutely super, because it was his way, his only way, of being in love.

His love and fidelity she had never doubted, and the Tom who had chased and fumbled before her time was dead, so that all the girls like Madge could never frighten her. All the girls, that is, except one. That had been in Long Island, soon after they were married. Tom had gone on business, and taken her with him. They had gone to the States aboard the *Queen Mary*, because he'd heard there was a wholesaler travelling aboard her he needed to meet, and Tom of course was right. Mr Kinsella had been Irish and terrible and drunk, but Tom had got his contract—made love to her every night. New York had been good, too, but one weekend they'd been invited to Long Island, that was all drinks and sailing and heated pools and charcoal grills, and there'd been a woman at a party. Very brown she'd been, with fair hair bleached by the sun almost to silver, a white dress by Balmain, and one jewel, a quite enormous solitaire diamond ring. Her name was Dagmar, and she and Tom didn't speak: but Tom looked at her as though he'd remembered a dream. They had flown back to England in one of those ghastly piston jobs they used then, and not even the memory of stopovers at Gander and Reykjavik could make her forget. Nothing, it seemed, ever would, until they went to another party.

This one was in London. One of those coming-out things it was so nice to get roped in for: all Jennifer's Diary and William Hickey and those quite hysterical photographs in the *Tatler*: plovers' eggs and Tattinger and prawns in aspic; girls who seemed full of eager terror and boys who were full of blended Scotch and parents whose one reaction seemed to be incredulity that the thing was still going on. But not at this house. This house still held assurance, absolute assurance. Its values and dignity were unassailable: tens of thousands of acres, a banking house, a fir forest, a copper-mine in Australia and a ranch in Mexico, all combined to make it so. Even the National Coal Board contributed its share in compensation. It was a house in Mayfair, filled with the ancestors of the plethoric, hasty, brilliant man who owned it. His daughter was beautiful, his sons commanded Guards' companies, or governed colonies, or chattered in faultless Italian to the Vatican Ambassador. His guests that night were beautiful, eccentric or brilliant, because beauty, eccentricity, brilliance, amused him. If he'd had a taste for dullness, he could have filled the place with bishops.

Tom she supposed was brilliant (commercial). That she herself was beauty she had no doubt: her host had told her so. And all around were the others: the outrageously Left M.P., the playwright with his swarm of pretty young men like pilot fish, the poet who this time did not dare to be drunk, the cricketer who'd scored the fastest hundred of the season, and was very drunk indeed. And there too was Dagmar. Her skin had paled this time to a creaminess like roses; her gown was blue and Balenciaga, and the solitaire this time was a sapphire. With her was her husband, tall and lean like a cowboy, but with a face of cheerful wickedness: twenty-seven million dollars' worth of chain stores, she heard one pretty boy whisper to another. She looked at once for Tom, and he was staring, as she had known he would be. But there was no remembered dream on his face; it showed, for the first time, a concentration of hatred she had not believed possible. Then as she watched, the woman moved, and Tom continued to stare. Behind Dagmar, three people stood: two men and a woman. One man was old, and dressed appallingly in what must have been a very expensive suit of evening clothes forty years before. His face was at once aristocratic and reptilian—and as much a part of the house as its owner. The woman was slender, pretty, but not nearly so elegant as the dilapidated old man. To Sybil she seemed to be intensely angry, and only just controlling it. It was the other man who was the cause of her anger, a big, powerful man who wore his dinner jacket and black tie as if he despised them. It was the other man Tom was staring at.

She gripped his arm, hard, and the hatred died, but oh so slowly. It was like a fade-out in a film.

'I'm sorry,' he said. 'I was far away for a minute.'

She moved away towards the ball-room, and the comfort of other people who didn't know hatred, the cheerful thump of a dance band.

'Darling, who was it?' she asked.

'An old enemy,' he said.

It was the first time he'd ever referred to Jim Moulton.

After that he took her on the floor to dance, and then to eat supper with a fat and cheerful couple who had some ideas about the way commercial television would go, and an endless fund of stories about show business. Tom listened and laughed, and never once looked back to the old enemy and the woman with him, or the distinguished, dilapidated man who sat beside them, eating cold salmon, waiting for their quarrel to end. For that was obviously what he was doing: waiting for them to finish so that he could start something of his own. At last the girl had gone away, and Tom's enemy had looked after her. There was no anger in his face, only a regret that deepened to despair.

The fat and cheerful man said, 'We've got some brainy ones here tonight.'

Sybil saw that he was looking at the old man.

'That's Bennington,' he said. 'Order of Merit. Father of the atom. All that stuff.'

'Bennington?'

'Our gracious host's uncle. Cambridge don. Some kind of a genius, they say. He's after the young feller. Another genius. Comes from up your way, Tom. Bit of a Red.'

'You're very well informed,' Tom said.

'I have to be, son. It's my living.' The cheerful fat man swigged—it was the only possible word for it—his Champagne. 'Those two could blow us all to hell and gone any time they felt like it.'

'Make the party go with a bang, like,' said his wife.

'And every other bloody thing as well,' said the cheerful fat man.

TUNBRIDGE WELLS WITH PALM TREES

SHE had never seen Moulton again, until that night. But she had seen the woman not long ago. They had met in an ice-cream parlour on Sunset Strip, the year Tom had put some of his dollar holdings into a film T.V. series. It had been her first visit to Hollywood, and she had found it clean and provincial and warm, a sort of Tunbridge Wells with palm trees; the flamboyance of its 'characters'—how damning to put 'characters' in quotes—mildly endearing: Tunbridge Wells in carnival week. There was another point of similarity, too: Holly-wood also was boring. Not for Tom of course: he had meetings with men who used words like 'growth-rate' and 'Hooper ratings' and 'throughput', aggressively well-washed men, fleshy for the most part, all mildly surprised that Tom could use the words too, because he was British. For Tom it was all very exciting: but she had been bored. Of course there were bus trips: Disneyland, Farmers' Market, The Homes of the Stars, but in between nothing very much except new movies at the cinema in air-conditioned darkness, and old movies on T.V. in one's room in air-conditioned light. It was a relief sometimes to go out, and hunt for a taxi, and tell the man to take you just any-where. And anywhere, in Hollywood, must at some point include the Strip.

It was, she thought, essentially a sad place. There was so much energy expended there, with such incredibly small results to show for it. Cafés and clubs and restaurants, all with the glossy impermanence of film sets, and the people, so many of them actors, with a glossy impermanence of their own. Even the palm trees shared the unreality, waiting, she thought, to be struck at any moment and re-erected round the Queen of Sheba's palace, or the villainous Don Pedro's castle in Spain. She walked past the topless bars, where the ad stills assured her they were bottomless too, the movie theatres, the real-estate offices, the gift stores, and into the coolness of the ice-cream parlour.

There was far more space than she had expected, and far, far more women. (The number of women on their own in Hollywood, so many of them young and pretty, was always to surprise her.) There were girls in cowboy clothes, in pedal-pushers, in Bermuda shorts, and one tall dark girl in doeskin and beads and eagle's feathers who was ready to go on right that minute as Minnehaha (from a story by H. W. Longfellow). The place chattered like an elegant aviary, the kind where the cockatoos and mynah birds pay twenty dollars an hour to get their vowel sounds right.

She sat down at a table on her own, behind a couple of men eating the most enormous chocolate sundaes. One of them was lean and handsome and deadly, the wild boy whom only love can redeem; the other was grizzled, muscular, paunchy, the ageing sheriff who's still got what it takes. They held hands discreetly and talked about agents. She tried not to listen, because she liked stories about wild, deadly boys and ageing sheriffs, but she was unsure whether one was permitted to read or not when on one's own (well, not permitted exactly, but was it a thing one did?) and the size of her orange freeze dismayed her. It looked like the dessert course at a dinner party for six. She became confused, and dropped her book. The wild cowboy and the sheriff ignored her: it was the woman next to them who picked it up.

'Thank you so much,' Sybil said, and the woman smiled at the Kensingtonian precision of her vowels. She was younger than Sybil, and very much taller: slender, with an eager quality that might become neurotic under stress. But she was kind too, with that vast and unthinking Californian kindness.

'You're very welcome,' she said. At that moment Sybil had no idea who she was.

'You look as if all this was new to you,' the young woman said, and Sybil assured her that it was, and they moved from kindness and politeness to the transient intimacy of a shared table, and later a single bill which Sybil paid. It was her Englishness, the Englishness of voice, restraint, desire to know precisely what was done and— more important—not done, that drew the young woman to her; the awareness of the impermanence of their relationship that coaxed her into speaking, as soon she did, of love and its inevitable corollary, unhappiness.

'Where I made my big mistake,' the young woman said, 'was in marrying a genius.'

In London such a statement would have disconcerted Sybil: in Hollywood she expected it. In Hollywood almost everybody who isn't a genius is married to one.

'What kind of pictures does he make?' she asked.

The girl's laughter was immediate, and joyous at first, but ultimately frightening. It went on for so long. Yet nobody else stared, or even looked up.

'I'm sorry,' the girl said at last. 'That was rude.'

'Not at all.'

This time, she got a smile: wide, delighted, sane.

'I love you people,' said the girl. 'My God, I must do. I married one.'

'The genius?'

'None other. But he's not in pictures. He's a scientist. My name's Moulton. Tracy Moulton. Professor Moulton's wife. Ever heard of him?'

Fair play, decency, whatever embarrassing, unfashionable word one used, had dominated Sybil's life since she first picked up a hockey-stick. It was too late now to deny her formative years.

'My name's Sybil Laidlaw,' she said, and Tracy Moulton's face remained just as it had been, so that Sybil realized that she had never heard the name, that Moulton had not even mentioned Tom; and hated him for it. Even fair play had its limits, she told herself, but that wasn't true. It was love for Tom that produced the lie.

'I'm afraid I don't know an awful lot about science,' she said.

'Believe me, you don't have to,' Tracy said. 'Just read the newspapers.'

It seemed that Moulton had had a big press in the United States even before McCarthy. A brilliant physicist who was not only a war hero with a D.S.O. but a poor boy who'd made good: all right-thinking journalists had loved him at first, and Tracy had loved him too. They'd met in New England, when he'd been week-ending away from M.I.T. and she'd been in Summer Stock. (What *you* call repertory. A little place in Vermont. You'd love it there—honestly. All maple forests and old stone farms.) To be in love with Moulton wasn't easy. Her friends disliked him, her father and mother, when at last they flew the weary journey to Los Angeles, detested him. But she persevered: they married. And then came McCarthy, and hints and smears and investigations—and a new job that never material-ized, so that her parents knew they'd been right all the time. The funny thing was that *she* had been the one who was indignant. To him all the uproar and denunciation had been simply the final proof of a theory that had all along held strong probability of success. The thing that was likely to happen had happened: he saw no reason for anger or dismay in such an obvious fact, even when he lost his job; even when it proved impossible to find another. But she had rebelled, and with anger. Her job soon went too, and after that her life was absorbed in pickets, meetings, rallies, and Moulton had helped her not at all. When she asked him why, he told her it was because he wanted the whole system to go: not just McCarthy, but all the things that she and her friends were battling to preserve, at considerable cost to themselves. It was all romanticism, he said. Mysterious, excit-ing and quite useless. She hated him for that. . . .

The orange freeze melted, and Sybil paid the waitress in gingham so crisp it almost crackled. Back on the Strip they found that the heat at least was a reality, and Tracy suggested a drink. When Sybil hesitated, it was not from fair play: not by then. She wanted it to go on and on, and alcohol was the best way to keep it going. What bothered her was the thought of two women drinking unescorted.

'A bar?' she said. 'Can we?' and again Tracy smiled her delight that Sybil should be so perfect a specimen.

'I know a place,' she said.

Voodoo masks, a false ceiling of straw, sulky Negro waitresses in Mother Hubbards, but a chill, persistent air-conditioning, Bloody Marys, and Tracy drinking with a kind of amateurish ferocity.

'I don't go to an analyst,' she said. 'My father wants me to but I won't. Like Andy says, anybody who goes to a shrink ought to have his head examined.'

'Andy?'

'The guy who wants to marry me. He collects dividends and old jokes.'

Sybil had no use for Andy. Her whole business here, sipping a distasteful mixture of vodka and tomato juice, was to spy on Moulton. Andy—rich, benign, a little stupid—had no place among the voodoo masks.

'But he can't anyway,' said Tracy. 'I'm married to Jim. If you ever see him, you might remind him of that no doubt unimportant fact.' She paused. 'When do you go back to England, anyway?'

'Next week,' said Sybil. 'Why did you mention psychiatrists?'

'Because you tell them things,' said Tracy, and drank. 'I loved him and then I hated him. I hate him now.'

'Can't you divorce him?'

'Sure,' the younger woman said. 'Any time. But I guess I don't want to. Isn't that horrible? I don't want to.'

'You want to go back to him?'

'Yes. I do.' She signalled, and ice, tomato juice, vodka, went into a pitcher. 'I can hate him better when we're together.' Suddenly she sighed, and willed herself back to the calmness of the ice-cream parlour.

'I'm sorry,' she said. 'That was just Hollywood—and rather self-indulgent.'

'I don't understand,' said Sybil.

'I was playing a scene,' she said. 'Acting what I want . . . and what I can't have. That's what Hollywood's about.' She sighed again. 'I'll divorce him all right. I may even marry Andy.' Then she talked of other things.

But there was still plenty for Sybil to tell Tom when they met for dinner, and afterwards he made her drink margaritas, then made love to her in a way they'd never tried before. It was delightful.

'THEY were holding hands when we found them,' said Laidlaw. He said it without laughter: no mockery, no salaciousness. For that at least I could be grateful to him.

'How did you find out they were dead?' he asked.

'Silverstein told me.'

'Bloody old voyeur,' said Jim, and I wanted to argue: to tell him about the goodness in Silverstein, the wit and warmth I had needed so much. But the weight of memory was too heavy, even for protest, and anyway it was true.

At first it had been necessary to avoid Silverstein: to keep away from him and the memories he immediately invoked: cherry red blankets and iodoform and sweet tea; Freda on compassionate leave, and the two of us standing like strangers beside the coffins, already screwed down. (What they contained was not fit for human beings to see, though human beings had done it.) And then the cemetery, cold and brown and neglected by war—except that the Germans had dropped a bomb on it too that night. There were all sorts of jokes made about that, I remember: about how thorough the Germans were. So the funeral procession picked its way among a litter of smashed headstones, swerved once to avoid a monstrous marble set-piece rammed casually into the soggy earth, its angels, once peacefully recumbent, now garishly vertical. *At Rest,* it said. The mud flicked at Freda's gleaming uniform shoes, the Co-op undertakers' men struggled and faltered in the mud, and the Reverend Mr Fowler strode ahead, tattered cassock, white hair flying, like a Lear who'd got religion.

It was the final irony that Fowler should have buried them. The Reverend Cuthbert de la Pole Fowler was the man they feared most in life, but even in death it seemed they weren't going to be allowed to escape him. My parents had been gently and undemandingly religious, in a C. of E. sort of way. And this was surprising. Most people of our class and income, if they worshipped God at all, did so like the Irish Catholics, because they'd inherited Him: or else went out and grabbed Him, like the Salvationists and Seventh-Day Adventists or the Primitives, the way they'd grab a bottle of brown ale, and for much the same reasons. But my mother, probably because she'd been in domestic service, had been Church of England, and they were married at St George's. Normally that would have been the end of it, but my father found he had a taste for the ritual and the poetry; the confident harmonies of Anglican hymns. They kept it up, and the hope of the life everlasting became, for them at least, a reality: communion a duty, and evensong a pleasure. If it hadn't been for the Reverend Cuthbert de la Pole Fowler.

Fowler was certainly an eccentric, and quite possibly a saint. His lineage was aristocratic and impeccable, like his manners; his acceptance of Christianity total, his poverty legendary. He was also capable of a very elegant kind of wit. Fowler could and did pray aloud while sitting on the lavatory and fill his house with tramps and derelicts: though most of them didn't stay. His huge Victorian vicarage had long since decayed, and its plumbing and cuisine were decidedly inferior to those of Rowton House. Very early the tramps had robbed him of everything he owned that had a resale value, and his stipend went as fast as he received it. He ate only because a group of church-going women like my mother had made up their minds that he should, and stuffed him with stew or Scotch broth or baked herrings whenever he came to call.

It was the visits that inspired the fear. My parents were inured to eccentricities of a kind: the foolishness of drunks, the neuroticism of World War One's shell-shocked, Mrs Baxter, next door but three, in a hypnotic trance recording messages from Disraeli. But Fowler, you see, was a gentleman. And yet he didn't take enough baths, and his clothes were ragged, and he quoted Crashaw and Herbert and New Testament Greek. Once he burst into tears at the thought of the eternity of Hell that awaited the Impenitent Thief. These things embarrassed them, and they feared him because of the embarrassment he inevitably caused. And yet they fed him, and tried not to look when a former Oxford scholar daintily sopped up the last of the gravy with his bread. 'He hath filled the hungry with good things,' he would say, then launch into extempore prayer: eloquent and multilingual, in a voice so booming that old Hunter upstairs, who was on shift-work, would rattle the fire-irons if he went on too long.

Yet in the end it was Fowler who paid them their last tribute. Death meant little to him, who was surrounded all his life by evidences of eternity, but sin and its consequences were to him very real, and very terrible: and in the middle of that war sin was strong indeed: so that his great voice reading the burial service was a blending of joy and pain in which joy finally triumphed, as joy must: as Heaven must eventually prevail against Hell. It hurt me almost more than I could bear: but it healed me too. The Burial of the Dead is very beautiful, and old Fowler that day brought to it a sense not only of its beauty but of its reality to my parents. *In sure and certain hope of the Resurrection to eternal life.* The words were like trumpets. I wished and doubted that they could hear them.

The funeral was a wartime one: there were no baked meats, no gaggle of aunts washing up after ham and tongue and salad while black-tied uncles wriggled off to the pub; but there had been a fair turn out at St George's, and at the cemetery too: relatives, and representatives from my father's union branch, a scattering of neighbours and the Mothers' Union. Freda and I shook hand after hand, and watched how some people wept and others tried not to, and others peered at us, inquisitive for our own signs of grief. Prominent among these was Old Bickersley. I could think of no reason for his coming, and, after the terrible splendour of Fowler's voice, was too dazed to think of one.

'Arnott, poor lad,' he said. 'I read about your sad loss in the newspaper. Terrible, terrible. These are terrible times we live in, my dear boy. Terrible times.'

'Thank you,' I said. For what? My sad loss? The terrible times? And Freda, more honest than me, stopped crying and stared her amazement.

'And you,' he said. 'Alone now——'

'This is my sister Freda,' I said.

'Good afternoon.' He grimaced; he had always hated interruption. 'Alone now,' he continued. 'How will you live? You have work, I hope?'

'I'm a medical student,' I said. It hadn't been two years since he'd written my reference for the university, and he'd hated my going. It seemed he still did.

'But now ... you see how things are altered. We must talk this over, Jim. Come and see me.'

'Bob,' I said, and he was grimacing again as Fowler came up, lean and hungry and instantly aware of sin.

'Ah, Mr Fowler,' said Bickersley. 'I was just explaining to this poor lad——'

'Not now, not now,' said Fowler sharply. 'No explanations now. Only solace.'

'But his affairs—he tells me he was a student. He'll need to find a job.'

'My kingdom is not of this world,' said Fowler. 'You should remember that, Bickersley. He will eat or starve each day as I do'—he looked at Bickersley's stomach, straining the houndstooth waistcoat—'as you should do—but today his grief is in his soul. Not now,' he said again, and turned, blocking off Bickersley from me. 'The rich shall be sent empty away,' he said. It was the other half of the text he had quoted to my mother so often. He smiled then, and his dirty, shapely hand touched my shoulder. It was as if he were saying 'Watch this'—and perhaps he was. He turned once more.

133

'Don't think me rude, Bickersley,' he said. 'This young man's needs are pressing.' And then with the air of one who makes amends: 'I found a teaspoon the other day. It was one of a set of six: the others were stolen from me years ago. It was made for my family in the reign of Queen Anne—and I'm told is very fine, by those who value such things. Come to the vicarage some time and look at it.'

Bickersley snorted, and left us in peace.

'Dear me,' said Fowler. 'Have I offended him in some way? I often do, you know.'

His wit, as I said, was elegant, but not always easy to spot. He went on without a break: 'You have lost two good and Christian parents, and today the two of you are only aware of your sense of loss. That is human, natural, and by no means a sin. But tomorrow, and the days that follow, you should turn your minds from your loss to their gain.' He looked sharply at us both. 'I fear that you will find that difficult, particularly *you*.' His hand came down on my shoulder again, and this time he shook it hard. 'But there is a lesser consolation, and one that I'm quite sure you will avail yourselves of: the sweetness of memory. Emotion recollected in tranquillity.' He paused. 'Do you not think Wordsworth would have been happier as a learned pagan—perhaps in the time of Marcus Aurelius? . . . Forgive me, I too often digress. You will remember, I say, and take happiness and comfort from remembering, but I doubt if you will pray for them. Rather rude, when you come to think of it. They prayed so often—and so earnestly—for you. God bless you.'

And there he left us, for tea at my aunt's, and her memories of my mother's youth. No wireless, no pub, no pictures. My aunt, a spinster, hadn't been inside a church since my mother's wedding, but she knew what was fitting. Grief was already yielding to boredom when Silverstein called to see me. . . .

'Stupid old sod,' Jim said. 'Prying all the time. Not as bad as Fowler though.'

'You really consider Fowler bad?' said Laidlaw.

'Not wicked,' said Jim. 'Far from it. But irrelevant. In the way.'

'Silverstein was hardly that,' said Laidlaw. 'Surely he was one of your lot?'

'He tried, I suppose,' said Jim. 'Pity he couldn't have done a swap with Fowler. Nobody minds a nosy parson.'

I minded Silverstein too: but it didn't stop me from liking him—or seeing him. Not that night, or for many nights to come. His visit impressed my Aunt Bet for a start, and increased my social standing. He was a doctor, after all, and he'd called out of friendship, not professional necessity—to see me. That was important, and he'd recognized the fact at once. In the time to come, he never hesitated to make use of it. He'd come, it was clear, because he liked me. I was shy, awkward, upset and churlish about it, but he liked me anyway. Aunt Bet installed us at once in her 'front room', where the japanned gas-fire soothingly popped, left us alone, and took to Freda her memories of my mother. Anything would be better than that. I tried, without much success, to be polite to Silverstein.

'It was a nice ceremony, so they tell me,' he said.

'Yes,' I said. How much Christian ritual could you discuss with a Jew? I'd only known four Jews in my life, and the other three were medical students. The only thing I'd discussed with them was *Gray's Anatomy*.

'Fowler's pretty good at that sort of thing,' Silverstein continued. 'I've seen him in action. You've no idea how useful a good parson can be to a doctor.' And he went on to talk about what a G.P. really was: doctor, oculist, analyst, obstetrician, health visitor, adviser, dietician —and creditor too. In those pre-health-service days, the poor never had enough money to pay, and yet they needed a doctor for almost every event in their lives that was not routine: from childbirth to death certificates. If they were not religious, he was the only educated man they ever saw. Silverstein talked fluently about something that was very dear to him: the colossal need of his patients, and his unending struggle to fulfil it. He talked with a kind of justified pride, that awakened in me, as it was meant to, my own determination to be a doctor, and an awareness of his own part in its inspiration. Then he switched—suddenly, and, that first time, with staggering effect, though I was later to recognize the signs, and brace myself for the impact.

'D'you suppose Fowler's a virgin?' he asked.

I squirmed in my chair. What the hell was he up to? Saying: As a virgin yourself, do you recognize the symptoms? He was a good and educated man, making unkind speculation about just such another—to a youth twenty-five years his junior. It wasn't just nasty, it was bloody unfair.

'He isn't married,' I said.

'He told me once there wasn't a day he could remember when he hadn't believed. The whole rigmarole.' I must have squirmed again, because he said, 'They're all rigmaroles—Islam, Christianity, Judaism. The whole lot. Surely you know that? . . . But getting back to Fowler, if he's always believed—he wouldn't, would he? Not out of wedlock. D'you know I bet he's never had a bit in his life? Maybe that's what gives him his drive.' He went on to give me a lecture on sublimated sexual energy as a source of good: the first I'd ever heard. As I remember it, it was an excellent lecture, but it was still bloody unfair. I didn't want to sublimate my sexual energy anyway; and it was a long time before I realized that he did—in his own embarrassing way.

'Silverstein changed you, Bob,' said Laidlaw. 'Before he came along you were just a savage learning to use a stethoscope. He made you an intellectual—perhaps even an aesthete?'

This was good, but not quite good enough. Before Silverstein the need had been there: for books, for music, the theatre; it was Silverstein who had persuaded me to earn the money that fulfilled the need, even though my father's last wish had been that I shouldn't. It had taken tact, and compassion too, to achieve that.

'Aesthete?' I said. 'I went on playing rugger.'

'And chasing girls,' said Jim. 'But maybe he was the one who made a man of you—and watched while you were doing it?'

Laidlaw gave a little sigh of content, while Jim, unnoticing, refilled his glass. It was the first time he had done so without waiting for Laidlaw to fill his first.

I said, 'Don't be so fucking rude,' and he blinked for a moment, then grinned.

'So you haven't forgotten how to talk to me?' he said 'The trouble is, when I get started on old Silverstein——'

'That won't do,' I said.

He sat rigid for a moment, his glass lifted, then: 'Oh. I see what you're after. I'm sorry. That what you want?'

'It'll have to do,' I said.

'Parties,' said Laidlaw. 'Our Bob went to a lot of parties. Dark grey suit, and a plum-coloured waistcoat, with his grandfather's watch in the pocket. And do I remember a cane? Yes ... I think I do.'

'You never,' said Jim. It was a cry from his childhood; a cry engendered from amazement and disgust.

'For God's sake,' I said. 'I was eighteen years old.'

'You were away at the wars,' said Laidlaw. 'Your dress was fancy too—but not eccentric.'

'My dress was normal enough at the time,' said Jim.

'But our friend here became—ever so discreetly—noticeable. Spoke in debates, joined the dramatic society. He made—I'm told—a very convincing Iago.'

'Convincing?' I asked, but Laidlaw wouldn't be drawn.

'And his spots cleared, his voice deepened; he became quite pretty in a manly way. And we mustn't forget he was muscular too. A swift and accurate wing three-quarter. Silverstein groomed him well ... and one by one the shy maids came running ... and lost their shyness as they ran. The parties must have been a great help, Bob—in your study of surface anatomy?'

'For God's sake,' I said. 'What is all this? I was eighteen years old and I groped a few girls——'

'Not groped,' said Laidlaw. 'Not then. The word hadn't been invented. We had another expression then—"touched them up"? Wasn't that it?'

'All right then—touched them up. Didn't you both?'

'Unfortunately not,' said Laidlaw. 'I was too shy. D'you know I had to wait another five years? What a waste. But our friend here...' he turned to Jim.

'I was busy,' said Jim. 'And the women were all starving anyway. All they wanted was food.'

'But not here,' Laidlaw said gaily. 'Not in embattled Britain. Here they all had tenpennorth of meat and two pennorth of corned beef and oranges on the ration. More than enough—eh, Bob?'

'It was a monotonous diet,' I said, 'but it was sound enough.'

'*Sound?*' His voice was delighted. 'Was that what it felt like when you and Madge——? *Sound?*'

I said, 'I think I've had enough of this,' and waited for Laidlaw to argue, but it was Jim who spoke.

'When he and Madge what?' he said. Laidlaw didn't answer, and Jim slammed down his glass, the wine slopped, stained the table-cloth's whiteness.

'Symbolism?' said Laidlaw. 'So late in the evening?'

'Bloody funny,' said Jim. 'I don't think. When he and Madge what?'

'I don't know,' said Laidlaw. 'I wasn't there. Ask Bob here.'

'How do you know we did anything?' I asked.

Laidlaw said promptly, 'Harry Lewis told me. He went to the parties too. But he didn't have your success. Perhaps he needed a cane.'

'Symbolism yourself,' I said, and he chuckled at that, but his eyes still glittered with excitement. The joke was an irrelevance.

'You better tell me,' Jim said.

'For Christ's sake,' I said. 'She's a grown woman—a guest here. We can't sit and snigger over——'

'Nobody's sniggering,' said Jim. 'I want to know.'

'There's nothing to tell,' I said.

'Don't tell me you've turned into a bloody coward as well,' said Jim.

'As well as what?'

'A bloody bourgeois.'

'All right,' I said. 'I'll tell you since it's so important. There was a party at Dolly Cousins's. You remember Dolly?' They nodded. Dolly, now married to a solicitor, had been gregarious rather than nymphomaniac, and extremely memorable. 'Madge was there. She'd had two gins and I took her pants down. Then I found out how old she was and pulled them up again.'

'How old was she?' Laidlaw asked.

'Thirteen,' I said. 'She didn't look it.'

'You bastard,' said Jim.

He started to get up then. He was a little drunk, and very dangerous. I was angry too, but compared with his, my anger was foolish and middle-aged.

'Come, come,' said Laidlaw. 'This won't do at all.' He made no move to stop us.

I got up too. No one in his senses would have faced an angry Jim Moulton sitting down. But the muscles I would need were long since flabby: I had eaten too much and I was slow on my feet ever since Malaya.

'Grow up,' I said. 'For Christ's sake grow up.'

He moved round the table and I did the only thing left to me: I picked up a bottle by the neck, the Gevrey-Chambertin, the '63. Really a quite excellent year. When I did so, Laidlaw's sigh was ecstatic.

'I did nothing,' I said. 'Not a bloody thing.'

'So you say,' said Jim.

'It's the truth. And if you start anything I'll crack you with this.'

'Me marrer,' said Jim. 'My fucking friend.' He sat down.

'You must forgive him,' Laidlaw said. 'But he had high hopes of Madge Innes once—till he found she'd been . . . corrupted.'

'I wanted to marry her,' said Jim. 'I would have, too.'

There was mourning in his voice for the death of love; and there were less admirable things: self-pity, and amazement that a girl, any girl, should not have waited for him until he was ready to take her. Laidlaw rose.

'Time to join the ladies,' he said. 'Thank you for the table talk gentlemen. I did enjoy it. So virile.'

A LATE ARRIVAL

MADGE INNES thought that the other two had almost run out of small-talk when the men appeared, but the silence hadn't bothered her. There had been so much to think about, and so much of it a pleasure. The way she'd got on. Peter Knowles never made the *Guardian*; he'd gone to London instead as a literary editor—*very* exalted, and he'd taken freelance pieces from her even while she was still at Manchester. He'd got her a job afterwards, with Ruthven Press, and she'd gone to bed with him. That had been a disaster, but a necessary one. He had at least been offered what he wanted. After that she owed him nothing. And after that there were others, anyway. Bigger and better Peters; bigger and better jobs. Tom Laidlaw for instance: what a surprise he had been. A very *elegant* sophisticate, and with such useful friends. He'd introduced her to that magazine syndicate, and that had been the end of Hope Still and the *Evening Courant* and Old Boys' Reunion Dinners. It had been the end of Tom Laidlaw too, and in that there was cause for regret, but little Sybil had him, that was obvious, if not by the balls at least by the cheque-book. But the others had been fun, too. She'd seen to that. And the work had been marvellous. All very petty no doubt, all those bank-robbers' women and mothers of seven and Paris says and Kitchens Are Fun and always and always love. LOVE. But never sex. Sex is vulgar; love is fulfilment. All petty as hell. But if you only saw the pettiness, you missed the point, which was work—exhausting work: circulation-building, delighting the advertisers, fooling the twits out of their ninepence a copy. My God, that was work. And it was great, especially when Larry came down for a weekend. He'd loved the excitement of it almost as much as she had, and he'd had a flair for it too, a flair he'd been too rich by then to use. But he'd been delighted just watching her, and afterwards ... their sex had been vulgar all right. Until the disaster—and after that he'd got married. But even then he'd played fair. He'd got her into television—and a block of shares and a house on the moors and a flat in Majorca. It had been good, all right. And now it was going to be great.

Poor Bob Arnott looked shaken. Tom had had plans for him too, and it looked as if they were working out. Straight over to his wife, and as close beside her as he could get. And she not spotting it ... no. Not like that at all. She was on to it all right, and touching him—well, well, well. On the biceps, but maternal. ... And then her eyes went to

Laidlaw, then fixed on Moulton, and her eyes were angry, but cold, too. It looked as if she'd misjudged Sunshine Susie. Those eyes were waiting to see somebody hurt, and if somebody turned out to be Jim, she'd love it. Nobody must hurt Mummy's boy.

Laidlaw was pouring out brandy, large ones, *very* large ones.

'We're all a bit drunk,' he said. 'Better to keep it that way.'

He handed them round like a waiter, and his wife reached for the coffee-pot, but Laidlaw shook his head. 'Later,' he said. 'If ever.'

Madge Innes said, 'We've had our share too.'

'That's nice,' said Laidlaw. 'I wouldn't want anybody to feel . . . inhibited.'

Susan Arnott said, her eyes still on her husband, 'I don't think anybody does.'

'My dear Mrs Arnott,' said Laidlaw, 'please excuse us. We've been talking over old times. It can be . . . a little uncomfortable, occasionally.'

'Yes,' she said. 'I know that. I'm not terribly clever—but I know that.'

'We have a little business to wind up,' said Laidlaw. 'That may be painful too. If you'd like to leave us for a while . . .'

'Is Bob staying?' she asked.

'He's very much involved,' said Laidlaw.

She turned to Arnott. 'Are you?' she asked.

'Yes,' he said.

'I'd like some more B and B,' said Susan. 'I don't think I'm drunk enough.'

Good for you, lady, Madge thought. And my apologies. I misjudged you, girl. Then, saving him to the last, she looked at Moulton.

Jesus, he's had it rough, she thought, and that's usually the way he likes it, but not this time. Somebody's hit you hard, she thought. Hit you where you can feel it. Just look at all that outrage.

'We're sorry to have been so long,' said Laidlaw. 'But really, there's been so much to catch up on. And it was all *so* interesting. But now we really must get down to business. Don't you think so, Jim?'

'Business?' said Moulton.

'You must excuse him,' said Laidlaw. 'You particularly, Madge. We were discussing certain episodes of our carefree youth. They appear to have shocked Jim, rather.'

Madge Innes thought, Oh, no, baby. Once you get a whip in your hands, you don't care who you hit, but don't try it on me.

Aloud she said, 'I'm surprised any of our memories of each other could be painful,' and it was Sybil's turn to look wary.

'Just so,' said Laidlaw. 'But that's all over, I hope.' So long as you know, thought Madge. 'Now it's time to help our friend here.'

'Can't he help himself?' Susan asked.

'I always have,' said Moulton. 'I've had to. Ever since I could walk. But Goofy wants to talk, and I don't mind listening.'

'His name is Tom,' said Sybil.

'It's not important,' Laidlaw said. 'We're here to help after all. And really, old chap, you haven't come up with anything constructive so far, have you? All that mercenary nonsense——'

'Guevara's dead,' said Moulton. 'There's nobody else I want to get shot with.'

'Exactly. And the universities won't have you—or am I wrong?'

'You're not wrong,' Moulton said. 'I've sickened them almost as much as they've sickened me.'

'What about Prague or Leningrad or Warsaw?' Arnott asked.

'I'd sicken them too. They make bombs.'

'Poor Jim,' said Madge. 'Not even Belgrade?'

'They can't do the stuff I'm after. No country can—that doesn't have the money to make bombs.'

'West Germany doesn't make bombs,' said Madge Innes. 'And they've got money.'

'The only ones,' said Moulton. 'That's why I'm here.'

'Not really,' said Madge Innes. 'There's Japan as well.'

Moulton laughed. 'I can't work in Japan,' he said. 'That's been taken care of.'

'Who by?'

He shrugged. 'Who knows?' he said. 'Some Fascist fixed it up somewhere. Moulton's out. Let's hear what you've got.'

'Let's hear what you want,' said Laidlaw.

'I want the bloody moon,' said Moulton. 'And a slice of the sun and a couple of stars. I want to go on with my work.'

'And for that you need a university?'

'I need a bloody lab with a cyclotron. And half a dozen blokes who know what they're doing—and an I.B.M. computer for three hours a week—four if it's acting up.'

'And that's all you want?' Madge Innes asked.

'It'll do for a start. There's electricity and equipment—materials. Plutonium costs a bomb——'

'Fifty thousand?' said Laidlaw. 'Could you do it on fifty thousand?'

Moulton looked up at the ceiling, calculated, then, 'Just about,' he said. 'Why? Are you going to give it to me?'

'It's possible,' said Laidlaw. 'Provided your work isn't classified, of course.'

Moulton looked warily from Madge Innes to Arnott, then back to Laidlaw. Only in Arnott's face could he see amazement.

'It isn't, is it? Classified, I mean?'

'I wouldn't touch it if it was.' Moulton gulped at his brandy. 'What you on about?'

'Fifty thousand pounds,' said Laidlaw.

'And a cyclotron. I suppose you've got one in the garage?'

'Not in the garage, no. But it'll be there when you need it.'

'And the computer?'

'Some Germans have just built a new toy of that sort—those typewriter people I told you about. I have an investment in it myself. A car company's buying it. I could get you your four hours a week.'

'The Germans,' said Moulton.

'I'm afraid so,' Laidlaw said.

'And a lab and the other equipment? The assistants?'

'They'll be provided.'

Moulton's wariness intensified. 'What you after?' he asked.

'A research institute. The first of its kind—in this country anyway. I've just been involved in a merger—with a group called Aliment. Ever heard of them?' Moulton shook his head. 'Too bad. They jumped four and a penny a share. They make things.'

'What kind of things?'

'Aliments—grub. Soups, canned meals—you know. Beef stew, chicken and rice, chopped ham. And they're in medicines too. Pain relievers, indigestion tablets. They've got a lot of assets they don't use—mostly property—and they want to realize them. They *could* be used to finance your lab.'

'Pep-pills and pickles,' said Moulton. 'Why should they help me? Why should you?'

'Why shouldn't we?' said Laidlaw. 'The money's there. Look—when the merger's through we'll be big stuff—not in the top twenty yet, but on our way. We'll be image-building. Science is good for that.'

'The kind of stuff I do?' said Moulton. 'Come off it.'

'Anything,' Laidlaw said. 'So long as it's science. White coats and test-tubes and intense-looking people with heavy spectacles.'

'Just like the telly ads.'

'Exactly. But this time it won't be a fake. It'll be the real thing—and we'll have your work to prove it. Quantum's gift to the nation.'

'Whose gift?'

'Quantum. That's what we're calling the new holding company. You'll be there, working, and it'll be our money that keeps you there. . . . Or at least that's what the public will think. Actually we'll come to an arrangement with the tax people——'

'But why me for Christ's sake?'

'Two reasons,' said Laidlaw. 'You're the best—and you're available. We were rather lucky there.'

'But you know my reputation,' Moulton said.

'We're going to change that.'

'You're what?' Moulton's incredulity, Arnott thought, was totally uncontrived. In certain ways the man's naïveté was incredible.

'Well, your image, anyway,' said Laidlaw. 'It shouldn't take long. Not if we do a crash on it. What d'you say, Madge?'

'What's it got to do with her?' Moulton asked.

'Oh, she's in. Handling the P.R.,' said Laidlaw. 'Put us in the picture, darling.'

Madge Innes looked at Moulton as if he were a product with problems. The sales potential was obviously there, but the tendency to inspire sales-resistance was equally manifest.

'He's not easy,' she said at last, 'but I think we can work it. To begin with he's a local boy—and that's good. We'll start the thing up here and let it spread. Then he's a war hero, and that helps. He's also world-famous—not like an actor, but he's *known*. Genius—a wild genius. More like a poet, maybe. Behan—or Dylan Thomas. Doing crazy things when he's not working—that's his way of relaxing—letting off steam, but deep down where it counts he's a dedicated scientist, working to push back the frontiers of knowledge.'

Her voice was flat, consciously devoid of excitement. She made no effort to hide the awfulness of the clichés she uttered.

'Go on,' said Laidlaw. 'I like it.'

'Like all geniuses he's a bit naïve,' she said. 'The simplicity of genius.'

'Sancta simplicitas,' said Laidlaw. 'Oh, it's gorgeous.'

'We'll save the Latin for the Sundays,' said Madge. 'Being a simple man—and a man who sprang from humble folk to the dizzy heights of eminence he has now achieved'—her voice was no longer flat, but actively malicious—'he was guided by one principle only: to do his best for the ordinary people he loved. People like you and me. Oh, he may have been misguided and misled, but he loved them always, and worked for them. It was for *them* he worked and struggled, and lost job after job, just as it was for them he was wounded when he fought to free the world from Hitler.' She paused, the irony vanished. 'Will it do?'

'Beautiful,' said Laidlaw. 'I love it.'

'It's terrible,' said Moulton. 'Disgusting bloody lies.'

143

'Lies?' said Madge. 'I hardly think so. You were wounded fighting Fascism, you do work for the proletariat——'

'Not the way you say it,' Moulton said.

'It's the way people will read it,' said Madge. 'What's the matter? Don't you want to be liked?'

'I don't want to be smarmed over,' said Moulton.

She shrugged. 'You have to be accepted,' she said, 'and this is the way to do it. . . . Oh, just one other thing.' She paused, and the irony came back, deliberate and cruel. 'We're selling a scientist—a brain-worker. He can be wild in some things—but not in others.' She turned to Susan Arnott. 'What do you think?' she asked. 'Would you mind if you read in the paper that a scientist was idealistic and went on protest marches?'

'Of course not,' Susan said. 'That's what they're like.'

'What would you mind, darling?'

Susan thought for a moment. 'Well, scientists are good people, aren't they? I mean they're clever, but they're good. They help everybody.' Moulton winced. 'So they ought to *be* good. I mean act like it.'

'Like what?' Laidlaw asked.

'Nicely,' she said. 'You know . . . normal.'

'Married perhaps?' asked Laidlaw. Susan hesitated.

'Married most definitely,' said Madge. 'But we're covered there. Moulton *is* married.'

'Was,' said Moulton.

'You mean you got divorced and I didn't hear of it?' said Laidlaw.

'No divorce,' Moulton said. 'But I haven't seen her in years.'

'Get her back,' said Laidlaw. 'Go over to Los Angeles and *woo* her.'

'A second honeymoon,' said Madge. 'She'd like that. Any woman would.'

'I bet it's what you want to do anyway,' said Susan.

Moulton hated the deadliness of cliché, ironic in Madge's mouth, sincere in Susan's: that could take the truth and turn it into travesty.

'It's what you're going to have to do if you want that lab,' said Laidlaw.

'A baby would be nice,' said Madge. 'Babies are so normal. Think about it.'

'To hell with you,' said Moulton.

'To hell with the lab,' said Laidlaw. 'It'll have to be Morrissey.'

'Morrissey? I *trained* Morrisey,' Moulton yelled. 'He's competent when he's properly led, but he's second-rate. He won't *get* anywhere.'

144

Arnott realized then how much he enjoyed observing Moulton being outraged.

'You do it then. The job's yours,' said Laidlaw. 'Join us, old man. Quantum needs you.'

'Quantum,' said Moulton. 'You know what Quantum means to me? Nils Bohr, Planck, Kapitza, Rutherford. The best minds of a generation. And you've turned it into a tin of semolina.'

'It's semolina that drives the cyclotron,' Laidlaw said.

'Tell me something, Goofy,' said Moulton. 'That property that Aliment owns. Is it possible they sold it to you cheap so you could build more supermarkets?'

'Some of it,' said Laidlaw placidly. 'The rest they sold dear—to other people.' He beamed at Moulton. 'The best minds of a generation, I think you said. We'd settle for yours, old son. Any time. Think it over. Now if you like.'

'Now?'

'We don't *want* to rush you, but it would help if you could give us an answer tonight.'

'I've got a hell of a lot to do,' said Madge.

'Use the study,' Laidlaw said. 'I'll show you where it is. There's pencil and paper—brandy too if you need it.'

'It's no use,' said Moulton. But he went.

As the door closed, Arnott looked quickly at his watch. Eleven twenty. Jesus! Only eleven twenty. Less than four hours to recall so much. He looked up at his wife. There was a tension in her, a watchfulness on his behalf, that he had not seen since before their children were born. That time he went to see her father. . . .

'It's been lovely,' Susan said. 'But I really think we must be going.'

'Oh, please,' said Sybil. 'Not yet. Do wait a little while. I'm sure . . . Tom . . . wants you to.' The word 'Tom' made her hesitate. 'That man,' she said. 'How could he? . . . Call Tom by that ghastly name?'

'Tom doesn't mind,' said Madge. 'It's all the poor bastard's got left.'

Arnott said, 'You would be very foolish if you believed that.'

'Still in love with him, Bob?' Madge asked.

'Now? No more than you are,' said Arnott. 'But I don't hate him enough to forget what he is.' He swallowed more brandy and smiled at his wife. 'You're driving, darling,' he said.

The door-bell sounded, and there was a stir of movement in the hallway, and Laidlaw came back in. With him was a heavy-bodied man, not tall, but deft and strong, a man careless of his clothes and dress with a carelessness that came close to arrogance. Susan gasped.

'Ah,' said Fitzgerald. 'So you haven't forgotten me?'

'I'll never do that,' said Susan.

'I'm told you married Bob here?'

'That's right,' said Arnott. 'How are you, Fitz?'

'Canny,' Fitzgerald said. 'Mustn't grumble. Evening, Mrs Laidlaw. Sorry I'm late.'

'That's all right,' said Sybil. 'Have a drink?'

'Scotch,' Fitzgerald said. 'A big one. Bloody London train. Living there.' His voice was dejected. 'Bloody great barn in Belgravia.'

'You?' said Sybil. 'But why?'

'Bird,' said Fitzgerald. He drank the Scotch neatly, but in quantity. 'I'm doing murals.' He turned once more to Susan. 'You mad at me, Mrs Arnott?'

'Should she be?' Arnott asked.

'Up to her,' said Fitzgerald. 'I upset her old man.'

'He got drunk after you'd gone. Beastly drunk,' Susan said. 'Mummy and I had to look after him. It was your fault, I suppose.'

'No, love, it was his fault,' Fitzgerald said.

'Anyway I had to learn. So I'm not mad at you. In a way I wish I could be grateful—you made me grow up after all—but he's still my father.'

Fitzgerald nodded. She had made a point that to him was valid.

'I didn't feel all that proud of myself,' he said. 'Not when I saw what it was doing to him. But there again I couldn't help it, could I? There was seventeen men died when he hit that landing-craft. I knew them all—and three of them were mates of mine. I'd put it off too long as it was.'

'Mummy told me he'd been recommended for the V.C. the day before.'

'He never told me that,' Fitzgerald said. 'What did he do?'

'Saved a lot of wounded. He led a boat's crew himself. Dived in under fire.' In her mouth the phrases had no reality: were part of a dreamworld. But Fitzgerald had lived there.

'And the next day he went and did that to us. Ironic, that is.' He drank again. 'And he never said a bloody word. Well he wouldn't, would he?'

'I don't understand,' said Susan.

'Toffs,' said Fitzgerald. 'What makes them tick. Even you don't know—and you are one, so how the hell can I? Nice to see you anyway.' He nodded, and turned to the Laidlaws.

'Have you eaten?' Sybil asked.

'Eaten?' The word seemed to have no immediate meaning. 'I think

146

so. Oh, aye. I had some swill on the train.' He looked around. 'Where's Moulton then?'

'In my study,' said Laidlaw. 'Thinking.'

'Thinking,' said Fitzgerald. 'He would be. He was always a great one for that.'

'You don't approve, Fitz?' Madge Innes asked.

'Not my business,' said Fitzgerald. 'Only—where's it got him? Where's it got the bloody world he was thinking about? Time enough to think when you've learned to feel.'

'You may have a point, but I don't think I should quote you,' Madge said.

'Still at it, are you?' said Fitzgerald, and laughed. To Susan Arnott's amazement, Madge Innes laughed too. The words had sounded so *rude*.

'Perhaps I should explain why Fitz has come to see us,' Laidlaw said.

'Don't they know?' Fitzgerald asked.

'We don't,' said Arnott.

'It's a commission,' said Fitzgerald. Nice one too, or I wouldn't be here. I've come to paint Jim Moulton's portrait.'

INSIDE JOHN FITZGERALD

THEY'D had a hard night of it, you could see that. Bob Arnott looked as if he'd been kicked in the ballocks by a bull elephant, and that frilly-drawers wife of his had grown up in a hurry too. Nothing like tension for maturing people. Old Goofy looked pleased with himself, but a bit whacked, so the wife was looking pleased too. She'd be looking whacked an' all before the night was out—or he didn't know Goofy. The only one not showing anything was Madge . . . no, wait a bit. Madge had that before-dinner look when she knew the dinner was going to be something special. Usually that meant she'd found a performer—bloke with a bit of stamina—but not tonight. Tonight it meant she was putting one over that mad bugger Moulton. Ah well, she'd waited long enough for it, but it was all such a bloody waste of time. She should stick to screwing if she wasn't going to use her brains properly. Funny bitch. With a mind like that and looking as if she was trying to decide if she was a Rubens or a Matisse. If he ever painted her he'd have to remember she was greedy.

Rigmarole. Then more bloody rigmarole. Labs and cyclotrons and P.R. jobs. Cock. He could have been banging that bird in Belgravia, even listening to her talk about Larry Rivers. Anything was better than rigmarole. Only there was Moulton to paint. Nice that. The intellectual tearaway. Frustration too. Funny. He looked like a stud—only he hardly ever got any. Every time he was nearly in he talked himself out again. He could hit though. That was something to remember. He could hit like a mule—only he didn't know enough tricks, not like the commandos. So in the end you'd duffed him. Duffed him proper. Stitches and cracked ribs and a week in hospital. A right bashing. And he'd said nowt to nobody—and he'd never come back for more either. Mad sod.

And thinking. Always thinking. He could think the arse out of your breeches that one. Build bloody bombs and when he didn't fancy them he could prove it was all your fault and get mad when you wouldn't join his bloody marches or design his bloody posters. Christ, he'd got Picasso for that. What more did he want? And all that Up the Workers clart. Aye. Right up. With a jammy stick. The way he went on you'd think the miners had invented breathing and we should all pay them commission. Christ! His bloody father was a miner—and what a fucking credit to the human race *he'd* turned out to be. People were all right till they joined things—unions, churches, factories, offices, political parties—even football crowds. Then they were just lumps, masses. Like Moulton's bloody molecules. You were better off on your own—and for God's sake stop thinking about it, you're not an anarchist you're a fucking painter, you stupid bugger.

Mumble chatter rigmarole squeak. On and bloody on. And all it meant was they'd got Mad Moulton by the goolies and now they were going to give them a squeeze just to hear his voice rise. They were off their stupid nuts. Bloody Guy Fawkes plot, wanting you to join . . . All that stuff about insults. All right. Moulton had insulted him. It was his privilege. All right. His privilege because he'd paid for it—with your boot in his ribs. You could have done more—Moulton was past arguing—but a boot in the ribs was about the right price. It was fair.

'I'll take another whisky, Mrs Laidlaw.'

'Sybil, please.'

'I'll take another whisky, Sybil.'

Give her nowt—else she'll rigmarole you. Jesus, she's going to any-way. One crafty eye on the glass in case you drink too much, but carrying it all dainty—like a fucking Hebe.

'And what are you working on now, Fitz?'

Oh, Jesus, not the work in progress bit. What did *Art and Artists* say you're doing?

'The murals? People mostly. It's the way you organize the masses of course. And the colour. Colour's tricky. It's got to be right. You know. Significant.'

That's got her off. Significant form and colour. She's memorized bloody Roger Fry. A bit old-fashioned, aren't you, hinny? Nice though. Bit small but a canny build on her, like a robin on a diet. Red breast. No. Not red you daft bugger. Ivory—touch of yellow. But warm. She'll have good tits—but Goofy wouldn't let her. She's a fucking asset—like his factories. If I ever paint her it'll be in a dress designed by some poof Eyetalian.

'I love the way you get your figures sort of floating in space. That gorgeous sense of . . .' rigmarole mumble.

Jesus, they do go on. Think about Moulton. Father-and-son pic-ture. Good that. Do a cartoon maybe. The mad sod in a pit helmet and the old bastard in Doctor of Science robes. Maybe he'd belt you one again. Belt you. Back in 1941 that was, and you'd left the com-mandos and gone to sea—deckhand—because you'd had some ideas about Mexico. And you'd been right. Jesus—what a country. Specially south of Vera Cruz. That jungle. Greens that were almost black; black that was almost purple. There'd been a nightmare of pigment in that 'almost', but he'd got it at last, painting the same bloody landscape fifty, sixty times while the Dagos were practically organizing trips to come and look at the mad Englishman. *Loco.* Well, it looked like it. Every cent he'd made when he was paid off from that floating madhouse of a Greek tramp. Captain with D.T.s and a poof bosun used to perform in a ballet-skirt—then six months' graft on the same subject and tortillas and beans and chillis that cut your tongue out. But in the end he'd got it—and the others came easier—though nothing ever came easy, and if it did you would worry. When it's easy you end up a fucking P.R.A.—and back to New York. The dealers all thought he was a clever sod because he went to New York, stupid bastards. He'd gone to New York because that was where the bloody boat paid off.

Hallo, she's going. Thinks you're drunk. About time you were—all this rigmarole.

New York was all right then. Get to New York. Learn the bugger. No place to paint though. Not for you. Jackson Pollock maybe: not John Fitzgerald. Not a bad place then though: not like now. Bop was going then. Bebop. Bebop she bam she deedle bop. Good kind of music for what you'd been doing. Purple black. Energy. Feeling. In '47 you could still go down to Harlem. You'd gone. Found a girl. She worked and you didn't—made no bloody difference. She expected it. Three kids an' all. And they expected it too. A marvellous fuck though, and feed you to bursting. Southern style. Fucking or eating. Yams and okra and collard beans. Pigs' feet and chitterlings. Red devil sauce. Hot—Christ. You had to start doing lightning portraits to keep yourself in cold beer. Up on 112th Street by the shoeshine parlour—*Living Portraits. Only 25c. Satisfaction Guaranteed. One Quarter. Be the Envy of your Friends for Only Two Bits.* Funny. There were hackies and short-order cooks and stillroom maids wandering around with bits of paper they could sell for fifty dollars—if the poor sods had hung on to them. It'd been good—and better when the pictures clicked. In the Village that was. The Renoir Gallery. What had poor old Jean done to them? Partners. You had to laugh. Geoffrey the queer one, and Roy who ran home to his missus every night at six and caught a dose of clap off a high yaller when his wife went off to see her mother in Chicago. Partners! Jesus. They'd even lend each other paper-clips. But they'd sold the first of his pictures—and Geoffrey had fancied him. 'Oo Fitz. You're so brutal. So masterful, darling.' What the hell. It cost him nothing and it helped to sell his pictures. When he'd told the coon she'd roared her head off. Then the first picture went, then two more, and this geezer from Park Avenue swooped down in a Cadillac and gathered him up and poor sweet Geoffrey cried himself to sleep. Schloer. There was a name for you. Sounded like a drunk talking rigmarole. Schloer. Not even

150

Schloer Gallery. Just—Schloer. Clever as a wagonload of monkeys—but cheerful with it. Jew with Jew jokes. Couldn't tell a Geordie from a Hottentot—but he knew his pictures—and his money. Christ, you were rich, and the coon had a mink stole.

Then it started. John, my sweet angel, you must paint me some more. I haven't got any more.

John, darlink, please. I'm begging you . . .

He was about as camp as a boilermaker's underpants, but he always talked like that. The clients expected it.

. . . John darlink. Don't make trouble. Look, I tell you a story.

Good act. Good stories come to that—only the coon never got the point.

Two Jews are sentenced to be shot—in Mexico—in the *Revolution*, darlink . . .

What's two Jews doing in a Mexican revolution?

Making uniforms. What else? So they are marched out—left right—and they are tied to a post each man—and the rifles of the firing squad are aimed—very dramatic: the drums roll, prrrr—when suddenly one Jew says, 'I demand a blindfold,' and the other Jew says, 'Sh. Don't make trouble.'

Crafty sod: he knows you'll laugh.

So please, darlink. Don't *you* make trouble little joy-goy. *Paint* me some more pictures.

Ah, hold on a minute. What's he think you are—a bloody Mexican Gauguin factory? So you went to Vermont instead and cut a new seam and Schloer loved those pictures so much darlink he wanted you to take out papers. So you went back to England bloody fool, where nobody had ever heard of you. What d'you think you are anyway? A fucking patriot? You missed the coon too—and the kids. Nice kids they were. There'll be four of them by now. Another boy mebbes. Black Panther if he's got any sense. You're daft to join anything but if you have to do it—join what's for you.

Back. But not right back. Moving on really. Mexico —Vermont—then Tyneside because you're ready for it. All that bigness—that's easy: shipyards and pit heaps and that; but now you're ready for the subtlety *inside*. Like that mad bastard's father. Took a lot that did: worse than the fucking jungle. Cantankerous old sod. Jumpy bugger too. Wanted a piss if you showed him a picture of a puddle. Then this Lord High Executioner son of his comes touting his conscience like it was his tassel. Worse than bloody Queen Geoffrey. Come and have a drink and I'll prove to you how wicked the world is and you are too for letting it all go on. Hiroshima and Korea and the C.I.A.—and all he gives you back is a brown ale. With Geoffrey at least you got Manhattans and California burgundy and sirloin steaks you'd never even heard of before. Impossible steaks that flopped over the sides of the plate.

Half of brown ale—and he wasn't even a bloody poof. Or maybe he was—inside. A bit rosy anyway. Brother. Comrade. It wasn't all that far to darlink—not the way he said it.

Then it was time to stand your corner. *Buying* the bloody stuff just so you could stand there and be lectured at. That was when you wanted to hit him. He didn't want to hit you till we got on to his da.

'Gives the wrong idea of pitmen,' he said.

'It's what he's bloody like.'

'I'm not denying that.' Fucking marvellous! You knock the old bugger to his face and all he does is agree with you. 'All I'm saying is you're not helping any of us if you paint a picture like that.'

'Any of who?'

'Us, man. The workers. The lads in here.' He waves his bloody arm round the pub—two old-age pensioners and a day trip from Shotton, sneaking a sly one while their wives queue for chips. 'The lads in here, you and me.'

'If I make your old man look like a hero, it'll help this lot here?'

'A bit,' he says. 'It'll get the image right. Anyway he is a hero. All miners are.'

'If he's a hero it's there—and if you want heroic statuary go to the Moscow Underground. Your da *is* that bloody picture.'

True that. That's why it hurt him. That's why he started on me—with no da at all. What d'you expect anyway? The old girl was on the batter long before I was born. Norwegians.... Daft on Norwegian sailors. Bet I'm a bloody Olaf an' all. Half anyway. So on he goes—on about your mam till you said we'd better settle it outside and you went to the Salt Pans. Full of memories that was—for him anyway. He'd been on about the place since you first played tiggy round a lamp-post. Riot Acts and demonstrations and Righteous Wrath and Militant Action. Mad sod. Anyway that's where you went to the scene of his triumph and now he was going to do it all again and hammer you. Militant Action against decadent artist: righteous worker triumphs for the cause.... Only he didn't. He had guts and he had stamina, but he knew nowt. Not for the advanced class anyway. Just bull charges and windmill arms—Ferdinand and Don Quixote—Disney and Daumier—with a couple of nobby fists on the end of them. Bang in the gut and your boot raking his shin and your hand at the side of his throat (thyroid was it?) when he came forward. Then down the bugger went and you put the boot in—enough, not much—and you went back to the pub and drank more brown ale and thought what a waste of bloody time. Then you had another one and thought, Still he asked for it, and listened to the ambulance bell. . . .

And here he is now. Jesus—he looks worse than the last time. They've worked you over, you mad bugger—you and Bob. Sod them for that. Bob's all right. He's not joining things all the bloody time. B.M.A. because he has to, and after that he's happy on top of frilly drawers. But you—just look at you. You're like St Paul on the road to Damascus, man. Struck by lightning. No. Bloody banderillas. Ferdinand the bull. And El Goofy coming in for the kill. Olé, Goofy—and mind where you're sticking your espada. Come on, get on with it, you stupid sods. It's all a waste of fucking time.

TWO PAIRS OF STAR-CROSSED LOVERS

It was not going to work: he knew it wasn't. The whole trip was a colossal waste of time: time that could have been better spent on . . . The racing thoughts stopped there: the runner at the end of the precipice. There was nowhere to go: if he didn't get that lab there was nothing to spend his time on. And he wouldn't get it. Tracy would see to that. Tracy would stay exactly where she was—and Goofy would wriggle out of his deal, his revenge complete. He would face nothing, because nothing was all there was, and Goofy would have the laugh he'd worked so hard for, Morrissey would run the lab. Nothing. The thought of the inactivity frightened him. Without his scientific work there was only politics, and nobody wanted him for that either. Even Harry Lewis had turned him down. Nothing. When he was a child, just starting to feel his way into pure mathematics he'd tried to imagine nothing, not to realize it as an intellectual concept, but actually to visualize, experience it in his imagination. Infinity had been easy; infinity was stars; galaxy after galaxy, drifting across his mind in random patterns for ever and ever. Amen? But nothing: nothing eventually became his nightmare. You took a pair of scissors and a piece of paper—and somehow in his mind it had always been black paper—you cut the paper in half, then halved the half, then that half, then its half, over and over, till you had to use a scalpel and microscope instead of scissors, but always, no matter how often you cut, there was a piece left over. Small, tiny, microscopic. But always something there. Something tangible. Knowledge just couldn't be. It had taken all the powers of his newfound logic to overcome what his imagination told him was impossible. Now logic and imagination alike told him he was wasting his time.

He looked down at the ground, twenty-seven thousand feet below, and there was the Grand Canyon, just as the Boeing's captain had promised them there would be, a shaft sunk deep into the endless plains and mountains. Hot dogs, he thought, and marshmallows round the camp fire, cowboys and dudes and transistor radios. And selling. Always selling. Heinz and General Motors and Dupont—ask your Friendly Finance Company for when you go broke. Even there. In that incredible upheaval of the earth, the most beautiful joke Nature had ever played, that was still a miracle no matter how explicable it was. Even there they sold and advertised and ballyhooed. They never stopped.

The fat man beside him heaved and stirred like a disturbed swamp. He was lucky all right. Only woke up when food or drinks came round, then passed right out again—as if the food were full of meprobamate. He'd even slept through the movie. And yet when they took off in New York that had been all he'd talked about, with an obscene gusto that was curiously innocent because it was so obviously ineffective. Its blonde star had inspired him to heights of salaciousness that had embarrassed Moulton, yet in the way he had described her, the proportions of her flesh, the creaminess of her skin, the breasts like cupcakes, he'd made her sound edible. He'd even called her a dish. But the real food had the stronger pull. He'd eaten everything in sight then slept. Maybe he dreamed of edible blondes.

Moulton couldn't sleep, couldn't work either, what was the point, when nothing was so near? But it was important, it was essential, that he should think about Tracy. Edible Tracy. There had been times when he had considered her that, though she might not be up to the fat man's exacting standards. Not enough cream, not nearly enough; but all there was smooth and firm and tender. Not dairy produce at all. More like a steak maybe. But that wouldn't do either. She had nipples like cherries. You read that in books, but hers really were. Steak and cherries—maybe you could get that, in Hawaii or somewhere, but it sounded ridiculous. He had no talent for metaphor. Leave that to Bob Arnott, but don't start thinking about Bob. Not *now*. Think about Tracy.

Tracy in the shower ,Tracy cooking with a deft unconsciousness that reminded him of his Aunt Sarah, despite the glaring contrasts of their kitchens, Tracy riding a bike, tongue out, brow wrinkled in concentration, as if a bike had a Jumbo jet's complexity, though she could handle a Cadillac with ease; Tracy reading. Those books. Those bloody books. Stanislavsky and Tynan and Granville-Barker. Got right up his nose. Even Brecht. His attitudes were right, his politics were right, even his emotions were right, and yet he couldn't stand Brecht. His people were all so *wrong*, and wrong in a way he couldn't verbalize. The irony of it, when Tracy raved about him. Tracy, who didn't believe in one thing the man stood for. And when he'd tried to argue, to explain, it was all 'But I thought you believed' and 'But you always say'—and how could you argue with that? Because he had believed, and he had always said, and so they had a row about it. Tracy having a row. That was the one he remembered most clearly. She hated rows, but she'd had a talent for them. She could hit and hurt more accurately than he. It was only because she hated them that he'd managed to win so often.

And because he was stronger than she. He liked to finish things, and used all the strength of his mind and body: she said it was be-

155

cause he couldn't bear to lose an argument. They had had enough, God knew. About politics, about religion, about love. And about money too. Over and over about money. About not accepting cheques from her father, about driving a Ford when a Buick cost so very little more, about the money she spent on clothes, and the money he didn't. Money had dominated their quarrels and their lives together almost since the honeymoon. She could never understand how he hated money, and her involvement with it. Once he had got her to read William Morris's story of the future in which money had become so obsolete that it is only vaguely remembered: something for scholars to study in their specialists' museums. She had seen no point in it. For her, money was an obvious and necessary part of life, as inevitable as food.

The fat man stirred again, nudging Moulton into an awareness that his mind still wasn't working for him. The quarrels were over—they had to be—now was the time to remember happiness. But the happiness he could remember best didn't involve Tracy at all. He had been happy in Libya, looking up at the unending stars while beside him his platoon lay, relaxed, vulnerable in a sleep so sound because he was their lieutenant, or looking at the sudden riots of colour the desert can provide—ochre red rock, silver sand, the green explosion of a palm tree. The only thing he could have talked to that maniac Fitzgerald about—and never had. The greedy bastard. Wouldn't even try to help the people he belonged to, the people who had made him. . . . Stop it, man. Stop it. Get back to happiness. In the labs. At Cambridge, M.I.T., London. That was happiness; no—that was ecstasy. The initial inspiration: the solitary exploration of an idea, the slow disentangling of relevance from irrelevance, the mathematics like music, lab work tense as drama, slow ritual of publication. Hypothesis, experiment, proof. There had been a happiness that only a tiny fraction of everyone who had ever lived could even begin to understand. Leadership and science: he'd found happiness in both—and both were solitary occupations. He was happiest alone, and Goofy Laidlaw knew it, had made it part of his punishment. And yet he had been happy with Tracy—dammit, he must have been. In the early days . . .

She had had a vital quality. Among that crowd of second-rate actors, all of them automatically trying to dominate the scene, she had succeeded in dominating without trying at all. The rest had done it on technique—not a bad technique, since they were working, but not the greatest, or what were they doing in Vermont?—but Tracy functioned on vitality alone. She had so much of it. Vitality, zest, élan. All the active words, the busy ones, whose business was fruitful.

They had just performed *Major Barbara*—he had seen it that night—and she had directed it. Next week they were going to do *The Doll's House*, and she was going to play Nora. He had seen the rehearsal. They were at a party. House beautiful. Split level, shingles, Old Colonial furniture, a garden as big as a municipal park, and meadows behind it full of cattle: the expensive kinds, Friesians and Guernseys and Ayrshires; and one Charollais bull in isolated splendour that looked as if it could have charged a tank. Their host had called the fields his home farm, and laughed—but looked forward to the day when he wouldn't be joking. An advertising man, a big one. Madison Avenue crash helmet and clothes imported from England; but that night he wore a plaid shirt and jeans—just like everybody else—and told actor after actor how much he hated dressing up. Actor after actor looked bored: they loved dressing up. Then he told them how ephemeral Madison Avenue was: the true core of life was here, by your own house, by your own farm. This, he told them, was reality. And the actors still looked bored. Reality held no interest for them.

Tracy said, 'How savage you look.'

'I've been listening to our host,' he said.

'You could hardly help it,' said Tracy. 'He never lets up.' She looked at the empty glass in his hand. 'Let's eat.'

Already she was keeping him out of trouble.

They went to the barbecue pit, the only part of the garden that wasn't illuminated, so that the red glow of the charcoal lit only what was near, leaving the rest in a warm, rich darkness, and even there the vitality pulsed inside her, an almost tangible force. It was incredible that she'd never made it. She'd had everything there.

'Steaks,' she said. 'We must have steaks.'

'Don't you people ever eat anything else?'

'Our host's own beef, Doctor. His very own. Come on now.'

He laughed then, and took a steak. There were potato chips and salad and a table on the lawn that had got itself isolated because it was badly lit, and actors cannot bear to be badly lit. She sat down and began to eat at once, carbohydrate and protein to fuel all that vitality. Then a man appeared in the half-light and put a bottle of wine and two *cunning* Italian wine-cups on the table.

'That feller works here. He's a servant,' said Moulton.

'Your exquisite reason, sir knight?'

'He's better dressed than the rest of us.'

Tracy put down her knife and fork. 'You're a little naïve aren't you, Doctor?' she said. 'He's also a Negro.'

'The first bit was supposed to be funny,' he said.

'The first bit was funny. The second bit was serious.'

'I wish you wouldn't call me Doctor,' he said. 'Makes me sound as if I'd been writing prescriptons all day.'

'Let me tell you, sir, doctors are very respected in this country. They make——'

'. . . a lot of money. I know. All the same, if you don't mind?'

'O.K., James,' she said. 'I don't mind at all.'

'Not James either. Jim.'

'O.K.—Jim. What's wrong with James?'

'It's a footman's name.'

She laughed then and drank wine—more fuel for all that vitality. Later they had walked away, down to the meadows in the night's soft darkness, a darkness so still that they could even hear the breathing of the sleeping cattle. He hadn't touched her, hadn't even held her hand, when suddenly she said, 'I really think you should kiss me now.'

He hadn't even thought of doing so. The vitality to him had represented not sex but potential achievement. The women who excited him were big, laughing, lazy: like Madge Innes, not like her, so that at first he was clumsy. Her lips tasted of steak and wine: her mouth met his eagerly, softening, but not yielding. She would never submit. Not even when his arms tightened round her so that she gasped.

'You're different,' she said. 'Different all the way.'

'What you on about?'

'What you on about?' Her voice was a deft, mocking imitation of his own. 'Even your manners.'

'I didn't think I had any.'

'You don't,' she said. 'That's what's different. And my God, you're strong.'

'I'm sorry,' he said.

'Don't be. Control it—and be glad.'

The kiss and all that led up to it had been her doing, so that for once in his life he had been passive, a follower—and unsure at that. Unsure even that he had enjoyed the kiss that said so clearly: 'No submission. Only equal terms.' And that was the pattern for the rest of his stay there. When performance and rehearsal permitted they went out together—to inns, movies, on walks, that she suggested and he agreed to. And her kisses never varied. Always kisses, never more. He never asked for more. He was still unsure, because she was different too, from the three Cairo whores, the frustrated wife of a miner paralysed in a pit fall, the female postgraduate who were the only sex he knew. Big women, opulent women. Not like this one at all. Sex hadn't been the main reason, not at the beginning anyway. He

158

had responded to that eager vitality of mind, as if she'd been a mate of his, the kind of raw young bloke with an unschooled intelligence who gave him the most satisfying kind of emotional relationship. He didn't want to think about that.

The chief hostess's voice sounded then, soothing, innocuous as a chocolate malted, full of good cheer about weather reports and time. It was five p.m. in California, and wasn't that nice, the voice implied. Time for a cocktail before you face the delights of the freeway. The weather was fine too, sun shining at a temperature of seventy-eight degrees, as if God and Southern California had come to a special relationship. Beside him the fat man ponderously heaved as the undercarriage rumbled down, the Boeing tilted for its long descent. Below him freeways rose to meet him, expanding as he watched. High rises, factories slipped by him, a deserted drive-in movie looked like a monument to man's futility, and still the Boeing nosed downward till the tyres gripped the runway with a smooth, accustomed care, reverse thrust came and went, and the Boeing taxied to its waiting terminal.

'Nice to meet you,' said the fat man, and stood on his toe as he left. The hostess too offered him sweet, uncaring farewells, and he walked out to find a redcap and his luggage—and his first real worry. Would his wife be there to meet him? The time-lag had caught up with him now—in New York it would be close to eleven at night, and he had the first faint consciousness of fatigue. Fatigue could never cope with that informed vitality.

She was in the main hall by the cocktail lounge. It was the first time he had seen her in a mini-skirt, and he found it shocking. The prettiness of her legs and thighs in no way mitigated his sense of shock: other women could expose themselves if they chose, but not his wife. Anger struggled with fatigue. It was going to be a bad start.

'Hallo, Jim,' she said, and kissed him on the cheek. There was a sense of caution in her, but that was to be expected. It was the weariness that dismayed him, as if she had played this scene over and over to the point of boredom that could develop only into despair.

'Hallo,' he said. 'You're looking well.'

'I'm fine,' she said.

'Pretty, too.'

'I never look pretty,' she said.

They walked across the reception hall, wary as fighters in the first round of a return match. It was true. She never looked pretty: never could. That vitality did, on rare occasions, flower into beauty, but for the rest of the time it existed in its own right to be prized only for its self.

Behind them the redcap trundled the luggage-truck, supremely bored. A married couple having a spat. About all that ever happened in the terminal, except when they were shooting a movie. He began to whistle, but not too loud. Whistling soothed a man's nerves, but sometimes it affected the tip, especially in the middle of a quarrel. Better just to look at the woman's legs, the way her skirt slid up that cute little ass as she walked. Except he wanted to whistle, so he whistled—softly, and the doors flew open, the heat hit them and they walked towards their car. A Cadillac convertible, man. He cut out the whistling.

'Yours?' Moulton asked.

'Dad's.' She waited in silence while the redcap stowed his luggage in the boot, then her hand dipped into her purse and she gave the redcap his tip, received his Uncle Tom smile in return, as valueless as Confederate money.

'There was no need——' he said.

'You wouldn't have known how much to give him,' she said.

It was true enough. He'd probably have insulted the poor sod as well. Tipping revolted him.

She got in behind the driving-wheel, opened his side. The tinted windscreen shielded his eyes from the sun, the overstuffed seat cosseted his back. It pushed into the traffic with about as much noise and fuss as a well-maintained sewing machine. Dreamboat. Passion-wagon. On the freeway it moved up to seventy without even trying, the mechanics about as perfect as human ingenuity could make them; all that skill and brains to power a monster, a salmon pink parlour on wheels. There was America for you: brains and technology no one could match, and conspicuous waste straight out of a Marxist textbook. He looked across at Tracy. As she drove the thing her skirts rose higher, almost to her crotch. The bloody minis were all part of the world's craziness. Why couldn't she wear pants? Or even those godawful Bermuda shorts? He looked away again, waiting till she found her lane on the freeway before he spoke.

'Where am I staying?' he asked.

'Our place.'

'I told you I didn't mind going to a hotel.'

'That's right,' she said. 'You did. But you didn't ask me if I minded.'

'Do you?'

'Yes,' she said. 'I do. I really do. We're supposed to be finding out if we're still married, right?'

'Yes,' he said.

'How can we possibly do that if you're living in a hotel?'

'You could live there too,' he said.

'Oh, no. Oh, my God, no. That married we're not.'

'So we go to your parents' house?'

'That's right.'

'And find out if we're still married while your parents watch?'

'It won't be like that,' she said. 'Not this time. I promise you.'

'You expect me to live in Bel Air and act normal?' he asked.

'You never act normal.'

The words were cool, but not angry. A statement merely.

'Your father must have been doing very well,' he said.

'Burbank to Bel Air?' The smile, as always when she spoke of her father, was mockingly affectionate. 'That's better than all right, darling. He's made it.'

The 'darling' could be discounted. That was just Hollywood claptrap. But the content was important.

'Made what?'

'It, lover. The *big* it. One zero zero zero zero zero zero.'

She flicked a glance at his face, overtook a truck, straightened out. Weight and power squeezed out like toothpaste.

'You would have been happier if I'd told you I was pregnant,' she said.

He tried hard not to show his feelings: it wasn't on. He always showed his feelings. If that podgy bastard Schiller was a millionaire he'd had it. He couldn't compete. Not with that.

Her father had vitality too—where else would Tracy get it? Not from her ma—not from her Ladies' Guild Imported Wedgwood Book of the Month Club ma. Vitality was her old man's department: her bouncing, screaming, grab-it-now old man. Squandering his energy like a gambler scattering chips. Coffee and hero sandwiches and quarts of ice-cream while he yelled down the phone getting fatter and fatter. Choice lots and superior homes and developments with style. Vitality gone to waste: more than that. Vitality turned to evil. Built-in obsolescence; shaded contracts; suckers. Add 'em all up and it comes out a million.

'That's some competition,' Tracy said. 'Think you can handle it?'

'It doesn't surprise me, anyway,' he said.

It didn't. If Schiller hadn't made a million he'd have burst by now.

'He's made me into a princess,' said Tracy. 'Are you going to turn me back to a goose-girl?'

He had dragons, too. Cold-eyed men with uniforms that owed nothing to the city or county: men with long .38s at their hips and blackjacks imperfectly concealed. They stood in front of the entrance to the canyon where her father lived, and looked at the sticker on her car, one of them by the door, another at Moulton's side, well clear of the bonnet, a third behind them in a Mercury hardtop. A classic cross-fire, Moulton thought, and looked in the driving mirror. The geezer in the Mercury had an automatic rifle. . . . But the sticker was in order, and the two men in front of them smiled their servitors' smiles to a Cadillac convertible and a house in Bel Air; one of them pressed a button and a gate sprung open, a triple-mesh gate with a live-wire on the top and the Cadillac whispered through because noise was vulgar.

'Welcome to Jacaranda Canyon,' Tracy said.

A twisting road; eucalyptus, jacaranda, palm. Behind them lawns, green, lush, close-shaved, as obvious a sign of wealth as the Cadillac itself, the sprinklers scattering diamond-drops in ironic symbolism. And every quarter of a mile or so the houses—the *homes* you had to remember to call them: if a cantilever split-level failed Corbusier people-factory could be called a home. No Hollywood-imitation Loire châteaux here. No Spanish castles with Cotswold thatched roofs. This was functionalville. Ferro-concrete and steel and tinted glass. Launching-pad modern. And sometimes it worked. It worked, Moulton saw, in Schiller's place, an elegant curve of tinted glass that caught and retained the sunlight till it glowed like jewels: light that echoed the olive trees and cedars and the pool's unwinking sapphire: light that could even live with the lawn's true green and the never-ending flowers. They pulled up on the car-port, between an Alfa-Romeo and a Rolls-Royce with a custom-built body by Hooper. Tracy glanced across at it and chuckled.

'Dad bought it yesterday,' she said. 'He wants you to feel at home.'

'It looks as if jokes are expensive this year,' he said.

'Baby,' said Tracy. 'Baby, baby. You've got to realize something. Dad can afford it.'

Almost he believed that she was trying to help him.

They had eaten California grapefruit and sirloin steaks from Chicago and tossed salad and babas-au-rhum. They had drunk Californian wine because Schiller had no patience with de Gaulle, and if Schiller's self-denial left the old man back there in Colombey-les-deux-Églises unmoved, the Republic of France was still out ten bucks. Now they were drinking Armagnac because even self-denial has its limits and where else would you get brandy anyway? And Moulton was sitting, sipping Armagnac as he marvelled. For Schiller had moved on. That much was obvious. From a noisy irritant Schiller had evolved into a brooding threat. The noise now was reserved for minor irritants, like France: to major issues, such as his daughter Tracy, he brought a new and unnerving quiet.

The funny thing was that it didn't please his wife. ('Call me Adèle,' she had said first time they had met, detesting him.) Mrs Schiller—Adèle—had been the one for culture so far, prettily apologizing for her husband's noisy money-hunger the while. Adèle was the one who read books with hard covers, and bought reproductions of Gauguin and Van Gogh. Adèle had been to the theatre in New York—and not just to musicals either. In London she had even been to the Old Vic, not once but several times. Adèle was culture in the Schiller family, and that culture, she told Moulton bitterly, she had bequeathed to her daughter. (The bitterness had nothing to do with her bequest. Whenever she addressed her son-in-law, Adèle's voice was bitter.) Moulton accepted the bitterness as he would have accepted a punch on the cheekbone if he could land one in the gut in return: and with Adèle he usually could. Adèle was an easy target, who had given Tracy nothing. There had been nothing to give. Tracy had culture—if you had to use the word—because she had turned her energies to it, and now old Schiller it seemed was doing the same, coached by his daughter.

Schiller had chosen the house, commissioned the garden, right down to the olives and cedars that had to be transplanted there to give the place that lived-in look. Schiller had started buying pictures: a Jackson Pollock and an Ivone Hitchens glowed at Moulton where he sat; jewels inside a jewel. Schiller had chosen the music they listened to on the Hi-Fi as they ate: music for the harpsichord by Scarlatti, suave and polished, exquisite flattery for the rich at table. Moulton bet he'd even chosen the dinner. And he enjoyed it. Moulton, exhausted—the time his body responded to said four in the morning, though his watch said ten o'clock—could not avoid the realization of Schiller's happiness. The man was exultant. He had even lost weight. No coffee and cream, no quarts of strawberry and vanilla; he had even refused the babas-au-rhum. Not that he bored on about calorie counts, or how to balance protein against cholesterol: he was too happy for that. He had his daughter, his house, his land, his music, his pictures, even his dinner to enjoy.

Moulton doubted if he enjoyed his wife. To respond to Adèle's subdued gloom would necessitate a rarity of taste Schiller did not possess. Adèle was unhappy. In this temple of sensuous delight Adèle was unable to worship. It was all too real for her, Moulton thought. Too genuine. Adèle liked her culture ersatz, the feeling filtered, the impact cushioned. Here her senses were battered by an honesty too great for her to bear. Brought up on ketchup, she was too late to adjust to sauce béarnaise. It seemed to Moulton that Schiller regarded her as he had regarded a Kokoschka he had bought. An early mistake: a fault of his own exuberance. All right in its way, but not for Jacaranda Canyon. It didn't fit. He had been sat beside Adèle too. The two of them facing Tracy and her father. Impermanence facing solidity. Suddenly, the mind unbidden, Moulton found himself thinking of Goofy, and the hopelessness of his task. Faced with a million dollars, you can't just put your head down and charge.

'Well, that's about it,' old Schiller said. 'You've got the whole history of the place. What do you think of it, son?'

Don't let 'son' fool you, Moulton told himself. He makes it a pejorative word, the kind he throws at elderly Negroes.

'Splendid,' Moulton said. 'Everything's splendid.'

He had to say it. Even the bastard's clothes were right: lightweight grey pants, blue linen shirt, covering a stomach flat and hard as a board; hard and colourful, like his palace.

'No faults?' said Schiller. 'No gripes?'

'Not so far,' Moulton said.

That was better. Schiller had thought it was going to be easy; but it wasn't going to be that easy; and now he knew it.

'Show you the rest of the place tomorrow,' he said. 'When you've rested.' The sneering kindness of that last word. Strong men need no rest. 'It ran into money, of course.'

'Of course,' said Moulton, and Schiller paused again, remembering that even insults have to be paid for, when presented to his son-in-law. Then suddenly he laughed, and this was new too.

'Commy bastard,' he said, but without anger, without even conviction. There was only laziness, and a tolerance very hard to bear.

'Fred!' said Adèle, the note of rebuke exactly as Moulton had remembered it, but with the dismay stressed more than ever. This was a temple after all: Pollock and Hitchen were present.

'He knows what I mean,' said Schiller.

'He means everything's meaningless. His money—my convictions. Everything. He's wrong.'

Schiller looked up at him again: eyes bright and hard. Still no pity—Christ, who wanted pity? But at least there was respect.

'You were all grab, even at school,' Madge Innes said.

Fitzgerald said, 'You're quoting.' She nodded. 'Moulton?'

'That's right.'

'Mad bugger,' he said.

Soon it would be necessary to get off this bed that was so wide and comfortable. Soon it would be necessary to deny himself the tactile comfort of her left breast, round and splendid in his hand, the nipple delightful in its responsiveness. It would be necessary to get her off the bed too, out into the studio, back in the pose: and she wouldn't want to do it. She'd rather lie there and talk till he was ready again. When you got down to it, Madge was a lazy cow. The fact that she knew her stuff just made his work more difficult: he had to fight not only her but half himself as well.

'Were you all grab?'

'For grub I was.'

'Grab for grub. Grubby grabber. Greedy feeder grabbing grub. How Joycean we are.'

He slapped her thigh hard enough to make her yell.

'Never mind the culture,' he said. 'I was hungry so I grabbed.'

'Hungrier than Moulton?'

'He could eat his books.'

'And you?'

'I was after life. Not reading about it. Doing it. You get hungry if you do that.'

'Food . . . liquor . . . women . . .'

'Blokes,' he said. 'Anything. . . . Funny.'

'Why funny?' she asked.

'Queer then. You know. Strange,' he said. 'It's all paint really.'

'Now you're misquoting Turner. Art—it's a rum business.'

He slapped her again, and again she yelled. 'Stop that,' she said.

'Don't quote,' he said. 'That's culture an' all.'

Unheeding. No. Not even that. Not hearing. And hurting her. *Her.* A world of his own; all the time. No one can get in. That was worth more than a couple of slaps.

'Why does he hate you really?' she asked.

'I thumped him,' he said. 'He's a bad loser. So am I, come to that.'

'How?' she asked. 'How did you thump him?' And he told her. 'Oh I like that,' she said.

Her hand touched his inner thigh, moved upward, teasing, playing.

'He wanted to marry me,' she said. 'I was fifteen and he went off to war and he never said a word. I suppose I was supposed to *guess.*'

'He came back,' said Fitzgerald.

Ten minutes. I can wait ten minutes. The light'll be better. And stop that, you bitch. It's bloody marvellous.

'To university. Like a monk. Saving it all for his protons and neutrons. He used to write to me. Then he got his research fellowship. That meant he was worthy of me. You'd have thought he'd won his bloody spurs.'

'You should have told him to piss off.'

'Don't you remember how beautiful he was?'

Greedy bitch all right. Greedy as hell. But she was right. He had been beautiful. Big and beautiful—and lost. Like Lucifer in that long-winded *Paradise Lost* thing—worse than bloody Latin—he'd read when he'd been gone on Blake. Her fingers still moved. He put his hand over hers, slowing her rhythm.

'He came to see me,' she said. 'He'd brought an engagement ring.'

'Right out of your bloody women's mags,' he said.

'Well . . . not exactly. I was in bed with a bloke called Larry.'

'You shouldn't have opened the door.'

'We'd forgotten to lock it,' she said.

'Mad bitch.'

'I don't know why I'm telling you all this. I never told anyone else.'

'Because I don't bloody care,' he said.

'Child of Nature, how shrewd you are. And I don't want you to care. I only want you to listen.' Then she sensed his restlessness, turned in towards him, pleasing him gently.

'He gave Larry a terrible beating,' she said.

'And you lay there and watched?'

'He . . . beat me too.'

'It's a risk you take for being so generous.'

'I'd never realized—a naked man has no chance at all.'

'Catch them with their pants down. It's the first thing you learn.'

'And Larry had lost half a lung in Korea.'

'He should remember to lock his bloody doors then.'

'You know it all, don't you?'

'I can take care of Moulton. Fully clothed or bollock naked.'

'I wish Larry had. Moulton blacked his eye, knocked his teeth out, kicked his ribs——'

'Not his goolies?'

'I was screaming,' she said. 'Then he hit me. He was hitting me and I was screaming and he was crying.'

'Mad bugger.'

'Then he talked. I was trying to look after Larry and he talked. On and on. We should have been hand in hand, fighting the class struggle, working for the overthrow of capitalism. He thought he was talking about love. It was all fighting. Then Larry said he would kill him.'

'Too busy, I suppose?'

'Larry had pride,' she said.

So he was the one, was he? You've got pride yourself when you say it.

'I talked him out of it—but it finished us.'

'Call the coppers?'

'How could I? I was running a woman's magazine.'

He looked down at himself. She followed his gaze, and grinned.

'All right,' he said, 'but after this you pose and I paint.'

Her body moved, the heavy curves rich but pleasing as she mounted him, but he didn't respond.

'He should have kicked that Larry in the goolies,' he said. 'You know what I think? Looks to me as if Moulton's a bit of a puritan.'

Damn you, Fitzgerald. What a time to make me laugh.

The time-lag had really got to him this time. Always before he had slept it off: twelve, fourteen hours in a blackness deep as a shroud. But this time he had dreamed a nonsense of protons, neutrons, electrons, dancing in elegant patterns to the music of Scarlatti. All the atomic particles in the world, changing, reforming as the elegant notes clipped out. And he, pure Spirit, the sun his throne, the moon his footstool, had looked down on the dance and rejoiced because on all the earth there had been no places, no people: only neutrons, protons, electrons, changing, reforming. In the morning he had hated his dream, but not enough, he told himself. Not nearly enough.

In the morning he had drunk California orange-juice and coffee, eaten dollar cakes with maple syrup, listened to Adèle. (Schiller had left for his office hours ago: black coffee, dry toast; Tracy was playing golf with some weirdo called Andy. He had to be a weirdo. Adèle approved.) And he had breakfast with Adèle. They had opened a glass wall of the breakfast-room—look, you press a button: it whines and slides—and now house and garden were one, green lawn smooth to the edges of parquet, sun sidling in like a good servant, cautious not to hurt the eyes of rich people. But even so, Adèle sat in the shadows. You can't trust *any* servants nowadays. Not even Filipinos who live in: not even the sun. A live-in Filipino brought fresh coffee, and Adèle sighed. Adèle sighed well: she'd had lots of practice.

'Who is this Andy anyway?' said Moulton, and she sighed again, a big one: her pas-devant-les-domestiques sigh: lots of brio.

When the door closed she said, 'Andy is a very, very dear person.'

Moulton thought: you are protons, neutrons, electrons, but you are a human being too. I will not let you defeat me.

'I mean what does he do?' he said.

'Andy? Why he's in everything. Golf, the country club, his yacht.

And he's a hunter too. One year he went clear up to Canada. Moose, I think that was—or some kind of bear.'

'For a living?' said Moulton. 'What does he do for a living?'

Don't yell, he told himself. Yelling is unfair to this one—even foolish.

'Andy? Oh Andy doesn't *work*.' Adèle laughed, but not very well. Laughter was an unfamiliar exercise. 'He just doesn't.'

'Rich?'

'Rich? Oh, my. I should think *so*. His family's one of the ... insurance, you know? and banks? and oil? But not vulgar. Certainly not vulgar. Andy has taste. And humour. A very well-developed sense of humour. Andy is lots of fun.'

'That's nice,' said Moulton.

'Oh, very nice. Everybody says so. He's devoted to Tracy.'

'That would be nice too—if Tracy wasn't married to me.'

Moulton, you stupid fool. Why do you say these things?

'Divorce isn't a crime in the state of California,' said Adèle. 'It isn't even a social handicap.' He'd asked for that one, but as he watched her he could see her wishing she hadn't said it.

'It's up to Tracy,' he said, and she said, 'That's very true.' They were back where they started.

'Your husband's looking well,' he said.

'Fred's fine,' she said. 'I mean so healthy—all that weight—it wasn't good for him. But now he's lost it he looks so much younger. Don't you think he looks younger?'

'Yes,' said Moulton. 'He does.'

'Do I?' The words were anguish, terror: a cry for help.

'You're looking fine,' he said.

'Why, thank you,' she said. 'I take these pills, you see. Three times a day, imagine. Over five dollars each for pills. Rejuvenation.'

'They're working beautifully,' Moulton said.

Each of them knew that he was lying.

'It's difficult,' she said. 'Men like you—and Fred.'

Moulton said, 'I don't understand.'

'You both travel so fast,' she said. 'Sometimes I think it would be better if a man stayed in one place for a long, long time.'

It occurred to Moulton that his mother-in-law had been drinking.

It occurred to her daughter, too, when she came back from golf. Adèle was told it was time for her nap and whisked upstairs before Moulton had time to open the door. It was time for him to change anyway. He had to lunch with Schiller at the Beverly-Wilshire, and that meant a tie. It meant another shower too, if he was going to be fresh enough to face Schiller. When he came down again Tracy looked him over quickly, expertly, the director's look that could tell at once if the clothes fitted the part. It seemed he would do.

'Nice,' she said. 'Very nice. Who's been looking after you?'

Laidlaw and Innes: image-builders.

'It's easy,' he said. 'You just go into Simpson's and wear what they tell you.'

That was it: the chat was over. She waited for him now to start on Adèle. Stupid. You didn't start on victims.

At last she said, 'Adèle's drinking.'

'Yes,' he said.

'You don't mind?'

'I mind,' he said. 'It isn't my business.'

'You have suggestions perhaps?'

'Analysis?'

'We've tried that. She says booze is more fun.'

'I think she's trapped,' said Moulton. 'Trapped and scared.'

'Trapped I've heard—but scared . . . scared of what?'

'Of your father,' Moulton said. 'Scared of keeping him, scared of losing him. She's scared either way.'

'That cold analytical intelligence,' she said. 'So accurate, and so displeasing.'

'I can't help it.'

'I'll drive you to Wilshire Boulevard,' she said.

'You don't have to.'

'Dad asked me to.'

So it was orders. They went in the Alfa-Romeo, that snarled in Italian, and argued all the way about Vietnam.

She left him at the door and the doorman saluted her, and Moulton went in past a painted Sicilian cart in the lobby that reminded him of bitter battles over ground like flint, olive trees and malaria and the prodigal ruins of the Greeks. Behind him the drugstore, and three hundred voices all convinced that the movies were coming back. Just one more *Sound of Music*, that's all it needed. Just one. Just one. In the bar, so cool, so very dark. Why did Americans turn the lights out to drink? Did it all stem from prohibition when the booze was so nasty they couldn't bear even to look at it? And Old Schiller, not looking old at all, grey suit with a fine red stripe, white shirt, red tie striped with grey, and a redhead who might be brunette next week, but the figure would still belong in *Playboy*'s centrefold. Schiller saw him and the girl was alone in a place where unescorted ladies are not allowed. She gulped at her martini.

'What'll it be, son?' Schiller asked.

They were back to that again. Look, man, why bother? Your wife's done it for you.

'Scotch and water,' Moulton said. 'No ice.'

'No ice,' said Schiller. 'I remember.'

The drink was enormous, the liquor strong after the stuff in English pubs. He looked at Schiller's glass.

'Tomato juice,' he said. 'That's new, isn't it?'

Schiller slapped his stomach, pleased at its flatness.

'I like my gut the way it is,' he said, and the redhead passed him, smiled and left.

'My secretary,' said Schiller. 'I've been working right to the minute you got here.'

Pull the other one, Schiller. It's got bells on.

Schiller drew him over to a window-seat, leaned forward, and suddenly the aggression was gone, his eyes were lit with an insincerity so patent that Moulton wondered how anybody was ever fooled.

'Tell me, Jim. This trip of yours—what's it all about?' he asked.

'Tracy,' said Moulton. 'It's about Tracy.'

'Sure, sure. I appreciate that.'

'And me,' said Moulton. 'It's about us getting together again.'

'You really think it's a good idea?'

'I do. Yes,' said Moulton. 'But I don't know if Tracy does. I've come to ask her.'

'You gave her a rough time,' said Schiller. 'When she left you that kid was really broken up.'

'I was feeling pretty bad myself.'

'Yes sir, she was in rough shape. Marriage gone, career gone. It took *time*, Jim. Lots and lots of time. And patience. And understanding. Things only her dad could give her.'

You bastard. Stop quoting soap-opera.

'And time was the most precious commodity I owned. Time was money, sure—but it wasn't just money. Time was what made more money. Time—why, in the real-estate business it's raw material. But I didn't grudge Tracy a second. She's my child, after all.'

What the hell was Adèle then? An incubator?

'And I was rewarded for it. I made the money anyway.'

'So I've seen,' said Moulton.

'Some,' said Schiller. 'Not all. I've got shares in orange-groves, Jim, in the trucking business, electronics. I've got a private plane and a place at Lake Tahoe. You wouldn't believe the things I've got. But most of all I've got Tracy—whole and well and happy to be home. And now you want to take her away from me, and start it all again.'

'That's only half true,' said Moulton. 'I want to take her away—yes. She's my wife and I want her with me. But I don't want to start anything.'

170

'She's your wife,' Schiller echoed. 'You want her with you. That's nice, Jim. Frank and manly. It has style. But I ask myself two questions. One: since she's your wife, why have you kept away from her so long? And two: why do you want her with you? Let's try a third: what's happening now that hasn't happened before?' He rose as Moulton finished his whisky.

'Come and have lunch,' he said, 'and we'll talk about it.'

The lunch Schiller chose for him was exquisitely cooked, decorously served, elaborate and long. Schiller himself had a salad and a steak done rare. While they ate, he talked about Tracy, her abilities and talents, her successes of the past. ('And she's still a young woman, Jim. Young—but more mature. What she's done once she can do again—and better.') There were her wit and charm too, her impact on the unattached male. ('I tell you, Jim, the phone never stops. But she's done right by you—you must know that. You know Tracy.') There was her love for her father too, and her dependence on him, after the terrible things that had occurred. ('But we won't go into that side of it, Jim. We want to stay friends, whatever happens.') It was only with the coffee that he got back to his three questions.

'You got to admit I played fair, Jim. I've given you time to think.'

'I kept away from her so long because I needed time, too,' said Moulton.

'Time for what, Jim?'

'Time to heal, like Tracy.'

'Oh, come on now. You saying that you were hurt, too?'

'That's right.'

'You're saying that poor, hurt little girl made you ill just like you made her?'

'I'm saying exactly that,' said Moulton.

'Son, I just don't believe you.'

The booming insincerity switched off: they were back to aggression again.

'That won't get us anywhere,' said Moulton.

'I don't *believe* you.'

'All right,' said Moulton, and rose to go. 'Thanks for the lunch.'

Schiller said, 'Sit down.'

'Say please,' said Moulton.

'All right then. Please.'

Moulton sat.

'Is "please" such a big victory? Did you get anything out of me I couldn't afford to give?'

'I'd better,' said Moulton.

'Tell me.'

'Cut out this "I don't believe it". Just let me tell it. Don't interrupt.

'O.K.'

'She hurt me too. I needed time. I'm all right now—and you tell me she is, too. That's fine. If she hadn't been I wouldn't have stayed. Why do I want her with me? Because I need her—and because she needs me, unless she's changed more than you've told me. What's happening now that hasn't happened before? I'm admitting it, Mr Schiller, to her, to myself, to you, to anybody who cares to ask.'

'And I'm in Dunn and Bradstreet.'

Moulton said, 'I don't know that one.'

'Last year I grossed over a million dollars. You get a copy of Dunn and Bradstreet, you could look it up.'

Moulton laughed. 'I don't think we'll count that one, Mr Schiller,' he said.

'That's right,' Schiller said. 'You never asked for money. Not once.'

'I never will,' said Moulton.

'What's your angle then, son?'

'Everybody has to have an angle, I suppose.'

'Not everybody, no. Not even most people. But you do.'

He looked at his watch.

'Your secretary waiting?' Moulton asked.

'Secretary?' Schiller chuckled: a zestful, innocent sound, that belonged to a Schiller that Moulton knew nothing about; a man pleased with his life and even—incredibly—at ease with his conscience, remembering an innocent yet satisfying pleasure. 'You know darn well she's not my secretary.'

'Why tell me, Mr Schiller?'

'Because you won't tell Adèle.'

'You know me that well?'

'I have to. You're after my daughter.'

'You have an angle too,' said Moulton. 'This lunch, this talk, saying please, hearing me out. It's all an angle.'

'That's right,' said Schiller.

'Will you tell me what it is?'

'It's Tracy,' Schiller said. 'She made me do it. Now you're one up on me, son.' He rose. 'The Rolls is outside. Harry will drive you home.'

Harry was a Negro who drove fast, well and in silence. He said nothing to Moulton, and answered the gate guards in monosyllables. It was clear that when white men didn't frighten him they bored him.

He went up to his room still weary, his brain dulled by food and wine. Nothing stirred in the house. No Adèle, no live-in Filipinos. No Tracy either, till he got to his room. She lay on his bed, her hair damp from the shower. She wore a robe of white towelling and her legs, her neck, looked brown against it. There was a cigarette in her mouth and she squinted through its smoke at a treatre magazine, but her absorption in it, he knew, was an actress's. As he watched he saw her hand was shaking.

'Nice lunch?' she asked.

'A gastronomic experience,' he said. 'What you after?'

'You,' she said.

'Don't make jokes,' he said. 'I'm too tired to enjoy them.'

'I'm joking then?'

'You have to be. Servants all over the place——'

'It's their afternoon off.'

'Your mother——'

'Mother has passed out cold. We call it migraine. Take your clothes off.'

'Tracy, for God's sake——'

'You don't even like it very much do you? You never did after the first few months.' She sat up in bed, tugged at the belt of her robe. 'But like it or lump it, you're going to do it this time, lover—if only to oblige me.'

She had been sun-bathing naked for weeks. Her body had an even golden tan.

'Like it?' she said. 'Dad built me a private patio so I could get like this and integrate with the servants.'

Moulton took off his jacket, began to loose his tie.

'That's what I like to see,' she said. 'Action.'

He kicked off his shoes, fumbled with shirt buttons.

'You're coming back to me?' he asked.

'That's what I'm here to find out,' she said. 'Get those pants off, sweetie. We're all broad-minded here.'

When he was naked she said, 'My, my. Some of us are out of practice. Never mind, lover. Just you come here. Momma knows how to fix it.' Then later: 'I guess momma doesn't. But you've got to admit she tried.' She stood up, put on her robe. 'What's the matter with you anyway?' she said. 'Am I that hard to take?'

'I'm sorry,' he said.

'Jesus, you should be. You just insulted me.'

She moved to the door.

'Let's try again,' he said.

'It won't be any use.'

'Please,' he said. 'I want you to try again. Please.'

It was the unfamiliar word that did it. She took off the robe once more and lay beside him, her face hidden in his shoulder so that he should not see her despair.

He was in the studio at last and painting. Christ, those curves. Like they'd been poured in a mould and allowed to set. And the flesh tints were right too. No need for any wish-fulfilment. No bloody poetry. Just what was there: what he saw was there. Bit cold in that north light maybe—but she had a couple of oil-stoves, and all that beautifully distributed fat.

'How long?' she asked.

'A minute. A minute.' He didn't even hear the words: it was what they always said. When they broke it was seventeen minutes later. He could see the teethmarks where she'd bitten her lip not to cry out.

'You're a tough one,' he said.

'Is that how you're painting me?'

'It's part of it.'

She huddled inside her quilted dressing-gown.

'Tough and beautiful,' she said. 'Like Jim Moulton.'

'Do us both a favour,' he said. 'Talk about something else.'

'All right,' she said. 'Let's talk about you.'

He poured her coffee laced with rum: sweet as molasses, scalding hot. With that inside her she'd be good for another hour at least.

'What about me?' he said. 'I'm painting you. That's me.'

'That and a big cock.'

'Don't talk dirty,' he said.

'Did I shock you?' She looked delighted.

'It might get me started,' he said. 'And I'm too busy.'

'That's all you do—paint and . . .' she hesitated '. . . go to bed.'

'It's all I'm good at. I drink a bit too. That's relaxation.'

'Moulton——'

'Back to that, are we? What about him?'

'You're bisexual, aren't you?'

'Is that why you're keen on me?

'Never mind,' she said. 'It's true isn't it?'

He leaned forward, loosed the big button below her breast, opened it, pulled on the lapel. Her breast swung out, the nipple bridled to the cold air.

'I didn't ask you to prove anything,' she said, but he was already back at the easel, the brush in his hand.

'Rosy Fitzgerald,' he said. 'I don't bother much now with fellers.'

'Why not?'

'They take up too much time,' he said. 'All that "Do you love me?"

and "You're different. Tell me I'm different too." Worse than bloody women.'

'Did you ever fancy Moulton?'

'That sod?'

'The word has its relevance,' she said.

'All that suave pedantic wit. You've been talking to Goofy.' She scowled at him. 'No. Not Moulton.'

'Too muscular?'

'Too spiritual,' he said. 'Like a bloody Ariel with muscles. Once he started on about the suffering masses he wouldn't know *what* you were doing to him. Wouldn't care.'

'But you're going to paint him.' He said nothing. 'Because he's spiritual?'

'That's part of it,' he said.

'What else?'

'Don't try to get me to analyse,' he said. 'Because I won't.'

'All right. But if he's so bloody spiritual, why did he fancy me?'

'You're a lot like his Aunty Sarah,' he said.

Child of Nature, why must you be right every time?

But aloud she said, 'That dumpy old bag?'

'You've never looked at her,' he said. 'She's strong. She's beautiful. And . . .' The words left him.

'Go on. Please,' she said.

'She fights. Like one of those bloody Amazons. The way a man fights. I don't mean blows. It's ideas—attitudes. Everything.'

'And I'm like that?' she asked.

'You could have been,' he said.

Her gasp of dismay went unnoticed. His whole mind was on mixing pigment: the words he uttered were accurate noise.

Madge said, 'What you're saying is, the way I've turned out I'm not like that at all.'

This time her voice pierced his concentration. He put down his palette and looked at her.

'Is that right?' she asked.

He looked puzzled. 'You know it is,' he said. 'Let's have your gown off.'

'She took her time about it, because her fingers were clumsy, and naked her body suddenly assumed a hunched, vulnerable look which he didn't want at all. Wearily he tried to undo what she'd just asked him to do.

'You turned out different,' he said. 'That's nowt to cry over. Now is it?'

'I don't know,' she said.

*

They'd had the golf-scene. Eighteen holes subjected to Andy's piti-less analysis. Now it was the arts, and the arts meant television, and television meant Andy telling the jokes he'd heard and getting them wrong. He looked at the others. Adèle, sober after four hours' sleep, was listening as if his voice were dollar bills set to music; Schiller was listening as if he were going to get Andy to invest: and Tracy . . . with a shock he realized that Tracy was listening as her father listened. Andy had something she wanted, and listening, among other things, would get it for her. It would be as well to find out more about Andy, but the voice was a water torture, on and bloody on.

'So this guy—the first guy I mean, said, "Would you let your daughter marry a Negro?" and you find yourself thinking: My God. On a comedy hour. I mean discussing inte*gra*tion. And then the sec-ond guy, you know the other one—the one that used to have a moustache, didn't he, about two three years ago?—doesn't matter. It's not that important—Well, anyway, the other guy says, "Certainly not. I've got nothing against Negroes. Certainly not," he says, "I've got nothing against Negroes." D'you get it? I mean, integration didn't come into it. The guy was knocking his daughter.'

'The second guy,' said Moulton. 'The other one.'

'That's right.'

'The one that used to have a moustache.'

'Right again.'

Moulton gave up.

There was brandy on the table, because Schiller had put it there. Moulton hadn't gone near it. Schiller put down brandy the way the Afrika Korps put down landmines. Because it exploded. Into rows. Preferably with Tracy, but even a quarrel with Adèle would count against him. He looked at Adéle. She had a coke. That would be Schiller's doing. No boozing while Andy's around. But Tracy was refilling her glass. It was a hard way to earn what you wanted. Listening to Andy. It was hard to have lived through the afternoon, too. Naked and perfumed, and nothing happening, no matter what she did. But Christ, it was bad for him too. How did she think he felt? Not being able to act like a man. All that wanting and willing—and nothing happening. Maybe it was this house, that was so full of Schiller it was like trying to do it with the old man looking on. . . . Suddenly he became intensely aware of the brandy decanter. It was a modernistic thing, a tall shaft of perfectly blown glass with a circular base. The brandy decanter was very important, so impor-tant that Andy's voice disappeared into the background, harmless as the buzzing of a bee in a garden. The decanter had information: vital information. He knew it as he always knew these things. His hands were sweating and yet his body was shivering slightly. It was the excitement of knowing that his subconscious mind was on to something, and that something might, with luck, come to the surface of his consciousness. This was his gift, his Muse, the thing that put him in the top rank. There were literally thousands of first-class physicists, but only a handful had what he had, when the palms sweated, the body shivered. And it was all there; in that decanter, if only he could see it. It had something to do with the tray on which it stood. The decanter was a nucleus——

The very word was a trigger. Simultaneously Moulton recalled his dream of the dancing particles and saw the relationship of tray, decanter, and the glasses that surrounded it. The dream, or rather the edited part of it, the part that had validity, was factual. If he used the cyclotron, the thing would work. It was all a question of changing the atomic rate. Maybe if he used alpha particles for that—old stuff, almost an obsolescent technique it was so slow—but slow or not it worked. It would give him what he wanted till he could think of something better.

'So the first actress said to the second actress, "Who are you calling a Thespian?" Now I don't get that,' Andy said.

'It must be one of those in-jokes,' said Tracy. 'If you don't join the crowd you don't get it.'

Her father snorted. Adèle said, 'I think you're right, dear. It's silly making jokes for just a few people.' She looked sharply at Moulton, suspicious as always that he belonged to every in-crowd going. But Moulton's face was serious. Adèle relaxed. And then he stood up. He was preparing to leave. In front of a *guest*. Really, that *man*.

'Can you excuse me just a minute?' he said. 'There's something I've forgotten to attend to.'

Schiller didn't like that, but Tracy said, 'Go right ahead.' There had been times before when she'd done that, when she'd understood. Wonderful times. He left, only just not running.

'What the hell's got into him?' her father asked.

'Something,' she said. 'Something important. It's what happens to geniuses.'

'You mean that guy's a genius?' Andy asked.

'Certainly not,' said her father. 'He's a pretty bright guy for a teacher, that's all.'

'He's not a teacher,' said Tracy.

'He was when you met him.

'That was just to make eating money. Actually he's a research scientist.'

'So he stinks out a lab,' said her father. 'Come on, Andy. Tell us about your yacht. Where you thinking of heading for this year?'

'I only ever met one genius in my whole life,' said Andy. 'He owes me eighty dollars.'

It was a warm night: no breeze. The scent of the flowers was heavy, in the darkness the cicadas chirred away, loud and distinct as cicadas in movies. They were always there, shrill and significant before the night attack when the cameras cut from faces registering determination to close shots of hands preparing weapons. That was probably accurate, too. In Sicily, Italy, Normandy, Belgium, it had probably been like that. His hands fiddling with the Sten gun's magazine, reaching down unbidden to feel for the handle of his combat knife. Cicadas and bowels loosening, fingers trembling, adrenalin flowing. No. Not Normandy, not Belgium. In Normandy there were grasshoppers, and in Belgium it had been too cold. Christ, it was cold there. Dead men frozen. To trees, to doorsteps, even to burned-out tanks. Old men some of them, and some just kids. Good-looking kids too. Sturdy, brave. Bloody lethal. Come out hands up and a stick grenade up their tunic. Kill themselves and kill you. More like Japs than Germans. So you never let them get too near—that was what the Sten was for. And sometimes they didn't have a stick grenade, but you didn't chance it. You had to think of your blokes, the ones who relied on you, and did what you did. You were the captain after all. Their sins were yours; because they trusted you. They hated Fascism like you did, the best ones: the politically aware. But even the others, the boozers, the ones who chased women, they were more than your company, your responsibility. They were your mates. Your own kind.

He moved to the pool. It was lit from beneath, and there were chairs beside it, half in shadow. The blue light glowed in the darkness, warm, welcoming. Light, warmth, Hollywood. When this fucking war is over I want—Lana Turner and a barrel of beer, Hedy Lamarr and a valet called Jeeves, Betty Grable and a coal-mine of me own. No matter who they were, when it came to sex they wanted Hollywood. Water-slick cuties swimming in a pool, just like the pictures. They'd all wanted it, some of them had died wanting it, and he was the one who'd got it. For a while, at any rate. He was also the one who'd rejected it. He thought of the dead ones: Adams, Birkinshaw, Smith 063, Shorty Stevens. If they'd known about it they'd have thought him mad. But he wasn't mad, only possessed, and that was perhaps an even harder thing to bear. When you're possessed—you know all about it.

Moulton became aware of a black shape in the darkness. It moved closer to the pool and became an azure Andy.

'Hi,' he said.

178

'Hallo,' said Moulton.

'Tracy and her dad are playing chess,' Andy said. 'I said I wanted to talk to you. They said O.K.'

'What's Adèle doing?'

'There's a movie she wants to watch. *The Moon and . . . Sixpence*? Is that right?'

'It's right for Adèle,' Moulton said.

'I hope I'm not disturbing you or anything.' Moulton said nothing. 'I mean you were so still—I thought maybe you were . . . meditating?'

'I was thinking about some people I used to know. They're dead now.'

'That's too bad.'

'It was also the war.'

'Yeah—Tracy told me you'd been in the war. I was too young myself.'

'You sorry you missed it?'

'Yes,' said Andy. 'I am.' There was defiance in his voice. He'd been over this ground before, and obviously this had been the wrong answer.

'You might have got knocked off.'

'Knocked off? Like killed?'

'Exactly like that.'

'It wouldn't have made all that much difference—except to me,' Andy said.

'And whoever gets your money,' said Moulton.

'My money? I don't even get it myself. My money's a trust-fund. When I die it goes on to my sister's kids, and when they die it goes on to theirs . . . or mine—if I have any. You know something—my money will still be going on when there aren't even people around.'

'I dare say the computer will spend it.'

'Yeah,' said Andy. Then: 'Hey that's a joke. A genius-type joke.'

'Are they saying I'm a genius?'

'Tracy is.'

'Schiller?'

'He doubts it. If you're a genius it makes it a lot harder—so naturally he doubts it.'

'Makes what harder?'

'I'm stupid,' said Andy. 'Oh boy, I'm stupid.' He paused. 'You don't deny it. Usually they deny it on account of I'm rich, too.'

'You were stupid in the house,' said Moulton. 'You're not stupid now.'

'Now you're saying things because I'm rich. The insult's just to show you have integrity. I've met your type before.'

Moulton said, 'Forget about your money.'

'You should write for television yourself,' said Andy.

'Try to put it to one side then. Just listen and think. You *were* stupid in the house. All that golf and television. It was worse than stupid. But here——'

'I get nervous,' said Andy. 'Oh boy, I get nervous. And then I have to talk. And people listen—on account of the trust.'

'. . . but here you were making sense.'

'I think I was. Funny. You know, strange. It was on account of you I got nervous.'

'Do you have to say "on account of" so much?'

'What should I say?'

'Because.'

'Oh,' said Andy. 'All right. I was nervous because of you.'

'Because of Tracy.'

'That's right,' said Andy. He stopped then, moved from one foot to the other.

'Sit down,' said Moulton. 'You're getting nervous again.'

'That's right. I am,' Andy said. 'I can feel myself wanting to talk stupid.'

'If you sit down you won't see me so well,' Moulton said. 'That'll make it easier.'

Andy sat, staring straight ahead into the pool.

'You're right,' he said. 'You must be a genius.' He stiffened. 'I'm in love with Tracy, Mr Moulton.'

'You've called me Jim all night,' said Moulton. 'Why get formal now? Are you going to challenge me to a duel?'

'Wouldn't that be something?' Andy laughed, delighted. 'Unless it was pistols. Then I'd probably kill you. I'm a very good shot. I don't miss, Mr . . . Jim. Never have. That's why I should have been in the army.'

'You love Tracy'

'Honourably,' said Andy. 'I want you to understand that. Honourably. If you two divorce I want to marry her.'

'You mean you tried the other way and it didn't work.'

Andy bounced to his feet on the words, so that Moulton, rolling out of his chair, hands ready to grab, was seconds slower. Andy didn't take advantage of it, but stepped back, fists cocked, waiting for him.

'I didn't mean that at all,' he said.

He moved in, weaving in some weird way of his own, and Moulton swayed to take a left on the muscles of his shoulder. It felt like a love-pat. Andy followed it up with a terrible right, fist wrong, arm wrong, stance wrong, and Moulton brushed it impatiently aside.

'You really meant that,' he said.

'Certainly,' said Andy, and moved in again.

'Knock off,' said Moulton.

Andy threw another left, and he took it on his forearm.

'Knock off.'

A right this time, signalling its intentions like a rapist. Moulton grabbed the fist and threw Andy, very carefully, on to the lawn behind him.

'Will you listen?' he said. 'I wanted to apologize.'

Andy got up then, brushing at his clothes.

'I'm glad you said that,' he said. 'Anyway I'm no good at fighting.'

'You're terrible,' said Moulton.

'I guess I am. You're pretty good.'

'I've had lessons, said Moulton. 'Why don't you?'

'There isn't time,' said Andy. 'Don't you understand?'

'Tell me about it.' Moulton motioned to a chair, and they sat.

'I want Tracy *now*. And you're what's in my way, Jim. The opposition. And she says you're a genius and I know you can fight. You're quite a man, Jim.'

You should have seen me this afternoon, Moulton thought. Me and my all too honourable love.

'Why tell me all this?' he asked.

'Because I like you,' Andy said. 'I really do. And because I'm going to beat you. I'm sorry, Jim.'

'Wait till it happens,' said Moulton.

'Oh, it'll happen all right.'

The certainty of his voice was ridiculously unnerving.

'Why?' Moulton asked.

'I'm going to buy her—and her dad. He wants me to invest in his business.'

'I thought you had a trust.'

'I can do what I like with the interest, Jim. You ever figure the interest on a sixty-million-dollar trust? What it can borrow?'

'All right,' said Jim. 'Schiller's a poor millionaire and you're a rich millionaire, and there's nothing wrong with you that money can't cure. All right. I believe you. I saw it coming anyway. But that's Schiller. You're not trying to tell me you can buy his daughter too?'

'But I can, Jim. Not for cash, but I can buy her.'

'What with, for Christ's sake?'

'A theatre,' said Andy.

Experiment to prove which Fate will decide more important: a cyclotron for Moulton or a theatre for his wife. We took a spring balance. In one pan we placed a cyclotron, in the other a theatre ...

'It's what she needs, Jim,' Andy said. 'What she needs most. To help her. Besides being what she wants, I mean. And I can give it to her.'

'You're not stupid at all,' said Moulton.

'I'm certainly not bright—let alone a genius. But money's all I've got. I guess I couldn't help learning how to use it.' He got up then. 'That's what I came to tell you, Jim. I'd better be going now.' He moved towards the pool, became again blue Andy.

'I'm sorry about the fight,' he said.

'That's all right.'

'I guess it is. You won—dammit. Be seeing you, Jim.'

He moved again, turning at once into shadow, then blackness, then part of the night. A nice, well-meaning, honourable feller. Money hadn't touched his niceness, or his honour. It had made him a bore when he was nervous, and it had stopped his mind developing as it should have developed, but it hadn't stopped it developing altogether. Andy could still think, simply perhaps, but clearly enough. A theatre of her own—it would be like buying him the California Institute of Technology. It was everything. She could act, direct, train other actors, other directors, commission plays ... all the daydreams she'd had when he'd first met her, all the aspirations that had been systematically knocked out of her when they'd married, because his Muse was a selfish one, and couldn't bear a rival in the same house, never mind the same bed. But they were more than aspirations: they were needs. To take them away was to change her—as he had changed her: to turn her vitality into argument, rows, reconciliations; all the stereotyped farce of china-ornament-throwing and kiss and make up instead of work: valuable, creative work. The denial of a right. The denial of a basic tenet of his creed. 'From each according to his ability, to each according to his needs.' He'd never even let her realize her abilities, but Andy would. He wondered how much interest sixty million dollars yielded a year. A million and a half? Two million? Even after tax—and his trustees would make sure he paid the minimum of that—there'd be the hell of a lot left over. And probably some crafty corporation lawyer would set it all up as a cultural enterprise, or whatever the jargon was, and they'd escape tax anyway. She'd have everything she'd ever dreamed of, and he'd be left with nothing. No Tracy, no cyclotron, Goofy had made that plain; and without equipment, his Muse was valueless.

DAY IN NORTHUMBERLAND; NIGHT IN L.A.

THESE places were all the same. It could have been Hamburg or Kobe or Minneapolis: the architecture would give you no clue. Not ugly, yet by no means beautiful. Designed so as not to draw attention to the frantic activity going on inside it; discreet as a valet. Contemporary ... functional ... inoffensive. It could have been a students' union or a palace of the nations of the free world or a Trade Union H.Q., instead of a complex of labs. If the experiment failed, it might yet become one of those things. Tallish, squarish, a cantilevered roof. Space for a lawn round about, and statues inside the lawn: something modern but not outré by a trendy R.A. ... But this wasn't Kobe or Minneapolis or Hamburg. This was Tyneside. A fact of which the architect seemed unaware; either that or one which he'd resolutely ignored. The building was screened by trees, real trees that had grown there for a century at least, not the orderly rows of pines that looked as if they'd been planted by a mathematically minded sergeant-major, and beyond the trees was a headland. That was the sum contribution the architect had made to aesthetic; a negative one. The building couldn't spoil the view from the sea. But Tyneside was the sea. Not only should the building not spoil the sea-view, it should enhance it.

If one were to walk past the trees to the headland one would see it: grey quickening to green where the shoal-sands waited, dull against the piercing blue of the sky, that bright sky that comes only to northern waters. Yet it wasn't a dull sea. Row after row the whitecaps would be lifting, gleaming like sugar-icing, the nearest tossing up a spray that would flash like diamonds in the hard sunlight. There would be gulls too, wheeling, planing, screaming their outrage when the whitecaps teased them; and ships, always ships, eager for the harbour. They built them so big now. A hundred thousand tons, a hundred and fifty, two hundred. Ships long as streets, wide as factories, but reduced by the sea's immensity to their proper scale, their proper value. Reduced already, by their very nature, to the need for a pilot—the pilot boat bobbing like a toy under their lee—their need to make harbour, to nestle between the twin arms of the piers that reached out to protect them. ... And there were still the small craft too: foy-boats, tugs, seine-netters. Boats with a jaunty beauty that told of the dangers run, the fitness of each craft for its purpose. The men who sailed such craft might well be blackguards, they were certainly heroes, who accepted danger and hardship as the inevitable price of freedom. The architect had ignored them too, and their boats, as he'd ignored the dun-yellow sands, the freakish, lordly heaps of rocks, the vivid orange of the crumbling cliffs. He'd built a box of the fashionable size and shape. It was what he'd been paid for.

'Like it?' Laidlaw asked.

'What a question,' Madge Innes said.

'Now, now,' said Laidlaw. 'Enthusiasm is the keynote of the day.'

She sighed. 'All right ... who says the North-East is backward? Who says we're being left behind in the race for new industries, new development? Yes—and new beauty, too? We've all heard them, the knockers, the stick-in-the-muds. ... Well—next time *you* hear them tell them to go and look at the new Quantum Laboratory at Marburn Bay. The building alone cost three-quarters of a million. England's leading architect designed it. Quantum's gift to the people of the North-East, a mark of respect for the practical yet go-ahead folk who know a good thing when they see it. That's why they eat Aliment Foods—the only foods that are scientifically wrapped to keep in the flavour, keep out the germs. ... Shall I go on?'

'I could listen to you for ever,' said Laidlaw. 'Such lyricism.'

He looked again at the building.

'It's pretty awful, isn't it?' he said, then: 'No, I'm wrong. It isn't even pretty awful. I wish it were.'

'Potatoes without salt,' said Madge. 'It tastes of nothing.'

'Ah, well,' said Laidlaw. 'It was cheap, anyway.'

They walked down the makeshift path that led to the main door, passed through from sunshine into fluorescent light still afflicted with nervous tic.

'Those bloody electricians,' said Laidlaw.

'Now, now,' Madge mocked. 'They're practical yet go-ahead folk too.'

'Not when it comes to wiring,' Laidlaw said.

They moved past the office-block, the vast lab, two floors high, big as a theatre, that housed the cyclotron: a thing so huge that it had had to be installed first, the building completed around it.

'That's the weirdest-looking piece of P.R. I've ever seen,' she said.

'Getting nervous?' he asked.

'It's a sprat to catch a mackerel. I know that,' she said. 'But when did you ever see a sprat that size?'

They went on to the place where the technicians would eat. Here the problem was one of nomenclature. What do you call a place where technicians would eat? 'Cafeteria' is square, 'canteen' insulting. Yet 'dining-hall' might inspire delusions of grandeur. At the moment she was working on 'refectory'. The academic overtones might compensate for the prevalence of chips.

They climbed a spiral staircase that swirled to an office-block. In the main office tables had been set out; cocktail snacks, a bar. Aliment Foods had given of their plenty, but there were salmon, asparagus, caviare too. And Scotch of course. Whole crates of it, for today was Press Day and the Parliamentary Secretary was flying from London. Laidlaw looked round at the waiting plates, the eager rows of glasses. Men in white mess-jackets, girls in mini aprons stood relaxed as runners waiting for the start. A nervous catering manager hovered, but Laidlaw didn't call him. It was all satisfactory. He helped himself to a caviare-smeared biscuit. Beluga—and quite delicious. So it should be, the price it was. He moved the plate farther back, then turned to Madge.

'You won't have one?'

'Not yet,' she said. 'When I do it'll be the whole pot.'

'New boy-friend?'

'Don't be nosy,' she said. 'You don't have to be with me. I'm on your side.'

She turned away then, and a man came in: neat-suited, brisk, carrying his bag like the badge of office it was. Bob Arnott. Laidlaw hurried forward.

'My dear Bob,' he said. 'How nice to see you.' He looked at the bag. 'But I didn't invite you here in your professional capacity.

'My car lock's broken,' Arnott said. 'There are drugs in this.'

'We'll put it in the *safe*,' said Laidlaw. 'I'm sure we have a safe. Come and get a drink. We haven't seen you since our little dinner. He's neglecting us, Madge.'

Arnott said nothing.

'I think he is,' Madge said.

'Here.' Laidlaw brought Champagne. 'For the chosen ones. Good of you to be so early, Bob.'

'I've got a patient near by,' Arnott said. 'Sorry if I'm too early.'

'My dear Bob. I said it was *nice*. And so it is. Where have you been hiding yourself?'

'In my surgery.'

'And where have you been hiding Susan?' Madge asked.

'She sends her regrets. She couldn't come,' Arnott said.

'Couldn't?' said Laidlaw. Arnott sipped Champagne.

'Very nice,' he said.

'She couldn't go to Sybil's for tea either.'

'She's rather busy.'

'Sybil called her three times.'

185

There was no look, no signal, but Madge went to check a pile of P.R. handouts.

'She's avoiding us,' said Laidlaw.

'That's right.'

'But my dear man—why? Didn't she enjoy our little dinner?'

'Of course she didn't.'

'Of course not. Stupid of me. How could she? But didn't she find it useful?'

'I think the word she used was futile. And cruel, of course.'

'Cruel? My dear Bob—it was positively surgical. You of all people should appreciate that. Surgical—and useful, too.'

Arnott said, 'I must confess that aspect of it had escaped me,' his voice as lightly mocking as Laidlaw's.

'But think, my dear fellow. Isn't it always useful to know who your friends are . . . and your enemies?'

Arnott put down his glass. It was still almost full.

'I'll thank you for that then,' he said.

'Bitter,' said Laidlaw. 'My God, you're bitter. Just because I destroyed your idol——'

'He destroyed himself.'

'Surely,' said Laidlaw, 'I deserve a little credit?'

Arnott didn't shrug, but he was very obviously a man who refrained from doing so.

'What is it then?' Laidlaw asked. 'Enemies? Surely you don't think that I'm one?'

'You use such big words,' said Arnott, 'for such unimportant things.'

That one got through. It hurt. The oh-so-quizzical smile cracked like glass.

'Because I reminded you about your parents? After all these years?'

'You meddle too much,' said Arnott. 'You cast profit and loss accounts on people and you meddle.'

'And yet you're here—at a meddler's party?'

'I'm curious,' said Arnott. 'It's my besetting sin. If I weren't I'd never see you again. But I am.'

'Your weakness is my gain,' said Laidlaw.

'It almost always is—but not this time. I'm curious about Moulton.'

'And so you came to see his mansion? Nice, that, don't you think—Moulton's Mansion?'

Arnott looked about him. 'From what I've seen—he should be very happy here. Where is he?'

'In Los Angeles—enjoying the sunshine. Lucky dog.'

'But . . . surely he should be here? I mean, it's his big day.'

'Let's hope so. But don't you remember—at our dinner-party which has such unfortunate memories for you—it was suggested that Moulton should be married not just theoretically but practically?'

'It won't make the slightest difference to his work.'

'But to his image——'

'Balls,' said Arnott.

Again Laidlaw turned off the smile. Quizzical wit time was over.

'I want him married,' he said.

'But what bloody difference will it make?'

'It will make him unhappy,' said Laidlaw.

'Suppose she won't come back to him?'

'Then he won't get the job,' said Laidlaw, 'and that will make him unhappy.'

'Heads you win, tails he loses?'

'How well you writers put these things.'

'Suppose he found out what you're up to?'

'I think he already knows,' said Laidlaw, 'but it doesn't make any difference. He has to have that lab. Don't you think our Madge is looking well today?'

Now the private audience is over too, thought Arnott. 'She usually does,' he said.

'A feast of good things, said Laidlaw. 'A banquet. And each course prepared by an artist.'

'I can see why you bought into Aliment Foods,' said Arnott.

'Don't you ever feel a nostalgia for the adventures you two shared in your youth?'

'I do not,' said Arnott.

'Strange. I'd have thought they would have been even more exciting now that you've both reached maturity. I rather think Madge thinks so too.'

'Profit and loss and meddling,' said Arnott. 'You're still at it.'

He wanted to go, but it wasn't the time. Just as he turned away the Parliamentary Secretary arrived, and the Parliamentary Secretary was Harry Lewis, who was determined to have a few words with his old mate Bob Arnott before he got on with this P.R. nonsense. Life was mostly business after all, but a place had to be made for pleasure, and what more pleasant than a chance meeting between old friends?

He was as red and breathless as ever, but now the air of ruddy haste was a pose, Arnott observed, a pose to con the voters that Harry Lewis was always there chasing the rights and privileges to which all who supported him were entitled. Family allowances; housing; social services. Harry chased them all and herded them back to the voters.

Only now his tracksuit was made in Savile Row, his running-shoes were hand-lasted. Yet Harry was Harry, and inside the con man there was a hell of a nice feller, and maybe the nice feller picked up as many votes as the breathless runner, Arnott thought, though Harry would be the last to know it.

He looked at Arnott with affection.

'You've done well for yourself Bob,' he said.

'So have you,' said Arnott, in duty bound to do so.

Harry looked down at the perfection of his clothes.

'It's me Parliamentary Secretary's suit,' he said. 'The P.M. likes us all to have one. Tat always shows on the telly.'

'It suits you,' Arnott said.

'Glad you think so. Mind you'—he smiled—'I'll have to change before I see my constituents tonight. Something a bit more homely. They see Savile Row close up and they think you've joined the Opposition.'

He means it, Arnott thought. He really does. This isn't cynicism, it's Harry Lewis's version of Realpolitik.

'You'll go far, Harry,' he said.

'Do you know,' Lewis answered, quite seriously, 'I rather think I shall.' He paused as a waiter put a glass in his hand, then said, 'What's Goofy up to?' The deliberate change of subject was without offence: the inevitable tactic of a man who had to husband his time.

'Making money,' said Arnott.

'He does that in his sleep. Still, he's saving us some at the same time. So we'll go along with him for this once. Is he putting Moulton in?'

'He wants to,' said Arnott.

'He'll have to. Excuse me.' Lewis turned, and Arnott saw Laidlaw moving in on them. 'Tom, old man. How nice to see you.'

'You've gossiped long enough,' said Laidlaw. 'Now it's time to work for your Champagne. Come and see . . .' He drew Lewis away, and Arnott looked round for his bag once more. It was by the P.R. table: so was Madge Innes. Arnott found that he did not want to face Madge Innes after what Goofy had told him. It was his annoyance at what Goofy had done that took him to her.

'So soon?' she said. 'The party hasn't even started.'

'A doctor's lot is not a merry one,' he said.

'I'm sure it could be,' said Madge. 'All you have to do is get the habit. Start with a glass of Champagne.'

'It's a funny thing, but I don't want any,' he said.

'Ah,' said Madge. 'You know—I liked your wife.'

'She didn't think so.'

'I'm not surprised. You see at first I got her all wrong. I behaved like a berk. I'm sorry.'

'It's not important,' he said.

'Oh, but it is. Please tell her what I've said. I'd love to see her again.'

'I'll tell her so.'

Madge said, 'You're judging us, aren't you—you and Susan? You're sitting in judgement.'

'We have our lives,' said Arnott. 'They don't overlap with yours.'

'They could—if you would let them.'

'Madge, Madge,' said Arnott. 'I'm a doctor. People get sick and I do my best to cure them. That's what I'm for—and that's all there is. You don't need me—or Susan—any more than Laidlaw does.'

'Your judgement says we're guilty and you despise us,' she said.

'You're wrong. That's why we need you—to show you you're wrong.'

He moved away.

'You don't believe me, do you?' she said. 'Isn't that a terrible thing. I make my living out of being convincing.'

The whisper of footsteps on grass again, then the tap-tap of heels on the stone flags that bordered the pool. But there were stars now, soft and tender, without the icy brightness of home: stars that grouped and formed in patterns, comforting stars that absorbed the mind yet were undemanding. He sat motionless in the shadows, hoping for the footsteps to pass. They came up to him.

Tracy said, 'I won. Twenty-one moves. Dad's smarter than I am, but I always win. I think it has something to do with my being a director. All those movement patterns.'

'He isn't smarter,' said Moulton. She ignored it.

'Andy left. He asked me to say goodbye to you. He seemed to like you.'

'Aren't you surprised?'

'Mother was.'

Adèle would be. Surprised and shocked. But she wouldn't show it. How can you show disapproval to sixty million dollars?

'What did you do to him?'

'We talked.'

'What about?' she asked. 'Vietnam? The Bomb? Saint Che Guevara?'

'About you,' he said. She shied away from it.

'Something hit you tonight,' she said.

He thought of Andy, and laughed.

'Don't try to kid me,' she said, 'I've been around you too long. Something happened to you.'

'I had an idea,' he said.

'It's funny—I've watched it happen so often, and every time I can see it. It's so obvious. Yet other people don't even notice.'

'That was Andy,' he said.

'You should have seen yourself. Like you were on mescalin or something. Staring into that decanter.'

'Was I rude?' he asked.

'You can't be rude if nobody notices. . . . Did you write it down?'

'That's why I went out,' he said.

'Does it work?'

'I won't know—till I get in a lab.' That brought them back to Andy. Andy was going to buy her, and he'd never get in a lab.

'Andy loves you,' said Moulton. 'Honourably.'

'He told you that?'

'He did.'

'And you believed him? About the honourably bit, I mean?'

'I did eventually.'

'Andy's very sweet,' she said.

'I think so too,' said Moulton. 'He's also very rich.'

'It's strange,' said Tracy. 'Weird in a way—all that money, and he loves Tracy Moulton.'

'Don't start knocking yourself.'

'Oh, come on, lover,' she said. 'Come on now. What would you buy—if you had sixty million bucks?'

'A cyclotron,' he said, and she laughed.

'All right. You're different. You proved that this afternoon—but let's put it this way—what would any red-blooded Ivy Leaguer buy with sixty million bucks?'

'The centre pages of *Playboy*?'

'Right. And that's not me, Jim baby. I haven't got the tits for it.' He said nothing. 'Forgive my uninhibited use of the vernacular,' she said. 'I had another brandy.' When he still didn't answer she said, 'Tits or no tits, I'm trying to talk about us. It'd be nice if you helped me.'

'Go on about Andy,' he said, 'and the strange, weird spell you've cast.'

'It's too early for you to get nasty,' she said. 'But what you're saying is true. It is like a spell.'

'How like a spell?'

'When we broke up,' she said. 'You remember when we broke up?'

He remembered. She'd thought she was pregnant and didn't want the child. Neither did he, but the thought of an abortion outraged him. They had rowed for days, at a time when the work he was doing was crucial, and the rows exhausted him. The expected results wouldn't come. One night he had knocked her unconscious. Next morning she was gone. Two days later he'd got a cable from Los Angeles: *Don't worry about the custody of the child there isn't one.*

'I was—sick,' she said. 'Sick in the head. Oh, I don't mean I was going crazy—nothing like that. It was just the yelling and screaming—all that stupid noise—and watching your fists and never learning to roll with the punch. You scared me, honeybunch. Scared the hell out of me. Did you know that?'

'No,' he said. 'I didn't know.'

'Never thought about it, I suppose. You were so busy. But I did. And that made me sick too. I'd never been scared of anybody in my life. And when I came back—here—the only thing that did any good was quiet. Oh, brother, did I need quiet. Dad wanted me to go to an analyst——'

'Maybe it would have helped,' Moulton said.

'Shrinks never help people like me,' she said. 'Or people like you either. They can't cure *us*, lover. All they can do is change us.'

'Into what?'

'Normal people,' she said, surprised. 'People who don't have rows and don't go into trances and see atoms splitting and don't stay awake eighteen hours and produce plays. You know. Normal. Breadwinners. Homemakers. That desperate I wasn't. I took to quiet instead.'

'Here?'

'It's possible,' she said. 'Difficult, but possible. Anyway I kicked off at Dad's place in Lake Tahoe. Stuck a stack of cans in the car, and off I went. It was the off-season. I didn't see a soul in three weeks.'

'Your parents let you?'

'I didn't tell them. Left them a note. But Dad called a shrink anyway, as soon as he'd found I'd gone. The shrink said to let me stay so I stayed.'

'He trusted him that far?'

'You've got to trust somebody,' she said. 'Shrinks may not be much, but they're the best priest-kings we've got. . . . It was great at Tahoe.'

'What did you do?'

'Walked, swam—hid from people.'

'Were you drinking?'

'From time to time,' she said. 'It was part of my therapy.'

'Like Adèle?'

'Most unlike Adèle. But don't let's start on her. She's not your problem.'

'But she's yours?'

'If I let her be—and the odds are I will. Anyway Lake Tahoe worked its healing magic, and one day I found myself talking to the birds like St Francis and wishing they were people instead. Quiet people. And I figured that even in Hollywood there must be some quiet ones so I came back and started looking for a Society of Amateur Trappists. I wound up with Andy.'

'Andy a Trappist' said Moulton.

'Throws you, doesn't it? D'you know I was spending whole days with Andy and we'd neither of us say a word?'

'What in hell did you do?'

'Now, lover. Unclench those fists. Andy is an honourable man. We fished, we swam, we surfed, we sailed. And we didn't talk.'

'Did he like it?'

'Of course not,' she said. 'Andy's a talker, you know that. He hated it.'

'Then why on earth——'

'He loves me—honourably—and he's very sweet. That silence was about the hardest thing he could give me. He didn't even hesitate.'

'Where did you meet him?'

'At the country club. I looked like Schizophrenia's Last Stand, but he didn't think so. I told him I wanted quiet—and he gave it to me.'

'And then?'

'I got to be O.K. Not all at once—but now and then I needed noise. Not to make it myself—but just to hear it. And as you know, Jim baby, when it comes to noise-making, Andy's in a class by himself.'

'You needed that kind of noise?'

'It was a damn sight more restful than yours,' she said.

'I can't help being the way I am.'

'Oh, Jim baby. Come on now. Everybody can help *that* and you know it. Unless they're crazy. Are you crazy?'

'Sometimes,' he said. 'Like everybody else.'

She sighed. The pool was very bright, very clear. It was right that Andy should have stood there, just as it was right that Jim belonged in the shadows, as she did.

'You're saying you aren't going to change, but I should come back to you anyway.'

He made no answer.

'I hope you're not saying that you're still carrying a torch for corn-fed cuties with a weight problem, because I never put on weight, especially when I'm living with you.'

Still no answer.

'You're supposed to help me, baby,' she said.

'I'm trying to,' he said. 'It isn't easy.'

'We're not easy people. . . . Why did you marry me, Jim baby?'

'I needed you,' he said.

'All of me?'

'Yes.'

'You can still say that—after this afternoon?'

'I wish you'd forget about this afternoon,' he said.

'How can I, baby? It was an insult. I never forget insults. Not any more. You taught me not to.'

'You're so alive,' he said. 'You understood whatever it is that drives me.'

'Not understood. No,' she said. 'The word you're looking for is envied. Coveted. I wanted what you had. I thought if I married you some of it might rub off on me. Osmosis or something.'

'You had it made,' he said. 'You were so——'

'Competent,' she said. 'One hundred per cent competent.'

'All that energy . . .'

'I needed it. Every scrap. You always need energy to make a hundred per cent—even in competence. But you've got inspiration, baby —and it doesn't rub off. I know that now. Or maybe you won't let it. You're a very selfish feller—you know that. Take this afternoon——'

'Please,' he said. 'Don't go on about it.'

'That was selfish too,' she said. 'They were your sperm after all—so why should you give them to me? Why should you give any part of yourself to anybody?'

'It wasn't like that,' he said.

'What was it like then? Like I disgusted you?'

'You were very kind,' he said. 'That's a quality you have.'

'It would help, it really would, if you could lapse into stupidity just once,' she said.

Perhaps no one but himself could have detected the tears in her voice.

She stood up then. 'I better go,' she said.

His body moved in the darkness, transformed itself from a shapeless blur to a series of beautiful masses, smooth-flowing lines, shallow, elegant curves without one hint of weakness, and the head above it, noble, handsome, arrogant as a Bourbon king's. My peasant, she thought. My proletarian activist.

'Let's try again,' he said.

Bastard! Bastard! Will you never fight fair?

'You've already made your point, baby,' she said. 'Or rather you haven't.'

She turned away and he grabbed her, and even then her mind was noting the irony of the fact that for him only an insult could trigger love, even then, when her body responded at once, and totally to the feel of him against her.

'Hey!' her father said. 'Hey there. Tracy? Jim? Where are you, boy?'

His hands slid to her waist, lifted her effortlessly from him, pushed her into further darkness. She was grateful for that: her father must never see her so vulnerable.

'Here,' Moulton said. 'Here by the pool.'

Schiller's body in motion had an aggressive energy that was totally ugly. It made no concession to his new-found elegance of life. To Schiller, the length of time his daughter had spent with Moulton was a threat, and threats had to be confronted at once. Ugliness had no relevance. He hurried, that was all.

Moulton stood solid to meet him, weight evenly planted, hands curved at his sides. In the darkness Tracy thought, I have watched you and admired you ever since I can remember, and watching and admiring made up my love. That—and envy. Because you have inspiration too—you inspired yourself into a million dollars. But a million is only a million, Dad, so don't tangle with Moulton. He uses the infinite for change. She stepped forward then, and her father's face flicked from Moulton's to hers. There was anxiety in his look; even a kind of terror. Moulton showed only the calm serenity of a man who had dined well and impressed a pretty woman.

'What the hell you doing out here?' said Schiller.

'Talking,' Moulton said.

'You've been gone for hours.'

'We've got a lot to catch up on.'

'You shouldn't stay in the dark. Tracy, you should know that,' Schiller said.

'What's wrong with the dark?'

'It's—dangerous. You get all kinds in California these days. Hippies, muggers, kidnappers.' He glowered at Moulton. 'It isn't funny.'

'I was just thinking,' Moulton said. 'Even the rich have their Central Parks. Only theirs are private. Anyway, what about your private army?'

'They could be bought,' said Schiller.

'Aye,' said Moulton. 'Mercenaries always can.'

'Let's go in,' said Tracy. 'We've talked enough for one night.' On the way back to the house she smiled at her father, even when her hand touched Moulton's, her fingers curled, fleetingly, around his thumb.

194

The living-room was lit by an orange light that warmed the creamy texture of walls and furniture. In the centre of the room was a chess-table, made up of alternate squares of clear and clouded glass. The chess-set was very old and very beautiful: white carved from ivory; black from jade. Moulton looked at the game. She had risked her queen, lost a knight, but queen and surviving knight held down Schiller's king. Symbolic chess? He looked at Tracy. Who survives?

'I see you still play rough,' he said.

There was a giggle behind him. He turned to see Mrs Schiller, stretched out, elegantly at ease, on a cream leather davenport. Schiller, his daughter and son-in-law looked at the decanter beside her. It was empty. For once in her life, Adèle looked smug.

It was nice Arnott hadn't brought frilly-drawers. She had the looks, and he'd no doubt she would strip all right, but she reminded him of her da, and anyway Arnott wouldn't want her to take her clothes off, and she probably would. They usually did once they knew it was for art. Look at Mad Madge.

'I'm interrupting you,' Arnott said.

Too bloody right mate. Caked in bloody paint, and the palette knife still in my hand. Of course you're interrupting me. What you don't know is I want to be interrupted.

'Come in,' Fitzgerald said. 'It's about bloody time I saw you.'

Arnott looked at the semi-detached's neat entrance. Shaved lawn behind him; gleaming plastic tiles in front, daring him to have mud on his shoes. He walked in.

'A bit untypical, isn't it?'

'Renting it furnished,' said Fitzgerald. 'Schoolteacher bloke off on an exchange to Canada.'

'What's he teach?'

Fitzgerald glowered at a terrible reproduction of a Turner.

'Art,' he said. 'He's got his bloody nerve. Still—the studio's not bad. He knew that much. Ha'way in the kitchen.'

They walked past drawing-room and dining-room, that looked like set-pieces in badly assimilated taste, and into a large square kitchen in which it seemed Fitzgerald did everything but paint and sleep. Besides kitchen equipment it held two armchairs, a shelf of books, sketching blocks and a T.V. set. It was spotless, and finically neat.

'Sit down,' said Fitzgerald, and pointed to a chair. The other, Arnott noticed, had a strip of canvas laid on it, that was quite obviously there to absorb the paint. He watched Fitzgerald pour out whiskies, and laughed.

'What's up then?'

'A bit early, isn't it?' said Arnott.

'I never know things like that,' said Fitzgerald. 'I fancied one.'

He passed over a glass.

'Cheers,' said Arnott.

'Oh, aye ... cheers.' Fitzgerald drank. 'What can I do for you, Bob?'

'Amuse me,' Arnott said. 'Unless you're losing your touch.'

'I don't think so,' said Fitzgerald. 'I'm still at it. And I still don't bloody know I'm doing it.' He laughed. 'Been worth a lot to me has that. You ask me gallery chap. Has me on parade all the bloody time. He says I'm so bloody weird I have to be a genius. And the customers think the same. Man, I keep them in stitches.'

'Don't you mind?'

'Mind?' Fitzgerald had never considered the matter, but he did so then, handling it as if it were an unusual shape and colour that he might or might not reject. 'It doesn't bother me,' he said at last. 'And it helps the pictures.'

'It helps a doctor too,' said Arnott. 'The customers like an eccentric.'

'There you are then,' Fitzgerald said. 'It doesn't stop you curing them.'

'It doesn't stop you killing them either,' said Arnott. 'But it gives them something to think about while you're doing it.'

'Things bad, are they?'

'No. Things are good if anything. Oh—you mean killing the customers? That was just talk. I don't do much of that nowadays. I leave it to the specialists.'

'Making a bit, are you?'

'Quite a bit.'

'Not as much as Goofy though.'

'I don't want as much as Goofy,' said Arnott.

Fitzgerald drank more whisky.

'You got kids . . . All that.' Arnott nodded. 'I'm glad. You were the one who should have had. You got a cracking little wife too.'

'I think so,' Arnott said.

'That business with her da——'

'It's over,' said Arnott. 'Don't worry about it.'

'Not worry. No,' said Fitzgerald. 'I think about it though. It was big for me—all that.'

'Big?'

'Important like. Joining. All that. Meeting the blokes.' He gulped at his drink. 'Oh Christ, I hate bloody words. I get lost in them.

'You can control them when you want to,' Arnott said. 'I've heard you.'

'Thanks, Doctor. Don't start diagnosing. Drink some more medicine and belt up.'

He passed the bottle; Arnott poured.

'You remember me when we were kids?' Fitzgerald said. 'Arse hanging out of me trousers. No boots half the time. Funny that. Me ma made enough money to buy the street. Only by the time she'd finished a night's work she was too bloody whacked to go shopping.

Except for grub. She ate like a bloody navvy. It gets me that way an'
all. Looked funny, didn't I?'

Politeness was lost on Fitzgerald. 'You did,' said Arnott.

'Funny even to *you* lot. Men's coats cut down, me mam's blouse.
Anything to keep the cold out. Lazy cow. She was all right other ways
though. Did you know I passed for the grammar school?'

'Indeed I didn't.'

'Me and that mad sod Moulton was top of the school. She
wouldn't send me.'

'I thought you said she was all right.'

'Well, she was. *She* wanted me to go and I wouldn't. Waste of
bloody time. All that mensa, mensa, mensam and πr^2. She bought me
books instead. Cartridge paper. Water-colours. Oils. Anything I fancied so long as I fetched it meself. She *hated* going to the shops.'

'You must have been lonely.'

'Because of ma? It didn't stop you playing with me.'

'Kids are different.'

'That's true. But mostly the wives took it out on ma. They were
sorry for me.'

'You didn't mind that?'

'Where's the point? I couldn't stop it happening. She died in '41.
Had a bloke all night, cooked him his breakfast and dropped down
dead. She left me eight hundred quid. So what did I do? I joined the
bloody Commandos. Under age.'

'Why?'

'Uniforms,' said Fitzgerald. 'There was something about uniforms.
About looking the same as everybody else—and not looking bare-
arsed neither. Anyway, it was time I did a bit of travelling. All I'd
done up to then was inshore-fishing. The way I looked at it, Commandos was bound to get around a bit. I was right an' all. We went
straight up to bloody Scotland, lived like bloody Red Indians. Off the
land. You never got fat off that bloody land. But you got hard. I
could run up a bloody wall them days. Kill you with me left bollock.'

'You wanted that?'

'I didn't know what I bloody wanted. I was seventeen and a half. I
fished on weekdays and painted on Sundays—and hoped nobody
would find out and start laughing. But if they did I wanted to be
ready for them. The Commandos made you ready for anything. We
got blooded in Norway. Killed a lot of blokes there. Catch 'em. Kill
'em. When you know how it's dead easy. You remember Daft Scully
at the rope works?' Daft Scully had haunted Arnott's nightmares for
years, and still menaced the frontiers of his dreams. A thin and violent man, invalided out of the Indian Army after sunstroke; a night-

watchman with a couple of mongrel terriers as violent as himself. Half the time he talked Hindi to himself aloud, and because Hindi was unintelligible he was thought to be daft, but his English was soft and persuasive when he found it, and used to persuade boys to go to the rope works with him and watch his terriers catch rats while he interfered with you. Or so Arnott's father had told him, one night of agonizing embarrassment when he'd seen him talking to Scully. What 'interfered with' meant Arnott had no idea and was far too frightened to ask. Even conjecture was terrifying.

'I remember,' Arnott said.

'You never went with him?'

'No.'

'No.' Fitzgerald's echo of the word was not mocking: betrayed only the recognition that Arnott was of a different breed. 'Nowt there for you. He taught me a bit though. . . . Where was I?'

'Catching Germans and killing them.'

'Oh aye. I wish you'd seen Scully's dogs in among the rats. Grab the neck, over the shoulder. Neck breaks. Next one. If you know how to do it—it's that easy. We scared them, Bob. Scared the shit out of them. . . . Norway. They say it's beautiful. I dare say it is. The colours didn't work for me. Next job was France. Blowing things up mainly. Big things. Radar and that. You ever smashed anything big?'

'No.'

'It's funny. You know—exciting. Dirty an' all. Man, the shapes you make. I was glad to get off that. I was getting too fond of it. Good at it an' all. It was different in Italy.' He looked at Arnott and grinned. 'You're used to this, aren't you?' he said.

'Listening? It's half my job.'

'It's a bit more than that if you ask me.'

'You should tell fortunes,' said Arnott. Then, reluctantly: 'I'm trying to write.'

'I knew there was something,' Fitzgerald said. 'I'm glad it's writing.'

'Why?' Arnott asked.

'If it had been painting you'd have wanted to show it to me.'

'You're quite right,' said Arnott. 'You *don't* bloody know you're doing it.'

'Upset you, have I?'

'Not in the least. Tell me about Italy.'

'Great,' Fitzgerald said. 'Spring and autumn. That's the times. Colour! Man. The whole place sings hymns. It wasn't that I wanted to paint it—not then. Bob—it was just living in it. And wine and grappa and Strega and brandy. And all those bloody women. Starving for it. And fit like we were—I've seen the bloody steam rising off us. It was like the wine, man—once you got started you couldn't stop.'

'Fear,' Arnott said. Fitzgerald's eyes flicked to him like a bird's: the understanding total.

'You've seen it, haven't you?'

'I lived it,' said Arnott. 'In Malaya.'

'Aye. Pull the cork and open their legs. I might be dead next week. Lot of us were. But I didn't mind. I mean—I didn't mind enough to stop.'

'I know.'

'Then a daft thing happened. I went and fell in love.'

'With an Italian girl?'

'With a fucking replacement. 073 Pendexter R. R for fucking Rodney.'

'An officer?'

'Should have been, Bob. With a name like that. He wasn't though. Swaddy like me—only by that time I was a corporal. Black sheep of the family. Daddy was a governor-general.' The mimicry of his last words was mocking, affectionate and quite inaccurate. 'The lads thought he was a joke. He wasn't though. They found out sharp enough.'

'Did he love you?'

'Aye,' said Fitzgerald. 'He did. Right off. He'd been bent since he left school. We got on fine.'

'No more women?'

'Sometimes—when he wasn't looking. He was jealous as hell.' Fitzgerald paused. 'We came out of Italy to regroup before D-day—and he was offered a commission. Daddy was that pleased he sent him fifty quid. But Rod wouldn't leave me. He turned it down.' Fitzgerald turned square on to Arnott. 'He was on the landing craft your pa-in-law hit. I dived for him five times. Couldn't reach him. He was washed up a week later. They identified him by his paybook. You never saw anyone as beautiful as he was.'

Arnott said, 'Is it over, now?'

'It was nearly over then. Like the war. I wanted it finished. By then I knew I had to start painting, you see. There wouldn't have been room for Rod once I started. Only—I had to go and talk to old Jennings. Or I thought I had to. It was wrong of me, Bob. . . . Rod's dead, and the poor old bugger's simple. Tell your missus I'm sorry.'

'All right,' Arnott said. 'I'll tell her. But I would have done what you did.'

'Don't tell her *that*,' said Fitzgerald.

Arnott smiled. 'I wasn't planning to. You really like her, Fitz?'

'Aye,' said Fitzgerald. 'She's all right. Got something for her.' His eyes ran across the row of exactly aligned sketching-blocks. 'Not here. In the studio. Bring your glass.' He picked up his own, and the bottle.

It was a gaunt, bare room, whitewashed and chill, the sun piercing in from the skylight brought no warmth. Arnott observed how, instantly, Fitzgerald was at home in his surroundings, like himself in his surgery or Goofy behind a desk. Fitzgerald went to a pile of drawings, began to flick them over. The mere act of handling paper with lines on it erased Arnott from his consciousness, and Arnott knew it. The thought failed to irritate. In twenty-five years he had seen Fitzgerald eleven times, and each occasion had been memorable, not least for Fitz's gift of erasing you from his memory when he had to look at drawings.

Arnott looked about him. There were sketches and fragments of sketches, tiny shorthand notes in oils, charcoal, pen and wash. There was a heap of cushions like a jumbled pile of refracted light: reds, yellows, blues, greens, purples, shouting at the whitewashed wall behind. Facing the cushions was an easel, and the painting on it was of the pile of cushions, glowing now as if their light came from inside themselves, and on the cushions Madge Innes, mother-naked: sly and sensual as he knew her to be, and of an abundant, a quite incredible richness. Texture and colour and shape assured him that this was a superb piece of painting; the slyness, the smugness of the eyes told him that it might be even more.

'Got it,' Fitzgerald said, and Arnott walked across to him. He was holding a water-colour: a seascape. The sea was of an intense blue-green, a colour that Arnott knew at once belonged to a country whose winters were cold. Beyond the sea was a beach, the sand of so light a gold that it faded almost to silver, and beyond the sand were cliffs, the hard texture of the rock immediately apparent: the visible sky was of a light and very pure blue, with white puffballs of cloud that brought no rain. Sea, sand, cliffs and sky were alike deserted, except that in the sea a body floated, face-upward, almost vertical in the water, thighs and legs foreshortened, so that thorax and head seemed huge, and yet not menacing, not even grotesque. The body wore British army uniform, but beneath the clumsy outline there was a suggestion of a slender, nervous beauty brought suddenly to an end; the unflawed face was beautiful also: beautiful, and dead.

'That's him,' Fitzgerald said. Arnott looked at it in silence.

'Forgive me,' he said at last. 'There doesn't seem any point in trying to look for words.' He handed it back. 'It's brilliant,' he said.

'Aye,' said Fitzgerald, and Arnott marvelled that such colossal self-assurance could also be objective. 'It's yours,' he said, 'if you think your wife would have it in the house.'

'Of course she will—but don't you want it?'

'I've got eleven more like it, and forty-seven sketches, and next year I'll have an oil. A big 'un. Mebbes I'll keep it. Mebbes not. It's funny, man. Once you've finished them you don't need them.'

'Even him?'

'Love dies or the lover dies. One or the other,' Fitzgerald said. 'Where's your glass?'

He looked, bird quick, across the studio. Arnott's glass was on a painter's horse beside the easel.

'Oh,' he said. 'Been looking at me contribution to *Playboy*, have you? What d'you think?'

'Bloody brilliant,' said Arnott. 'But then you are bloody brilliant, so I expected that.'

'What else then?' Fitzgerald asked.

'The eyes,' said Arnott. 'Those eyes are a dead giveaway. Tell me—do you always make them take their clothes off every time you paint a portrait?'

Fitzgerald roared with laughter. 'By God, I like you Bob,' he said. 'You know how to look.' He turned back to the picture. 'There's an assault course for you,' he said. 'A fucking Olympic steeplechase. Like a feather-bed stuffed with trampolines. She fancies you.'

'She fancies everybody.'

'Everybody except Moulton. I'm painting him an' all.'

'So I hear. In the nude?'

Fitzgerald grinned. 'Not that sod,' he said. 'Head and shoulders and he can think himself lucky.'

'What are you doing it for?' Arnott asked.

'Goofy asked me to.'

'Don't tell me you're doing Goofy favours.'

'Five thousand quid isn't exactly a favour,' Fitzgerald said. 'Anyway I want to paint him. It's the kind of face I'm good at.'

'Five thousand quid?'

'Yeah,' said Fitzgerald. 'Bloody madness, isn't it?' He looked again at Madge Innes. 'I'm doing that one for nowt.'

'For love?'

'That's what she thinks. I'm keeping the bugger. She thinks she is.' 'Did she tell you she hates Moulton?'

'Aye. Worse than Goofy. Same, anyway. It's all daftness.'

'It's sick,' said Arnott.

'Money,' Fitzgerald said. 'It all starts with money. Rewards and punishments. They think they're gods.'

'You never liked Moulton, did you?' Arnott asked.

'Not since I first laid eyes on him. But it won't affect my painting him.'

'Do you think he's as bad as Laidlaw—or Madge?'

'No,' Fitzgerald said. 'He wants to be a bloody sight worse; but he hasn't got the power.'

'You wouldn't consider helping him then?'

'I would not,' said Fitzgerald. 'Let the bugger stew.'

There was a sudden staccato of heels clicking on oilcloth. Fitzgerald looked dismayed.

'Bloody hell,' he said. 'I'm in it now. I forgot——'

'Forgot what, for God's sake?'

'Her all-over portrait. I promised I wouldn't show it to anybody.'

'Cover it,' Arnott said.

'No bloody fear. The paint's not dry.'

He turned to the door, his face showing the supreme unconcern of a man who is completely in the wrong and equipped to cope with the fact.

Her reactions were noisily dramatic, and Arnott was at once aware that Fitzgerald revelled in it. All the 'How dare yous?' and 'You promised mes' awoke a response of sheer delight. There was also the fact that, enraged, Madge looked even more splendid than usual: eyes flashing, breast heaving; a Venus facing Mars with a rolling-pin after he'd had a night out with the boys. Then the voice grew shriller, the comedy faded, and Fitzgerald's air of indulgent connoisseurship faded also, to be replaced by a look of wariness that was familiar to Arnott, yet elusive too.

'To show it to *him* of all people,' Madge was saying.

'Bob?' Fitzgerald said. 'What's wrong with Bob? He got it right first time.'

'He knows me,' she said.

'So he knows you. So what? Now he knows you better.'

'You had no right to let him see me like that.'

'I'd take it as a favour if you'd both admit I'm here,' Arnott said.

'All right then.' She turned on him, hair swirling, plump hands crooked like claws. 'How do you feel now you've looked at it?' Before he could answer she said, 'I'll tell you how I feel. Dirty.'

'Puritans,' said Fitzgerald. 'We're all Puritans.'

'Not you,' she said. 'You don't bloody care.'

'But why should you?' Arnott asked. 'You're beautiful. So's your picture. Isn't that all that matters?'

'No it's not,' she screamed. 'I didn't want you—anybody who knows me—to see me like that.'

'But surely they're bound to?' asked Arnott. 'It'll be exhibited, won't it?'

'No, it won't. That picture's mine. He——' She broke off then, looked at Fitzgerald. 'You promised me,' she said.

'It was the only way I could get you.'

'But it *is* mine.'

'No.'

His denial was absolute.

'You bloody liar.' There was a palette-knife on the bench beside her. She grabbed it and ran at the picture, arm raised to strike. Her body, so beautiful in repose, was awkward, ungainly when she forced it into violence. It was Fitzgerald who achieved beauty in movement, with the economic grace of a dancer in a familiar routine. His body pivoted, one hand shot out, hitting the inside of the arm that held the knife, then, as she swerved away from the pain his other hand clenched, the fist clubbed down in a carefully calculated blow to the side of her neck. She fell like lead.

Arnott remembered then where he had seen that wariness before. It had been on the face of the Gurkha jebadar. He went over to Madge Innes, knelt beside her.

'She'll be all right if her heart's all right and her nervous system's normal,' Arnott said. He felt for her pulse.

'Is it?' Fitzgerald asked. A minute crawled by. Arnott continued to examine her.

At last he said, 'This time you're lucky. Help me to put her on those cushions.'

But Fitzgerald carried her himself, her inert weight almost an irrelevance. Arnott went to a tap, soaked his handkerchief in cold water, bathed her temples.

'What a bloody menace you are,' he said.

'It's all in the training. Once you've had it you never forget.'

'You don't even care,' Arnott said.

'You don't think I enjoyed it, do you? She was going to cut my bloody picture.'

'And that's important?'

'Of course it's important——' He broke off.

'You better watch it, Fitz,' Arnott said. 'They can get at you, too, if they want to.'

'I could have killed her,' Fitzgerald said. 'You believe that? I'm a middle-aged man and I could have killed her. Or you. One wallop—you're dead. But I didn't, Bob. I didn't even hit her hard. I didn't want to hit her at all. It was just the picture . . .'

Arnott's rage died. It had been a familiar rage, anyway; almost routine. The rage a doctor feels when people damage each other and instantly expect the doctor to put it right.

'Watch them, Fitz,' he said. 'For God's sake be careful.'

She stirred then, moaning. He chafed her wrists.

'It . . . hurts,' she said. Her head moved, and she winced as her neck muscles hurt her. She was looking for Fitzgerald; he stepped at once into her line of sight.

'You bastard,' she said.

'What's up then?' he asked.

'Shock,' said Arnott.

'Shock?' She was screaming at him. 'This bastard hit me.'

'Shock,' Arnott said again, and turned to Fitzgerald. 'Don't let it upset you,' he said. 'They often hallucinate as they're coming round.'

'You saw him hit me.'

'I saw you pick up a palette-knife. You were making some sort of joke about the picture and you pretended you were going to destroy it.'

'I was going to——'

'Your own portrait? Surely not. A psychiatrist would say that's a symbolic destruction of self. I'd hardly call you suicidal.' He waited, but she said nothing. 'You were playing a game. But you stumbled and fell. Hit your neck on that stool. You were lucky I was here to look after you.'

'It's all lies. You know it is.'

'It's what I saw,' he said.

'Chums,' said Madge. 'Bloody boyhood chums.' Her fingers moved, cautiously, towards the pain. 'Am I marked?' she asked.

'Bruised,' Arnott said. 'No more than I would have expected. It won't last.'

Her legs moved, her shoulders pushed back into the cushions. A man leaned over her. Without conscious thought she was presenting her body to its best advantage.

'You hate me,' she said. 'You hate Tom Laidlaw.'

'No,' Arnott said. 'I don't hate either of you. I'm not involved.'

The posturing vanished. She tried to turn her body once more into a threat, a weapon. It was foolish of her, Arnott thought.

'I shan't forget this,' she said.

'Neither shall I.' He felt her pulse once more. 'You'll be all right soon. Can I give you a lift anywhere?'

'No,' she said. 'I'm staying here.'

Arnott looked at Fitzgerald.

'She can please herself,' Fitzgerald said.

'Put the fires on,' Arnott said. 'Keep her warm.' Fitzgerald did so as Arnott picked up a quilted dressing-gown, spread it over her, then scribbled on a prescription-block. He tore off a sheet, laid it by her.

'This should take the soreness away,' he said. 'You've nothing to worry about.'

'But you have.'

He shrugged. 'Doctors always worry. . . . I'd better go, Fitz.'

'I'll see you out.'

They went back to the kitchen, and Fitzgerald rolled up the water-colour, placed it carefully inside a plastic tube.

'When you have it framed keep it simple, he said. 'It doesn't need any bloody commercials.' He handed over the tube. 'I'm in your debt,' he said.

'Friends shouldn't talk like that.'

'Friends?'

Again Arnott had the sensation that the echoed word was an unfamiliar object handled and observed. 'Oh, aye. I'll give you something else——'

'There's no need.'

'Souvenir,' Fitzgerald said.

He pulled out a sketching-block, flicked through it. Studies, impressions, drawings, and towards the end his preliminary sketches of Madge.

'I draw well,' said Fitzgerald. 'These are good.' He might have been quoting his own reviewers. 'They're worth a bob or two—if your patients all get well.'

'Thanks,' said Arnott. He looked again at the final study: all that glorious opulence. 'You know something,' he said. 'When she moves she's clumsy.'

'Daft bitch,' Fitzgerald said. 'She needs paint. It keeps her still.'

'You'd better get back to her.'

Fitzgerald shrugged. 'Not to worry,' he said. 'She's a quick learner. Watch out for yourself, Bob.'

When he got back to the studio, she was naked. He found that it didn't surprise him. She *was* a quick learner. Already she'd realized that her body wasn't a club to strike with, but a pillow to smother.

'Bob said keep warm,' he said.

'I am warm.' She turned slightly, her breasts turned to rose in the glow of the fire.

'You don't need to pose any more anyway,' he said.

'I don't want to pose.'

'What then?'

She lay back, crooked one knee.

'I clobbered you,' he said.

'Maybe that's part of it.'

'Your neck'll hurt.'

'Maybe that's part of it too.'

He pulled off his painter's smock.

'All right,' he said. 'But you touch that painting and I'll belt you again.'

TWO BREADWINNERS WITH IN-LAWS

ARNOTT drove back home by the coast road. It was the longest way, but he needed time. There was so much to think about, so much that he was not yet ready to discuss with his wife. The two whiskies had been strong ones, the adrenalin still flowed inside him, the inevitable reaction to Fitz's violence, and he knew he would start shaking if he surrendered to the assault on his senses. He drove slowly. Sex and violence. The catchphrase that looked like lasting out a generation. And now at last he had shied away from it. He remembered the other younger Arnott who would have leaped to meet them both: what Madge had offered, what Fitz had threatened. The young feller would deliberately have blacked out his mind to obligations: commitment. It was Old Man Arnott who took sides; helping Madge, defending Fitz. That incredible body. It was incredible, it was downright mad, that he didn't want it; had even ignored the hints, subtle enough in their offering, that he could have it. And all for what? Because Fitz had seen something in her eyes, and caught that something on paper?

He was leaving the open land behind, the bents grass, scrub, sandy places where sea-fowl still nested: blackcaps, herring gulls, even a puffin or two. Now on his right were the semi-detacheds, red-tiled, picture-windowed, with already a Zodiac or a Cresta pulled up here and there in front of the garage, a breadwinner with field-glasses, home from the office, staring out to sea till it was time to go in for a drink. On his left was a strip of grass, mile after mile of it, unending playground for the day-trips of summer development; but he longed still to see the place as it had been in his youth, tumbled rocks and spear grass and sand, and wherever you looked, seabirds squabbling over Lebensraum. They never came there now. Seabirds didn't like neat grass any more than he did.

'I'm getting old, Arnott thought. Pernickety. Resentful of change. That grass is for kids. My own kids play on it. Let the seabirds find somewhere else. Suddenly the grass narrowed, the road bit into it to make a lay-by. Arnott drove into it. When he got out the air was cold, spiteful still though the sun was shining. Shoulders hunched, he walked on to the grass. From a distance he could hear cries, the shrill, combative cries of children playing 'Tiggy', the Tyneside name for tag, 'block the bay', and football, always football. Nowadays boys prepared for football the way Spartan kids had prepared for war.

And what's wrong with that? You and Fitz and Jim Moulton—you did prepare for war—and look where it got you.

The trouble was he couldn't think it out—Fitz, Madge, all that. He'd acted on reflex, emotion, not rationalizing at all. The result was he'd ended up with a vicious enemy and a water-colour and drawings worth—what? Hundreds? He'd have to find out: his insurance broker would insist on that. Have to show them to Susan, too. Those drawings and Susan. The idea embarrassed him. 'We're all Puritans,' Fitz had said. And Madge had added—except Fitzgerald. They had both been right. And yet once it hadn't been so. When he first loved Susan he had been open and honest, and she with him. Marriage and children had dulled all that. Inertia blossoming into shame. . . . This Laidlaw business was wrong. Evil, consciously chosen, must be wrong. . . . Then there was the problem of Moulton. That friendship had died that night, fading to nothing like the spilled Burgundy that spread across Laidlaw's tablecloth. He didn't want to help Moulton, not any more, and couldn't decide whether he ought to. For once his instincts brought no reaction.

Suddenly he found himself thinking of Silverstein. This was very much a Silverstein problem, this worry over the moral commitment of a Peeping Tom. He'd talked to Silverstein about Madge once. The night after that party. Oh boy, he'd fancied himself in those days. Goofy had been right about that. The smart suits, the dandy's waistcoats, the cane. But Goofy forgot how well he'd done at Medical School, going up the ladder year by year, never a failure, never referred back. Silverstein had insisted on that. Working hard and loving it, loving being right. What's wrong with this patient, Mr Arnott? And the answers, fluent, sure, straight out of the textbooks. Only there was no love any more. Just fortnightly letters to Freda and a present for his Aunt Bet at Christmas and birthdays. His relationship with Silverstein was the closest he got to love: the stories about his girls that set Silverstein giggling, the tribute that affection always has to pay.

Silverstein had adored the one about Madge. It had everything. Eroticism, drama, even a happy ending: her pants pulled up as the curtain pulled down.

'Frustrating for you. Very frustrating.'

'Too bloody true,' he said.

'Nubile,' Silverstein said. 'That's the most erotic word in the language. Don't you think it's erotic?'

'I've never thought about it.'

'Too busy doing. Think about it now.'

'The "nu" bit's obvious,' he said. 'That's nude. But "bile". Can you really get excited about bile?'

'There's a ring about it all the same,' said Silverstein. 'I take it she was?'

'Oh yes.'

Always after that, nubile meant young Madge, skirts over her thighs, pants tangled around her knees, dress unzipped at the back, bra loosed on breasts already rounded, firm, yet with a freshness like dew. He'd never touched, fondled a body like hers, never awakened such responses. It was the age thing. To her he was a man then, a mature man, and his hands had moved with a man's assurance while she'd shuddered and clung. There'd been the gin she'd drunk too, easing her, opening her to him while she'd shuddered and clung, cried out aloud in her delight. Yet when he found out her age he'd reacted at once, sealing her up again in her knickers, seeing her to her home intact, warding off the others so anxious to take what he had rejected. She had been so very beautiful, and yet he had refused her without thinking. Tears, pleading, it made no difference. She was too young; she must go home. Silverstein had praised him for it. If Arnott had seduced the girl he couldn't have borne it, but even so that automatic withholding had earned praise. Silverstein hadn't stinted it. Yet in the end he had said one curious thing.

'What you did was admirable,' he said. 'Splendid even. It lacks only one thing.'

'What's that?' Arnott asked.

'You don't seem to have felt either the good you did or the bad you could have done. You don't seem to have felt a damn thing. . . . Now let's see what you've learned about obstetrics.'

He'd never felt a damn thing—in Silverstein's sense—until he'd met Susan. And that hadn't lasted.

Then another thought hit him. On two occasions he had insulted Madge in the sexual way that would hurt her most deeply—denial. She had cause to hate him all right. He walked to the edge of the grass. Below him cliffs cascaded down to a yellow-brown beach, blotched with the debris of winter gales, piled shale, rocks, festoons of seaweed. Beyond that the sea, blue-grey today, but with a light in it, the incoming tide as calm and steady as the beat of a strong heart. Across the harbour two seine-netters moved towards the fish-quay, their wakes reduced to ripples in the calm water. No big ships now. He looked behind him. A bend in the bay showed him Goofy's laboratory, featureless, fashionable, about as exciting as bread. Arnott looked down. The beach was almost empty: a couple of tramps beachcombing, two steps ahead of the tide, a bunch of kids in the distance, huddled round a fire (who were they today? soldiers? pirates? spacemen?), and one lunatic wading out into the icy water, hoping it was virile, sure it was good for him because it felt so cold. (We're all Puritans. Except one.) How far up am I? Arnott wondered. Eighty feet? A hundred? If I jumped now I'd hit those rocks. I'd be dead. Inexplicable suicide of undemandingly happy doctor.

'Balls,' he said aloud. 'All that stuff in your mind. Leave it. It's balls.'

He walked back to his car, looked at the water-colour Fitz had given him. It could be Brittany; it could equally be the place where he'd just been standing, in July, at early morning, before the trippers come; the waves the colour of summer. He saw now that there was a dignity in the dead man that from what Fitz had told him could never have existed while he lived. What Fitz had made was a requiem.

She was waiting for him. No surprise, no drama, only a mocking unconcern.

'If at first you don't succeed,' she said. She made no effort to lower her voice.

'Won't they hear us?'

'Jim baby, this is Tracy's pad. She works here. She makes a noise. So naturally it's sound-proofed. Then we're married, Jim baby. We've got the preacher's word for it. Don't tell me you've forgotten we're married?'

'It's why I'm here,' he said.

'I thought it might be.'

He looked around the room.

'Like it?' she asked.

Shelves of books, the same ones he remembered, playbills, a complete hi-fi deck, a Pollock theatre beautifully assembled. That was background. But there was urgency too: the interleaved directors' scripts, the model stage littered with shapes cut out in cardboard, three dimensional notes, costume designs, actors' photographs, letters and bills, the apparently haphazard chaos that she could sort out in seconds. This part of it he could understand. It was the way he worked himself.

'It's what I'm used to,' he said.

'Work.'

She'd said it as a nun might say 'prayer'.

For a moment she lay still, then she pushed back the sheet that covered her, and got out of bed. She was wearing shorty pyjamas with a sleeveless top. As she moved a book fell from the bed, bumped softly into the carpet.

'Forgive the rather workaday outfit,' she said. 'I wasn't sure that you would come.'

She was sweating a little: as he watched she went into the shower and came back with a towel, dabbing at herself, careful not to show her body.

He picked up the book: a collection of Pinter plays.

'Are you glad I did?'

She was busy now at the dressing-table, putting on lipstick, combing her hair.

'That remains to be seen,' she said, and picked up a scent-spray.

'This is Ma Griffe,' she said, and squeezed the spray.

'Nice,' he said.

'Sure it won't put you off?'

'Why should it?'

'Griffe means claw,' she said. 'Also it costs twenty-eight dollars an ounce.'

'I'll try not to breathe,' he said.

'My, my. So confident we are.' The bulb squeezed again, her hands rubbed her body, preparing, perfecting, then she swung round on the stool.

'I want to see you,' she said. 'Take them off, sweetie.'

He felt that he was blushing; hated himself for it.

'Oh that's *sweet*,' she said.

'Please, Tracy,' he said. 'Help me a little.'

'I tried to help this afternoon.'

'Not like that. What I mean is—you first.'

'O.K.' Her hands moved, the towel fell and she was naked. 'I haven't got any fatter,' she said. 'Now you.'

He pulled off his robe. Below it he wore pyjama trousers.

'Don't be shy,' she said. 'I won't bite you. Not where it'll show anyway.'

He took them off.

'Well, well,' she said. 'I'm glad to see your confidence was not displaced.'

Then he reached out for her, drew her in to him, let her feel his strength till she had no more need of words. Her body was moist, the perfume fragrant; she was active and eager as he remembered. When he picked her up, dropped her on to her bed she cried out, but in anticipation, not in pain, when he covered her she was ready for him, yielding at once. This time for him too the act was one of pleasure, the mind drugged, the body intensely aware of what it gave, was given. Suddenly she cried out again, a high and keening cry, pleasure that sounded like despair, her body became submissive, slack, and he rolled from her, lay still.

'You've forgotten some——' she began, but his arms came round her, drew her to him. 'No you haven't.' She kissed him on the mouth, for the first time. 'It was marvellous,' she said. 'Was it marvellous for you too?'

'It's never been like that before,' he said. He wasn't lying.

'You're as strong as ever. But you didn't hurt me. Not this time.'

'Did I hurt you before?'

'It doesn't matter.'

'It matters to me,' he said. 'I shouldn't have hurt you.'

Her hands moved over him, and this time he welcomed them.

'It was because you worked it out, wasn't it?' she asked.

'What you on about?' he asked her, knowing it would make her laugh.

'That decanter,' she said. 'All that inspiration stuff. It worked so you got your cock back.'

Even her using the word was a test: she knew he hated her using it. But this time that didn't matter either. He lay passive to her hands, gently squeezing her to the rhythm she set.

'I don't care why you've got it back so long as it's there,' she said. When the time came, he moved to her again.

Her body now had infinite power to please: the slenderness, the unsuspected strength, even the aggression; it was all delight. Tender skin, strong muscles, the flash of teeth against the redness on her lips, he wanted, needed it all. To touch, to be touched was good, but to make it perfect you had to see, be seen. Ma Griffe was right for her: she fought love all right, like a tigress—and yet there was no wounding—unless pleasures were wounds. Next time, after the wailing cry, she got up and ran the shower. Without thinking, he got up too, followed her, watched by the door as the water streamed on to her, smooth on her smoothness. Then he got in too, took her in his arms as she soused them both. Water ... kisses. ... Her hands too, kissing in the water—then, 'Darling,' she said. 'Let's rest awhile.'

She wrapped them both in bath sheets, and he sprawled on the bed.

'Let's drink,' she said. 'Let's make it last.'

That she had a miniature bar up there didn't surprise him, but that she should have a tiny refrigerator for ice cubes did, yet this time there was no mockery in his laughter. When she brought the drinks he took her bath sheet away, spread it on the bed, covered it with his own, made her lie naked on top of it, himself lay naked beside her.

'I love you when you're like this,' she said, then turned to face him. In her eyes there was no trace of the melting look he had expected. They were cool eyes, appraising eyes. 'It mightn't make any difference.'

'I realize that,' he said.

'We're having fun.' Still she had that appraising look. 'Please don't say that's banal. I know it's banal. But it's the only way I can say it—unless I write poetry. I write very bad poetry. Only—our bodies are being honest with each other. Why not our minds too? Just once. It might never happen again.'

'All right.'

'Why do you want me back?'

He told her at once, and when he had finished she laughed.

'Jesus,' she said. 'I'd forgotten how brave you are.'

'Brave?'

'It took some nerve, insulting me like that.'

'What we're doing is an insult?'

'Call it a bonus,' she said, but she made no effort to escape from him.

'You asked for the truth.'

'I got it. "I could not love thee dear so much, loved I not physics more."'

'I think that's true too.'

'Tell it to me again. All of it.'

He told her about the dinner party, the corrida-like teasing, himself the bull; about Bob, Madge ('So that's why you like big girls,' she said), about the wives.

'Sybil Laidlaw?' she said. Her face furrowed, then: 'Sybil Laidlaw. The bitch. The Kensington Crown Derby bitch. Did you know I'd met her?'

'She never told me.'

'Darling—I *talked* about you. Bitch,' she said. 'Bitch bitch.' Then, 'Tell me about Quantum,' and he told her.

'And that's what you want?'

'It's what I can do.'

'You need a whole building just because you saw a decanter?'

'What they're giving's the minimum.'

'Who else was there?'

'Nobody. ... Oh—Fitzgerald came in after dinner. He's a painter.'

'You mean John Fitzgerald?'

'Yes. We called him Fitz. ... You've heard about him?'

'Darling, he's world-famous. Dad's been after one of his Mexican pictures for months. You never told me you knew him.'

'He's a nut,' he said. 'Round the twist.'

'People say that about you too.'

'Obsessives aren't always crazy,' he said. 'But they get things done.'

She lay flat on her back again, took away his drink.

'Make like an obsessive,' she said.

The last person he had expected was Sybil Laidlaw. He'd had Goofy, he'd had Madge. After the Mongols had passed, it was a bit much to get the camp-followers as well. But there she was, daintily sexy, at ease among the crystal that his wife hated to hear described as best. Two elegantly sexy women, but not at ease with each other; the first casual friendship of the dinner-party ripening now to an intense dislike.

'Look who's here, Bob,' his wife said.

Arnott realized that he was doing so all too obviously; was aware too of the picture and drawings he held.

'Mrs Laidlaw,' he said. 'How nice. Excuse me while I get rid of these.'

'Pictures?' said Sybil. 'How exciting.'

'Nothing so splendid,' Arnott said. 'Just case-notes.'

He was damned if the little bitch would see them, but there was no time to think of why that should be so. He fled.

When he came back, they hadn't moved. The room was still filled with an atmosphere of glacial dislike—his wife was very good at glacial dislike. But Sybil's coldness was of a different sort. There was a quality of defeat in it, and defeat was something to which she had yet to grow accustomed. He took refuge among the crystal, topping up gins and tonics, pouring Scotch for himself.

'I could say I just happened to be passing,' Sybil said. 'It would have been a lie. I very much wanted to see you both—so I came.'

Little Lady Bountiful, Arnott thought. Giving of your presence to the poor.

'In a Jensen Interceptor,' he said.

'Clever of you to know it was mine.'

'Round here we have Rovers,' said Arnott. 'When we don't have Hillmans.'

'Please don't,' she said.

So languidly weary of the yelps of her inferiors.

Arnott said, 'To what do we owe the pleasure, Mrs Laidlaw?'

'I asked you to call me Sybil,' she said.

'I remember,' said Arnott.

The languid weariness returned.

'I've asked your wife to come to us for dinner or drinks or a theatre-party or *any*thing, any time in the next three weeks. She doesn't seem able to find a date.'

He looked at Susan, standing behind the elegant one, foraging for ice-cubes. She shook her head and scowled.

'That's too bad,' he said.

'Wouldn't you also say it was incredible?'

'Not unless I were being deliberately rude.'

Sybil Laidlaw's face showed nothing, except that she was a lady.

'Why us, Mrs Laidlaw?' he asked. 'Why pick on us?'

'Tom *likes* you.'

'I find I don't respond to his brand of affection.'

'You're referring to the dinner-party?' He nodded. 'But that's just it. He showed you what a monster that Moulton was.'

'He did rather more than that. May I offer you another drink?'

'No thank you. Please visit us.'

'No,' said Arnott.

Sybil Laidlaw said, 'It's because of our parents, isn't it? Your father and my father. That's why you dislike us.'

'Your father committed a vindictive and spiteful act——'

'He certainly did not.' It was strange how quickly the glacier could melt.

'. . . in my opinion. It had nothing to do with you.'

She struggled to resume her ladylike calm, as if it were a coat and she couldn't find the sleeves.

'Well then?' she asked.

'I did love my father,' he said. 'And my mother. I love even their memory. I think one day you'll do that too. You won't enjoy seeing that memory used in a smear campaign—any more than I did.'

'So you're still on Moulton's side,' she said.

'Oh, for God's sake!' The words were rage, and all three of them knew it. He stopped, sipped whisky, tried again. 'I'm on Susan's side, and my children's, and my patients'. They're the only side I have. Please go, Mrs Laidlaw.'

She left in silence. In silence he saw her to the door, watched the Jensen whisper down the street, went back to his wife, who was weeping.

'Hey, what's this?' he said.

'I hate her,' Susan said. 'I hate what she's doing.'

'I'm not letting her do anything,' he said. 'That's why I've sent her away.'

The tears flowed faster, and he put an arm about her, fumbled for a handkerchief. The movements were clumsy. Susan so rarely cried.

'All because of a dinner-party,' she said. 'It's so *stupid*.'

'Symbols so often are,' he said.

'Please don't be clever, Bob. I'm too tired,' she said.

'I mean, another dinner is nothing—just some damn good food and wine. It's what it stands for—the Laidlaws and Madge and ourselves against Moulton.'

'I knew that as soon as she asked us.' Susan hesitated. 'I don't like Moulton either.'

'You detest him,' he said. 'I'm the one who dislikes him.'

Behind them a voice said, 'It's very naughty to make people cry.' Arnott turned to look at his son. On Andrew's face was the look of smug satisfaction that comes to even very nice children when they can put an adult in the wrong.

'Who told you that?' he asked.

'Miss Addison.'

He turned for guidance to his wife.

'Miss Addison's the new nursery-school teacher,' said Susan.

'Miss Addison said I was naughty when I made Bobby Henderson cry. She said Jesus would be crying too.'

'Jesus?' said Arnott. His wife gripped his arm.

'Daddy didn't make me cry,' she said.

'Who did then?'

'The lady who came here,' Arnott said. 'But she's gone now. Why don't you go back to the television?'

'It's the news,' said Andrew. 'Will Jesus be crying now?'

'Not for me,' said Arnott firmly. He picked up his son. 'Where's Jane?'

'Sleeping,' Andrew said. 'Are you going to throw me up in the air?'

'I certainly am.'

'Super,' said Andrew, then he remembered something. 'We'll have to be quick,' he said. 'After the news it's *Wagon Train*.'

The night was an easy one. Harkness had the surgery, and there were only two calls, an appendix and a child suspected of swallowing a marble. Both ended up in hospital: so often these days one abrogated responsibility from the start. But that night he didn't care: he felt a tiredness that slowed him like chains. There was a need to talk to Susan too, but when he returned from the hospital the second time she'd gone to bed. Perhaps she'll be reading, he thought. He'd wanted so much to show her the picture and the drawings, but even the easy cases took up time. He went into his study, fetched them from the case-notes drawer where he'd locked them, and climbed the stairs to the children's room—Andrew asleep under a mound of teddy bears, Jane, fists clenched, ecstatic in dreams—then on to their own. Susan was sleeping, the bedside light still on her. Arnott was conscious of a great wave of disappointment, and yet, holding the treasures he'd brought her, he looked at her with love. Sleep usually softened her face, but tonight he was conscious of a strength he hadn't seen before. Her mother's daughter.

The blankets had slipped from her, and he pulled them up to cover the sleek shoulders, the dark shadow between her breasts that still had so much power to move, if only he had the time to indulge pursuit of such happiness. He changed in the bathroom, brushed his teeth, then came back to the coffee that waited every working night on the bedside table. He couldn't sleep before he examined Fitz's gifts. Cautiously he drew out the water-colour, quietly unrolled it. At once it filled his world. . . . She had said, 'Pour me a cup,' and he broke free at last from the serenity of sea and sky, the ultimate remoteness of the dead. She was sitting up, alert, beautiful as if it were morning, yet with that maternal look she used on him as much as on the children. The look he detested.

'I'm sorry,' he said. 'Did I wake you?'

'No. I just knew you were there,' she said.

He poured her coffee. One shoulder-strap had slipped: she adjusted it, brisk as a nurse.

'I liked it the way it was,' he said, and she smiled the smile she gave to Andrew and Jane when they asked for something they couldn't have.

'What are you reading?'

'Not reading,' he said. 'A pressy.'

'Let me see.'

'It's from Fitzgerald,' he said.

'A picture? Oh super!'

'You may not think so,' he said. 'In a way it's not exactly tactful.'

'Let me see.'

He gave it to her and waited. Time lengthened. It was impossible to read her face.

'Dear God,' she said at last. 'It's so beautiful.'

'You don't mind?'

'I don't think he hates Daddy,' she said. 'I don't think he hates anyone.' She looked at it again. 'I want you to tell me about it.'

'He gave us these too,' he said.

'Let me see.'

'Wait till I tell you.'

'No.' She grabbed for them but he held her off till she sensed the threat of desire in his hands, and submitted, scowling. 'I want to see.'

'After I've told you.'

She listened at first with reluctance, but soon his words were reaching her, demanding her attention, her allegiance even, as she responded to his sadness in what had happened.

When he had finished she said, 'We're never going to see any of them again, are we?'

'Not if we see them first.'

'We will,' she said. 'I'll see to that. Please let me see, Bob.'

He gave them to her, sat beside her on the bed as she began to look. When she came to the nudes she gasped aloud. It took her a long time to see them all.

'He's clever, isn't he?' she said at last.

'Of course he is.'

'I mean clever like Moulton.'

'Not clever like me.'

'Bob, you *are* clever. It's your job—you have to be. But Moulton's different. And Fitzgerald is too.'

'It's called talent,' Arnott said. 'Maybe it's called genius.'

'You have to pay for it,' she said. 'Look at mummy.' She turned back to the drawings, and giggled.

'What's so funny?' he asked.

'It's ridiculous,' she said and giggled again. Arnott moved closer.

'Tell me,' he said.

'Do they make you feel sexy?'

'Not particularly.'

'That's what's funny,' she said.

He put a hand on her breast.

'I married a lesbian, did I?' he said.

'I think it's the competition,' she said. Then, 'Bob it's late. You're tired.' But this time she stayed where she was. He had reached for her shoulder-strap when the door opened, and they sprang apart. Arnott turned to face his son once more.

'What is it?' he asked.

'Jane can't sleep,' Andrew said.

'Tell her I'm coming,' said Susan. 'Go along now.'

Andrew peered at them, suspicious as a prosecuting counsel, and left.

'I'll go,' said Arnott. 'She may need something.'

His wife was probably the only one in the world who could tell his voice was bitter, and yet, when he bent to kiss her, his lips were gentle. There was a cry from the children's room, Jane's cry, soft and petulant, not Andrew's outraged bellow. He hurried out.

Susan lay back and thought about her husband. She was married, it seemed, to a good man. Not just kind, or considerate. Good. With the sort of goodness you expected from parsons. It was the goodness that had made her so sexy—all through their affair. She could be fearless in her love-making because there was nothing to fear. With her marriage, and the children, the sexiness had gone. He had needed so much she had used it all up. Had turned instead to Andrew and Jane. He was a man who needed sex beyond the average, and she'd reduced it to a routine that fulfilled neither of them. She looked again at the pictures. Competition. Gorgeous competition. She couldn't match that any more; she didn't want to, because if they started again, this time she would be as vulnerable as he. Giving as well as taking. Giving, she knew, would hurt her. . . . Sex and goodness. Such a ridiculous mixture. . . . Her mother would laugh. But her mother would also understand. She turned a page. When Arnott came back she was asleep, the book still open in front of her.

THE YOUNGEST MAN IN THE CABINET

'The Minister is rather busy.'

'My appointment's for two forty-five,' Laidlaw said.

She looked at her watch.

'It's five past three,' said Laidlaw.

'I make it nearly ten past,' she said.

'Couldn't you phone through?'

'I'm afraid not.'

Nothing for it then. Rage only made you stupid. Better to sit down. Better even to smile before you did it. That shook her. She'd expected a tantrum.

He went back to his leather armchair and his briefcase. There was enough in that to last him the day, and the armchair was comfortable. Whither he went, Aliment went also. He got out the Quantum Lab file and started on the figures, but was aware still of the girl at the desk. Secretary bird. You called them P.A.s nowadays, and paid them twenty a week at least if they were any good. And this one obviously was. Not bad-looking either. Good legs for a mini. So often nowadays the legs were too fat, or else they were spindles. The voice was nice too—if a little over-refined, the bank-manager belt—and she guarded her lord and master well. Harry Lewis. Still running. But now he was running up—towards the top, or very near it. He wasn't cut out for Everest, but he might just scale Kanchenjunga. Did he ever stop and feel those legs? Laidlaw wondered. Harry Lewis and a dolly bird from Esher? It was impossible. But so was Harry Lewis the minister who was too busy to see him. Chubby red Harry and middle-class legs. If the legs responded to power, Harry had it made.

At twenty past three her buzzer sounded, she murmured refinements into the intercom as he kept his eyes on his figures. He still looked down when the man came for him, the bright, alert young man they all had: smooth-shaven, neat-suited, discreet tie inside a gleaming collar. This one's was Balliol. Was that just acquiescence on Harry's part? Or shrewdness? Or even—was it possible—wit? Harry Lewis hugging himself that Balliol should obey Harry Lewis, late of the Gateshead Training College for Teachers?

'Mr Laidlaw?' Balliol said.

'Yes?'

'The Minister will see you now.'

Laidlaw took his time putting away his papers, and Balliol was too well bred to fuss, though not fussing took its toll. Then past the P.A., soft tap on panelled door, and into the presence at last. Nice room. Big. Panelled in white. Another door to leave by when you'd finished—no chance of informal chit-chat during the to and fro. Couple of pictures, flowers just so—did the legs arrange them every morning? The room was a very elegant setting——

'Mr Laidlaw, Minister,' said Balliol.

And Harry was its jewel. Harry rising from behind an imposing chunk of Edwardian mahogany, advancing with his greeter's smile, hand outstretched.

'Mr Laidlaw and I are old friends. Tom, how are you?'

He looked tired. They always looked tired. But behind the tiredness there was a sense of fulfilment that he hadn't had when he was Parliamentary Secretary. Then he'd had a chance; a good chance, but still a chance. Now he had arrived. All he had to do was stay where he was, and the honorary doctorates, the decorations, even the directorships would come in like the tide. And when he got old, Lord Lewis of Gateshead, p.c, c.m, k.g.v.o., ll.d, etcetera, etcetera. Read his memoirs in the *Sunday Times*.

'It's good of you to spare me a few minutes, Minister,' Laidlaw said.

'Always glad to see an old friend,' said Lewis, the greeter's smile expanding. Still new to it. Likes the sound of that 'Minister' even in the mouths of those who've known him longest. Maybe especially in those mouths.

'Run along, Michael,' he said. 'I shan't need you.'

Run along. I shan't need you. Harry, Harry. How soon you have adapted to this rarefied air. Laidlaw waited as Balliol departed, then: 'Are congratulations in order, Minister?' he asked.

'You're very kind,' said Lewis.

'Not at all,' Laidlaw said. 'Believe me I'm delighted. The youngest man in the Cabinet. It's marvellous news.'

'Of course I'd learned the job as Parliamentary Secretary,' said Lewis. 'That helped.'

'Nothing helped,' said Laidlaw, jovially brusque. 'You were the only possible man, so you got it. Congratulations again.'

He thrust out his hand, and Lewis took it, and for the moment the smile was honest in the relief it showed. Harry Lewis had stopped running.

'Come and sit down, Tom,' he said at last.

'Thank you, Minister.'

'Harry,' said Lewis. 'I hope I'll always be Harry to my friends. At least in private.'

They sat, and Lewis at once became brisk.

'I've kept you waiting for thirty-five minutes and I can spare you ten,' he said. 'I'm sorry. There's just too much to do.'

'Good of you to see me at all,' said Laidlaw. 'I thought your Parliamentary Secretary would handle it.'

'Strictly speaking it is a P.P.S.'s job, but I like to think of this one as my baby,' said Lewis. 'Especially as it involves an old friend.'

And it's happening right in the middle of your constituency, Harry old friend.

'How is it doing?'

'The lab's almost finished.'

'You're in a hurry, I see.'

'When you believe in what you're doing, you like to get started.'

'Quite so. . . . Your equipment?'

'All housed.'

'You're still . . . enamoured of the German computer?'

'I'm enamoured of its price.'

'And of course you have a certain amount of investment to protect.'

'Harry,' said Laidlaw, 'I really do congratulate you. But the price is paramount. We're stretched to the limit as it is. Anything British would be too expensive. We'd have to abandon the project.'

'We had rather hoped for an all-British project.'

'Not at the price. We haven't any more money.'

He stressed the 'we' a little. Lewis shook his head.

'Nor have we,' he said. 'Gratitude, encouragement, recognition, even tax provision, but no grant. We'll accept the German computer if we must.'

'Thank you, Harry. I'm very grateful.'

'What about Moulton?'

'He's been offered the job.'

'I know that.' Lewis's brusqueness was not jovial. 'Will he accept?'

Careful, for Christ's sake, Laidlaw thought. He's saying you've got to have him.

'He already has. Verbally.'

'I suggest you contract him at once.'

'You're saying you want him?'

'No, Tom,' said Lewis. 'I'm saying you've got to have him.'

'Are you threatening me, Harry?' Laidlaw asked.

'No threats,' said Lewis. 'With you they'd be foolish. Please listen to some facts. We have five minutes. Fact one,' he struck one forefinger with the other. 'Quantum's after publicity and tax-free research. Fact two'—the middle finger—'you're buying it with a bit of

222

spare time atomic physics. Dress it up all you like Tom, but that's what you're doing.'

'Go on,' Laidlaw said.

'Fact three—under normal circumstances you wouldn't get this Government's curse, let alone its blessing, but Moulton isn't a normal circumstance.' He paused, and looked at Laidlaw. His eyes told nothing but power. 'What I'm going to tell you now goes no further.'

'I give you my word,' Laidlaw said.

'Because if it does you have no deal at all. I spoke with Bennington some weeks ago. He's old and smelly and his memory's gone. But he still knows his physics. In fact it's all he does know. He tells me Moulton's very near a breakthrough. A big one.'

'And you'll let him make it with us?'

'Where else can he go?' Lewis asked. 'The universities won't have him.'

'He could try abroad,' said Laidlaw.

'No,' said Lewis. 'He couldn't.'

It was nice, Laidlaw thought, to have one's theories confirmed.

'Moulton won't do classified research,' he said.

'He may not have to. But what he's working on is completely unpredictable. It could lead anywhere.'

'Bennington says so?'

'He says very little else. Please do as I ask.'

'Moulton's in California,' said Laidlaw. 'Visiting his in-laws. We expect him back very soon. I'll sign him up at once.'

'Please see that you do,' Lewis said, then added: 'Not his in-laws. His wife.'

'Your homework was always thorough, Harry,' Laidlaw said.

'It had to be.'

'May I ask something?'

'Briefly.'

'What do you get out of all this?'

'If you don't get Moulton nobody gets anything.'

'I'll get him. What'll you get?'

'Acclaim,' said Lewis. 'A great deal of acclaim. You think you're using us—but you're not. We're using you. You put up all the money—but you can't move without us. That fact will be made known. Moulton's work will be British work, sponsored and encouraged by this Government. Once that is known—but not until then—we won't grudge you a few crumbs.'

'Suppose I decide not to go ahead?'

'You can't,' said Lewis. He had no need to say more.

'Your terms are acceptable—just,' Laidlaw said.

'There's one other thing I should like you to consider,' Lewis said. 'Moulton is a problem. That problem is totally yours—after all he's your employee—and must remain so. We want only his results.'

Laidlaw said, 'You can have a seat on my board any time you want it.'

'You're very kind,' Lewis rose. 'Ten minutes,' he said. 'How quickly the time goes.' His hand moved towards a switch, withdrew. 'A little gossip,' he said. 'Let's make time for that. You were a civil servant yourself, I believe?'

'Ministry of Economic Warfare,' said Laidlaw. 'I left when peace broke out.'

'To begin your career of rugged individualism?'

'To learn it. I worked for Charlie Dodds.'

'So I believe. Dodds is about to be prosecuted.'

'What's he done?'

'Illicit trade. The penalties can be extremely heavy. I trust you didn't allow yourself to be involved.'

Laidlaw said carefully, 'It would be impossible to prove I ever did anything illegal when I worked for Charlie.'

'Naturally. I'm delighted to hear it. The trouble is that mud of that sort does rather tend to stick.'

'We'll have to make sure none is thrown then.'

'You'd be very well advised to do so.' This time Lewis touched the buzzer. 'It's been most interesting to talk to you.' Then Balliol appeared. 'Show Mr Laidlaw out please, Michael.' He made no effort to shake hands. 'And drop me a line as soon as you have a contract, won't you, Tom?'

It occurred to Laidlaw that, years ago, Harry Lewis had stopped running long enough to hate him.

He had slept late, and the sleep had been dreamless: black and deep as a tarn. When he woke he was conscious at once that his body was simultaneously relaxed and easy, and yet clamorous for food. He lay remembering the last tempest of their love-making, the furtive sneaking back to his bedroom, the sound of Tracy's laughter. Married, she had said, and acting out a French farce. In California yet. It had seemed funny then, and it remained so. Old Schiller couldn't hurt him today. He showered and shaved, and went down to breakfast. There was no one there but Adèle, looking vague and dreamy, sipping tomato-juice. When he came in she began to read *Vogue*, and the Filipinos supplied ham, eggs, dollar cakes. He was glad Adèle had *Vogue* with her: he was much too busy to talk.

Once she said, 'What a splendid appetite you have, young man,' which might have been insult or might have been envy, then later: 'I can see you're not so fond of tomato-juice.' This was meaningless, but so often Adèle was meaningless. When he'd finished he poured himself coffee, and turned to grapple with Adèle, wishing that Tracy would come down.

He could see that Adèle was fond of tomato-juice. There was a jug beside her which had been full of the stuff and was now almost empty. In her hand she had a glass containing a third of a pint at least. He could see also that she wasn't all that fond of *Vogue*. She was reading it upside down. The Filipino male appeared, and Moulton said, 'Not now. We'll ring when we want you,' and the Filipino grinned. He was always grinning, but this time the grin seemed to widen when he looked at Adèle and *Vogue*. Then he left, and Moulton wished once more that Tracy would come. Adèle drank more tomato-juice.

Moulton said, 'That was a delicious breakfast.'

Adèle was past it by then: she stayed with upside-down *Vogue*.

'It looks like another beautiful day,' said Moulton.

It was like talking to furniture. Adèle went on staring at *Vogue*, then drank again. Moulton tried coughing. Adèle drank.

What in Christ's name was he supposed to do?

Then Adèle drank again, and her glass was empty. Moulton marvelled as she filled it up; she didn't spill a drop. But she had to turn to do it: she became aware of him at last.

'I know you,' she said.

'Of course you do.'

Moulton hated the spurious kindness of his own voice, but he didn't know what else to do.

'You're the rude one,' Adèle said.

'I'm sorry,' said Moulton.

Adèle looked at the magazine in her hands. 'I don't like *Harper's Bazaar*,' she said.

Moulton said, 'That's *Vogue*.'

'There you go,' said Adèle, and drank more tomato-juice.

'I wasn't even reading it,' she said. 'I just didn't want to talk to you.'

'I wish you didn't feel like that,' Moulton said.

'You eat funny,' she said. 'British style——'

'I am British,' said Moulton.

'. . . That's got nothing to do with it. You make Fred nervous. That's why I didn't want to talk to you. I'm afraid.'

When she began to cry Moulton gave up, retreating behind a mumble of embarrassment, racing up the stairs, bursting into Tracy's room. She was in the shower again, but this time she made no move to show herself to him when she came out. She wore a robe that covered her from neck to ankle, and was furious.

'I thought we agreed——' she said.

'It isn't that——' he began.

'You're spoiling it,' she said. 'Oh, you *fool*. You spoil everything.'

'I didn't spoil your mother,' he said. 'Somebody else is doing that.'

'Mother?'

'She's drunk as a fiddler's bitch,' he said.

She was past him in a flash, hurtling down the stairs, so that he watched in terror. So easily she could trip and fall. He hurried after, not caring what she had said, only pleased that she was there to cope and nervous for her safety. In the breakfast-room Adèle had stopped crying; had almost, it seemed, stopped living. Her face was blotched red, she sweated and breathed heavily, but she made no movement.

'Oh, Mother,' Tracy said. 'You promised.'

Her mother made no answer: probably hadn't heard. Suddenly she pitched forward, head slumped towards the gleaming tiles. Moulton's body moved, he caught her across her narrow breasts, eased her back in the chair, head flopping, limbs already rigid. She weighed so little, it was pitiful. He picked up the jug, drank from the dregs in the bottom.

'Vodka,' he said.

'Bloody Marys,' Tracy said. 'I drank them that day with that Laidlaw bitch. I *hate* Bloody Marys.'

Moulton said, 'I can see you're not so fond of tomato-juice.' Tracy turned to him. 'That's what she said to me.'

'I'll have to get her to bed,' said Tracy. 'You'll have to help me. I'm sorry.'

The Filipinos still chattered Spanish in the kitchen. He plucked her out of the chair, clumsy with her inert clumsiness, and followed Tracy.

Her mother slept alone in a room that was all silk brocade and lace and Tretchakov prints. Racks of *Vogue*, *Harper's Bazaar*, *Queen*. Book after Book of the Month. Hi-Fi and sound-track of *Oklahoma*, *Dolly*, *Sound of Music*. A neat room, a refined room, a sad room. Moulton laid her on the bed.

'We'd better leave her,' Tracy said.

'No.'

He eased her forward, piled pillows behind her, found a towel and spread it across her.

'She might vomit,' he said. 'If she did she could choke.'

'You're remarkably well informed.'

He looked at her. The irony was directed inward: a defence mechanism only.

'I've had some funny friends in my time,' he said. There was a pitcher of water beside her. When she woke up she would be desperately thirsty, but that was provided for. Moulton left. There was nothing else he could do. He went back to his room, found a pair of swimming-trunks and went down to the pool, swam in the warm, acrid-scented water, up and down, up and down, his body soothed in warmth and repetition. Poor cow. Poor, sad, defenceless cow.

There was movement, a procession. Male Filipino with table, female Filipino with tray, Tracy with nothing, only the long robe trailing; Princess Tracy who could fuck like a goose-girl. The word came unbidden, and he didn't reject it, but swam on as she sat by the pool to her breakfast, raised one hand in greeting as his body barrelled past. When he came out she was sipping coffee and smoking, legs stretched out to the sun.

'Want some?' she said. He shook his head, conscious of his fishbelly whiteness against the even brown of her legs.

'I insulted you this morning. I'm sorry,' she said.

'It was a pretty accurate insult.'

'And now you're helping me. I'm grateful. Grateful for my mother too.' She hesitated. 'Can I ask you another favour?'

'Of course,' he said.

'I want to take you somewhere—but if we go, you must do exactly as I say.'

'All right.'

They went to her patio: a screen of trees, walls of frosted glass beyond, a garden inside a garden. Clipped yews, shaved grass, roses that lived only because the sprinklers let them.

'You're so white,' she said. 'I want you brown like me.'

She took off her robe, stepped naked to him, kissed him on the mouth.

'Thank you,' she said, then stepped away. 'The favour's this. I want you to get brown—and talk. That's all.'

He stepped out of his trunks and lay down on the grass, moist from the sprinkler, springy, alive. She knelt beside him, began to rub him with suntan oil. Oh Adams, Birkinshaw, Smith 063, Shorty Stevens! When she'd finished she sprawled on her back beside him, lit two cigarettes, put one in his mouth.

'That's Hollywood for you,' she said.

'What you on about?' The words a lovers' secret now.

'All this naked symbolism,' she said.

'What you after?'

'You're the only other person who's ever been here,' she said. 'Except the gardener. And he has his clothes on—and I'm not around. When I'm naked I find I think better. It's the grass maybe. Or the flowers. I don't know. Sounds like some phony Beverly Hills guru.'

'Sounds more like Wordsworth,' he said.

'I keep forgetting you read books. . . . But it works, phony or not. Maybe it'll work with you too.'

'Maybe.'

'Darling,' she said. 'What am I going to do about Adèle?'

'I've been back three days,' he said. 'D'you think you're being fair?'

'Of course not,' she said. 'I'm being desperate.'

He looked at her, the desire muted, and yet the appraisal was one of pleasure.

'With a body like yours you have to be honest,' he said. 'What can you do?'

'Stop her drinking.'

'Not here,' he said. 'You'll never do it here.

'Why not?'

She was thinking only of her ability, her strength.

'If we go on I'm going to hurt you,' he said. 'We'll quarrel.'

'Please darling,' she said. 'Please.'

'All right. You'll never stop her here because she can always get booze here.'

'We can keep it from her.'

'*You* can.'

'You're talking about Dad,' she said.

'That's right.' When she was silent he said, 'I'm sorry, love, but you asked me.'

'Don't be sorry. I *did* ask you. I want you to go on.'

'Your dad—he's not a fool. By now he'll know about alcoholics. Has he talked to her doctor?'

'Her doctor—the shrink, everybody.'

'So he knows how dangerous it can get. But he doesn't send her for treatment—and he doesn't hide the booze. She's even got it in her bedroom. I saw it.'

'But why?' she asked. 'Why would he do that?'

'I don't know why,' he said.

'But you must have a theory? You always have a theory.'

The irony this time like a sword between them; the point could turn either way.

'The theories are up to you this time.'

Her arm reached out to a stone behind her, to squash out her

228

cigarette. The movement tautened her breast, accentuated the curve of her rib-cage as it narrowed to her waist. The need for her was deep inside him, but not urgent yet. He was concerned now with the special quality of her beauty, her honesty.

'He wants to get rid of her,' she said at last. 'Is that what you're saying?'

'Is it what you're saying?'

The outstretched hand clenched, became a fist. Not menace there; suffering only.

'Yes,' she said.

'It's what I think too.'

'I love my father.'

He was silent now. The statement was an unarguable fact.

'He's an impossible human being and I love him. What am I going to do?'

'Take her back to England with us,' he said.

She sat up quickly, breasts shaking.

'You're clever,' she said. 'You're bloody clever.'

'Is that all I am?'

'Generous too maybe,' she said, 'if you've won. Victors can afford to be generous.'

'Have I won?'

'Not yet,' she said. 'Not here. This place is for thinking. Decisions come later. Turn over or you'll go red.' He obeyed her, and she rubbed him with oil again; again knelt beside him. It was too much: reluctantly, inevitably he grew erect, and as he did so pushed back his arms, rested his head upon his hands.

'A promise is a promise,' he said.

'Why, Jim Moulton—you're a gentleman,' said Tracy.

'Can't help it,' he said. 'I went to Cambridge.'

She kissed him lightly on the mouth, then lay on her stomach beside him.

'If I went back there would have to be conditions.'

Andy with your terrible stance and sixty-million-dollar trust—are you listening?' Last night you made me think even 'if' was impossible.

'Let's hear them.'

'I'd guarantee you a year. Would that be enough to get you started?'

'Yes.'

'In that year I'd live with you—and we'd see mother got treatment. But I'd work if ever I got the chance.'

'All right.'

'And if we started to quarrel I'd leave you till we both cooled off.

O.K.?' He hesitated. 'Only we wouldn't tell anybody. We'd say I was touring Europe or taking Mother to a specialist or something.'

He lay immobile, eyes closed, wincing at the sunlight.

'O.K.?' she said again.

'I think it's our only chance,' he said.

She let out her breath in a sigh, cautious that he shouldn't see.

'It's not definite yet, you understand.'

'I understand.'

'Jim,' she said,' 'what's happening to you? Why aren't you shouting?'

'Protons, neutrons, electrons,' he said. 'No people.'

'You may think me wayward,' she said, 'but I don't understand you.'

'It was a nightmare I had. You learn from nightmares—if you're lucky.'

'I want to go away,' she said, and this time he shot up, eyes open, shock, hurt, quickly masked. She moved, pushed him down again.

'Just two or three days,' she said. 'That's all. Just to be sure.' He was wary still, and she added, 'You're making me too happy. Happy now, I want to think about the future.' The sun beat on his eyelids: spots danced, red as coals against a black nothingness, danced and formed patterns.

'All right,' he said. 'Two or three days.'

She looked down at his thighs: the need had left him.

'Jim,' she said. 'Please look at me.'

When he did so she sat beside him, arms clasped behind her head, one hip jutting. She laughed with the joy of her body's power as he rose for her, and knelt astride him.

'I'm not a gentleman,' she said. 'I can't help it. I didn't go to Cambridge.'

When they went back to the house there was a cable waiting for him. PLEASE WIRE DECISION NOW. LAIDLAW.

'I'm surprised he said "Please",' she said.

'Goofy should have been a dentist,' Moulton said. 'He always hurts you politely.'

He was leaving for a hotel in Long Beach. She had promised not to tell her father, and Adèle was incapable of being told. Adèle would have a nurse, Tracy promised, until she got back. They left to face the gate and the guards, canyons, boulevards, freeway, sprawling, unending city, palms and petrol and sun. Mostly they travelled in silence. Their talking was finished, and what remained was the happiness of the present. It still wasn't time to talk about the future.

DIRTY SILK PILLOWS

DODDS still had the penthouse, so he couldn't be doing all that badly. Laidlaw hadn't even thought about him for years, except for that one time at the dinner-party, so he couldn't have been all that active financially either. The charges against him, according to the Press, all related to the period immediately after Laidlaw had left him, so that was all right, but they had been vaguely worded and there might be more to come. It would be as well to make sure. ... One of the newspapers had had a picture of Charlie, burly as ever, snarling at the cameraman, and beside him the kind of solicitor Charlie would have, flash-brilliant and expensive. Very expensive, the kind that briefs barristers even more expensive than himself. What with that and the penthouse, Charlie must still have a bob or two left. Laidlaw was glad about that: he'd have hated to think the poor old bastard was broke.

The first shock was when he paid off the cab. He had forgotten how ugly the block of flats was; or perhaps at one time it had become so integral a part of his life that he simply hadn't seen it, as one is unaware of the suit one wears, the pen one holds, when one is signing a vital cheque. But now, the crudeness of that white-glazed brick was awe-inspiring. The thing was a monster, and a decrepit monster at that. Even just after the war, that period of impossible repairs when builders rode in Bentleys, it hadn't looked as bad as that. He went inside. Carpet not clean, floor not polished, porter, jacket off, drinking tea, an occupation far more important than the opening of lift-doors.

The lift dragged too, *rallentando*, then gave sudden, feverish spurts, struggling to regain lost ground. Laidlaw left it at the penthouse floor with relief: he had reached the level of wealth where all gadgets worked, promptly, and preferably in silence. Dodds's lift had been given to a rhythmic clank he found ominous. And Dodds's front door was dirty, had been dirty for some time. There was a scratch that might have been administered by a shoe—most probably a woman's—and the door-bell needed polishing. He pushed it, and waited. A white plastic box beside him, the only clean thing in sight, squawked once, then asked in Charlie's voice, 'Who the bloody hell is that?'

'Tom Laidlaw,' he said.

The box squawked again and the door swung open.

231

Second shock. The hall was empty: of people, of furniture, even the carpet had gone. Laidlaw had expected to see what he remembered: more whores and suppliants than seats, stacked boxes of tinned food, radiogram playing Ambrose fox-trots. All gone, right down to the linoleum, a bright blue horror mottled with a rash of roses.

'Where are you, Charlie?' he shouted.

'In me bedroom. Come on through.'

Past the kitchen, gutted down to a tiny fridge and a gas-ring. No freezer crammed with hams, no cases of booze. His own room empty, office reduced to telephone, desk and chair, then Charlie's room: another scratched door, shut. He fought a ridiculous impulse to run away; another, even more ridiculous, to knock, opened it and went inside.

This room was crammed. Three-piece suite, last survivor of the tubular steel and silk monstrosities, colour telly, hi-fi, bar, same wall-to-wall mirrors, same canopied bed. But not the same Charlie. That was the third shock. The newspaper photograph had lied, conning him with half-truths to make the lie more convincing. In the picture, Charlie's stance had been right and his snarl had been right—and that was all of the picture he had seen; the rest he had filled in for himself. Quite wrongly. He'd imagined a lame gorilla at bay, defending his stolen bananas. What he looked at was a shrivelled and wary invalid on a canopied bed, in a suit three sizes too big for him. There was nothing left but the petulance—and perhaps the cunning. He would find out soon enough about the cunning.

'Tom lad—good to see you,' said Charlie. 'I won't get up. Doctor says I have to lie down this time every day.'

'Hallo, Charlie,' Laidlaw said. 'You've not been ill, I hope?'

'Aye,' said Charlie.'

Looking so sorry about it too? What's this then, Charlie? Is being ill the only pleasure you've got left?

'Bit of a heart,' said Charlie. 'Got to be careful. No over-exertion.'

'I'm sorry,' Laidlaw said.

'You get used to it,' said Charlie. 'How you doing, lad?'

'Pretty well.'

'Aye.' The eyes bland, not telling him anything, but that 'Aye' meant 'Just what I expected'.

'And you?'

'Bloody awful,' said Charlie, and Laidlaw was alert at once. He'd expected bluster, excuses, *reculer pour mieux sauter*; expected and been prepared for it; but such forthright honesty from Charlie demanded caution.

232

'I'm sorry to hear that.'

'Aye,' Charlie said again. Sorrow, his voice implied, could be offered without obligation. 'Have a drink.'

'It's a bit early for me,' said Laidlaw.

'It was usually was,' said Charlie. 'Either that or a bit late. Fetch me one will you? Brandy. Doctor says it's good for me heart.'

Laidlaw went to the bar. Brandy was all it contained: two bottles, one half full. Spanish. . . . He poured the old, familiar dose.

'Christ almighty,' Charlie said. 'D'you want to kill me? Give us a couple of tablespoonfuls.'

Laidlaw tipped the liquor back into the bottle and poured again, measuring, then carried the dose back to Charlie.

'This is all I'm allowed,' Charlie said with pride, and struggled up among the pillows. They were all of silk, and they too were dirty.

'What can I do for you, lad?'

'I heard about your trouble,' Laidlaw said. 'I was in London anyway—so I came to see you.'

'You haven't heard a tenth of my bloody trouble,' Charlie said.

'But what went wrong? You were right on top when I left you. You'd just made a quarter of a million.'

'The deal with de Groot? Tom lad, Tom lad. You know what a bloody liar I am. It was eighty thousand.'

'It still isn't ha'pennies,' said Laidlaw. 'And you had all the other stuff as well.'

'Aye,' said Charlie. 'I did. Pushing a million I was. Pushing a million.'

'You can't have lost all that.'

'Who says I can't?'

'But man alive—how?'

'I got married,' said Charlie. He glared at the rigid composure in Laidlaw's face. 'I wish you'd laugh,' he said. 'It'd be more natural.' He got no laughter from Laidlaw. 'I must have been stark, raving bonkers.'

'Who was it?' Laidlaw asked.

'Tart,' said Charlie. 'Bloody Irish tart. She could do things that could drive you crazy—only you had to pay for them. I worked it out once. Seventeen all nights and fifty-five short times. And you know what it cost me? Quarter of a million quid.'

'But how on earth could she——'

'Cartier,' said Charlie. 'Asprey. Boucheron. It soon mounts up. House in her name, bank account, Ferrari. She skedaddled to Rome with the bloody chauffeur. Christ knows where she is now.'

'All right,' said Laidlaw. 'That's two hundred and fifty thousand. What happened to the rest?'

233

'I invested it,' Charlie said.

'In what, for God's sake?'

'Anything I knew bugger-all about. I went mad, Tom.'

The matter-of-factness of his voice horrified Laidlaw. He meant it.

'Model gowns, car-hire, property. I even financed bloody films.'

'That wasn't very wise.'

'It was mad. I told you. I was mad. Booze and worry and not enough sleep. I should have had a breakdown. I started investing instead. When I come to they'd all left me—Pretty Flynn, Harries, Lardy Rigg, Booker. You remember Booker?'

'Very well,' said Laidlaw.

'Aye. Even Booker had gone, and he was no bloody good. They'd all helped themselves before they left, an' all. I was down to next to nowt. So I started doing deals again.'

'Who with?'

'De Groot.'

'Oh, my God.'

'No—you were wrong about de Groot,' said Charlie. 'Nobody ever got a thing on either of us, thank God. They'd put me down for life if they did.'

'So you got some back?'

'A bit. Not much. De Groot got the big share—then he wanted to turn respectable. Like you.'

'Some of us like it that way, Charlie.'

'Aye—it makes more money. I'd have liked it myself, but I was too old to learn, and them as could teach me had all scarpered.'

This self-pity was an irrelevance; it wasted time.

'So how did you end up?' Laidlaw asked.

'Me flat, enough to live on, a few thousand put by for insurance.'

'No more girls?'

'I'd had enough,' said Charlie. 'Bit of a film-show, that's all. You can get some right good 'uns nowadays.'

'Insurance?'

'You don't want to talk about films, do you?'

'Not particularly.'

'No. But you're forgetting something aren't you? I'm a dirty old man. Have been ever since I've known you.'

Self-pitying, querulous. Almost certainly not shrewd, ten to one against. But he'd need longer odds than that. And with querulousness there might just possibly be danger, threats.

'You've had your fun.'

'You're right there,' said Charlie. 'And that's one thing they can't take back off you. Once you've had it—it's gone.'

'That's something you taught me, too,' said Laidlaw. 'One of the many. I'm obliged to you, Charlie.'

The querulous look went, and the old man took a sip of brandy. His first.

'Tell me about the insurance,' said Laidlaw. 'I'm interested.'

'Maybe you ought to do it too,' said Charlie. 'You never know. Work out your risks, turn 'em into solicitors' fees and counsel's fees, lock it up on deposit—and don't touch it. That's insurance.'

'What you're up for—is it bad?'

'No. . . . Sort of a high-class smuggling. That's all.'

'I'm glad.'

'Just one thing bothers me, Tom lad,' said Charlie.

Laidlaw thought, So now I'm about to know.

'What's that?' he asked.

'The fines. They reckon they'll tot up to about eight thousand quid.'

Laidlaw whistled.

'And if I don't pay it'll be gaol. Eighteen months more than likely. I couldn't face that at my age.'

'And you don't have eight thousand?'

'It's about all I bloody have. If I pay up I'll be well-nigh skint.' He paused, waiting. Laidlaw waited longer.

'I was that glad you came here,' Charlie said at last. 'Matter of fact I was going to write to you—and I was never much of a hand at writing.'

'It's my pleasure to be here,' Laidlaw said.

'We'll see. You know, Tom, I've always taken an interest in you.'

'I know you have, Charlie.'

'Watched your career with interest. My old schoolmaster said that. Not about me though. If he'd watched my bloody career he'd have turned green. You've done well, Tom. Very well.'

'I wouldn't say that exactly.'

'Better you shouldn't. But I'm bloody saying it. You've come out on top lad. Supermarkets, Aliment, this Quantum merger. You're going to pass me soon. How much would you say you're worth as you sit there?'

'It's impossible to say,' said Laidlaw.

'No it isn't,' said Charlie. 'I'll tell you.'

He was accurate enough; within seven and a half per cent. The ten to one shot had come up after all.

'I'm near enough and you know it,' said Charlie. 'So don't let's waste time arguing.'

'Go on.'

'You could spare me a few thousand,' Charlie said.

'A few?'

'Twenty-five thousand.'

'Oh come on, Charlie,' said Laidlaw. 'Why on earth should I?'

'Old times,' said Charlie. 'Old pal that needs a bit of help.'

'A *bit* of help?'

'Twenty then,' Charlie said. 'I could manage on twenty.'

'I should think you could. You're managing on eight now.'

'With twenty I could retire,' Charlie said. 'Buy a place in the sun somewhere. Warm me bones. North Africa maybe. I've always fancied North Africa. Little house. Buy an annuity. House in your name, Tom. When I passed on it would revert to you. That way it wouldn't even cost you twenty.' Laidlaw shook his head. 'There's some would say you owed it to me, Tom.'

'We parted square,' said Laidlaw.

'I won't deny it. You took no cash from me. But knowledge, Tom? Tricks? Opportunities? You took them fast enough, didn't you?'

'I worked for *you*, Charlie. You got all the cream.'

'Right again. But look where you are now—and look where I am.'

'No, Charlie,' said Laidlaw.

The old man sipped again, and then another. He *needs* the brandy, thought Laidlaw. Those little, cautious sips. It's all the strength he has.

'I'm wondering why you came here,' Charlie said.

'I told you. To see how you were.'

'Aye. Well. We needn't waste time with lies. You were worried.'

'About you? Why should I be?'

'That's what you came to find out. What can old Charlie do to a respectable businessman? Well I'll tell you. I'm going to write me memoirs.'

So there was danger too.

'I don't believe you,' Laidlaw said.

'Suit yourself. I'm not actually doing the writing, you understand. They have a young chap does that for you. I talk into a tape-recorder and he types it up. Ghost, would you call him?'

'Ghost for who, Charlie?'

'National Features. They sell it to the papers. Make a right good thing out of it.'

'How good?'

'I was a celebrity in me day,' said Charlie. 'Film stars. Theatres. Horses. Rags to riches. And all that sex. Oh, they'll pay well.'

'And I'm in it, I suppose?'

Charlie said, 'Of course you are, Tom lad. You were my blue-eyed boy.'

'If you libel me——'

'Only facts, Tom. Only facts. But it's the way they slant them, you see.'

'What do you get out of it?'

'Ten thousand.'

'And you're asking me for twenty?'

'Today I am. Keep me waiting and I'll go back to twenty-five.'

Laidlaw said, 'No money.'

'Suit yourself,' said Charlie. 'I'm glad in a way. I'm going to enjoy writing about you. You've turned out a disappointment to me, Tom.'

'Just free board and lodging,' Laidlaw said.

The hand that held the glass trembled.

'You'll have to be clearer than that, lad,' said Charlie.

'The Burma deal, de Groot, strategic materials,' Laidlaw said. 'You won't be fined for that, Charlie. It'll be prison. A long time in prison. You'll probably die there.'

'Nobody can prove a thing,' said Charlie.

'I can,' Laidlaw said. 'Not all of it, Charlie. But enough to start them digging. And didn't you say you've done other deals since with de Groot?'

Charlie said bitterly. 'I can't seem to keep me bleeding mouth shut these days. Ever since me heart.'

'I think prison would kill you anyway,' said Laidlaw. 'You print a word—and that's what you get.'

Charlie sat for a long time in silence, then gulped down what was left of his brandy. A faint pink flushed the greyness of his cheeks.

'I meant it, you know,' he said. 'I am disappointed in you. Did you notice I asked you first? That was treating you like a pal.'

'Don't be foolish, Charlie,' Laidlaw said.

'Foolish. Aye. But I thought you might *be* a pal you see. Admit there was a debt.'

'A debt of honour perhaps?'

'Oh you're a witty gent all right,' said Charlie. 'You——'

And then the words came, all the old obscenities, copulatory, lavatorial, the same old phrases, same old emphases. Laidlaw was surprised that such hackneyed filth had power to hurt: but it had.

At last he said, 'You're not doing your heart any good, Charlie.'

But Charlie raved on anyway. Laidlaw stood up; the vileness of the language was all the proof he needed. Charlie was safe. When he turned to leave, Charlie said, 'Just wait a minute will you?'

'Well?'

'One last favour, Tom. Pass us the brandy.'

Laidlaw went over to the bar.

'Both bottles.'

Laidlaw stiffened, then picked the bottles up, brought them over to Charlie. The old man was panting, spent: the faint flush of colour had died. He looked at Laidlaw.

'You don't give a bugger, do you?' he said.

'It isn't my business,' said Laidlaw.

Charlie poured brandy till the glass became half full.

'It won't work out for you, Tom,' he said. 'Remember what I'm telling you. It won't work out.'

Then he started to say more, but Laidlaw left. He could not bear the relish in the old man's voice.

Arthur Harkness said, 'And Mrs Gurney?'

'Placebos,' said Arnott. 'Keep her on placebos.'

'Any particular colour?'

'Anything but mauve,' said Arnott. 'She's just painted her bathroom green.'

Harkness grinned. 'I'd like to talk to her,' he said.

'You mean you're going to talk to her.'

'I ought to, Bob, surely? If we don't talk I won't find out what's wrong.'

'Nothing's wrong,' Arnott said. 'She's a good wife and mother with a nervous tummy.'

'The nervous tummy's wrong.'

'The good wife and mother's right.'

'You don't suppose I'd interfere with that, do you?'

'Not if you can help it,' Arnott said. 'You may not be able to help it.' He looked at Harkness's face: young, smiling, unsatisfied. 'Gurney's all right,' he said. 'But three or four times a year he gets blind drunk. And Mrs Gurney has a nervous tummy. It gets her some sympathy—yours or mine—and some funny-looking stuff in a bottle that makes her feel important. What's wrong with that?'

'It's a compromise,' said Harkness.

'I'm at the compromising age,' Arnott said. Harkness noticed that he said it without a smile.

'Mrs Gurney shall have her bottle,' Harkness said. 'Orange, I think. It should show up well against that green.'

'Thanks,' said Arnott.

'Anything else?'

'Yes,' said Arnott. 'A favour. I've got this damn St John's Ambulance lecture at eight o'clock, and my in-laws are due in at the City Station at ten past. I was wondering——'

'If I'd pick them up?'

'They *could* get a taxi, but——'

238

'The bold Commander,' Harkness said

'Exactly. The bold Commander. There's something about trains,' Arnott said, 'that takes him straight on to gin. It's like a ruddy conditioned reflex.' He hesitated. 'Or maybe it's the thought of seeing me,' he said.

'It's here,' said Harkness. 'This place. He hates it.'

Arnott's face tensed and Harkness thought, There's no need, Bob. Honestly there isn't. I like you too much to ferret for your secrets.

Aloud he said, 'Not to worry. I'll see he gets to your place in one piece.'

'Thanks,' said Arnott. It's an imposition I know, but——'

'It's about time I did you a favour,' said Harkness.

The astonishment on Bob's face was genuine, Harkness knew. The man was too nice for his own safety.

'I'd better let my wife know it's all arranged,' Arnott said.

Harkness went back to his own surgery. A bit sparser than Bob's but then he hadn't been in the money all that long. Still, it was pleasant, more like a living-room than a surgery. Good carpet, easy chairs. People responded to it. Bob had shown him the value of that, and he'd learned it from an old chap called Silverstein. People had thought he was mad, apparently. In those days illness and discomfort had always walked hand-in-hand. Up here at any rate, where sickness was regarded as a punishment. He pressed his buzzer.

'I'll see Mrs Gurney now,' he said.

Something orange and preferably nasty, so that she would know it was doing her good. And a nice cosy chat about her symptoms. But he'd have to leave in good time for the train.

For Mrs Gurney it was enough that a new medicine was to be tried out on her, but there were others who entered as they left, without hope, accepting the fact of their illness as a permanency of life more terrible to Harkness than despair.. When he left the surgery he had, deliberately, to empty his mind of them before he drove away. Once in his early days he brooded on a peritonitis at seventy miles an hour, and nearly killed himself and a lorry-driver. From then on he had made brooding a static occupation. Motoring was best endured to sound supplied by the B.B.C.; that night the sound of Brahms and Hindemith. String quartets. The trick was not to listen consciously to the music: one hoped to be possessed to the point where time had no relevance.

That night it worked so well that he found himself beneath the portico of the City Station before he had time to readjust to people, places, the omnipresence of motor-cars. Only one space going, and that one marked *No Parking*. He pulled into it anyway, and a policeman appeared at once, like a genie whose lamp has just been rubbed.

'Good evening, officer,' said Harkness.

'Good evening, sir,' the policeman said. 'You can't park here.'

'That puts us in a bit of a difficulty,' said Harkness.

'I hardly think so, sir.'

'Oh, yes,' said Harkness. 'You see, I'm a doctor. I'm meeting a patient on the eight ten.'

'Serious, sir?' the policeman asked.

'Very sick,' said Harkness. Very sick indeed if he knew the Commander.

'Stretcher case?'

'No,' said Harkness. 'I shan't need an ambulance.' Jesus, I hope not. 'My patient can just about walk to here.'

'You'll be all right here for twenty minutes,' the policeman said. 'That should do you, Doctor. The eight ten's on time. Need any help?'

'No thanks,' Harkness said. 'I'll manage.'

Inside, the station was ugly yet functional in the Victorian manner, in contrast to its elegant exterior. But it fascinated Harkness, who visited stations rarely. His generation used cars and planes: stations were an anachronism; the kind of thing you saw in war-films, black-out, steam puffing and soldiers kissing goodbye the most oddly dressed women. He looked into the bar, the buffet, the cafeteria. It was like walking into a novel by H. G. Wells. Still pleased, he put three pennies into a massive machine of wrought iron that spluttered then disgorged a platform ticket. Harkness was enchanted.

Even the train's arrival was pleasing. No steam—at least they'd heard about diesels—but the long snake of carriages coiled in just like the movies, the faces appeared at the doors, anxious or eager or bewildered. And a restaurant that moved, and utilized space as cleverly as a ship's cabin, and people actually eating, and drinking *wine*. Harkness remembered the bold Commander, and hurried towards the first-class carriages. There was Mrs Jennings, mink coat, court shoes, severe hat, just right for a train. Harkness called out to a porter, and she smiled when she saw them hurrying to her. She liked Harkness.

'In here,' she said, and the porter climbed aboard, came out with her suitcases. Mrs Jennings followed, her movements wary, but graceful enough.

A bit much, Harkness thought. Am I going to be left to cope on my own?

'Where's the Commander?' he asked.

'Rupert?' Mrs Jennings said. 'Oh, I didn't bring him. He doesn't travel very well, you know.'

She makes him sound like an inferior Chianti, Harkness thought.

240

'My car's just outside,' he told the porter, and the barrow trundled off. Mrs Jennings fell into step beside him.

Suddenly Harkness said, 'You've been quite ill.'

'My dear man,' she said, 'I'm perfectly healthy.'

'No, no,' said Harkness. 'You've been very ill indeed. Don't walk so fast, and take my arm please.' She looked at him. His mind was absorbed, that was obvious, but he seemed sober enough, and she was an expert on sobriety. God knew. Harkness was frantically trying to remember if he'd mentioned his patient's sex as Mrs Jennings took his arm.

'No, no,' said Harkness. 'Lean heavier. Limp a bit.'

She obeyed him, convinced she was overdoing it, but Harkness showed nothing but concern, and deference to her imagined frailty. The policeman was still there, and went at once into action, helping the porter with the boot, opening the car door so that Harkness could ease her tenderly into the car. Mrs Jennings enjoyed it, especially the pitying look the policeman gave her.

'All right, sir?' he asked.

'Fine,' said Harkness. 'You've been very helpful, thank you.'

He tipped the porter, and the policeman held up traffic to let them out. Mrs Jennings leaned back in the seat, allowed her head to droop. The policeman had earned that at least.

'I think I understand,' she said at last. 'You were being prepared for Rupert, weren't you?'

'That's right,' Harkness said.

That he made no attempt to deny it delighted Mrs Jennings.

'You were quite right,' she said. 'Rupert's last arrival was positively epic.'

An outraged bar steward, stupid policemen, and Bob in the background quietly coping.

'I take it he's never quite so bad at home,' Harkness said.

She hesitated, then said at last, 'I don't terribly mind discussing Rupert with you—at least I don't think I do, but for some reason not while you're driving a car.'

'You would prefer to face me.'

Again the total denial of social obligation: again delight.

'I really believe you're *clever*, Dr Harkness,' she said. 'Perhaps we could stop for a drink.' Her voice grew mocking, but affectionate still. 'Will that be symbolic enough?'

He chose a pub just off the trunk road, a long, low building set in a car-park like a football field. Its sign, a galleon, was six feet high and picked out in neon; from time to time smaller neon lights rippled across its gun deck as a broadside fired.

'How exciting,' Mrs Jennings said.

'And they say we're not civilized,' said Harkness.

They went into the Sir Henry Morgan Cabin: all plastic barrels and cannon and fibre-glass shot. Harkness bought Sherry in schooners and Mrs Jennings, a little disappointed, found that it was good Sherry. As she grew older she found that she wanted consistency above all things.

'You are *aware* of Rupert,' she said. His directness was infectious.

'I've had opportunity,' he said.

'And?'

'I'm not his doctor,' Harkness said. 'Or yours.'

'We're here talking,' she said. 'With two people like ourselves that's inevitable. Let's say I'm talking to you as a friend. . . . It may even be true.'

'It's obvious,' Harkness said at once, 'that is it's obvious to a friend of his wife's—that someone from this area hurt him deeply. Drinking is a form of defence against conscious recollection of that hurt.'

'And a very effective form.'

'It fills a need.'

'I've just acknowledged it,' she said.

'No, no. You misunderstand me. It fills a need in you.' Her face grew angry at once. 'You're about to face a choice,' he said. 'To reason—or to lose your temper.'

'Does it matter to you which?' she snapped.

'Not in the least.'

She swigged at her drink. Harkness signalled, and a pirate brought more Sherry.

'Go on,' she said at last. 'I'm hopeless at tantrums.'

His words had been like ice-water.

'There doesn't seem any other basis on which you could continue to have a life together,' he said. 'And you appear to want to do so.'

'I *have* to.'

'You're alone, the two of you,' he said. 'Your daughter is married—and provided for. In your profession divorce would scarcely be a handicap. If you *have* to, the reasons are inside yourself.'

'You mean I *like* looking after Rupert, keeping him, cleaning him up, putting up with his ravings?'

'Don't you?'

'Why on earth should I?'

'You know the answer to that. Whether you want to tell me or not is up to you.'

'He needs me,' she said. 'There's great comfort in that. He needs me far more than Susan ever did. He needs the power I have over him: the punishment I give him from time to time. I need it too. It doesn't sound very fragrant, our life together. But it is a species of love.'

'Exactly,' Harkness said.

'Some people would find you detestably clever,' said Mrs Jennings. 'I don't.'

'It's nice to watch one's theories proved,' said Harkness. 'Thank you.'

'I've done you a favour,' she said. 'You must do one for me.'

She noticed how little words like 'must' concerned him.

'My daughter,' she said. 'And Bob. What's wrong with them?'

Her daughter had no claim on him: that was obvious; it was equally obvious that Bob had.

'He's my partner,' Harkness said.

'She's my daughter. We're still talking as friends.'

'Bob's a superb G.P.,' said Harkness. 'At the moment he's at the very top of his ability. He's also a very good man. I'm lucky to work with him.'

'And my daughter?'

'She doesn't like me,' said Harkness. 'She finds me detestably clever.'

Mrs Jennings laughed.

'We'll have to be friends,' she said. 'Or allies at least. We have so much in common.'

'She's a good wife,' Harkness said. 'Very . . . loyal.'

'Perhaps an inherited characteristic. Bob needs loyalty, you think?'

'Now he does.'

'Why now?'

He sat for a moment. Mrs Jennings knew that he was deciding whether or not to break a confidence.

'This is between ourselves,' he said at last.

He told her of the dinner-party; the excerpts from Bob's journal that he had been allowed to read.

'Laidlaw I know,' she said. 'We did a piece on his wife once.'

'We?'

'The magazine. The-woman-behind-the-man stuff. How my cosy dinners win million-dollar orders. You know.'

'Wafer-thin mints,' he said.

'Exactly. She seemed all right.'

'And he?'

'Good mind. *Very* good mind. Witty. Charming. Not very mature.'

'Peter Pan,' said Harkness. 'He doesn't even want to grow up.'

'Why should he—if he's happy where he is?'

243

'He hurts people.'

'You mean he hurts Bob.'

'It's not all subjective you know,' he said. 'In my line it can't be He hurts Moulton, too.'

'And Moulton also hurts Bob.'

'He's another case,' said Harkness. 'Another problem.'

'But not yours—any more than Laidlaw is. Tell me—if Laidlaw's Peter Pan, what's Madge Innes? Wendy?'

'To be honest,' said Harkness, 'to me she's just an enigma. No morals—no values even. Just an enormous talent.'

'And a very luscious body which you haven't mentioned.' Then to herself: 'Are you queer, by any chance?'

'Let's talk about Bob,' said Harkness.

'Not Susan?'

'They're a unit,' said Harkness. 'I'm very much aware of that . . . I'm in no sense her rival, Mrs Jennings.'

'All women are nosy about other people's sex,' she said. 'Women journalists are impossible—even editors. Forgive me.'

'This thing's shaken Bob,' he said. 'Hurt him. You see he's not only learned to hate Laidlaw, he's been forced to reject Moulton too. Hate and rejection aren't easy for him. If it weren't that Susan were so loyal . . .'

'I see,' she said.

'Not all of it,' he said. 'Not yet. Do you want all of it?'

'Of course,' she said.

It was those two words that made him her friend. They epitomized her so well.

'Bob's monogamous by nature, Mrs Jennings—a surprising number of men are. He's also extremely passionate. Madge Innes could be very much more of a symbol to him than to me.'

He told her about Fitzgerald's sketches.

'What an adorable man,' said Mrs Jennings.

'He does sound adorable,' Harkness said.

'You've never met him?'

'I've chosen not to,' Harkness said.

'My daughter's missed the whole point of you,' Mrs Jennings said. 'You're not detestable at all.' She smiled. 'Oh dear. That was meant as a compliment. I'm terrible at compliments.'

'I don't think so.'

'. . . I'm terrible at passion, too. Maybe Susan's inherited *that*. No—that can't be true. What on earth am I to do, Arthur? Buy her the *Kama Sutra*?'

'I can diagnose,' he said, 'but this time I can't cure.'

'Do you want me to?'

'If you knew how important Bob is—you wouldn't ask.'

His friendship, it appeared, must be paid for in very hard currency indeed.

'It seems I'm to be a procureuse,' she said. 'But then so many editors are. And anyway—there isn't much else left at my age.'

SNEAKING FORWARD

The hotel had a pool of course; every bloody place had a pool. It also had air-conditioning, shower, radio and television that worked and room-service that didn't. Not that he needed room-service. He drank his Scotch without ice and there was water in the tap. When he was hungry he bought fruit, or went to the drugstore for hamburgers; when he needed exercise he swam. The rest of the time he worked: page after page of equations that all gave back the same answer: all right so far, but you'd better get your hardware soon. In a way the equations were useless, he'd come to that same conclusion the night he'd talked to Andy, made love to his wife, but they were training him anyway, conditioning, preparing, like work-outs to a boxer. They also helped him to forget the fact that Tracy might still turn him down. No cyclotron, no computer, no Tracy. No bloody life. Without them he really would be better off dead, and yet to kill himself was unthinkable. He had no religion, his system of ethics was social only, and yet he could not anticipate the time of his own death. To do so would be to acknowledge despair, not only for himself but for all the others—his mates, his own kind—to whom he had offered so much of his life. Social worker? Teacher? His dedication would serve nothing but physics: he lacked patience. Work was all he had left. Body work. Hard muscles and a fury in the brain that only exhaustion could dull. Road ganger, shipyard labourer, building worker. He had the strength for it; he could talk the dialogue. But he would be alone, and slowly, day after hard day, his mind would die. Sclerosis of the brain. Moulton faced a kind of fear he had never known before. In the past fear had been of death, of wounding. Pain, blinding, amputation. He had seen it, he had missed it narrowly, he had given it to others. That was all right, something you could live with, a part and parcel of the last justifiable war. But this new fear was something else again. It could lead only to despair. Moulton knew that it would be much harder to live with that. It would help to tell someone, but it could not be his wife.

When Tracy came to see him, in the afternoon of the third day, he was working still with that intensity of concentration that was his only way, even when the work was futile. He looked at her, she observed with relief, and saw only indices, surds, Greek letters. And yet behind all that was love, or at any rate, need.

'I left it pretty late,' she said. 'I'm sorry.'

'That's all right,' he said. 'It's a big decision.'

Oh please, she thought. Just this time. Please ask first.

'I had to talk to Dad,' she said. 'And Adèle.'

She had all his attention now.

'If it's no,' he said. 'Just tell me.'

'It isn't "no",' she said.

He looked at her; not moving, not touching, not even willing to touch.

'You're a hell of a woman,' he said.

'But the same conditions,' Tracy said. 'A year's trial. My work. Adèle.'

'Thank you,' he said. 'Thank you, my darling.'

As always he baulked at the word, but he'd said it.

'I meant it about the conditions,' she said.

'You always mean it. So do I. That's why there have to be conditions.'

'Three days on your own—and suddenly you're profound,' she said, and looked about her. Rexine, plastic, windows on to a parched, cracked court. 'Don't you hate it here?'

His eyes went to the four-inch pile of equations.

'I don't know,' he said. 'I never looked.' They laughed together: it was friendly laughter.

'But you haven't kissed me,' she said.

'I know.' The hard body moved, clumsy. He was like a man in a net. 'I was afraid.'

'But not now. Now I've told you.'

'I'm embarrassed,' he said.

He could surprise as easily as he could hurt.

'Embarrassed?'

'I want you so,' he said.

He had given, after all. He had asked, called her darling. It was her turn now. She moved to him, embraced him, till she felt his arms tighten as they kissed.

Drinks then, Scotch and warm water, no ice, shades drawn, love on the hard, narrow bed. Mature love, give and take, a dialogue. That splendid body, already beginning to brown, mature, beautiful, and yet learning still: learning to excite, to please; best of all learning to wait.

'My gentleman from Cambridge,' she said.

He had learned, for instance, how to caress when love was over: no, not learned, but instinctively realized the soothing prolongation of joy his hands and lips could give her, and him. He touched her in a friendly sensuality.

'I've got to ask . . . things,' he said.

247

'Surely.'

'Andy,' he said. 'What about Andy?'

'Andy loses,' she said. 'You win. For now.'

'The theatre he was going to give you?'

'I can still get it,' she said. 'If and when I need it.'

'I see.'

But his hands still pleased her. He accepted.

'And your dad?'

'He still hates you.'

The hands stopped then. She wriggled against him till he resumed.

'So nothing's changed,' she said.

'Does he still love you?'

'Yes. He does. But I'm an enigma now. You see—he can't buy me. Not with anything he's got. And believe me, he tried all afternoon. That bothers him.'

'D'you mind?'

'No,' she said. 'It's about time something bothered Dad.'

There was a smugness in her voice because she'd won. There was an assurance, too, because her dad still loved her. And that meant a separate peace, one that excluded him. A dress allowance, holiday trips, a 'proper' car; something in which money was involved. Moulton found to his astonishment that it didn't matter.

'What about Adèle?' he asked.

'Mother was experimenting with Dad's cologne,' she said. 'There was nothing else available. Fortunately it made her sick, so we had a chat. She'd love to come to England.'

'What did your dad say? About the cologne?'

'Dad was at the office, darling. I saw him there. By appointment.' His hands pleased more deeply. 'You were right,' she said. 'I may be getting a new stepmother.' Then, 'Please. Don't *do* that.'

'I like to.'

'We have to talk.'

'We *are* talking.'

'No,' she said. 'No, wait, darling. *Wait*, I said . . . Oh, *you*!'

Then later: 'I suppose you're proud of yourself.'

'I am that,' he said.

She grinned at him. 'You should be. Still you've got to admit I helped you. I'm randy.' The smile faded. 'So's Dad,' she said. 'Randy Fred Schiller. He never wanted to get married before.'

'It hurts you,' he said.

'No. I won't let it. I can't stop him—so where's the sense? But I can help Adèle.'

'If you're lucky,' he said. 'Alcoholics need all the luck that's going.'

'I wish very much that I loved Adèle,' she said, and swung off the bed. 'Show me how to work this terrible shower.'

He showed her, and they dressed and paid the bill, and the clerk said, 'Come again, folks,' and meant it. He knew an Alfa-Romeo when he saw one. As she drove she said, 'There were some cables for you. I forgot. What in the world made me so forgetful?'

'Where?' he said.

'In my purse,' she said. 'Open it, darling, it's faggot time.'

'Bitch,' he said.

Three cables, all from Goofy, all saying come home and please reply at once. Nice cables. *Polite* cables.

'My, my,' she said. 'He certainly needs you. When shall we go?'

'Tomorrow?' he asked.

'Maybe,' she said. 'Let's wait till he calls.'

'O.K.'

'She risked a glance at him.

'Maybe it will work,' she said.

'You've got a good mind,' he said. 'I admit it. But I'm damned if I understand how it works. It's like a series of knight's moves. When I think you're going sideways you suddenly sneak forward.'

'I'm glad you like lying on top of my mind.'

'Look,' he said. 'You said wait till he calls and I said O.K. and that's supposed to prove maybe it'll work.'

'It does,' she said.

COOL BEER FROM SUSAN

Mrs Jennings looked at her daughter with the old, familiar look of amazement that was at once mocking yet tender. She had unpacked, peeped in at the children, eaten; sat back now with coffee and the cheesecake she had brought from Harrod's because Susan adored it, and the tender mockery was there because the amazement could not be hidden. Susan, her daughter, *hers,* after a day of housekeeping and children, wearing old pants and last year's sweater, hair not set, mouth full of cheesecake; Susan, *her* Susan, was more beautiful than ever.

'Didn't Dad want to come?' Susan asked.

'A little,' her mother said. 'I talked him out of it.'

'I'm glad,' said Susan.

'Susan, darling,' Mrs Jennings said, 'I hope you haven't turned against your father.'

'Of course not. Dad's all right. I mean, I love him and all that—but I wanted to talk to you.'

The penalties for being sick in the bath might be slow, but it seemed they were inevitable.

'I'm very glad,' her mother said.

'Only I can't. Not now. I'm expecting Bob home any time—and . . .'

'It's about Bob?'

'Yes,' Susan said. 'It is.'

Defiance—and protection too. Protection for Bob? If so, how mature my daughter has become.

'You haven't quarrelled?'

'Oh *no,*' said Susan. 'I'm very fond of Bob.'

'I am aware of it,' said her mother.

'Oh, Mother. Please don't start.' So even mockery had lost its terrors. Susan gathered up plates.

'I'll help you,' her mother said.

'Thanks. Our daily left—*and* our au pair,' said Susan.

'Troubles never go singly?'

She got a giggle for that, at any rate. 'But it's murder being without all the same,' said Susan.

'Can't you get others?'

'Next week, thank God,' said Susan. 'One of each. Let's get these done.'

So that when Arnott came home from his lecture he found mother-in-law and wife together in the kitchen, washing dishes, chattering happily. And what could be more domestic than that, Mrs Jennings thought. Or more ominous? He kissed her as he always did, firmly, affectionately, the only way he could handle anyone he liked. How very *astute* of Harkness.

'How nice to see you,' he said. 'Did Arthur look after you all right?'

'He was very kind,' said Mrs Jennings.

'Good for Arthur.'

He looked around the kitchen.

'On top of the fridge,' said Susan.

A cool beer, taken out in time by wifely hands so that it wouldn't be too chill. Arnott drank in a ritual of relaxation and Mrs Jennings felt a quite irrational pride in her daughter. Arnott turned back to his mother-in-law.

'How's the Commander?' he asked.

'Well,' she said. 'But a very reluctant grass-widower.'

'I hope that doesn't mean you'll have to dash away.'

'I hope so, too. Grass widowerhood is good for Rupert. And the magazine is quite glad to do without me for a while.'

'I doubt that,' Arnott said.

'Oh, but it's true. I'm retiring, you know. My successor deserves a little trial sit in my chair—just to see if it fits.' She turned to her daughter. 'Darling, you look quite vulgarly surprised.'

'I am,' said Susan. 'I can't imagine you not working.'

'I can,' said her mother. 'Or rather working just enough for my own satisfaction, which is what I shall do. They've asked me to freelance, you know.'

'Congratulations,' Arnott said, and lifted his glass.

'Where d'you want supper, darling?' Susan asked.

'In here,' he said. 'I like to watch my women working.'

Really he was a most delightful man, Mrs Jennings thought. No wonder Susan loved him, and Arthur Harkness, and probably half his women patients as well. She could well have loved him herself. And he talked so well – even about his work that night; basic physiology from archaic charts in a ratty little drill hall. He was so intensely *aware* of things. It was just possible that he would make a good novelist: as a lover he would be splendid. There should be an unease when one considered one's daughter possessing, being possessed by this man, but she felt none, perhaps because she had never felt the urgency she sensed in others. Her love-affairs had all begun and ended in conversation. Yet others had other demands that were at best boring to her. Arnott was one of those others. For her sake she hoped that Susan was too. . . . Fitzgerald. He was talking about Fitzgerald.

'I saw his last exhibition,' she said. 'The retrospective.'

'You're a connoisseur?' he asked.

'Not precisely,' she said. 'When you're an editor they give you free Champagne. That makes it tolerable—that and the things people say.'

'Not the pictures?'

'I'm not awfully good at pictures. All my passion went into words.'

Really these aware, intense people. Now he'd lured her into a Freudian slip, and Susan was gaping because she'd said passion. Gaping as an angel by what's his name—Raphael—might gape, but gaping just the same.

'It's true,' she said to her daughter.

'Oh, Mummy—not passion.'

'What then?'

'I know you mean a passion for work,' Susan said. 'But it all came out like thinking.'

'Not really,' said Arnott. 'It was reason. A passion of reason. It does happen, you know.'

'Like Euclid getting all intense about theorems,' Mrs Jennings said. 'It happened to me. At my best, anyway. Words. The preciseness of words.'

Arnott thought of cold and glacial peaks blue or green in a thin white snow. Ice tinkling in the wind, the bold strength of pine tree. The savage purity of cold—and its cruelty to those who were exposed to it too long.

'Fitz's pictures made no impression?' he said.

'No. This time I really looked. They could hardly fail to impress.'

'Go on,' he said. 'Please.'

'It's so difficult. I suppose if I were colour-blind I'd have a ready-made excuse. But I'm not. I simply don't respond. That's why I adore the conversations so. Words like "rhythmic" and "organic" and "functional"—about lines and colours. Its all such a nonsense. But this time they *made* me look. He's good, they said after one glass. After two he was very good. Three made him great. If I'd stayed for a fourth I'd have heard the word genius.'

'You didn't stay?'

'The pictures upset me,' said Mrs Jennings.

'Upset you?' said Arnott.

She looked at her daughter, but the thing had gone too far to stop now, and anyway it was what Susan needed.

'Fitzgerald's passion is different from mine,' she said. 'Mine was a passion of reason, you said. His is a passion of passions. Passion for passion's sake. I had seen this before, in the work of other men, and I knew that their passion was coarser, more animal than mine. But Fitzgerald was greater, or perhaps merely more skilful than the others. He made me realize that their passion was healthier too. . . . I should like very much to meet him.'

'You must,' said Arnott. 'We'll invite him over. Did Susan tell you—he gave us some things . . .'

'Healthier?' said Susan.

'Oh much,' her mother said.

THE newspapers hadn't bothered all that much: it would have infuri-
ated Charlie, how little they had bothered. *Junk King Dies, Sudden
Death of Genius of Scrap*, and one mordant sub-editing wit, *Totter's
Empire Falls*. But very little else. Name; age; brief memory of past
glory—'a vanished era'. A vanished Charlie. Natural death. Over-
strained heart. Not long after he'd left, either. Lucky that. Laidlaw
put the last paper aside and relaxed. He hadn't been mentioned
once.

'Busy day?' Sybil asked.

'They're all busy.'

'Oh dear,' she said. 'Something's upset him.'

'Sorry,' Laidlaw said. 'It's that idiot Moulton.'

'Still no answer?'

'Not a word. I've got a call in.'

'Madge called,' Sybil said.

'About time,' said Laidlaw. 'Where the hell's she been?'

'Working from home.'

'And why didn't she call me?'

'She had a bruise,' said Sybil. 'It showed—and it embarrassed
her.'

'A bruise? For God's sake what's so embarrassing about——'

'Fitzgerald gave it to her.'

'Tell her to lay off Fitzgerald.'

'At the moment,' said his wife, 'it's the last thing she wants to
do.'

Laidlaw looked down at her, then smiled as she smiled.

'I'm glad I never had to beat you,' he said, but her smile became
preoccupied.

'Why's Fitzgerald important?' she asked.

'He's not important.'

'You act as if he were.'

'He's a bonus,' said Laidlaw. 'Like icing on top of the cake. No
icing doesn't mean you can't eat the cake. But it's better *with*.'

'I've never seen Fitzgerald as icing,' Sybil said.

'What I mean is this,' said Laidlaw. 'Fitz succeeded as Moulton
succeeded. As I did. That's why I want him. He's part of the pattern.'

'You want him but you won't keep him.'

'Nobody could ever keep Fitzgerald. Madge should remember that. But I don't want to keep him—after he's done his job.'

'Immortalized Moulton?'

'It'll be nice to have the canvas,' Laidlaw said. 'It'll be great to have the sitter.'

His wife said, 'You want this too much, Tom.'

'Now wait a minute—you agreed with me. We discussed it together.'

'I know,' his wife said. 'But it's getting too big. It's dangerous now. Dad——'

'You've talked to him about it?'

'Did you think he wouldn't find out?'

Old Jameson was seventy-three. Of course Laidlaw had hoped he wouldn't find out. It seemed that he had hoped in vain.

'Did you tell him how much we stood to gain?'

'He knew that, too.'

'What did he say?'

'He thinks it'll go wrong.'

Jameson had no right to say such things. He'd done enough already for Christ's sake, poking and prying, tying up Sybil's money till he couldn't bloody move. Sybil's money; a golden ball and chain. Buying him with it, then shackling him with it. No trust. Not even in his love for Sybil. Quantum was the only key to unlock that chain, and Jameson knew it.

'I'd better talk to him,' he said, then the phone rang, and he had reached it, picked it up even before she had risen.

'Yes,' he said. 'Yes. Thomas Laidlaw here. Yes, I'll hold on.' He covered the mouthpiece. 'Los Angeles,' he said. The door-bell sounded. He was dimly aware that Paco came in, handed an envelope to Sybil, but his whole being was concentrated on the telephone, and the sound of sighing wires that stretched back and back over seven thousand miles. The voice spoke at last with startling clarity.

'I see,' said Laidlaw, then, 'Yes, if you would please. . . . Thank you.' He hung up. 'He's been away,' he told his wife. 'He didn't even leave a forwarding address. When he knew how important it was——'

'But he doesn't know,' Sybil said. 'Not the way you know it.'

The sharpness in her voice alerted him at last. He had been making a mistake, but thank God it mightn't be fatal. He'd probably spotted it in time. He'd been a fool to be brusque with Sybil, to take out on her the worries of the past few days. Because he needed her. Desperately. How could he cope with her father except through her? And he had to cope with the old bastard. He had to be sure about the money.

'I'm sorry,' he said. 'I've been getting too tense lately. Stupid of me—and damned unfair to you. What have you got there?'

The voice was right: he knew it at once by her reaction.

'It's for you,' she said. 'It went to the Barker Street store so the manager brought it. He thought it might be important.'

On the envelope was written *Tom Laidlaw, Supermarts*, and the name of the town, and in the left hand corner *Strictly Private*. That was all. The handwriting was unmistakably Charlie Dodds. Laidlaw tore at the envelope, took out a single sheet of paper. Like the envelope, it was of very high quality, but old. It bore the printed words *Dodds Enterprises Ltd,* then the address of the flat in dreadful fake-Gothic lettering. Below that was printed: *From the Desk of the Managing Director,* in red. The letter too was handwritten; the writing was Charlie's.

DEAR TOM [Laidlaw read],

Well I said it often enough, didn't I lad? You'll be the death of me. And now you are. It's a bit of a comfort that we both know it—and you do know it so don't deny it. I could see it in your face when you passed them brandy bottles. So on you go Tom and good luck to you which I think you're going to need. Just one more thing—you're the biggest disappointment I ever had worse than the wife even. I want you to remember that lad.

C. Dodds

P.S. Nobody's going to know what we did now so you won't need any sleeping tablets. I'm getting the porter to post this for me but he's half-pissed and he can't read anyway. You won't have to kill *him*.

'Bad news?' Sybil said.

'Cranks,' said Laidlaw. 'They're worse than dirty phone-calls.'

'Let me see.'

'I'd rather you didn't,' he said. 'It really is very nasty.'

The smile she gave him was adoring. Chivalrous Laidlaw. He refolded the letter, put it back in its envelope, put them in his pocket.

'What does it say?' she asked.

'That I ruin people's lives for my own ends,' he said.

The words were out before he could stop them, and yet he was conscious of relief. The words had to be said.

'Do you?' she asked.

'I'm not ruining Fitzgerald,' he said. 'Far from it. He's in to me for five thousand. And how am I ruining Moulton? By offering him a job when no one else will?'

'Your job carries its own humiliations.'

'*And* its own rewards. I'm not a charity, Sybil. I like to give but I have to take. It's the only way to stay solvent.'

'Arnott? What about Bob Arnott? You took from him.'

'Only his friendship with Moulton. And that was something he was better without.'

'We offered ours in return. They refused it.'

'Their privilege,' he said. 'But I'm sorry. I liked Bob Arnott.'

'I liked them both,' she said. 'We're going to be awfully lonely. Let's hope it's worth it.'

But she came across to him and kissed him even so, and as he held her he thought: You didn't mention Charlie—but how could you? You didn't know I'd been to see him. Nobody did. Harry Lewis will guess. But he won't do anything. He can't. He's backing the project.

When the phone rang again he had to force himself to be gentle as he put his wife aside.

'Yes,' he said. 'Yes. That's very kind of you. ... If you would please.' (He covered the mouthpiece. 'He's home,' he said. The wires sang to him and he waited.) 'Jim? Jim, how are you? ... That's good. Excellent. ... Listen, when are we going to see you? ... Urgent? Of course it's urgent. ... We can't move till you've signed your contract. ... Of course now. ... Good. Do that please. ... How's your lovely wife? ... Good, good. ... I somehow thought you'd bring it off. ... Goodbye, Jim—and hurry home. Now that's an order.'

He put the phone down, smiling. Maybe he did need luck, as Charlie had written. But that was all right. He had luck. Now he had to persuade old Jameson of the fact.

Moulton hung up, and went to Tracy's room—their room now—where she had been listening on the extension. The impulse to rage was very strong. All that smarm, then, 'That's an order.' The sly comment of 'I somehow thought you'd bring it off'.

She was waiting, angry as he.

'You handled it well,' she said.

'I should have hung up on the bugger.'

'But you didn't,' she said. 'You're learning, darling.'

'Learning what?'

'To pay for what you want.'

'I don't pay for you.'

'Oh, but you do—all the time. By being nice to me.'

'That's no hardship.'

'It will be—when you want a row.'

'Not with you,' he said. 'I was a fool when I rowed with you. But Laidlaw—he talks as if I were his pet monkey——'

'There's a way to beat him,' she said.

'Do the bloody work and ignore him. I know.'

'A better way,' she said. 'At least I think it's better.'

'How?'

'Get rid of him.' There was a slyness about her, and an absolute assurance. Both were frightening.

'Tracy, for God's sake——' he said.

'I don't mean kill him, you nut. Take him over.'

'Take over Laidlaw? . . . He's got millions.'

'He's got eight hundred thousand sterling. That's just under two million dollars, most of it tied up in Aliment and Quantum. If we took them over——'

'We haven't got two million dollars.'

'Dad and Andy have.'

'That's a hell of a favour you're asking.'

'Not asking,' she said. 'Offering. Quantum's a hell of a good investment.'

She frowned at his bewilderment. It was all so *simple*.

'Dad's got some money locked up in Britain, and Andy's got a lot. They *need* a good investment. Quantum's it.'

'And the project?'

'It would stay as it is.'

'Including the research on dog-food and stuff? And the P.R. and the publicity and the advertising?'

'Yes.' There could be no compromising on that one. 'Except Dad's people would probably do it better.'

'And I'd wind up with Andy and your dad on my back instead of Goofy Laidlaw.'

'You'd wind up with me on your back.'

'Jesus!' he said. Bewilderment more marked than ever.

'Darling,' she said. 'What's the matter with you? Don't you like the idea?'

'You make it sound so easy.'

'It *is* easy.'

'You can really do it?'

It was already being done, but she did not dare to say so.

'Ruin Goofy?'

'Not ruin. He'll still have money. But he won't have power any more. Especially not over you.'

'Your dad will—and Andy.'

'Power's there,' she said. 'Power's always there. Somebody must take it.'

'Jesus!' he said again. 'Goofy without power—it's like cutting his balls off.'

'He'll deserve all he gets,' she said. Then: 'Darling, please. Make your mind up. I have to know.'

'You'll be mixed up in it?'

'Andy and I can handle Dad,' she said, and he nodded. Queen and knight take king.

'All right,' he said, and she kissed him.

'You worked it all out in Lake Tahoe?'

'And here,' she said. 'I had to talk to people who know.'

'The other night you said you were a hundred per cent competent,' Moulton said. 'You weren't kidding, love.'

'You're all the investment I've got,' she said. 'I know how to protect it.'

He had it all now: lab, hardware, assistants, a loving wife whom he had learned to love. And yet, when bewilderment faded, fear returned. His own balls were now lined up for the razor.

But it was party time and they went to Wilshire Boulevard and the Brown Derby, while Harry waited in the Rolls and sulked. Andy was there, and a man called Miron who knew about money, and a man called Ralph who not only knew about money but was a lawyer as well. Miron and Ralph had wives so alike as to seem interchangeable, bright, predatory-pretty, shiny as plastic. Andy had no one and squired Adèle, sullen and sober as she sipped a coke. Quickly the others hived off too, the plastic wives to gossip, Miron and Ralph and Schiller to talk the deal, courteous in their deferment to Tracy, totally oblivious of the others. Champagne cocktails, Niersteiner, Cheval-Blanc. They came in regular succession and Moulton drank them all. Early he had recognized that the deal was under way already, and he didn't want to think about it. Didn't want to talk to plastic wives either. He wanted to talk to Andy, who had put up a wad of money and got himself ignored. But Andy was still squiring Adèle. He stuck out a hand, and a waiter came up through the floorboards and put a glass in it.

'You getting drunk tonight, darling?' Tracy asked.

'Yes,' said Moulton.

'So am I,' she said and held out her glass. 'Gimme.'

As he poured he thought: Do you really love me or are you bloody clever or both? Then below the table her leg rubbed against him. Crude stuff. Sensual and obvious. Trouble was it worked. He forgot about this bunch of capitalists who were going to buy him from the other bunch of capitalists, and rubbed his leg against hers. The old Jim Moulton was dying—for want of causes, lack of youth, a new-found need for people, and the new Jim Moulton, sensible, mature, happily married, was bursting from the bud in the apposite air of the Brown Derby. But he'd keep his balls away from that razor.

Suddenly, no signal given, Tracy, Adèle, the plastic wives took off for the what d'you call it—the loo, the john; sudden and certain as migrating birds. At once the men hunched in together. Story-time. Broad talk. Moulton walked over and sat beside Andy. The bottle at his end was almost untouched. Andy looked flustered.

'Why, hello there, Jim. How you doing?'

Moulton said, 'Andy—you know very well how I'm doing. You must do. You just bought me.'

'Oh, I wouldn't say that, Jim. I certainly wouldn't say that.'

'What would you say, Andy? Come on, tell me. I like you.'

'You do?' Andy said.

Now why in hell should he sound dismayed?

'Of course I do,' Moulton said. 'You're likeable, Andy. I'm proud to belong to you.'

'Please don't say that,' Andy said. 'Me owning you—it's wrong. I mean you being a genius and all.'

'What's wrong with people owning geniuses?' said Moulton. 'It happens all the time. Mozart was owned by an archbishop—not even a likeable archbishop. Give me a likeable Californian millionaire every time. I want to say thank you, Andy.'

'Fred had a hand in it too.'

'Nepotism,' Moulton said. 'Family stuff. You are far, far finer than Fred and that's a lot of fs, Andy.'

'I guess it is.'

Moulton rose and took Andy's hand.

'Thank you, Andy,' he said, and bowed. 'For all you've done for me. And for Tracy.' He bowed again. 'Her indebtedness conjoined with mine.'

'I don't get you Jim,' Andy said. 'What you saying about Tracy?'

'Andy,' said Moulton. 'You're shy. That's nice. Old-fashioned, but nice. You don't meet all that many shy people nowadays.'

Schiller said, 'Come and hear this one of Ralph's, Jim.'

'In a moment,' Moulton said. 'I know I'm drunk because I'm using long words, but I have a message for Andy here.'

'It's an awful good story.'

'I look forward to it. Andy—I owe you for something no husband should ever owe to another man.'

Andy spilled his wine.

'Now there's an interesting phenomenon,' Moulton said. 'I'm drunk, polysyllabically drunk, and Andy spills his wine.'

Andy said, 'On my word of honour, Jim, you don't owe me for anything.'

'Oh, but I do,' said Moulton. 'I owe you for your priceless gift of silence.'

He estimated the passage of seven seconds before Schiller spoke.

'That's handsome of you, Jim,' said Schiller. 'Really handsome. Isn't it handsome, Andy?'

'Yeah,' said Andy. 'Handsome.'

It was a relief when the women came back and Andy could go on being nice to Adèle.

There was talk of going on, to a club, to Ralph's house, to a topless bar, but Moulton had no interest in Ralph's house, or in clubs, and one naked woman at a time was rather more than he could handle. Besides he had drunk a good deal and so had Tracy, and Adèle hadn't drunk at all, yet tomorrow they must fly five thousand miles. Schiller, Miron, Ralph, the plastic wives abandoned them to go to a place where money might still be talked. When Andy hurried after, Moulton felt only relief. Andy and he had talked enough. He addressed himself to the problems of getting out of the Brown Derby and into a Rolls-Royce. There was something fascinating in the fact that Harry could hold a door open and hate you simultaneously. A good trick that. When he'd hated people in the past, he'd tended to hit them with the door. Always something new to learn.

On the way back to Jacaranda Canyon he sang: 'When the Roll is Called Up Yonder', 'The Harlot of Jerusalem', surprisingly long excerpts from Handel's *Messiah*. Dimly he became aware that Tracy was nudging him. He beamed at her.

'What, love?'

'I think Adèle wants to say something.'

'I should like that,' he said.

Adèle voice was acid. 'I said you seemed happy,' she said. 'I said it five times.'

'Call no man happy till he dies,' said Moulton. 'He is at best fortunate.'

'That's cynical,' said Tracy.

'It's Solon,' he said.

'Cynical and defeatist,' said Tracy.

'Not if you're fortunate,' said Moulton, and beamed at Adèle. 'I'm fortunate,' he said. 'That's why I'm singing.' He stretched out his neck. 'And that He shall stand,' Moulton howled, 'at the latter day upon the earth.'

Suddenly Adèle screamed, 'I don't want to go to England with you.'

Moulton said patiently, 'I know that, love. But you have to——'

'You can't make me either. You haven't the right——'

'Not me, no,' Moulton said. 'I haven't the right because right is might and might is power.' He paused, checking that he'd got the words in sequence. 'But the power's always there love, and somebody's got to use it.' He turned to Tracy. 'Right?' he asked.

'Might,' she said.

'Power,' said Moulton.

Adèle began to weep, and he put his arm round her. She struggled against him, and he could feel her body shivering, with her need for a drink. She subsided at last against the power of his arm, and lay against him, shivering still, hating his strength as she hated her husband's, as she was learning to hate her daughter's.

'Why, thank you, darling,' Tracy said.

'You're entirely welcome,' said Moulton, and his voice sounded like Andy's.

His free hand reached out, found her lap, pressed into it, then Moulton, arms filled with women, passed out.

He hadn't wanted to pass out, because in doing so he missed the white men with guns and the politeness of Harry's hate and fear as he reacted to them. He'd wanted to see that. Harry was ... interesting: maybe even typical, but he missed it, and when he woke it was to find the car parked outside the house, and Adèle still imprisoned inside his arm. Even unconscious, Moulton was too strong for her. He became aware that Harry was leaning in towards him, trying to disentangle him from Adèle while Tracy lurched behind in the background, shouting directions, earnest and unhelpful.

'You'd never get away with this in Georgia,' Moulton said, and Harry smiled his servitor's smile that was also a grimace of rage and fear.

'Please help me, sir,' said Harry.

'All right,' said Moulton. 'Nothing to do with me.' His arm fell heavily from Adèle's shoulders. 'You follow your destiny, Harry. But watch out for the Klan, boy. Watch out for the Klan.'

As he helped Adèle from the car, Harry was sobbing. That was interesting too. You hated, but you had to eat, so frustration made you sob. The miners, back in the thirties, they'd been like that, when the strike hadn't worked, or the lock-out had. Going back down, hating, but hungry. Black an' all, once they'd got down-by. Interesting that. But not relevant. Not when you had a lab, and hardware—and Slasher Tracy. He swivelled round in his seat—his legs it seemed had grown tired of obeying the impulses his brain sent them—and watched his wife stagger towards the house, supported for once by her mother. The night had been filled with such ironies.

He said to Harry, 'Now it's my turn.'

'I beg your pardon, sir?' Harry said.

'I know you do,' said Moulton. 'That's what's so interesting. Lift me out while we talk, Harry.'

The chauffeur sobbed again, reached in for Moulton and heaved. Slowly Moulton rose, then fell back again, his weight too much for Harry, who tumbled in on top of him.

'The dignity of man,' Moulton said severely. 'I'd hardly say that we're preserving it.' Harry said nothing, but Moulton was almost sure his teeth were chattering. 'Let's try again, Harry,' he said. 'Remember Archimedes. Remember fulcrums, levers. Now.'

Harry, manic by then with rage and incomprehension, heaved

263

with such force that Moulton shot out of the car, knocked him flat and lay sprawling on top of him.

'Well *done*, Harry,' said Moulton. 'Give you a place to stand and you could lever the world.'

Harry was once again silent, even when Moulton discovered that his legs were working and scrambled to his feet, treading on Harry as he did so. Moulton peered down, almost falling again on Harry, and observed that he was unconscious. An amazing man; full of surprises. He decided to make a speech to him, unconscious or not; something might get through subliminally.

'Friend, Comrade, Fellow Worker,' orated Moulton. 'I applaud your rage, understand your fear, echo your sobs. If my teeth were as good as yours, I would bid them chatter even as yours chatter. But they're not.' He hesitated. Was it right to knock a tenet of his own beliefs? This time it was, he decided. Harry's need was great. 'Nothing like as good. National Health,' he explained. 'I empathize with you, Harry, because I know your kind, only my blokes were sometimes black and sometimes white, and you are forever brown. I empathize, Harry. You don't even know what it means, you ignorant sod, but I do it anyway. Gladly. Freely. And I tell you this. When you start to struggle they'll knock you down and when you get up they'll knock you down again. Up down up down up down till you take it for granted because vertical or horizontal Harry, life goes on. Then one day'—his arm shot up, dramatic, and he lurched again—'one day they *won't* knock you down. Remember what I'm saying, Harry, it's important. But don't look forward to it too much. Because you'll think you've won, you poor bastard, and you haven't won at all. You'll just have started another fight—and this time, Harry, you won't even know who's hitting you.' He stopped then, seeking a peroration. Subliminal empathy had shot its bolt. 'Good night, Harry,' he said. 'Sleep well. I shall watch your future struggles with interest, but if you'll excuse me, I shan't join them. I've got struggles of my own, old son. But don't go wasting your empathy on me. I'm not worth it.'

He turned then, walked to the house, legs better than ever. Mind not so good though. Atrophy of the conscience. Adèle in the living-room, unfriendly, looking for a bottle. Poor cow. Who'd give her a bottle? Help her man. Help her.

'You want to lay off it, Adèle,' he said kindly. 'Look what it did to Harry.'

'What's wrong with Harry?' she asked.

Snapping, nasty with it, but what does it matter? Be *kind*.

'He's drunk,' Moulton said.

'He certainly is not.'

'Oh, isn't he?' said Moulton, abandoning kindness. 'Then just you tell me this—If Harry isn't drunk, why has he passed out on the drive?'

Then up the stairs to Bedfordshire while Adèle peeped out at Harry and began wailing. But that wasn't his business: his sun was set, his race was done. His race was miners: big-muscled, beery, courageous. Blokes you could rely on. Fighting men. Anachronisms. They'd run out of bloody wars.

'Song,' said Moulton.

> When this fucking war is over
> No more soldiering for me.

Take out the magazine, off pack, train to the demob centre, civvy suit, single-breasted, brown, one.

> No more church parade on Sunday
> No more queueing for a pass.
> I will tell the sergeant-major
> Stick your detail.

Dirty train because there'd been a war on and who'd had the time to clean trains? Beer. York Minster. More beer and floods. Sandwiches at Durham Cathedral. One more beer and Newcastle Central. Grit under foot and your Aunty Sarah crying. Your da half-pissed but she'd got him there. . . .

'Darling,' Tracy said. 'You're crying.'

'I bloody should be,' he said.

'What happened, angel-baby?'

'I just knocked Harry unconscious,' he said.

FRILLY-DRAWERS' ma was all right. All Earl Grey tea and cucumber sandwiches on the top, but layer after layer underneath and all of it good stuff. She should have commanded the bloody landing-craft. Mind you, she knew nowt about paintings, but she had the common savvy to say so. And all the time keeping a tight eye on frilly-drawers. But nowt to worry about in that. She was in Bob Arnott's corner, whatever she was up to.

'More tea, Mr Fitzgerald?' she said.

'Don't mind. Thanks,' he said.

'I was telling Bob and Susan about your last exhibition in London. Free Champagne for editors.'

'I hope you got your share,' Fitzgerald said.

'Rather more,' said Mrs Jennings.

Now frilly-drawers was going to say something. Tensions inside her, pulling her body like wires. He'd seen a colt like that once, out in a Vermont riding-school. It thought the fence was too high and its muscles tightened till you could twang them.

'We haven't said thank you for the pictures,' she said.

'You're welcome.'

'That one of your friend——'

'You like it?'

'Adore it,' she said. 'It explains——' She broke off, looked at her mother.

'The apparently inexplicable,' Mrs Jennings said.

'That one's yours,' said Fitzgerald.

'I know. Bob told me. The others . . .'

'Oh, aye. What d'you think?'

'Are you trying to break up my marriage?'

A trick he'd never learned—make a joke and yet say what you mean—but if you were born into the nobs like frilly-drawers you absorbed it along with the cucumber sandwiches and the Earl Grey tea.

Fitzgerald said, 'Tell you how to find out. Let me paint you the same way.'

'Me? Oh I couldn't possibly,' she said.

'Why not?'

'Well I couldn't. How could I, Bob?'

'Don't ask me,' said Arnott. 'Fitz made the offer.'

She turned to her mother then.

'Better not ask me, darling,' Mrs Jennings said. 'Compared with you I'm a swinger.'

'It's a serious offer,' Fitzgerald said. 'And it'll cost you nowt.'

He could see it all happening in her mind. Her body was good, and she knew it, and though it had a few years left there weren't all that many. He couldn't immortalize her exactly—nobody could. That was a lot of cock. Nowt lasted for ever. Look at Leonardo—but she'd be around for a long, long time. Praised. Admired. Lusted for. He could give her that, and she knew it.

'No thank you,' she said.

'I should like to see the oil,' said Mrs Jennings.

'Any time,' said Fitzgerald.

'Would now be inconvenient?'

'No.' Fitzgerald was on his feet at once. 'Let's all go.'

'Sorry,' said Arnott. 'I'm on call.' He turned to his wife. 'You go, darling,' he said.

'No,' she said. 'I can't. Not today. The children——'

'I thought they were at a party,' Arnott said.

'They'll be back very soon. I can't leave you with them. Not if you're on call. Why don't you go, Mummy? Bob and I can see it some other time.'

'I hope you will,' said Fitzgerald.

They went, Susan's mother driving Susan's car. Fitzgerald neither desired nor intended to own a house, or a car, a boat, or land. Not even an animal. The claims of any possession were a threat to the totality of his freedom. He resisted them, and used other people's, fiercely or graciously. It depended on the people. It amused Arnott to see how at ease Fitz was with Mrs Jennings, and she with him. They'd been absorbed in each other from the moment they met. How many pink gins would the Commander need if he knew? He closed the door softly, and went back into the living-room, to observe his wife choking down a quite enormous Scotch. She whirled as she heard his footsteps, and the liquor slopped in her glass. He remembered the night at Goofy Laidlaw's: the Burgundy see-sawing in Moulton's glass. A good year for Chambertin.

'Do you mind if I join you?' he said.

He poured one, as large as hers. Four thirty. When Fitzgerald appeared one always seemed to drink at the wrong time.

'Are we allowed ice?' he said. 'Or soda?'

'You shouldn't drink at all,' she said. 'You're on call.'

'My dear girl,' said Arnott, 'if you're going to get drunk I'm not going to stay sober.'

'I'm not going to get drunk.'

'Very well then.'

She sipped from her glass and so did he, gauging his intake against hers.

'Oh Bob, *please*,' she said.

'It used to happen when I was a boy,' he said. 'Married couples drinking, I mean—one trying to stop the other. Only it was the woman who tried to stop the man in those days. And it was beer of course. Pints. There's a story about it. This bloke was a terrible boozer, always coming home drunk, and one night his wife saw him going out and said, "Where d'you think you're going?" "Pub," he said. "Oh are you," the wife said. "Then I'm coming with you." "Now, pet," he said, "the pub's no place for you," but she insisted so off they went. And when they got there the barmaid asked what they were having and she said, "Same as him," so the husband called in two pints. Now the wife had never drunk beer before, but when the husband took a big swallow so did she. She hated the stuff. "Why, Jack man," she said, "that tastes terrible." "Aye," says the husband, "and you think I'm enjoying meself." '

'That's a very funny story,' said Susan.

'If you'd laughed I might believe you.'

She drank again. At once he drank.

'Bob,' she said. 'Please stop it. I need this drink.'

'And I don't?'

'Only this one, Bob. I promise you.'

He put down his glass.

'All right,' he said. 'If you'll tell me why.'

She took a longer swallow, and choked. Arnott waited.

'I've been talking to Mummy,' she said at last.

'About the Commander?'

'Daddy? No. Why on earth should I?'

'In your family he does tend to be linked with alcohol. And now you've started——'

'Good God,' she said. 'I'm not an alcoholic.'

He struggled not to laugh at her vehemence.

'Not yet,' he said, 'but you've made a good beginning.'

'Bob, I'm *nervous*.'

'Because of your mother?'

'Because of us,' she said, and drank again.

'I make you nervous?' he said.

'No of course not,' she said. Then, after a pause, 'Well yes, I suppose you do.'

'Is this what your mother says?'

'It's what I said to her. I wanted her advice.'

'Advice?' he said. 'What about? What am I supposed to be doing to you?'

'Let me finish this,' she said, and struggled again with the Scotch.

'Susan, for God's sake.'

'Bob, it's no *use*. If I was sober I couldn't utter.'

'Suppose the kids come back?'

'The party won't be over for ages. Anyway Mummy's going to pick them up.'

'Did your mother plan this?' asked Arnott.

Susan said, 'No. I did. For God's sake let me drink.'

She had no head for alcohol, had always been a sipper, even in her social drinking. A quadruple Scotch hit her like hammers, flushed the flawless skin, moistened the brilliance of her eyes.

'The Scotch was my idea too,' she said. 'So don't go blaming Mummy.'

'I won't,' he said.

'Promise?'

'Promise.'

That made it binding, and she finished the glass. As she did so the telephone rang. Arnott moved towards it.

'Bloody hell,' said his wife, and threw her glass at the phone. The glass missed, bounced in pieces off the wall.

'Dr Arnott,' he said, and looked at Susan. She was going towards his almost untasted drink.

'I'm sorry, you have the wrong number,' he said, and hung up. She didn't touch his whisky; Arnott was aware of what an enormous strain it was, not to touch his whisky. He lifted the receiver and dialled again.

'Arthur,' he said. 'This is Bob. I'm sorry but I'm going to have to ask another favour.' He went on talking: from time to time Harkness replied, but his whole mind was concerned with the sight of his wife, her back to him, the tension of her neck and shoulders. He was suddenly aware that his palms sweated, and he felt an overwhelming desire to yawn and stretch. It had been like that in Korea: Malaya too; always a⁺ the beginning of action. He hung up again.

'Arthur's taking my calls,' he said. 'He'll tell the exchange.' He waited. So often people thought he had limitless patience, but it was a very exhausting virtue. 'Susan, you must turn round.'

When she faced him she looked as Andrew looked when he'd been naughty; when Jesus had been crying.

'Is it money?' he asked.

It had often enough been money in the past, but the practice could withstand most shocks now. She shook her head.

'What then?'

'It's . . . hard,' she said. 'Difficult.'

'I love you,' he said. 'I love you and I'll help you.'

She drew a deep breath, shivering still, like a swimmer preparing for a fierce race in icy water. Arnott realized that she too was anticipating violent action.

'Mummy says——'

'No,' said Arnott. 'Let's start with Susan says.'

'I asked Mummy here,' said Susan.

'I know that.'

'Because I wanted to talk. About you. About *us*.'

'Go on.'

'We aren't . . . happy, Bob. Not any more. Not the way we used to be.'

She waited, but it would be wrong to help her now.

'Before we were married,' she said. 'It was all different then.'

'Sex?' he said. 'You're talking about sex?'

She nodded. 'It's all—part of it. We had sex and it made us happy. 'I *know* I made *you* happy. And I was, too. It was something I could *do*. Please you.'

'Don't stop now,' he said.

'Only it didn't last. For me. After Andrew and then Jane. It got . . . different. For me. Not for you.'

'How different?'

'I didn't—don't—want you.'

'I had observed it,' he said.

'Don't make me cry, Bob,' said Susan. 'You just said you loved me.'

'I do love you,' he said. 'And because I love you I want you. But you don't want me.'

'I can't help it,' she said. 'You're . . . kind Bob. And I don't like to see you hurt. But that's all.'

'It's a pity you had to tell me,' said Arnott.

'You knew anyway——'

'But not from you. Coming from you it hurts.'

His voice was trembling now, but she hadn't noticed her mind was concentrated solely on what she was driven to say.

'Mummy said that too,' she said. 'But I *have* to tell you. That bloody dinner-party——'

'Go on,' he said.

Moulton's letter was in his pocket. Moulton's New Testament:

'People can be as important as causes. You can spend too much of your life chasing abstractions. Think about love. I mean really think. Go on. Try to analyse it. You can't, can you?'

Arnott thought about love.

'What happened at the party?'

'Moulton—Fitzgerald—Madge Innes,' she said.

'You're jealous of Madge?'

'No. I thought I was. When I saw those drawings—I thought you wanted her so I wanted you. But I was wrong.'

She took another breath; dived smack in the water.

'You don't love anybody,' she said.

'Oh my God——'

'It's true, Bob. Everybody's just people to you—and you're nice to people. All people. Moulton, Arthur Harkness, Sybil Laidlaw, me, the children. We're all the same. We're people and you like us and help us. And that's all.'

'I love you,' he said.

'You like to sleep with me. You need to, I think. But I can't, Bob. Not any more. I won't.'

'Did you tell your mother all this?' She nodded. 'And she knew you were going to tell me?'

'No,' said Susan. 'I told you. She said I mustn't. She thinks we're . . . going to bed.' He looked up then. 'I won't do it, Bob. Don't ask me to try.'

'I like people,' he said. 'I help them. Raping wouldn't help.'

'It really wouldn't,' she said.

Moulton had written: *I never knew about involvement before. I do now. It means this, Bob—you can only get to know yourself in terms of another human being. But I'm preaching to the converted.*

'Tell me something——' he said.

'If I can.'

'Who helped you to work all this out?'

'Madge Innes,' she said. 'She came here and I asked her to leave and she wouldn't. But she was . . . very nice. We had coffee and we . . . talked.'

'About me?'

'She's very fond of you, Bob.'

He had insulted her twice. The punishment for that was, it seemed, severe.

'I won't mind if you have *affaires*,' she said. 'I'm hardly in a position to, am I?'

'Divorce?'

She winced at that.

'I suppose so,' she said. 'If you want to. Bob, I'm sorry. Honestly I am. But when you touch me I can't bear it.'

He walked out on her. He had to. If she'd seen him crying, she might have felt obliged to touch him.

271

A 707, and then a Jumbo. Movies, muzak, martinis. More plastic women, this time dressed up as stewardesses, and Adèle drugged to the eyeballs, dozy and dreamy and no trouble at all. After that the Savoy, and Adèle starting to come out of it, and a discreet geezer from Wimpole Street, very convincing, and very anti-drug, even when it meant what he called 'withdrawal symptoms'—and you can't have withdrawal symptoms in the Savoy, it lowers the tone. But the discreet Wimpole Street geezer had a little place in Surrey—pines, pure air, gravel soil, formal gardens—'a clinic for those of a nervous disposition,' he said. A home for well-heeled drunks. Nervous disposition and loot; Adèle had both, and they whipped her off in a kind of bespoke ambulance before you could say Jack Knife, and he and Tracy went with her, and it was all just like they said. Pines and downland, Regency house, beautiful garden, pretty suite for Adèle on the first floor where even the wire-mesh in the window couldn't spoil the view. Kind nurses, considerate doctors, the very latest treatment. It was only when you looked at the other patients that you realized this was a well-heeled hell.

They ate in their suite that night and drank Perrier because their heads still ached. The travel had got at him again too, so that he didn't know what time it was, looked at his Sole mornay in surprise. He had expected eggs and bacon. He felt post-operative, like that time they'd sewed him up after his wound. No shock, no pain; only woozy, head stuffed with cotton-wool. Impossible to think, though he ought to be thinking. Or drinking. But he wouldn't do that again, not in quantity. That one good booze-up had told him all he needed to know. It was enough.

'Do you realize,' Tracy said, 'this is the first chance we've had to talk since L.A.?'

'Adèle took care of that,' he said.

'You don't mind, do you?'

'Of course not,' he said. 'It's part of the deal. And anyway it had to be done. Only . . .'

'Only what, darling?'

'I'm sorry,' he said. 'Maybe it's just me—I always react badly to hospitals—but I got a sort of feeling . . . nothing's any good.'

'I don't think anything is,' she said.

'But we've got to try.'

She looked at him. There was uncertainty in her eyes.

'You really mean that,' she said.

'Of course I do.'

'You and Andy had quite a talk at the Derby,' said Tracy.

Moulton said, 'Did we? I don't remember.' It was surprisingly easy to lie when your whole happiness depended on it. 'You may not have noticed but I was very drunk.'

'I was hardly in a condition to notice,' she said.

Still uncertain, that would last for some time, but she was beginning to allow herself a little happiness.

'Why the change of subject?' he asked.

'I was just thinking—Andy's fond of mother too.'

Fond was all wrong for him. Adèle was part commitment, part bargain, part obligation; fond didn't come into it. But he let it pass. It was surprisingly easy to let things pass when your happiness seemed assured.

'I think I could do with an early night,' said Tracy.

'Me too.'

'After the Derby you weren't any good to me at all. I tried for *hours*. All you did was giggle.'

'I haven't been drinking tonight,' he said, and they grinned together. That was because they were both greedy he thought. Kids locked inside a sweet-shop. Black mints. He'd adored black mints as a child, but why think of them now? He remembered Harry.

'Oh, Chist,' he said. 'The chauffeur.'

She loved the dismay on his face; she could fix it.

'Momma took care of it,' she said.

'How?'

'Money,' she said. 'What else?'

But the look on his face now was dangerous. Careful, Tracy; careful, baby.

'I apologized too,' she said. 'For both of us—but I don't think Harry's quite ready to take apologies from us yet. So I gave him money. What else do we have to give?'

Now he looks fine, she thought, and why am I reproaching *my*self anyway? I meant what I said.

'Bedtime, baby,' she said; and so of course the phone rang. Tracy picked it up before he could move.

'No,' she said. 'Not tonight. We don't want to be disturbed. . . . Yes, of course, say that if you like . . . But no calls. . . . Unless it's about my mother. . . . You're welcome. Good night.' She hung up. 'Laidlaw,' she said.

'But we're not talking?'

'Who needs him?' said Tracy. 'You're what I need, lover.'

Good beds in the Savoy. Just soft enough, just firm enough. Like his wife. His sexy, cunning, adoring wife. All those atoms so beautifully arranged. Greedy atoms. Drawing, sucking, squeezing. All of him. Into herself. All. All. Jesus how big you are. And you are big, Moulton. Big with love, with need, and maybe with forgiveness too. But soon you're going to be small. Quite soon. And your sexy, cunning, adoring wife will wait till next time for the bigness, and take it again, again leave you small, exhausted with her taking, your giving. Now now she says and it is now, because you can't help it. She says now and you obey. You must obey. She's stronger than you are. And younger. She'll even outlive you.

DRINKS AND THEN LUNCH.
SPOT OF BRANDY WITH THE COFFEE

'He wouldn't speak to me,' said Laidlaw. 'Said he didn't want to be disturbed.'

'I rather think that would be Mrs Moulton,' Jameson said. 'It's a long journey, Tom. They would need their sleep.'

He held up his glass to the light: pale gold liquid, delicate, dry, with a whisper of fire beneath the smoothness. At his age it didn't hurt to verbalize your remaining pleasures, even if it did make you think and act like that Innes woman's telly ads. And even Sherry had to be paid for in heartburn.

'Good Sherry this,' he said. 'I like it.'

'Sybil chose it,' Laidlaw said, and smiled at his wife. This time he had to play every card he had.

'Good girl,' said Jameson. He turned deliberately to Laidlaw. 'The Moultons'll be up here soon,' he said. 'They're seeing Harry Lewis this morning.'

'*They're seeing——*'

'I'm a bit tired, Tom,' said Jameson. 'Give me a few minutes, will you?'

'Of course,' Laidlaw said. The old bastard. Telling him where to go in his own house. He rose, and Sybil followed.

'Not you, Sybil,' said Jameson, and Sybil went to him at once. It was too much, but Laidlaw found he had to take it, was not allowed even to slam the door.

'What d'you reckon?' Jameson asked.

'He wants it,' she said. 'You've no idea how he wants it.'

'Haven't I?' It seemed to her that her father was laughing at her, with a familiar teasing that was gentle because it was rooted in love.

'You know what I mean, Father,' she said.

'I know you don't want to talk about it. But you're going to have to. I bought him for you after all. Did we get what we ordered?'

'I love him,' she said.

'You don't seem to be in the mood to answer my questions today,' he said.

'He needs Quantum,' she said.

'Needs!' He was brusque now, but the brusqueness wasn't aimed at her. It was all for Tom. 'In this life we get what we work for—

provided we do the work right. In this case I don't believe he did.'

'How can you say that?'

'By thinking.' He reached out a hand: large and mottled, powerful still, tapped her forehead. 'Up here. You've got it too. Use it.'

To deny her father was unthinkable.

'You mean he let personalities get in the way,' she said.

'He had a chance in a lifetime,' said her father. 'Aliment was out looking for him—like a rich widow looking for a new young husband. He'd have been worth seven figures inside a year—and he would have had control. And what did he do?'

'He worked,' Sybil said. 'Honestly he did. Contracts—negotiations. Night after night.'

'What did he *do*? I'll have to answer that, since my daughter doesn't want to. He antagonized people—and he didn't even take the trouble to find out if they were important or not. Or whether their wives were—or their fathers-in-law. Setting aside whether he was right or wrong in what he did——'

'I don't want you to do that, Father.'

Jameson said, 'Very well. He was wrong. And he was careless.'

'What's going to happen, Father?'

'He's lost,' Jameson said. 'You know he's lost.'

Sybil knew that she would not be allowed to cry.

'My shares?'

'I'm selling them to Schiller. He's offering a shade better price than you would have got from Tom.'

'You're destroying my marriage,' she said.

'You couldn't destroy Tom with artillery.' Jameson paused, groping for appropriate comfort. 'He'll still have money,' he said. 'And when he's ready maybe I'll let him use yours. He'll try again.'

It wasn't enough for his daughter, but he had no more to offer.

'He's what you wanted,' Jameson said again. 'I bought him for you.'

'Whoever would have thought it, Jim?' Harry Lewis said. Stiff napery, crystal, the elegant deference of waiters. Whoever would have thought it?

'You,' said Moulton.

'You think so?'

'I know so.' Moulton turned to his wife. 'Last time Harry and I ate together was back home,' he said. 'Old Boys' Reunion Dinner—the Three Leopards. Do you remember?'

'A terrible dinner,' said Lewis.

'Bloody awful,' said Moulton. 'But that gleam in your eye was the Savoy Grill Harry, even then. And now you're here.'

'You too,' said Lewis. 'I must say I'm surprised.'

'You're thinking about the last time?' Moulton said.

'Jim's changed,' said Tracy. 'You'd be amazed how much.'

'He must have done,' said Lewis. 'He hasn't lectured me once.'

Nor will I, my old school chum. I know what I'm after these days.

'Old Bickersley,' said Moulton. 'He started me off you remember? Christ, how I hated Old Bickersley.'

'Me too,' said Harry. 'But I lacked the courage to show it as you did.'

'I was never one to pass up a scene in public.'

'I was,' Lewis said. 'It might have lost me votes.'

Don't tell me I have to start liking you as well, Harry.

'I don't think you lack courage now,' said Tracy.

'You're referring to the project?'

'I am,' said Tracy. 'Risking your Government's good will on a bunch of Yankee capitalists.'

'I'm relying on Jim,' said Lewis. 'If you start pulling too far to the right—Jim will pull you back.'

'It's going to work, you know,' Tracy said.

'It has to,' said Lewis. 'We're all in too deep for it not to.'

'You're very perceptive,' Tracy said.

'Informed too,' said Moulton.

Lewis said, 'It's my living.'

After that they simply ate and drank, and Tracy examined the fact that she liked Harry Lewis though her father in Los Angeles hated and despised him, stayed in Los Angeles for fear he might meet him. Ralph and Miron might risk contamination, but her father and Andy were too important to be risked so, too *wealthy*. Andy, she thought, might also have liked Harry Lewis. But Andy must stay away. Must and would. He had given her his word.

'Will it be awkward for you if you see Laidlaw again?' she asked.

'No,' Lewis said. 'His dealings were purely financial. The Government wasn't concerned in that particular aspect. It may be rather awkward for you though—and Jim.'

'Awkward?' said Moulton. 'Meeting Goofy?'

He looked at his wife. Lewis observed their happiness as gratefully as if it were his partner's seven spades to the ace queen.

'It'll be *fun*,' Tracy said. 'We're looking forward to it.'

For this plethora of clubs Lewis was not grateful.

'I should hardly recommend that attitude at this stage,' he said.

'What attitude?' Tracy asked.

'He thinks we'll be vindictive, don't you, Harry?'

The stately inclination of the head implied regretful assent.

'Goodness,' said Tracy. 'We won't be vindictive.'

'We leave all that to Goofy,' said Moulton. It was nice to see old Harry cheering up.

'I'm glad,' Lewis said. 'We don't want to waste any time. In fact I'd like to send our technical people up next week.'

'I'm ready for them now,' said Moulton.

'I'm delighted to hear it.'

'Next week,' said Tracy. 'We'll need some time to settle, darling.'

'Then next week it shall be,' said Lewis. 'But get started soon, Jim. I'd like your work to be well on the way by the opening.'

'We all would,' Tracy said. 'You've nothing to worry about, Minister. It's going to work.'

'I'll leave you to your coffee,' said Sybil.

'A little formal, surely?' Laidlaw said. 'This is a family thing.'

'I asked her to,' said Jameson, and turned to his daughter. 'Go along.'

Laidlaw thought: In my house. In my own bloody house. My own wife. But he kept the smile on as he fetched the brandy. The old bastard liked brandy. He poured cautiously. A thimbleful. Jameson never took more. Charlie Dodds had asked for the bottles, but Jameson would never do that. Jameson was iron right through.

'A good meal,' said Jameson. 'I enjoyed it. You'll forgive me not talking business while I was eating. It would have spoiled it.'

He took out a cigar-case, and the two men unwrapped Montecristos. Jameson cut and prepared his with agonizing slowness, lit it with three matches as he always did.

'I'll come straight to the point,' he said at last. 'I've no doubt you'd prefer that?'

The old bastard was enjoying himself all right, and that was bad. It had to be bad.

'I wish you would,' said Laidlaw.

'You're out, Tom,' Jameson said.

He had known it as soon as he saw his wife's face, but when the words were said he couldn't believe them. It was impossible.

'I find that hard to believe,' said Laidlaw.

'It's quite simple. You didn't buy enough shares.'

'I've got thirty per cent,' said Laidlaw. 'And all the key people are behind me——'

'Key people are behind money,' said Jameson. 'You should know that, Tom. Money's what key people want to unlock.' He paused, and his mouth rounded like a baby's to his Havana. Laidlaw willed himself to wait for the cigar's withdrawal, the expulsion of smoke. 'Thirty from a hundred leaves seventy,' said Jameson. 'Did you never think of that Tom?'

I can't take much more of this bloody dialectic, Laidlaw told himself.

'I thought of it,' he said. 'But the key people had another twelve per cent, and you held fifteen for Sybil. Thirty and twelve and fifteen make fifty-seven.'

'And fifty-seven from a hundred's forty-three,' said Jameson. 'I see your reasoning, Tom. I see your reasoning.'

You do a beautiful act, Laidlaw thought. The stupid, painstaking old buffer. But don't try it on me. I married your daughter.

'But it still doesn't work,' Jameson said. 'Schiller's group went to the key people and offered more. Fifty-seven *minus* twelve's forty-five, and forty-three *plus* twelve's fifty-five. D'you see my point, Tom?'

'I see it,' said Laidlaw.

'I thought you would—bright lad like you,' said Jameson. 'So now you know why you're out.'

'Not quite,' Laidlaw said. 'I've still got Sybil's fifteen and my thirty. I could go to the other twelve per cent and improve on Schiller's offer.'

'Good, good,' said Jameson. 'Oh, very good indeed . . . but it won't work, Tom.'

'Why on earth shouldn't it?'

'Because forty-three and fifteen's fifty-eight,' said Jameson.

It couldn't be. It couldn't possibly be.

'*You sold Sybil's shares?*'

'One of Schiller's chaps stopped by the house yesterday. "Call me Miron," he said. Nice feller. I gave him one of these.' He waved the Havana. 'He says you can't get them in America. Something to do with Castro.'

'You sold them to him?'

'Got a good price too,' said Jameson.

'But why, man? Why?'

'It's a man's duty to look out for his daughter.'

'You call that looking out for Sybil?'

'I do,' Jameson said. 'Yes.'

'Don't you realize you've destroyed me?'

'You don't come into it, Tom,' Jameson said. He drank his brandy; one sharp, delicious swallow. 'On the contrary,' he said. 'You go out.'

'You're saying you hate me,' Laidlaw said.

'You're talking daft. I don't hate you, Tom, never have. I don't

279

like you very much, to be honest, but hate? No, Tom. If it was hate I'd come to you for lessons.'

'I see,' said Laidlaw.

'I've no doubt you do. You're sharp enough.' Jameson leaned forward. 'I was at a Licensed Victuallers do on Thursday. Down in Manchester. I like those dos. Nice and homely—and I've got a bit of money invested. Friend of mine was in the chair. The Earl of Hexham. You remember. I introduced him to you. Harry Lewis was guest of honour. We talked about Charlie Dodds.'

'What about him?'

'Dying drunk. Two bottles in his bed. We both thought it was funny.'

'Funny?'

'Excuse me, Tom. I don't always say what I mean. Old age, I suppose. And not being as well educated as you are. I meant peculiar. Dodds had a bad heart you see—but you must know that?'

'No,' said Laidlaw. 'I didn't. I hadn't seen Dodds in years.'

'Very good indeed,' Jameson said again. What he knew, what he suspected, were impossible to guess.

'Did Lewis put you off me?'

'He was a factor,' said Jameson. 'There were others. . . . I'd better be off.'

'No, wait,' Laidlaw said. 'What shall I tell Sybil?'

Jameson hauled his heavy body upright.

'She already knows,' he said. 'I wouldn't keep her in the dark.'

'You told her I was finished?'

'I told her you'll try again. I'm sure you will. Clever chap like you. Don't write this off altogether, Tom. It's been a chance to learn something. Better luck next time, eh?'

Then the young fool cracked up, started raving and screaming. Language, too. He used a lot of language. But at seventy-three you'd heard language before. You were used to it. And you could control this one if you had to, sharp as he was. Only there was Sybil to think of. His daughter. He was going to leave her now, lie down, rest a bit. He had to. That damn heartburn. Leave her to this clever fool who couldn't control his tongue—or his hate. Let him swear on. Wait till he gets his breath. Now.

'It was a mistake then, was it, the porter saying he saw you go up to Charlie Dodds's flat just before he died?' Jameson said.

'I don't understand you.'

'Chap that works for me—he showed your photo to the porter. The porter said he recognized you. But people do make mistakes,' said Jameson. 'We won't worry Sybil about it.'

'No,' said Laidlaw. 'We can't have Sybil worrying.'

'That's right. Funny mistake for him to make though. I got him to swear it—you know. Proper form. Notary public.'

'Why would you do that?' said Laidlaw.

'You do a lot of daft things at my age. I just took it into my head to have it all written out legally. Even made arrangements for it after my death. Just a fancy you might say. I better be off. . . . Take good care of Sybil, Tom.'

Laidlaw said, 'You know I will.'

'I do now,' said Jameson.

INVOLVEMENT, EXTRICATION

Madge Innes said, 'I'm leaving.'

Fitzgerald was cooking pan hagglety. It claimed all his attention.

'You don't seem all that interested.'

'What?' he said.

She had learned that any attempt to dominate Fitzgerald was useless. Wait or walk out. There was no other way. She watched him handle sausages, potatoes, onions, bacon. They seemed to him as important as paint.

'Plates,' he said, and she fetched them. Fitzgerald shared out, neatly and fairly.

'I haven't eaten this since my mother kept the shop,' she said.

'I bet you still like it,' said Fitzgerald. It was delicious. 'Where you off to?' he said.

'Holiday,' she said. 'I feel I could do with a holiday—after all this excitement.'

'What about Moulton's image?' he asked.

'That's somebody else's worry.'

'You told Goofy?'

'Laidlaw?' she said. It was funny, but even now she shied away from the nickname. 'No. I didn't tell him. He told me. Laidlaw's out.'

'What?' he said.

'O-U-T.'

'The project's over then?'

'Oh no. The project goes on. But Laidlaw goes out. His takeover backfired. Somebody else outsmarted him. Would you believe that?'

'I'd believe it was possible.'

'I doubt if you'll believe who outsmarted him.'

'Who?'

'Jim Moulton.'

'That mad sod? You're joking.'

'Laidlaw wishes I were. And so do I. But I'm not.'

'Moulton a bloody financier——'

'Not quite. I bent the truth a little for dramatic effect. Moulton's father-in-law. A concept so improbable that Laidlaw, I'm afraid, overlooked it.'

'Never mind the future,' he said. 'What about my portrait?'

'Do you know,' she said, 'in all the mad whirl of excitement I overlooked that overwhelmingly important point?'

'He's got a face that's crying out for it,' Fitzgerald said.

'Would you like to come to Majorca with me?'

'No.'

Sometimes he was funny even when he hurt, but only sometimes.

'Used me up, have you?' She looked at the one surviving sketch of her picture. Fitzgerald shrugged.

'There's a lot to do,' he said.

Madge Innes continued to stare at her naked self. It was absurd to take such pride in one's own body. One hadn't made it after all, assembled it as Fitzgerald had done. It had simply happened. An inexplicable gift. One had to look after it, that was true, clean it, polish it, keep it in trim, but that was all. It was just a gift but delivered into the right hands, like a Stradivarius anonymously sent to a poor violinist. And yet, one had it. It was one's own. A cause for pride in one's self—and envy in other women.

'The picture stays,' said Fitzgerald.

She touched the bruise at her throat.

'You've made that perfectly clear,' she said. 'Only . . .'

'Only what?'

'Please don't show it to anyone else.'

It was strange to have to say please and feel no shame, only desire.

'You're on,' he said. 'Not till my next exhibition.'

'When's that?'

'Year. Two years mebbe. When I've got enough stuff.'

By then she'd have moved on. The picture might even help her own P.R., if she got the job she was after.

'All right,' she said, then: 'You haven't shown it to anyone else?'

'No,' he said. 'Oh aye.'

The man was impossible.

'Who?' she said.

The man was also utterly, wonderfully dangerous.

'Please tell me.'

'Mrs Jennings,' he said. 'Bob Arnott's ma-in-law.'

He was braced for any reaction but the one he got. Madge burst out laughing. Not hysterical laughter neither, nor sarcastic. He'd made her happy. That was something. He went on eating.

'That's great,' she said. 'That's perfect.'

'D'you know her?'

'I worked for her once.'

'What d'you think?'

'She's the best there is. I wanted to like her, but——'

'She wouldn't like you.'

Right as always, my superman.

'I wanted to like her daughter too,' Madge said. 'It's just possible it may work out.'

'You've seen Susan?'

He was a friend of Bob's, and the desire to make him share Bob's hurt had something to do with her answer, but courage also had its share. To risk Fitzgerald's anger always took courage.

'Yes,' she said. 'We had a splendid little chat.'

'What about?'

'Married life.'

He ate the last of his food, laid down his knife and fork; looked at her. The real terror was in the fact that his eyes, his whole face, told you nothing.

He said at last, 'For a clever woman you're a hell of a bloody fool.'

He reached out to a fruit-bowl, plucked out two apples, threw one to her.

'The woman tempted me and I did eat,' she said.

'You're all bloody culture,' said Fitzgerald. 'You don't even think any more.'

'About what?'

'About yourself.'

'You obviously don't know what Susan told me.'

'Susan?'

'I told you. I think she likes me. You don't *know*, Fitz. If you did——'

'Of course I bloody know. She's gone off Bob.'

'Who told you that? Not Mrs Jennings?'

'Nobody,' he said. 'I watched them both—and I thought about it. You daft bloody bitch.' Contempt in those last words, but no anger. Contempt and pity. She hated the pity.

'Bob asked for it,' she said.

'*I* asked for it.'

'*You* made love to me.'

'So you bloody own me, is that it?'

'Nobody owns you.'

'Only myself. *I* own me. *You* own nobody.'

She looked again at the sketch.

'You don't even own that,' he said. 'You bloody give it away.' His teeth crunched noisily into the apple. 'One day you won't even be able to do that. You'll be on your own.'

'So will you.'

'I already am. It's what I want. It isn't what you want—but it's what you'll get.'

'That's not true.'

'Who then? Who? Once your tits start sagging. Who? Goofy? Moulton? Susan Arnott?'

'You're the only man who could ever make me cry,' she said.

'You're crying because you're daft. Because you bloody well won't give up. I'm sorry for you, Madge.'

'What are you going to do about it?'

'Being sorry?'

'About *it*. Me—Susan—Bob.'

'It isn't my business.'

He finished the apple and watched her cry. Tears were thick, translucent, not transparent. The skin behind them took on a different texture. The colour modified. Interesting. But it was late, too late for working, and if she was leaving, she'd want him. Bound to. They always did. Put their heart and soul into it just before they left. It was supposed to remind you what you were going to be missing.

'Fancy a drink?' he said.

They went to a club. The Old Chelsea, they called it. Doorman done up like Charles II and all the waitresses done up like Nell Gwynne. Upstairs a band and a floor-show that was mostly strippers and Geordie comics, downstairs roulette, blackjack, poker dice. Goofy Laidlaw had a piece of it. He has a piece of most things round here, Fitzgerald thought. But not of me—or of Mad bloody Moulton either it seemed. He ordered a bottle of whisky. It worked out cheaper in the long run. Madge was brooding, so he watched the stripper. No bloody good at all. Smothered in body make-up. Madge still brooding. He put a hand on her knee. No harm in cheering her up a bit. Then the lights came up and she stiffened, aware as a pointer bitch.

Bob Arnott three tables away, Bob in a nice grey suit and a discreet maroon tie. Bob with a touch of grey at the temples, all weary eyelids and civilized charm. Bob with a bloody ice-bucket and Champagne and a couple of teenage tarts that were lapping it up. He took his hand away.

'Didn't I tell you you were a bloody fool?' he said.

'But what can he possibly see in them?' she asked, and he told her.

'Is that all he wants?'

'What more were you offering?' Fitzgerald asked. 'Culture?'

'But I mean . . .' Madge Innes said. 'Just look at them.'

'The fair one's not bad,' said Fitzgerald. 'She fancies him.'

It was true. The brunette was bored, alert already for another, and preferably younger man, but the fair one was already responding to the looks, the experience, the charm; as Susan must also have reacted once, Madge Innes thought. From where she sat Bob was obviously acting, and not even acting well, but the fair one was loving it. Suddenly the brunette waved to a new arrival, then leaned forward, kissed Bob on the cheek, took off. At once the fair one snuggled closer.

'It didn't take him long,' Madge Innes said.

'Who are you so bloody sorry for?' Fitzgerald asked. 'Susan—or yourself?'

The fair girl whispered to Bob then, telling him he was being watched. He turned at once, saw them, smiled and waved them over.

'He's got a bloody nerve,' said Madge Innes.

'What did you expect him to do?' said Fitzgerald. 'Wet himself?'

She rose. 'I'm going over,' she said.

Fitzgerald started to follow, then went back for his bottle. He never trusted the catering trade, not since he'd been a ship's steward.

'Bob, how nice,' she was saying. 'Fancy meeting you here.' And Bob was saying, 'Madge Innes, I want you to meet Valerie Bowman, Valerie this is Madge and this is John Fitzgerald.'

'But I've seen you,' said Valerie. 'On T.V. Oh this is marvellous.' she turned to Fitzgerald. 'And you're the painter, aren't you? Oh, Bob—you know such exciting people.'

Not a tart then, or not an obvious tart any way. Madge didn't fancy that at all. Didn't fancy Valerie either, now she got close up. The hair was mouse, but thick and gleaming, the skin had a freshness you lose with your hangover after your twenty-fifth birthday. Body nothing special compared with Madge's but pretty enough, he'd bet, because it was young. Nice voice too, and nice, very nice blue eyes. A girl who wanted maturity, who had her hand on its arm.

'How's Susan?' Madge asked.

'She's fine,' said Bob, and the hand stayed where it was. 'We were just talking about her.'

Daft bitch, Fitzgerald thought. Do you think Bob's that stupid? Better let her get it over with.

He turned to Valerie. 'Want to dance with a painter?' he asked.

She did, very much. No doubt because he was not only mature but famous; but she didn't want to risk leaving Bob with Madge.

'Why don't you?' Bob said to her. 'Go on. I'll be here when you come back.'

No doubt about it, Fitzgerald thought. Bob's tricks might be a bit flash, but they worked.

She went with him to the dance-floor. To her surprise, he danced well.

'Champagne?' said Arnott. He reached for the bottle.

'No thank you,' she said. 'I'll stick to my Scotch.'

To her surprise he was completely sober. It annoyed her, as Valerie had annoyed her. She'd wanted him drunk, with a money-grabbing tart.

'When I said Susan was fine, I meant physically,' Arnott said. 'But of course you know about all that.'

'She told you then?'

'She told me. I hope it brought some satisfaction to you, Madge. It didn't do Susan any good at all.'

'And you?'

He looked at Valerie, laughing, struggling to match the easy relaxation with which Fitzgerald's body moved.

'It's a bit early to tell,' he said.

She had followed his gaze.

'Are you saying Susan's having a breakdown?' she asked.

'While I sit here with my Champagne and my nymphet?'

'Is that what she is?'

'Valerie's twenty,' he said. 'She knows I'm married and she's not my patient. There's nothing for you there, Madge—and Susan isn't having a breakdown.'

'You said she was all right physically.'

'She is. Mentally too. Except with me. She's nothing—with me.'

'I didn't cause that,' she said.

'Indeed you didn't. I caused it and she caused it.'

'So you've nothing to blame me for.'

'Hardly that,' he said. 'You persuaded her to verbalize it.'

'But it was already there.'

'We chose to pretend it wasn't,' he said, 'because we were trying to overcome it. To—what's the phrase?—work it out. Once the words had been said that was impossible. But of course you knew that. That's why you did it.' She was silent. 'I'm glad you don't deny it,' he said.

She looked again at Valerie. At all that freshness; that vitality.

'It would seem I did you a favour,' she said.

'It's an easy way,' said Arnott. 'It might be a very satisfying way. It isn't the best way. But you know that, too.'

'I don't understand you,' she said.

'My dear Madge, of course you do. The best way was what I had—the thing I was fighting for. That was why you killed it.'

He spoke as a teacher might speak to a bright but recalcitrant child refusing to make the effort to comprehend something manifestly within its compass. It frightened her. What she had expected, needed, was rage.

'If that's so—why aren't you angry with me?' she asked.

He said wearily, 'I haven't the talent for it. All I can do is treat people, Madge. Even you.'

But not myself, he thought, and not Susan either. He looked again at the dancing girl. She saw his look, and smiled, and he knew the smile to be a compliment. She was concentrating so hard.

'Don't work at it,' Fitzgerald said. 'Let it come.'

'Where on earth did you learn it?'

'Harlem,' he said. 'From a coloured lady.'

The coon had moved always as if dancing had been a prologue to love, and like love itself it must be highlit by passion, and a sense of style. White people, even the new young, found the trick hard to learn. When the band played a fox-trot she moved to his arms with relief.

'You know Bob well?' he asked, and she was at once defensive.

'I know he's married,' she said.

'So do I,' he said. 'That's not what I'm asking.'

'I'm a student,' she said. 'I like a few bright lights, and I like older men. I like Bob.'

'You don't have to hit me,' he said. 'What d'you study?'

'Pharmacy. I'm taking my exams soon. I met Bob at a First Aid class. St John's Ambulance.' She paused, then added, 'He's a very kind person. Kind and patient.'

'That's right,' said Fitzgerald.

'If that Rubens Venus there asks you if I've slept with him tell her no,' she said. 'But I intend to. Tell her that as well.'

'If she asks,' he said. 'D'you love Bob?'

'No,' she said. 'I like him very much but I don't love him—and he knows it. If I loved him he wouldn't be here.'

He thought: How cold the young are. Love in the Antarctic. Ice-floes for beds, snow for a pillow, while the penguins watched and took notes. Maybe it would suit Bob, but his own bones needed warming. He was glad when the dance finished, and it was time to tell Madge they were leaving. She resented his tone of voice or something, resented more the fact that Bob saw it all and smiled. But she stood up.

'I'm going to Majorca for a while, Bob,' she said. 'Several months in fact.'

'It should be nice at this time of year,' he said.

She opened her bag, took out a card.

'This is my address,' she said. 'Look me up if you feel like it.'

He made no move to take the card, and she dropped it on the table.

'Goodbye,' she said.

'I think so,' Arnott said.

Fitzgerald pulled her away then, and Valerie picked up the card.

'Tear it up,' said Arnott.

'I like the way you're rude,' she said. 'It's elegant.'

'Please tear it up.'

'Don't be silly,' she said, and tucked the card in his pocket, behind his handkerchief.

A PLETHORA OF CLUBS

THEY travelled up North in another Rolls-Royce, a dead ringer for the one in L.A., and Moulton wondered if his father-in-law bought them wholesale. But the chauffeur was different. The chauffeur was white, and his name was Tomkins. He neither hated nor feared anybody, just drove and kept his feelings to himself. Moulton enjoyed that.

'I've booked a suite at the White Hart,' Tracy said.

'Yes, dear.'

'It'll do till we find a house.'

'Yes, dear.'

'And make arrangements for mother.'

'Yes, dear.'

She nipped him, viciously.

'Less of the wit,' she said. 'Somebody has to be practical.'

'Do we really need a suite?' he asked.

'We need an office,' she said, 'and I won't use my bedroom for that.' She touched his hand, furtively. Tomkins awed her. 'It's going to be just great, darling,' she said.

The work would come out, and he'd make love to her at night, and after that . . . after that was too far ahead. He had no doubt that she was right.

'Just great,' he said.

Great car, great project, great wife. Doing everything for him because she loved him to the point where she functioned best as a part of himself, the practical, director's part he had always lacked: managing, manipulating, and so contributing to the whole of him, his achievement And once you'd swallowed that you knew that what she'd done with Andy, you had done too, because she was part of you.

'I can't wait to get started,' said Moulton.

Nor, it seemed, could she. There were messages, letters, appointments waiting when they arrived. There was Miron waiting also, to be congratulated because of old Jameson, and sent out glowing to look for office-space, armed with the power of Harry Lewis's mighty name. There were supplicants and well-wishers, and for himself some more of the technical people that old Harry had promised, and some of his own as well—to take him to the lab, explain and probe, and gradually to grow excited when they became aware of what he was after, as he had known they would. Oh, that was great, all right. There was no alloy in that. They were a good team—Harry and Tracy and he had seen to that—and the bigness of it didn't frighten them. They *wanted* it like that. Good lads. They would do the thing all right, if it was possible for it to be done at all. And that night, when he got back, he found his wife had arranged a treat for him. A cocktail party. Civil servants, minor shareholders, a couple of presentable scientists, and 'Mr and Mrs Laidlaw', the hotel waiter called out.

'How the hell did you manage that?' Moulton asked.

'Her father made them,' she said. 'Anyway they have things to sign.'

She surged forward, social and bright.

'Sybil, darling,' she said, 'how gorgeous to meet you again—after all these years.'

That was the rifle-butt, smack in the gut.

'You can't imagine how often I've thought about you . . .'

Head butt. The rim of your tin hat smack across the bridge of the nose.

'. . . and all that intimate gossip. I hope I didn't *bore* you, giving away all my girlish secrets?'

The boot going in. Over and over. And every kick just right. What you got you paid for, and this poor bitch had spent too much, even with all Goofy's money behind her—and old Jameson's. He turned to Laidlaw.

'Well, Jim?' Laidlaw said.

'Well, Tom?'

So now even you can afford to be magnanimous? Laidlaw thought. A waiter brought a drinks tray, and he chose Scotch; the victor, he noted, was sipping a Coke.

'You haven't met my wife,' Moulton said.

'No, I haven't,' said Laidlaw.

'No indeed,' said Tracy, 'but Jim has told me so much about you I feel I've known you for ever.'

'How sweet of you,' Laidlaw said.

'Not sweet at all. It's the *truth*,' said Tracy. 'And I want to say right here and now to you two lovely people'—her voice had risen; she had an audience now—'you two utterly lovely people—how sweet of you it is to come here today. It shows a wonderful spirit. Really it does. I doubt if Jim and I could be like that. I honestly do. What do you say, darling?'

'Wasn't I the one who told you how lovely they were?' Moulton said. 'What a wonderful spirit they had? Why—Tom and I have known each other since we were kids. A man couldn't wish for a nicer friend.'

'I'll drink to that,' said Tracy. 'And to you, Sybil. Come on, everybody.' She lifted her glass. 'Tom and Sybil,' she said.

And they all said, 'Tom and Sybil,' even the ones who didn't know them, while behind them reporters scribbled, a flash-bulb popped.

When you married a director at least you got a production, Moulton thought. He'd seen nothing like Laidlaw's face since he fell on top of Harry. Then suddenly he wanted it to stop, it simply wasn't important enough to go on with, but Tracy had only sipped blood so far. Now she wanted to swig it. They had to be photographed with the Laidlaws, arms interlinked, Tracy had to invite them to the official opening of the lab and insist, positively insist that they attended. She had to take them round and introduce them to the members of the board Laidlaw had almost chaired, the scientists and executives Laidlaw had almost hired. She had to ask Laidlaw, over and over again, if he wouldn't agree with her that he had the cutest old father-in-law in the world. And all Laidlaw could do was take it, and give his impersonation of Harry, and all Sybil could do was struggle not to cry, and hang on till it was time to go.

'I'm sorry Madge Innes couldn't be here,' Tracy said. 'Seems she's gone abroad. But never mind, darlings, we'll catch up with her some time.'

Laidlaw had no doubt she would. He finished his drink.

'I'm afraid we'll have to go,' he said.

'Oh, come on now,' Tracy said. 'This is fun. Isn't it fun?'

'We . . . we really do have an engagement,' said his wife. Her voice was a whisper.

'Before we've even had our little chat?'

'I'm afraid so,' Sybil said. 'I'm awfully sorry.'

'No, please don't apologize,' said Tracy. 'I hate apologies. Don't I, darling?'

'Indeed you do,' said Moulton, recognizing a cue. 'I've never quite understood why.'

'Because they always come too late,' she said. 'And they're usually insincere anyway.' She kissed Sybil. 'So please, honey, never apologize to me,' she said. 'And see Miron on the way out, will you? He's got some things for you to sign.'

She turned away then, and Moulton saw that she was frowning; but then Fitzgerald was announced, and the smile returned. The production it seemed still ran smoothly. When Fitzgerald joined them, she went through the whole routine again. She even thought up a new one.

'Please don't worry about your computer, Tom,' she said. 'Harry Lewis asked me to tell you. We've got a line on a new one—and it's all

British. Costs a bit more, but at least it's home-grown. Harry's delighted—and you know Harry. When he's pleased he helps everybody. Isn't it good news?' Before he could answer she said, 'I knew you'd be pleased.'

This time Moulton managed to edge away, have a word with the scientists. It was only after the Laidlaws had gone that Fitzgerald came up to join him. He broke away from the two men's questions. Fitzgerald was something else that had to be faced, and he wanted to get it over.

Fitzgerald said, 'Are you glad to be back?'

'I am,' said Moulton.

'Back among the lost causes?'

'My cause isn't lost,' Moulton said.

The man had been looking at him as if he'd been committing his last words to memory, but at last he let out his breath in a sigh—of relief it seemed.

'Which cause would that be?'

'My work,' Moulton said.

'Work,' said Fitzgerald. 'Aye.' He slapped Moulton on the shoulder. 'You're looking better than I've seen you in years.'

'I'm feeling better,' said Moulton. Fitzgerald's eyes flicked to Tracy, chatting, hovering, as the Laidlaws signed Miron's papers.

'That's a hell of a wife you've got there,' he said.

'I think so.'

'She can hit as hard as you,' Fitzgerald said. 'But she's faster.'

'And younger.'

'That's right,' said Fitzgerald. 'You better watch it, son.'

No point in watching it, Moulton thought. There's nothing you can do—except enjoy it while it's there.

Aloud he said, 'How's the work going?'

'Canny,' said Fitzgerald. 'And you?'

'There's a chance,' Moulton said. 'Quite a good chance.'

They faced each other, each reluctant to give up an old antagonism, but each aware too that the antagonism had outlived its point. A reporter scurried up. Fitzgerald had arrived late; he'd missed his name.

'Excuse me, Mr Moulton,' the reporter said, 'but is this gentleman a relative of yours?'

'Well I'll go to hell,' said Fitzgerald.

'I'm sorry, sir,' the reporter said. 'There is a resemblance . . .'

'This is John Fitzgerald,' Moulton said.

'I'm a painter,' Fitzgerald said.

'Oh, yes, indeed,' said the reporter, and backed off scribbling.

'Your wife says I can paint you,' said Fitzgerald.

'Her too? What in hell for, man?'

'Five thousand quid. Are you on?'

'Five thousand?'

'It's me going rate,' said Fitzgerald.

'That why you're doing it?'

'There's a bloody queue,' said Fitzgerald. 'Three years long. But you've got a face, son. Something I can get at.'

'Will it take a long time?'

'You can sit there and bloody think,' said Fitzgerald. 'It's what you're here for.'

'You're right there,' Moulton said.

The painter's eye was on him again, calculating, assessing.

'By God you've changed.' he said. 'It's more than you can say for Laidlaw.'

'It was my wife fettled him,' Moulton said.

'Aye,' said Fitzgerald. 'You can see it from here. Blood all over her. But that bugger—he'll start all over again. You watch. He's still after you.'

'I won't be so easy next time.'

'It won't stop him trying. He has to hate, that one. It's the only fuel his motor'll take. Like that poor cow Madge Innes.'

'Cow' should have angered him, but it didn't. He knew Fitzgerald now; knew it meant nothing.

'What did she do?' he asked.

'Fettled Bob, poor bugger. Bob was the best of us—know that? He mebbe still is.'

Tracy came up to them, and Moulton looked to the door. The Laidlaws had gone.

'Mr Fitzgerald,' she said, 'I can't tell you how glad I am to meet you.'

'Fitz,' said Moulton. 'He's known as Fitz.'

'Me too, Mrs Moulton,' Fitzgerald said.

'Tracy,' she said. 'Please call me Tracy.'

There was a rapport there at once, that Moulton instantly recognized. The power of creation in the man, and the woman's yearning for it, to serve it, foster it, become a part . . .

Andy, Moulton thought, we've just got ourselves a rival. Why the hell think of Andy—except that he liked Andy, and had just learned to like Fitzgerald. Look out for the razor, Fitz.

'We were just talking about Bob Arnott,' Fitz said.

'I asked him too,' she said. 'He couldn't make it.'

'You said he was the best of us,' said Moulton.

'What do you think, darling?' Tracy asked.

'Last time we met I was drunk,' said Moulton. 'Drunk and a bit scared. I hurt him. Badly. I shouldn't have done that. There was never anyone like Bob.'

'We're going to need an M.O. at the lab,' she said. 'That's one reason I asked him. What d'you think?'

'I could use him all right,' said Moulton. 'He's got the right sort of mind. But——'

'Round here everybody wants him,' Fitzgerald said. 'He's that sort of feller.'

'No harm in asking,' Tracy said. 'I'll get on to him tomorrow.'

'No,' said Moulton. 'I'll handle this myself.'

She's reacting to that one, Fitzgerald thought. But you don't care. Half of you doesn't even notice. This is your business, and you'll handle it your way. Even if you are daft about her. And you are, son. And I don't blame you. I'll be daft about her meself if I get half a chance. I'm sorry, son. But it's true.

AFTER I'd written up what happened at Goofy's I decided to abandon writing. My craft is medicine after all, and it demands all my time. Then too, I have seen Fitzgerald at work, and the concentration of energy and passion involved is one which I should not care to risk, even if I were capable of its achievement. Yet here I am. Scribble scribble scribble. More pages in holograph. But not the creative itch; not the mildest irritation for that most modest of creative acts, using real people, real situations, as patterns for embroidery. This is for my son Andrew, my daughter Jane. A record of what is usually called 'my side'.

It begins, my loves, with your grandmother, who I hope very much will be alive and near you when you are reading this, at the time when you are old enough, whenever the law says that will be. She visited your mother and me at our house in Tyneside (were you young enough, I wonder, to have forgotten that house completely?) at a time of crisis in our lives. The crisis was sexual in origin. Even to write this for you embarrasses me. To have to say it to you would be impossible. I am hypersexual: your mother is ... not. Not any more. She believes quite sincerely that I 'used her up', sexually. If I did so, I apologize for it. The best I can say in my defence is that I did it unthinkingly, and that it was once a source of great joy to us both.

Your grandmother visited us at your mother's request because Susan (forgive me if I call her sometimes by her name, but it seems to me more honest, certainly more realistic), Susan had asked her to do so. The state of affairs between us had worried her more intensely than I had realized, especially after a dinner-party at the house of some people called Laidlaw, of whom I have told you—and a meeting I had with my friend John Fitzgerald, which involved the gift of some drawings and a painting. The painting is still in Susan's possession, I hope. I hope, too, that you look at it and think about it often.

It was your grandmother's opinion that Susan and I should say nothing to each other about our problem. She believed that each of us had a gift of tenderness for the other and a liking and respect for the other, that constituted, in a sense, love. If this were fostered, she believed that passion would return. If not, liking and respect would have to do. Mrs Jennings had observed kindness in her daughter, and sympathy, which had informed her reaction to our meeting once again with Fitzgerald, who had twice been involved in crises in your grandfather's life. The reactions were those of honesty and affection, and were, so your grandmother tells me, acquired from me.

Forgive me, my loves. An attempt at objectivity in one's self can so often sound like boasting; or whining—as when I say that I never acquired the habit of loving from Susan. It seems I couldn't. I have her word for it—and she was told by a woman called Madge Innes, who by this time, for all I know, may be your honorary Aunt Madge. Your gay and giddy aunt. If so, and if you have grown up to be like me in your kindness and sympathy, treat her gently. She is a sad and tormented person. The gay and giddy ones so often are—and twice I have been obliged to hurt her—for her own good, of course. It's always for their own good when the smug wound the vulnerable. Be gentle with her. Make a little restitution for your father. Like the rest of us, she found Laidlaw's little dinner expensive.

I hope very much that I shall have seen you often before you read this, that I may show you all that kindness and sympathy I talk so much about. Love you will get from your mother and you'll get it in abundance. I have no gold to offer my loves, but you're welcome to all my silver. You see, love died for me with my parents, as I hope my account of their death will show: one more bereavement. But if I don't see you, there are certain other things that I still must tell you. For instance, I did see Laidlaw again, once, and wanted very much to hate him. Anyone who can hate must have at least the potentiality of love. . . . He and his wife were at the official opening of the Quantum Lab; so were most of the others involved in my affairs. God knows why they'd gone: I suspect Jameson, his father-in-law, had made them. . . . Jameson. Now there's somebody I did hate once. But by the time I was big enough to do anything about it I was sent to Korea—and by the time I came back I'd even got over that. The only other people I've known suffer as Laidlaw was suffering were Jim Moulton—and Madge Innes. It's true that their suffering—and Laidlaw's—was quite largely self-inflicted. But for me all suffering is irresistible: the alcoholic who prefers whisky can still drink gin. I looked at Laidlaw, and pitied him, and he knew it and despised me. I envied him that.

The opening was a very splendid affair. It was held in the main lab, which that day looked like a canteen for scientific millionaires: lobsters, salmon, Champagne, laid out on work-benches, cyclotron like the world's biggest juke-box in the background. T.V. cameras, microphones, Press. Oh, it was very splendid. A bit pompous too. You see Harry Lewis was there, so naturally he supplied the pomposity, and that was only fair. He'd supplied a lot of the splendour too. (I'm at it again, you see—being kind to people. Indulge me, my loves. It's my only trick.) Harry made a speech. It was all 'As I look about me' and 'This splendid achievement' and 'This Government will never cease to encourage the creative genius of its people'. You'll have grown used to those noises by the time you read this. Then he spoke of us Geordies: 'the rough good humour that you find up here' ... 'shipyards, the Roman wall. The coaly Tyne'. Harry was our M.P., you see—so forgive him the clichés. His majority was important to him. Then he spoke about our passion for justice, our hard-learned faith in the rightness of our cause, our fearless demands for social equality, and I knew he would soon get to Jim Moulton. But first we had to hear about the team, so I listened more carefully. You see, I was on the team. I was its doctor. I was also, Harry Lewis told me, one of a hard-working band of gifted, dedicated people. I thought that was nice of Harry, but then I'd had five glasses of Champagne, and I rarely drink more than two. My colleagues and I, Harry told me, stood on the threshold of a great achievement made possible by Harry's Government, which was somehow using American-owned capital to further British socialist ends. But that was beyond me: after five glasses of Champagne it would have been beyond Engels.

I thought instead of how I had come to join that gifted and dedi-cated band. It was mostly Tracy Moulton—Jim's wife. Jim had wanted me, so she'd bought me for him—as if I were a new set of golf-clubs. There was also my desperate need for a change, and soap, dog food, atomic nuclei, were a very big change from people with lumbago, ulcers, varicose veins. So I sold the practice and joined the dedicated band. Poor Arthur Harkness—who is also I hope a friend of your grandmother's still—begged me not to, but smug to the last, I hurt him for his own good. With the money he got, he's going back to study for a diploma in psychiatric medicine. He'll make a very good psychiatrist. Arthur was wasted as a G.P.: I ... wasn't.

The dedicated band had had their due. Now it was Jim's turn, and Harry Lewis made roguish jokes about the black sheep returning to the fold and the prodigal's return and how he'd better not go too far because Jim had had a tremendous right hook, even at school. Amid the merry laughter I looked at Jim—not glowering, not scowling. He hadn't even clenched his hands. Jim was smiling. He was also, I realized, putting on weight, and, true to my nature, I was sorry for him. He had a lovely wife, millions of pounds to play with, a great discovery waiting to be made—he *will* make it, I know he will—and your father was sorry for him. Or perhaps for the things that had been. All of them. And not just his and mine. All the terrible, wonderful things, while Jim smiled, at Harry Lewis, at his wife, at me. There was still a smile for me. We had both of us changed so much since our boyhood—but our friendship was still there, and that didn't seem to have changed a bit. Jim was still forging ahead, and I was still stumbling after. His acolyte, his Blondel, his Merry Man. When I joined Quantum I was told I would need a pharmacist, and that I might choose my own. I chose a girl called Valerie Bowman. She was young, but mature for her years, and wary of emotional commitment. Not in the least like Susan. Perhaps you will have heard of her, too, when you read this? . . .

Harry Lewis was still being pompous and splendid, but the Champagne had made me sleepy. I began to daydream, and soon I was back in Korea again. (Andrew, Jane, you have no idea how much your father longs to boast to you about his soldiering: how he fought, was wounded, survived.) It was very near the end of that particular war, and I had been invited to dine with some American marine officers. They were, I think, genuinely glad to invite me, but I took a bottle of Scotch anyway. After dinner they showed me something I shall never forget.

Their mess was in a defile between two hills. We climbed the taller one and looked about us. On either side, hills stretched out into the distance. Blue-grey, rough, deserted hills. Below, a road twisted its way, seeking for valleys. The north-south road that linked Pyongyang in the North to Seoul in the South, the only way an armoured column could move; the only way the war could be won. On the American side was wire, twenty yards deep, and before the wire mines to a depth of fifty yards at least. Behind the wire there was infantry, entrenched to enormous depth, bazookas, heavy-calibre machine-guns, napalm traps, all the bestial gadgetry of war, and behind the infantry there were guns, a primeval forest of guns: a hundred-millimetre cannon for every twenty yards of disputed territory. Then came no-man's-land, and then the Chinese positions. They were the same: except for one thing. They had even more guns, more men, more mines than the Allies. . . .

Arnott wrote it all down, exactly as he remembered it, Harry, his friend, Harry's final words: *'Yeah. The war's over. Now we got to fight the fucking peace.*

The word *fucking* made him hesitate, but he put it in anyway. By the time Andrew and Jane read it, they'd be old enough to realize that every word of Harry's had relevance. . . . He turned the page, then put down his pen. He had told them about his childhood, and Moulton's, about the dinner party, about his parents. It was enough. To add more could only lead to boasting—or whining. He sat back, easing his cramped fingers, then picked up the pen once more. He was a methodical man, and he hoped, an honest one. He would finish his journal methodically, and honestly.

c/o Innes (Arnott wrote)
Apartado 4,
Casa Murillo,
Calador, Mallorca.